SAINT
JULIAN

⸺✺⸺

SAINT JULIAN

A Novel

WALTER WANGERIN, JR.

HarperSanFrancisco

A Division of HarperCollins*Publishers*

ZONDERVAN™

Saint Julian is published by HarperSanFrancisco and Zondervan in the United States.

SAINT JULIAN: *A Novel.* Copyright © 2003 by Walter Wangerin, Jr. All rights reserved. Printed in the United States of America. No part of this book may be used or reproduced in any manner whatsoever without written permission except in the case of brief quotations embodied in critical articles and reviews. For information address HarperCollins Publishers, Inc., 10 East 53rd Street, New York, NY 10022.

HarperCollins books may be purchased for educational, business, or sales promotional use. For information please write: Special Markets Department, HarperCollins Publishers, Inc., 10 East 53rd Street, New York, NY 10022.

HarperCollins Web site: http://www.harpercollins.com
HarperCollins®, 📖®, and HarperSanFrancisco™ are
trademarks of HarperCollins Publishers, Inc.

FIRST EDITION
Designed by Joseph Rutt
Library of Congress Cataloging-in-Publication Data
Wangerin, Walter.
Saint Julian / Walter Wangerin, Jr.
p. cm.
ISBN 0–06–052252–6 (cloth : alk paper)
1. Julian, the Hospitaller, Saint—Fiction.   2. Christian saints—Fiction.
3. France—Fiction.   I. Title.
PS3573.A477 S25 2002
813'.54—dc21   2002032842

03 04 05 06 07 RRD(H) 10 9 8 7 6 5 4 3 2 1

Unto Emil and Emma Jochum
for their love and their lasting patronage
I dedicate the telling of this tale

"Fear wist not to evade,
As Love wist to pursue"

—Francis Thompson

CONTENTS

PROLOGUE

───⟨≋⟩───

TO THE TELLING
OF THE TALE

1.

SOME PRELIMINARY DISCLOSURES

I am a minor cleric. My parish is small and my parishioners poor—located, as we are, in the neglected center of a city of considerable size. But hither my vocation led me when I was a young man, light of foot, fresh from the halls of theological instruction. And here I have remained even down to these latter days and my older age—here, in this place, without notable successes or ecclesiastical advancement. I beg you, however, not to think that I complain of my life's position and its long career in an impoverished parish. For I have loved these people, both the members of my congregation and their relatives and the citizens of these rough streets. Aye, and my Savior knows how dearly do I love them still. Why, I am their intimate; I span their lives—for which they have become my purpose and the value of all my labors. 'Tis a common, consistent man that I have been, never grand nor extravagant. I am no luminary, I: a pastor. That plain and necessary thing. Their pastor. I have baptized them and confirmed them; have confessed, communed and married them. Yea, even the ones whom first I baptized have I since married. I have followed their wilder children into prison cells, there to kneel and pray for peace and for salvation. Year after year, Sundays and all the Holy Days, I

have preached sermons of quiet caution and quieter com-
forts, for that I lack rhetorical power, though I have, by
grace, a measure of good sense. My presence is as the siskin,
not the nightingale; and rather than the blazing fire, I am
the bricks that keep it in. I have preached. I have catechized.
I have shoveled the snow outside the door. I have begged
money of larger parishes and kept both food and coin in my
study against emergent occasions. Even still today I pray in
the dark of the early mornings; six mornings a week I shovel
out the cold ash in order to strike new fire, then kneel on
the chancel step and pray for the people whom God is
pleased to have placed beneath my care. At midnight I cry
out against the Devil that would oppress them. The daylong
I go visiting. I watch my people. I recognize when one of
them is borne down by wanhope, for that has been my own,
my private malady. And always, from the beginning of my
ministry until the day presently upon us, I've sat by the
beds of my people's diseases, have touched their brows with
the oils of healing, have sung soft hymns in unhearing ears,
have murmured psalms, have shriven their souls and closed
their eyelids upon their dyings and stood at their gravesides,
uttering over and over again the words that toll the deepest
rhythms of this existence: *We brought nothing into this world,
and it is certain we can carry nothing out. The Lord gave, and the
Lord hath taken away; blessed be the name of the Lord.*

   They that sow in tears shall reap in joy. . . .

   And these next words too, which I have by heart; and
though one might expect the older cleric to find them easier
than the younger did, it is not true. Every time I intone

them above the casket of another one of my beloved, I find them harder to pronounce, and so they come forth softer and softer, until perhaps none can hear them said but me:

Forasmuch as it hath pleased Almighty God in his wise providence to take out of this world the soul of our departed sister, we therefore commit her body to the ground; earth to earth, ashes to ashes, dust to dust: in the sure hope of the resurrection to eternal life, through our Lord Jesus Christ. . . .

("Harder and harder to pronounce," aye. But Julian is beginning, as you will see, to work a change in me.)

Except you know these things, you would know nothing regarding my person. Indeed, insofar as a life is behavior and event, there is almost nothing else to tell.

Yet of you, my gracious reader, I beg pardon for having visited even this much puffery upon your patience, pleading the necessity of such personal disclosure. It is not pride in me that asks attention to my words, as though I myself were the importance of them. I seek no praise. I seek, rather, your confidence and your profoundest trust. Moreover, and most delicately of all, I seek in you an obedient spirit.

For this, too, is the purpose and end of all my ministerial vocation: that I have prepared myself to tell you the tale which now this volume encloses, which is the life of Saint Julian, whom we call the Hospitaller.

As a tale, it is bright with interest, filled with wonders and warrings and such marvelous human accomplishment as can take your breath away.

As an account of the ways our ancestors lived their lives—yea, more than an age ago—the tale is as accurate as my own persistent studies can have made it. The quietness and the singularity of my life have together granted me the favors of time and scholarship. I have over the years accumulated a library peculiar to my interests, which are Old Latin, ecclesial history, the means of sanctity, the Sweet Rose of the Mystics, how a mortal might participate in the Holy, how mortals *have,* in fact, achieved divinest communion— and these communicants are the Saints, and therewith have I made a sincere study of the contexts of their lives, the lives of our spiritual ancestors, clothing, castles, worship, fears, faith and feignings and fightings, including even the brave spectacle of

"Trumpet, drums, flags and pennons,

Standards of horses white and black—"

as wrote the Provençal poet Bertrand de Born. I am assiduous for the small fact. Here, you see, I seek the lesser level of your trust. But in this next, the greater level:

For as it is a Saint's Tale, I declare unto you that the thing has sustained me! Why, it contains *my* life in whole—and in the end, hope for us all.

For though my external behaviors have been common and quiet and consistent; and though I have ever been steadfast in responsibilities, plain in pastoring, of no more ambition than my narrow parish permits, nevertheless, my interior spirit has suffered extraordinary turbulence, some few delights and after those, periods of the most doomful dejections. I have been Jacob at the Jabbok, alone and

wrestling in the night—in sunlight to discover that it was
the mighty God Himself whom I had engaged to fight, and
knew that it *was* the merciful God for that I had not perished.

It is not false to say that I have sinned Davidic sins,
though none save me and my God have known of them; nor
shall I recount them here (which recounting would come,
indeed, of a perverse kind of pride). Sufficient to say is that
the effect of such sinning was to send me into a howling
solitude. A spiritual solitude, perfectly enclosed within my
flesh, for I continued to preach, nor ever doubted the value
or the truth of my preaching, for the Spirit of God was in
the pastoring truly, even when it was not in me.

But in the midst of these my desolations I encountered
the tale of Saint Julian, Hospitaller, in the book of a French
man, and therein met my secret self. Or, to be more accurate, in the life and the deeds of Saint Julian my secret self
found form and direction and terrible truth and confession
and hope at the last.

Him, therefore, I did in particular study. Legends, pious
chronicles, the handwritten incunabula related to Saints and
to this Saint I read carefully, accumulating notes. Twice I
spent sabbatical time in the monasteries of certain monks
who devote themselves to the preservation of ancient memory; under their guidance I searched through the volumes of
their libraries. With prayer and patience I gathered the matter of Julian's ways and his days—yea, though the wealth of
this Saint's life is more to be found in the spirit than in the
history.

Into him, by the force of my imagination and the gravity of my own interior life, I entered; and there I have allowed my soul to dwell—in revealing and in healing—now many a year. The stuff of this Saint is my stuff now; and I need no other name than his name—knowing which, you *do* know all.

From him, then, from the terrible and beautiful Saint Julian, Hospitaller, and from the God which his tale has taught me to love, my little ministry among the poor has grown sweetly rich, if not in successes and advancements, then in wisdom and in mystery; and I have myself grown, as I wrote it above, altogether contented.

I was at the first, and still I am, a minor cleric. But now I am grown old. Wisdom knows the length of her days and does not count them more than what they are. Soon I shall cease to preach. Soon another hand shall baptize the children of the children of them that I baptized so long ago. My hams are weak; they hurt when I sit on the wooden bench. In consequence, I stand to read or else to write. I am standing now, addressing you. But my knees are becoming untrustworthy, and *that* is the measure of the time left unto my working, my ministerial life.

We brought nothing into this world. It is certain we can carry nothing out.

Therefore, I must now—this day and the next—begin to fulfill the second purpose and the second end of all my ministerial vocation. Today and tomorrow and every day it takes thereafter, I shall pour my learning and all my interior spirit into the tale this present volume encloses, of him, the Saint that shaped my life, Julian, Hospitaller.

He is the Saint of every ordinary mortal. He is, moreover, the Saint of them that have sinned uncommonly, whether by heart or by hand, and whose peculiar penitence grants them to know a most uncommon grace. Mystery attends both his borning and his dying, but such mystery as precedes our own consciousness and that follows it, too.

And I have disclosed to you, O most gracious and deliberate reader, my external ministries as well as my internal turbulence not (as I already have protested) to draw your attentions unto myself, but to draw your trust in my telling, that you might give your complete attentions, rather, to Julian. For if my personal confessions can have led you, too, into an open and obedient spirit, then you might yourself take up residence in the tale of this Saint—at the end of which, in truth, in the most glorious truth, lies hope for us all.

And when it pleases Almighty God in his wise providence to take out of this world my soul too, let those who would remember me assign unto my life, my ashes and all my dust but one name only, the name most accurate to that which I have been and that which I would be:

I am, my Lord, your Julian,
the Least of him.

THE FIRST PART

―――❀❀❀―――

BIRTH

2.

CONCERNING THE MOTHER OF
THE SAINT

I know not her name. In no account is the name of the
mother of the Saint remembered. It is in the light of the
name of her son that we see her at all, for his tale embraces
her. Nevertheless, the mother was whole ere the boy was
born, and it is in *her* that he came to be. Without Julian, his
mother would not have been remembered; but without his
mother, Julian would not have been.

Therefore, honor obliges us to grant her place and person-
hood here at the head of the tale.

Julian's mother, gracious in every regard, was a slender
woman with slightly caven shoulders and a quick, bright
eye. Her face, in sweet descent from the brow to the chin,
showed first the temples of stable thought and wise administration; next, the dawn-blush of joy and high-blooded
health; and finally the raised taper of noble certitude—
which, in her husband's presence, lowered to noble compliance. Ah, and then how glad was the Lord of the Castle
to find the gift of such compliance in the face of his lady!
And how rich was the issue of Compliance and Gladness

commingled together: for the issue was Julian himself, appearing pink and dimpled on the Feast Day of St. Michael, Archangel.

His mother bore her child quietly, as Mary must have delivered her own, for each woman was faithful unto God and of God she bore the fruit.

Quiet in childbirth, quiet abroad, devoutly quiet both at prayer and at table, this woman did nonetheless manage the estates of her husband when he was gone to court or to war—or else on pilgrimage. And daily after Mass had been said in the chapel, after breakfast had been taken in her own apartments, Julian's mother moved forth to direct the household staff in all its regular duties, *whether* the lord was in residence or not.

Her hair was abundant and beautiful. There was none who met her that did not remark—at least prively—upon its shining plenitude. Alone, the woman would gather the masses and cover them with a woolen cap for comfort and for the warmth. When busy about her common responsibilities, however, she wove her hair into a golden rope which dropped from a head erect straight down her back, where it swung like a censer in rhythm to her tread. Over her crown, on such days, and under her chin she bound a white linen wimple which she wore both indoors and out. When the weather looked kindly upon her, she covered her head with nothing but this wimple, and breezes in the bailey would catch at its shoulder-folds and puff them with air and lift them around her head as if they were the wings of the white swan of lazy waters, unfolding now toward flight.

Blue-eyed, with lily-white skin—Oh, how comely was the Lady of the Castle as she ducked her head and grabbed for the sailing linen and laughed at the whirling breezes as if they were sprites or dryads, the children of dreams and memories.

It was upon occasions of such unconscious abandon, occasions when his mother broke her silences and danced with the day, that Julian—watching through some high window or lattice above—was so moved with love for his mother that he fell to his knees and gave thanks unto Heaven for the rain of grace and goodness in his life.

Ah, but in the evening at banquets in the great hall, or else when her lord led her into the courts of their young king, then her golden hair was a heaven itself, abiding like cloud around her head, and God, I swear, forebore then to blame the love-locks fringing her temples.

3.
CONCERNING THE FATHER OF THE SAINT

Of Julian's father certain records insist that from his youth he was curious for every kind of knowledge—that after he had surpassed his tutors, this unusual lad had of his own accord read all twenty books of the Etymologies of Isidore of Seville, by which he conned an encyclopedia of subjects, from the grammatical subtleties of Latin to the nourishing properties of certain foods and drinks.

While yet his own father, Julian's grandfather, stormed in lordship, the lord-to-be, wisely to prepare himself to

follow his father, went to the vintners and learned from
them, to the plowmen and the scholars, all three. He put
particular questions to millers and smiths and knights and
counselors at law; to architects, strategists, tradesmen,
priests, and the monks bent over books on boards in the
abbey libraries.

And if these records are worthy of belief, then the grown
man's frame, his body and his massive skull, were the perfect casement for such a mind, since he was broadly built
and thickly muscled, arm and thigh; his grey eyes were generous and as widely spaced as the sun from the moon, stars
glittering in the oils of his black brows.

From God Julian's father had inherited the talents of foresight and steadfast responsibility. And this was providential,
since from his forebears—and from his sire, at the bloody
man's death—he had inherited a raw patchwork of properties requiring a governor of his qualities precisely.

And as he had done for himself when he was young, so
did the castle lord for his only begotten son.

Julian at two the Lord of the Castle bore on his shoulders;
Julian at four he bore on the neck of his post-horse, riding
forth with frequency to introduce the boy to estates which
one day would fall unto him: fields and villages, marshland
and valleys, lakes and streams, forests for hunting and
forests for timber, the which the lord both sold and used in
his own constructions. And when they reined around, father
and son, to return home in the green of the evening, there,
on high ground above a bend in the treacherous river, they
saw their castle ascendant, that solitary castle filling half the

heavens in magisterial silhouette. Dark, save where the torches winked on the wall and fires cast glows in the bailey. Solid, its timbered palisades defending the great hall, the great hall built of oaken beams, and below the hall, the stables, granaries, gardens, barracks, kitchens. A high, dark and solid power, the small boy saw; the *symbol* of power, saw his father: for the thing was more than a magnificent weapon, more than their residence, more than the seat of governance: it was command; it stopped the mouth; it was the sign and the very splendor of supremacy.

These, then—lands and castle—had Julian's father inherited in his thirtieth year, before he married, before the birth of his son, when the ravening heart of his own sire stopped, and the old man lay down dead. That one had been a blood-lusty lord, acquisitive and unkind. He had doubled his estates, for he loved to get and he loved to kill. And once when the king, a warrior fully as brutal as himself, had imprisoned the blood-lord's son, Julian's father, and had demanded liege obedience for the life of the boy—whom he planned otherwise to catapult bodily over his castle wall— that bloody lord and sire of the boy had roared back that he did not care, for he had "the anvils and hammer with which to forge still better sons!" 'Twas the king that had buckled then; for his own rough heart had been won by the grace and the intelligence of the boy whom he held captive, whom he therefore could not kill but kept and afterward welcomed as a member of his council.

But the blood-loving heart of the old sire, Julian's father's louder father, was won by nothing save delightful slaughterings. Hear him, his voice and his grandest sentiment: *I tell you I find no such savor in food or in wine or in sleep, as I do in hearing the shout "On! On!" from both sides, and the neighing of steeds that have lost their riders, and the cries of "Help! Help!"—as I do in seeing men great and small go down on the grass beyond the castle walls; and at last in seeing a field of the dead, the pennoned stumps of lances still in their sides, their bright pavilions empty. . . .*

It was in this manner that the cruel old man extended the properties that fell to his son when his hard heart cracked and he fell down dead.

And since it must be recorded how, from his thirtieth year forward, Julian's good father enriched his legacies, allow me here to detail four different sorts of additions which this more courteous lord made, each of which cannot but illuminate the character of the man:

The first sort of addition:

Ever moved by a restless love for the lands and their peoples, and guided by a deep sense of stewardship before God and every righteous authority, Julian's father brought economy and organization to every transaction of the castle and its territories; he brought a balanced judgment to the disputes of the villeins and all the souls within his care; he made his word trustworthy and true before ambassadors and powers abroad; and thereby did he both preserve the inheritance and cause it to flourish ere he would die and pass the enrichments on to Julian.

The second sort, more visible in prominence:

Immediately upon sitting in the seat of his lordship, Julian's father added to the eastern bend of his castle wall a great tower, which he caused to be constructed of dressed and mortared stone. All buildings else, save the chapel, were of wood; this would be superior to those in that it would not burn; therefore the new lord designed his stone eminence both as a watchtower landward, and as the final refuge for himself, his family, and his knights, should an enemy succeed in breaching or burning the wall.

Note that the tower was required on the *east* side of the castle grounds because the river that couched the northwest corner was wide and swift and silent, a nearly absolute demarcation between this lord's lands and the lands of his violent and vengeful neighbors (such vengeance being one more bequest the bloody sire left his son). When there was peace, Julian's father ran a painter-line from bedrock on his side of the river to great oaks on the far side, by which a ferryman was paid to draw a ferryboat across the waters with travelers to and fro—and so this castle became known as a "Point of Crossing" in that country. When hostilities threatened in the west, the painter was chopped at the oaks and coiled on the castle side.

But the direction of the lord's most common activities was eastward, for that way lay neighbors of closer blood and a greater concord; and yet farther east than these dwelt a new king whom Julian's father served with a genuine affection, and between them—between the courts of the king and his lord—was good order maintained and prosperity encouraged.

And this was *the third* sort of addition to the inheritance of his forebears: a powerful political alliance.

For Julian's father, who had earned the fondness of the old king when he was a captive, now enjoyed the reverence and the complete adoration of that king's son, a youth withal, whose life he had saved by a canny diplomacy. For this young king had been but a pale prince, the *second* son of his father, a quiet, observant lad more taken by books than by the quintain. He made no sound when he walked, infuriating his father by the surprise of his approachings; his speech was precise and spare and withheld at table; his beard was soft and his fingers long—and the old king despised him for these "milk-fed manners"! That brutal king swore to tonsure his second son. Likelier, he would suddenly, in a blind fit, have killed the boy with his two-handed sword, except that Julian's father interposed to preserve the boy.

At that time a member of the old king's royal council, thirty-two years old, the lord of his own demesne, and in liege obedience to his king, Julian's father asked to keep the lad as a *servus a manu,* one to write his dictations while he was himself acting in the court's service. The old king, thinking such an office appropriate for lisping striplings, agreed with a bark of laughter. He never laid eyes on the youth again. He occupied himself and his elder son with wars against Saracens approaching from the east, infidels he meant by force to baptize, but who instead slaughtered his heir and himself in an ambush most uncivil.

For several years thereafter Julian's father acted as regent, earning the love of the young king while establishing his throne securely. And there was peace in all the lands between these two, a thing their fathers could not accomplish and did not attempt.

The fourth sort of enrichment may be summed in a single name: Julian. This the man considered his greatest addition to the inheritance of his ancestors, for that he loved the boy more than he loved his own life, and he considered all his work to be done for the sake of this child, who would inherit the whole himself in the end.

"Come here, boy! Come to my bosom. Ah, let me heft my warrior still before the day when *he* must heft the bones of his withering, crippled father, bearing me from the hearth to my bed and back to the hearth again!"

Julian's father's hair was black; black were the sweeps of his moustaches and his beard, both of them divided in the middle and combed east and west away from a central white line. 'Twas *all* his hair divided so. Black were his brows that sparkled like stars as they bent over his grey eyes, and black the radiant lashes that opened and closed those eyes.

On the other hand, the lord's tunics, his mantles, his hose and his shoes—these were dazzling bright! By color the castle lord made boisterous his goings and his comings: blues and yellows, crimsons, purples, greens. His clothes were mostly wool, though at the young king's court he wore samite, sendal, damask; and the furs that trimmed his raiment were lambskin, rabbit, miniver, otter, marten. . . .

Julian's father boomed laughter at the goodness of life. If his mother's willow elegance was wrapped in silences, his father's was the generosity of these eruptions, and the pure equality of his affections for those that served the land with him.

And here was the real authority of this lord's governance: that as intimately as his lady knew the staff of the household, even so intimately did the lord know his knights . . . *and* his hostlers, *and* his smiths, his hawkers and huntsmen, villagers, shepherds, cowherds, swineherds, plowmen—yea, and the cottars too, and *all* his villeins! This lord did travel his holdings himself, fully as much as any bailiff ever did.

And in all the disputes, in every litigation which the people brought to him for adjudication, the man, Julian's father, was a just judge, making his decisions upon the convergence of three codes, and in the spirit of one. The codes? They were the venerable customs of his various peoples, even those folk whom his father had merely killed in order to gain their lands; they were, next, the laws of the kingdom entire; and finally they were the righteousness of God.

As for the spirit . . .

"Julian, my son, come sit beside me."

And the lad skipped through the great hall to the dais, where his father sat upon a wooden chair carved all over in curious figures, a pelican, a phoenix, a cross between.

"Look into this book. Canst read, lad?"

"Aye, father."

"Art easy enough in the Latin, then?"

"Aye, father."

"Then read this."

Little Julian leaned against his father's shoulder, reached toward the book open on his father's lap, then put the tip of his pointing finger upon the page where the letters were individually inked in a crabbed calligraphy. Slowly, shoutingly, the lad read:

"BEATI MISERICORDES: QUONIAM IPSI MISERI-CORDIAM CONSEQUENTUR."

It was the bellow of a boy at lessons. The hall re-echoed Julian's melodious *"consequentur,"* and the sharp edge of a massy battle-ax—a tremendous seven-foot weapon which hung from hooks above them—hummed.

With his own thick forefinger, Julian's father touched the back of his boy's hand. "And what is *misericordia?*" he asked.

And Julian, crossing one foot behind the ankle of the other, said, "Mercy. 'Blessed are the merciful'"—he was translating the whole without his father's further request: "'for they shall obtain mercy.'"

And the man with solemn instruction said: "Remember this."

And the boy, now winding his fingers through the tangled fall of the man's black hair, said, "I will, Father."

And thus the spirit of this lord's every decision: mercy.

It will have been noticed by my more canny reader that this account, as it knows no name for Julian's mother, knows none for his father either. Nor shall I invent the thing I do not know. I can only say "lord" and "grey-eyed" and "Julian's father," and otherwise let house and lineage slip into the clouds of the past.

Likewise, the identities of the kings of Julian's lifespan, as well as the hard placement of his lands and his itineraries, are lost in obscurity. But for the most part, I am not sorry to labor within this dimness surrounding the clear center of my tale. Except in the instance of one figure (she who has taken my own heart, too) I am not sorry that the tale must be told uprooted from the names and the dates of more cogent chronicles: for such unmooring grants a timelessness to the Saint and to all that I shall say of him, yea, though of the past, and of our deepest past, Saint Julian *ought* to seem to dog our heels, ever close behind us, in whatever age we—any of us—make our habitations and our meanings.

4.
THE CHAPEL

In those days and in other castles, the private chapel was commonly part of the main building: a single room two stories in height, the nave divided horizontally so that the lord and his family might enter the upper balcony directly from their chambers, while the rest of the household staff would enter at the level of the great hall.

The chapel inherited by Julian's father, however, stood alone, a building separate and isolated. Moreover, it was made of stone. And these stones were hewn so huge that no one could imagine what engines were used to place them here; hewn *both* huge and smooth, and so tightly fitted one upon the other, that mortar had been unnecessary. This was plainly the most ancient part of the inheritance, and the stone-carved cross within was of a runic character.

Julian's father appreciated that such a chapel made an equality of all who entered there, for all must worship on the same level, and all must needs experience the selfsame moods of heaven while walking to the mossy structure: rain and storm and sunshine and the spring breeze and snow. None was exempt from a wild sky, nor was anyone denied its milder smile.

Though the golden chain of creation demanded that here on earth some should govern and others be governed, yet Julian's father loved deeply this effect of the coming of the incarnate Christ, that in God's kingdom none was more important than another, and all were servants, all were mortal, all were one before the judgment seat of God.

There was an ax.

Julian's father's bloodier sire had done little to maintain this place, and nothing to improve it. But when the care of it had fallen to him, Julian's father commanded its complete repair; and so, in a vault below the flagstones of the chapel floor, he had found an iron battle-ax within the sarcophagus of his earliest known ancestor.

According to a legend alive in his own day, it was this great, great, and greatest of grandfathers who had, by seizing a beacon hill in the bend of the river, conquered the core of the lands now held. Legend described him as a small, bunch-backed, and angry pagan who killed rather by cunning than by brute strength. But after overpowering a minor chieftain of the riverland, and after building a crude motte-and-bailey castle where once the beacon had burned, the little man was said to have seen a vision of a Crucified King, standing wounded—as bent and quite as toadlike as the dreamer himself—outside an old stone chapel in the forest. When he woke up, the little man discovered that he had been made whole, tall and sweetly muscled. Straightway he sought the chapel of his vision; and finding it in the forest hard by his own new-conquered hill, and finding too that it was a Christian shrine with a priest to the place, and learning from the priest that it was Jesus Christ Himself had met him in his dream, this oldest of ancestors besought of the priest a Christian baptism. Next he cleared and claimed the chapel, worshipping there for the rest of his earthly days; and so the lineage seemed to have begun in the folds of our merciful Savior's robes.

Julian's father had wondered much about the truth of the meaning of this legend—especially since his ancestor's reputed coffin measured seven feet from the head to the foot of it. During the sacred building's repair, therefore, he ordered the stone lid to be lifted. By ropes and pulleys his servants inched the heavy granite upward, upward, until their lord could thrust a burning lamp within, and after that his head and a shoulder. Mutely he gazed into the stony space. Long he stood thus, in contemplation under the crushing weight of the lid of the sarcophagus, while the servants, holding rope, glanced dumbly at each other.

Within the great stone box the lord was looking at no body at all, neither hunched nor tall, for there was not so much as a bone within. Instead there was a marvelous battle-ax, gleaming even in lamplight, unrusted, massive, venerable, runic, ancient.

Look at you, the lord, Julian's father, spoke inside his mind, *at once so agèd and so fresh. Time must be as nothing to you.* He stroked his beard with the flat of his free hand. *Truth is like that, never changing, but often lost and ever new at being found again.*

Soon he laid the lamplight by and removed the ax with his own two hands and a terrible straining, for the weapon was of an uncommon weight. Saying nothing of its vacancy, he ordered the tomb closed down again and sealed.

Whence had he sprung, then, if not from flesh and blood? From a legend? From an ax? Or perhaps the legend itself was all an invention and a lie?

Julian's father next brought the ax up to the castle in a cart, then had it hung from iron hooks on the wall behind the high table and the dais where he administered judgment, and where he and his wife—at that time great with child—and the priest of the chapel sat to eat.

5.
THE BIRTH OF THE SAINT

Annually by the Feast Day of St. Michael the Archangel, the autumn crops had been harvested and winnowed and dried and stored; the villeins had come to the lord's court and had sung, as they called it, "harvest home" over the rich foods of his harvest feast; the castle lord himself—together with his steward for matters of the household and with his bailiffs for matters of the land—had totaled and closed his accounts for the year. Then, *after* the Feast of St. Michael, the villagers opened gaps through the field hedges so that cattle might enter to graze on the stubble the harvest left behind; at the same time the plowmen drove their oxen into fallow fields to prepare for the planting of wheat and rye. The autumn had ended, the winter begun, and Michaelmas—year after year, and every year the same—marked passage from one season to the other.

Every year the same, I say . . . except for one particular year when the lord walked to the chapel to celebrate St. Michael's Mass without the footfall of his wife beside him. He entered at the back and approached his solitary chair in the foremost row and sat and bowed his head and groaned. And though the chapel was full of his people, he did not know. He was alone, and no one interfered, for the man had twined his hands so tightly together that the fingers grew bloodless and yellow.

His lady's frame was slender, delicate, scarcely hardy. And the midwife that morning had called him aside to whisper, "Her hips, my lord. Her hips." Boyish, those hips, as the husband knew right well. Narrow. Perhaps the baby that would strive to pass between them today would be blocked, never to breathe. Or would break a bone, or would tear some necessary thing within his wife, and then what? Babe and mother striving against one another, though both would yearn the same, and he would wish it of them both. Ah, God: life and death it was, striving together in the person whom he loved, unto whom he had given his heart.

The Lord of the Castle groaned.

"*Et a Jesu Christo*—" said the priest at the lectern, which was carved to represent the head and the wings of an eagle. He was reading the Epistle Lesson appointed for this day: "*—primogenitus mortuorum, et princeps regum terrae, qui dilexit nos a peccatis nostris in sanguine suo. . . .*"

Morning light sliced the thick interior air. The entire chapel and all its worshippers were like that lectern, carven stone; so were all the servants in the castle and all the villeins on the land. Every heart beholden to this lord was mute in fear and sympathy: For what if their lady—? What if the firstborn of their lord—?

Only the priest was not a stone. Only he, standing in festal vestments, could open his mouth and utter words. But even he spoke not for himself, since these were not his words, but words that came first from the visions of John the Divine: "And from Jesus Christ, the firstborn from the dead and Lord of the kings of earth, who loves us and washed us in his blood from our sins. . . ."

The priest broke off. Silence rose up and walked like the rolling-shouldered panther through the room. In a moment the lord became aware of the silence. He lifted his eyes and saw that the priest now, too, was as fixed as wood, his grim gaze toward the back of the chapel. A shiver seized the lord. He turned his own gaze backward and saw his lady's

midwife standing empty-handed in the sunny doorway
there. Her right hand and her full right arm were bloody,
and tears were streaming down her cheeks.

At the motion of their lord, the worshippers likewise
turned. A terrible gasp went up, together with one woman's
stifled cry, which cry broke the stillness of the midwife, who
whispered the Latin word *"Monstrum"*—and straightway the
lord stood and strode the aisle to the midwife at the chapel
doors, and the midwife turned at his coming, and together
they went out.

"Good my Lord," the midwife puffed as the two of them
moved uphill toward the castle, her thick legs pumping,
"'Tis a marvel! 'Tis a portent, surely!"

"What?" the lord demanded. "Woman, what are you
telling me? How is my wife?"

"Well," the midwife declared. "She is well."

The lord crossed himself. His black hair streamed in the
wind of the speed of their going. His eyes remained steadfast, unrevealing.

"And the child?"

The midwife hesitated. She slowed her poor legs' pumping. Her face was bursting red from these exertions and her
breathing heavy.

The lord was torn between two desires: to break into a
hard run toward his lady in her chambers, or else to halt for
the midwife's words.

He restrained his legs and paused.

"Speak, woman!" he cried. "Am I a father? Am I rejoicing now? In name of Christ, *why* is your right hand covered with blood?"

The old woman swallowed and wheezed and seemed so suddenly weak that the lord grabbed hold of her elbow to keep her upright.

"God save us," she huffed when the breath returned to her, "it is the blood of my lady."

"The blood of—"

"For the child tore her flesh when he came. Tore her terribly—"

"*Salve Regina!*"

"The flow of her blood was like a fountain new-brast from the land. I held the babe by his ankle in one hand, while with the other I tried to stanch the crimson stream. I failed—"

"*Failed,* mistress?" The lord let go her elbow with such a snap as to be throwing her away. "Then 'twas *lying* when thou saidest she is well!"

"Nay! Nay! Hear me through, for 'tis a miracle I'm telling you, truly! *I* failed only. Only *I,* my lord. And yes, my lady's skin grew swiftly ivory-white for the losing of her blood. But the *babe,* your son, even dangling from my left hand, *he* did not fail his mother, my lord. Ah, no, he did *not!* For he was gazing at the lady, sir, with a knowing eye—and to that I'll swear upon my life! And the whiter her lower parts, my lord, the more aggrieved did the babe's face appear! He saw! He knew! And he was crying at the sight! It was a rain of compassion that fell from his eyes, and where the tears splashed upon his mother's flesh, both belly and thigh, the pink returned! And then, like a river conjoining, the tears gathered together and poured over her fallen womb, poured down her mons as down a grassy hill, finally flooding the fountainhead of his mother's blood, the place of his own borning, to wash the wound and to heal it, sir, as though it had never been torn. Oh, good my lord, at the laving of that baby's tears, your lady's bleeding ceased, and lo: she lifted up her eyes and she did smile at him as sunlight beams upon the morning.

"'Give me the child,' she whispered, and didn't I hand the baby quickly down? Obediently down upon his mother's breast, my poor soul wonderstruck for all that I had seen? And then she wiped the child of his many fluids, and even now they are nuzzling together. . . .

"My Lord? One final thing? My lady, your wife, did all in silence, never speaking, never making the first moan while laboring to bring your son to birth. Never."

The Lord of the Castle, himself speechless, suddenly kissed the midwife and then flew. Like a youth he flew up the stairs of the forebuilding, dashed through the great hall to an interior stairs, and up these to the private apartments, into the room of his lady—

—who lay serene and wakeful upon her bed, her long hair loosed and wild upon the pillows, a babe in the crook of her arm, a tiny infant sleeping, in whom the lord saw nothing prescient or else powerful.

His lady smiled at him.

And so he was at her side, and so he knelt and drew to his eyes the back of her slender hand, and he turned and kissed it, and he was weeping.

"Ah, my Lord," she breathed, "our Greater Lord has seen us through, and all is well again."

She took control of her own hand and began to stroke the high blush on his cheek.

"Here's news," she whispered. "The child may bear the image of neither one of his parents. Julian may become his own lad, truly. Look."

She raised her cradling arm to reveal the nape of the baby's neck, where a small blush of hair was growing. Not sun-golden as was his mother's, nor yet black as his midnight father's hair, the infant's hair was sanguineous, as red as the hart, or the western skies at eventide, or blood.

"Julian?" said his father. "Thou callst him Julian?"

"Hast thou another?"

"Well, in God's order his name might well be Michael."

"Ah, sir, but it seemed to me he asked for Julian."

"God asked?"

"Nay. The babe himself."

"Julian. Julian," mused the grey-eyed, black-bearded man regarding his sleeping son, in whom he perceived nothing unnatural, save that loving made it so. "I have read of pagan potentates bearing such a name in the days before the darling infant, our Lord Jesus, was born. Hum. Perhaps our lineage bears backward farther than I knew. . . .

"Julian," the dark man said. "Thou art Julian."

6.
CELEBRATIONS

And so "JULIAN!" the people of the castle cried; and by their cry the word went forth into the countryside and the villages, and then all the peoples of the Lord of this Castle sang: "AN HEIR! BRAVE JULIAN IS BORN!"

Already by noon of the day of his birth, the appearing of Julian had been noised north and east and south. Everyone learned that a new generation had sprung up to receive the inheritance of their present lord—and the Feast of St. Michael gained a precious *second* reason for celebrations.

Oh, how the grateful folk broke their morning's quietude with shouts and songs and jubilations. They danced in the bailey and the villages and the churchyards; they ate cakes dipped in honey, drank wine mulled with ginger, marjoram, wormwood. And "Salt him with goodness" they sang:

> "Salt him with goodness, good Lord!
> Let blood be his baptism white.
> Robe him thine heavenly ward,
> While earth-shod he rides as thy knight:
>   And anchorite. . . ."

By nightfall—so the gossip blew abroad (for who had *not* heard the story the midwife told?)—the little lordling had found his mother's breast and, after the first three pulls and after his first three swallows of her rich milk, had uttered in tiny, toothless piety: *"Benedico Domino!"*

I do not vouch for the truth of the slippery tongues of gossip; but unto the truth of the following I give my absolute surety as a scholar and a pastor and an intimate of a thousand private moments:

That by nightfall little Julian had indeed found his mother's breast and was sucking as skillfully as any newborn cub, while the woman bent tearful eyes upon him and ran her bended knuckles down the ruddy fuzz on his cheek and touched the sweat-beads on his forehead.

And then it was her husband himself who moved softly through her chamber, attending to tasks otherwise accomplished by her servants: he combed her hair; he drew the curtains around her bed; he drove out the cat and the dog; he placed first a basin of water on the table by the wall, then a urinal bedside on the floor—and finally he took his leave mannerly, that his lady might take her rest merrily: she and their babe, whose name, indeed, was Julian.

THE SECOND PART

YOUTH

7.
YOUNG SAINT JULIAN AND THE MOUSE

In the forefront of the nave, close upon the steps of the chancel, three carved and cushioned chairs were set in descending sizes: one for the lord, one for his lady, and one nearest the stone wall for their young son, Julian.

The lad had no choice, of course; nor was it assumed that he could *ever* choose to miss a Mass, however old or self-determined the man might grow. For in this household, as in the whole country east to the approaching Saracens and south to the kingdoms of the Saracens, worship was as natural and as necessary as the sunrise. Only the fool could doubt that his happiness came of sweet obedience to Almighty God and his Son Jesus Christ. For wasn't the very air inhabited by ranks of evil spirits?—who might plague a man's flesh as easily as plague his sleep and his everlasting soul? And didn't the adversary, the Devil, as a roaring lion prowl around, seeking whom to devour?

Quaerens quem devoret!

Indeed! And therefore even when his father had ridden to duties abroad and his mother was left home to manage affairs, the two of them attended Mass daily, and High Mass Sun-daily, and every festival Mass throughout the year.

Already in his lisping boyhood Julian was taught the Latin language for two pragmatic reasons: first, that he might speak easily with clerics and ambassadors who traveled from distant countries to his father's halls or else to the king's court, for by ancient agreement this was the language that bound the better world together, the language that had prevailed before the Saracens broke forth to destroy things orderly and holy; and second, that he might understand the language of the Mass (and, incidental to his father's spiritual ambitions and the freedoms of his father's high office, that he might also read the Vulgate of St. Jerome).

By the time the boy was four years old, he caused his parents' hearts to soar, for they saw how perfectly, how faithfully their son was murmuring the Ordinary portions of the Mass—word for word!—with the priest himself. Such a chaste and pliant expression in the child's face, his pink mouth mobile even to the suffrages of the morning: *"Dignare, Domine, die isto,"* the priest and the child uttered together, and the people responded: *"Sine peccato nos custodire. . . ."* His parents received and returned the meanings, for their duplicate priests, old and young, had said, "Vouchsafe, O Lord, this day," and then parents and people and all the devout had responded, "To keep us without sin."

Priest and Julian: *"Miserere nostri, Domine,"*

Parents and people: *"Miserere nostri,"*

The priest and little Julian: *"Fiat misericordia tua, Domine, super nos."*

"Quemadmodum speravimus in te."

With glowing souls at their son's most nimble participations, the lord and the lady engaged in a rich, textured exchange with him and the priest, upon which dialogue would be founded the rest of their morning and all their day till the darkness:

> "Have mercy upon us, O Lord:
> Have mercy upon us.
> O Lord, let thy mercy be upon us
> As our trust is in thee."

And it is almost certain that Julian, too, thought he understood the deepest meanings of these Latin phrases, for whole tapestries of story passed before his eyes as he mouthed the magical formulations. In fact, the boy's notions of "mercy" and "trust" and "sin" were vague, and *"Domine"* seemed to be some elevation of his father in the people's mouths; on the other hand, the stories which his mind's eye watched granted unto the lad himself mysterious powers by the mere uttering of the magical phrases. He could, *Julian* could, command the animals! They came at his call; they lay themselves down before him. And he imagined riding their backs, terribly swift aground, breathless under the vaults of heaven. Of particular power was the phrase which he and the priest intoned at the most dramatic moment of the Mass, a phrase surrounded by bells and bowings, then lifted high, and yet higher than the priest's head, in the shape of a flat and rounded wafer of bread:

"*Hoc est corpus,*" they cried together, and this same *hoc-est-corpus* Julian plucked up and saved for real applications in the real world, no longer for games in the false worlds of story or imagination.

For he had himself witnessed the effect of the phrase. For it was during the grey days of February, in the fourth year of his age, that Julian happened to cast his eyes to the side and so noticed how *hoc-est-corpus* seemed to bring forth a wee, white communicant from a chink in the wall beside him.

But the lad had learned to test the seeming of things. Therefore, he returned to Mass the following morning—and yet more mornings after that—with bright purpose and a growing delight. Indeed! Precisely at the old priest's sing-song whine of that commanding *hoc-est-corpus,* a pink nose appeared in the shadow of the chink, twitching, waiting.

Not to diminish the young boy's wonder, but rather at every point to ground this tale in fact, let it be recorded: he was a very old priest.

Perhaps a holy dread came upon him whenever he served the host. Or perhaps the years had stolen the steadiness of his arm. Whatever the cause, he trembled as he broke the bread he had declared to be the Body of our Christ. He trembled again as he tried to place its fragments upon the tongues of the faithful. And then it was that fine flakes sifted down from the priest's silver paten to the stones below. No one saw; no one stooped to pick the pieces up again. So here came that little four-legged knave, darting across the floor, snatching quickly the flakes for his breakfast, and for what? Were there others behind the chink to be fed?

Now then, by the fourth morning and the fifth, delight began to wane in Julian for the mouse of the Mass. On the sixth and the seventh his emotion had changed altogether: he hated the beast.

For wasn't the creature a thief, after all? A tiny grandee, proud of himself? And though *hoc-est-corpus* might compel him from his hole, after that he ran as free as a heathen, feeding, disdainful of the pieties while every Christian child must sit in a devotion of hunger!

Julian felt the heat of anger in his face. Ah, it caused a wordless surging, a craving and a hating in the lower bends of his bowels. He panted beside his mother, her blue eyes oblivious of the minikin blasphemies at her feet. But then the sound of his breathing drew her attention. She glanced down at him, lifting her eyebrows in silent questioning, then she laid the back of her fingers cool upon his flaming cheek. She smiled, showing beautiful teeth. Her son, therefore, contrived to smile back, which was his silent answer to her question, and which made the answer true; for his love for his mother was greater and deeper than the agitations in his abdomen. And so he lifted his eyes to the crucifix above the altar and the warm moods cooled within him.

Julian was a slight child. Nay, but he was already deft and accurate with every motion of his eye and his hand, and the expressions of his countenance could communicate a sunlit glory. These traits he had taken from her, his mother.

From his father the lad had taken spontaneous eruptions of emotion: a giddy joy in the stooping of a falcon, joy in

the mere *sight* of that frowning, peremptory bird—or else a
seething heat at the sight of some little break-law.

   All his own, from no *immediate* parentage, was that blaze
of blood-red hair spilling in tangles down his shoulders and
coiling upon his back.

Very early on the morning of February twelve, Julian rose
from bed, dressed as for worship, donned a pair of leather
boots, selected from his personal arsenal a small, blunt,
weighted bolt which had been fashioned for practice on a
juvenile crossbow, then crept silently down the stairs. Out
the forebuilding the small boy went, carrying the bolt in
one hand and in the other an unlit lantern; out into darkness
and the feathery descent of snow, and his forehead ached in
the cold. Softly he moved over the new-fallen snow, softly
down to the chapel. Once inside that place, however, he can-
celed darkness and quietness together: he lit his lantern, and
he caused his bootheels to crack as he walked up the central
aisle, up into the chancel, up to a little chamber in the eastern wall behind the altar. This chamber was closed by a
metal door. Almost never did the priest lock this door, despite the value of the golden monstrance kept within. Nor
had Julian come for the monstrance. Instead, he wanted the
consecrated bread which the vessel contained. Between two
fingers he took out a single flat and rounded wafer. After
closing the vessel and this its chamber, the boy moved to
the altar and trimmed his lamp to its greatest brightness
and set it there, and tucked his bolt in the round of his

boot, and then—precisely as the old priest would do were he here—Julian raised the wafer in two hands high above his head. Oh, his heart was pounding now! His breathing became constricted, causing a nearly lascivious pain in the regions of his abdomen. His face blazed with heat, yet all his motion was steady and controlled.

"*HOC!*" he cried, his voice grown wretched and seeming old. And then, as it were a sentence unto itself, he cried, "*EST!*" And then, again, the hammer-blow: "*CORPUS!*"

Immediately, soundlessly, the boy was at the wall by the mouse's chink. Flat against the stones he fixed himself, his left hand holding the host above the heathen's hole, his right hand lightly balancing the crossbow's bolt. He watched. He kept his keen eye blinkless.

But the hole stayed empty.

As a further expedient, Julian began to crack the bread the way the priest would, but with one hand. Again, croak-ingly, he uttered the potent phrase: "*Hoc est corpus*"—and suddenly there was motion! Tiny life! In the shadow of the chink, a pink nose twitched, waiting.

Waiting for what?

And in that instant, knowledge flashed in the boy's mind, and he knew where the truer power lay, and he crushed the host in his left hand, and a snow of fine flakes went fluttering down, abundantly down. . . .

And so the white mouse crept out into the open and began to feed, skipping from crumb to crumb, mindless of disaster; and Julian allowed the moment to stretch, experiencing spasms of glad domination and, at the same time, fears for the loss of his dominion; and then his right hand acted with deft accuracy, flipping the bolt, its blunt end downward, and knocking the wee mouse lightly on the top of its head.

The creature drew a tiny paw within his white pelt, paused thoughtfully, then lay down on his side and shivered and then was still. The moist bead of an eye gazed universally upward; a single drop of red blood emerged from the nostrils; and the white mouse died.

Julian watched unmoving while that black eye lost light. He knelt and put forth his pointing finger and touched the small body at its belly: warm; the white fur silken and expensive; the flesh so soft that, as he pressed, he could feel the ridges of a trifling backbone under all. There were exactly three long whiskers on either side of the mouse's nose and the nostrils and the crimson button there. Julian touched the blood drop to his finger and brought the wee pool up beneath his seeing; and here he held, it seemed to him, life, the thing itself, all that the small mouse ever was.

But suddenly the boy felt a stab of shame for the taking of this tiny life. *Wicked!* Shame had a mouth and could accuse him: *Wicked, wicked Julian!* it sang in his heaving chest. The blood drop cooling on his finger! Tiny dying, irreversible! He could not call it back again!

With something like a whip of briars, guilt struck the boy across his face and his eyes and his two ears stinging; and, feeling the stripes in his flesh and convinced that he was bleeding a rain of blood, Julian stood and stumbled and flung his wretched self on the chancel steps and cried out in genuine anguish: *"Salve Regina!"*

At the same time there passed through his bones another shuddering; and part of his soul recognized the shuddering as pleasant, for he liked the pain.

8.
THE EDUCATION OF THE SAINT IN MATTERS UNDER MOTHER'S HAND

In his fifth year, the boy Julian was removed from the care of nurses. He was removed, too, from the wide attic rooms where he'd slept on pallets with the other children of the castle, and was granted a room of his own near the sollar where his parents slept.

Likewise at five, Julian's particular education began, for wasn't he the only son of his father, heir to the castle and all its demesne? Aye: there were not then, nor would there ever be, sisters or brothers for Julian. Precious was he not only in the affections of his parents, therefore, but also in the hearts of them that loved peace and their present places, them that yearned a warless succession of the castle from one lord to another, for Julian was the sole continuance of this lord's lineage and, please God, the future of these lands.

It was his mother who undertook to teach him courtly manners and the courtesy of every occasion. She did so with few words, offering her grace and behavior as the model for his.

"*Imitator mei es,*" she urged him softly in Latin, one of the woman's many languages since she was as capable of statecraft as her husband, though discreetly. "Watch me. Do what I do"—and together they entered the great hall where the Lord of the Castle would be entertaining in large or in small: bishops or cardinals or foreign envoys, scholars, merchants, members of the king's court—aye, and sometimes the young king himself. Whomever Julian's mother met in the company of the lord, she greeted with titles and bows and murmurs most appropriate, her words and her gestures indicating the various ranks of the guests; at the same time she defined herself in the act, her power to please or else to wither, for the tone of her voice alone was benediction to one and malediction to the other.

Julian watched. Julian copied what he could—and soon it was seen how closely the boy's frame and his natural posture mirrored his mother's: lean, smooth-muscled, efficient, caven between the shoulders. Both mother and son had cream-white complexions, though Julian's was also freckled and easily burnt in sunlight. The mother moved with a high-born, self-confident progress, like a tall ship on calm seas. In time the son affected the same tread, and soon no ear could hear either one of them coming down castle halls, down castle steps, on floors of oak all covered with rushes.

But the banquet itself was more than entertainment and the body's nourishment. "'Tis the trigger of the crossbow," the lady instructed her son: "a mere pin with magnified consequences, even of life and death." And this was her meaning: that at bread and meat, powers threatened and preened and shifted, and some were lost and some were gained. Therefore, long before guests arrived and entered the hall, Julian's mother had already prepared the place and the tables, teaching her son every ceremony of their service, from the servant's duties to the lord's: how to lay the cloths; how to cut day-old bread for the trenchers which held, bowl-like, portions of roast meat; how to carve that meat. Steel knives, silver spoons, salt-bowls, silver cups, mazers—how to place each of these, and in what order. How many fingers to use when later he held the joint for his father to carve.

"For when thou canst perform the chores of every least servant in thine house, only then art thou lord of all and, at the same time, free of all."

And when they sat at the high table to eat, though Julian's place was near the end of it, he watched his mother's motion; he observed her manners with the greater guests beside her; and these were triggers of a mighty consequence, indeed: for she, who never allowed her spoon to linger alone in a dish, might pluck the spoon of her neighbor from his with coquetry or else with a smooth contempt. She never put her elbows on the board. She did not belch. Her mouth was never over-full. Her hands and nails were scrupulously clean, for didn't her guests take pieces of meat with their fingers from the self-same dishes? She wiped her spoon and knife after each use, again for the sake of those beside her. But her mouth she wiped before she drank. She did not dip her meat in the general salt-bowl. And she charged her servants ever to keep her own dish heaped with various meats, so that she could graciously give from it to guests both left and right of her. Her voice was musical; and though the sense of the words did not reach her son's ears, yet the effects of them did; for a fat man's eyes might suddenly bulge; a bishop smile; a knight laugh helplessly; an abbess bow her head and listen at great length, nodding. And when trestle tables filled the hall with lords and ladies roaring, and fools ran like rabbits about, and jugglers tossed bells and bat-sticks, and musicians labored at harps and oliphants and vieles, even *then* young Julian knew the golden thread of his mother's voice, serene, unbroken, binding them together. . . .

Yes, yes: that voice was flawless music, and a consolation.

For when the young boy's brains began to buzz with the merriment's million noises, and when his head grew heavy at the banquet table, the slender lady rose and smiled and turned his way. On the wings of her wimple she sailed from her place to his and, taking his hand, led little Julian away to his room; and there, in the light of a single taper, she lay down beside him on his bed; and having removed her wimple, and having with her fingers raked the braid from her abundant hair, she began to sing sweet songs. "Blow, northern wind," his mother sang, her head on her palm, her eyes measuring his jawline, her pink lips making a soft kiss on the B of the first word, *Blow:*

> "Blow, northern wind,
> Send thou me my sweeting!
> Blow, northern wind,
> Blow, blow, blow-ooo—"

That "oh-ooo" of the final word she allowed to linger, a low note, thrilling him: then she pursed her lips to a whistle and breathed a stream of thin air into the child's ear, which tickled and caused him to giggle; and oh! how the giggling raised strong feelings within his breast, and small tears too, because his love for his mother grew almost more than he could bear.

And softly the lady sang:

> "Jesu, great in every might,
> That madest man above all thing,
> Save my true-love, day and night,
> Oh, keep him in thy good liking.
>
> For he is full of courtesy,
> Julian nimble, whom I love;
> Sweet as the rose upon her tree,
> And true as any turtle-dove. . . ."

While she sang, Julian reached and curved his hand around the warm column of her throat and felt the source of her music—vibrations each way free. He stroked the column downward, then extended his pointing finger and touched the pure-white hollow at the base of his mother's throat. The Poking Place he called it, that small scallop above her breastbone which he loved and where he nestled, the place wherein he might, like a cub in a winter's cave, find rest and warmth and protection. . . .

Sleep caused the child to sigh and to close his eyes; and so it was as the murmur of dreams that his mother's voice enwrapped him and carried him away:

"Adieu, dear heart that is so sweet,
Thine hair vermillion, eyelids white;
Great Jesu keep thee in thy sleep
And make thee morning's fairer light. . . ."

9.

THE EDUCATION OF THE SAINT IN MATTERS UNDER THE HAND OF HIS FATHER

By his eighth year, Julian's father had engaged a tutor for his son, a cleric to teach him the motions of the stars and the planets and their meanings; the cycles of the moon and the seasons; the marvels of numerical calculations; the use of plain figures for business and accounting; the mind and the deeds, the laws, the jealousies, the will, the love and the triumphs of Almighty God; the blood, the sorrows, the sufferings and the death of the Lord Jesus Christ; natural sciences and ageless philosophies, much of which the young pupil memorized:

"What," said the tutor, "is speech?"

And Julian, leaning upon a window sill, crossing a foot behind an ankle, answered, "The betrayer of the soul."

"What is sleep?"

"The image of death."

"What is death?"

"Passage without a vehicle."

"Whither the passage?"

"The mansions of the Father."

"And, as there are two roads, whither goes the other?"

"The torments of perdition."

"In the light of which—?"

"In the light of which:

> "Keep well ten, and flee from seven.
> Rule well five, and come to heaven."

And so on: Julian's necessary catechetic.

During all his young age—both driven by his own curiosities and drawn by his father's daily questionings (for he was in both respects his father's son)—Julian came to know every room, every servant and person, every duty, skill and craft that kept the castle flourishing: in the kitchens he learned from the slaughterer, the poulterer, the baker, the brewer, the candle-maker. He watched tailors and launderers, sewing and washing. In the stables he talked to grooms, smiths, farriers, carters and clerks. He learned to repair a cart, replacing its iron fittings, greasing its axles. *(For when thou canst perform the chores of every least servant in thine house, only then art thou lord of all and, at the same time, free of all.)*

Still within the castle walls there were gardens for vegetables, gardens for herbs (and the sauce-maker), vineyards,
orchards, each requiring knowledge of the earth and the seasons and all weathers. Outside the castle walls, in the strip
of land between them and the river's shore, was a channel
cut in bedrock, flowing with diverted river water. Here the
ferryman kept his boats and barges for crossing with people
and goods, travelers and trade. Here was the painter tied to
hooks in the rock, strung thence to iron bands round massive oaks on the other side. Here Julian watched as the ferryman winched his boats by this long cord shore to shore.
And Julian, traveling with him, learned the moods of the
river, laconic in the late summer sunlight, disastrous in au-
tumns and springs, and deceitful between.

Inside the castle again, in rooms of quietude, Julian
propped his elbow on the table, his chin on his fist, and
watched intently as the priest wrote in tight strokes the
words of the epistles his father dictated—business transac-
tions, personal exchanges.

And at his father's insistence, young Julian spent many a
day assisting the Almoner, who had charge of offerings to the
poor. Together they gathered leftovers from the tables before
the servants could pilfer them; then they distributed even the
richest of foods in the highways and the byways. For charity's
sake they visited the sick, the lepers, widows and others in
want—even the prisoners kept in the stone vaults beneath
the great tower—granting bread to the hungry and alms to
those impoverished. They selected older horses from the

stables and gave them freely to poor peasant families. The Almoner himself cut a spare figure, as unaccommodated as any beggar that he served: thin, gaunt, threadbare, ever colorless, dressed in black; generous was he, as gentle as John on the bosom of Christ, and faithful in all his ways. Of all his teachers, none made so great an impression upon Julian's heart and his behavior as this Almoner, for he was a good man, taking nothing for himself, giving all and getting nought, and calm, withal, content in his existence. His was the voice of a pipet, his language a run of blissful squeaks, unimposing, uncommanding: kind. And ever he ended their days together by kissing the tips of his "lordling's" fingers and squeaking: "Ten for the hosts of Heaven."

Julian seemed to keep those kisses as tinglings on his fingerpads until he entered the coolness of the great hall. And his father, watching his son arrive, seemed likewise to recognize a difference in the boy when he returned from the Almoner's benefactions.

"Julian, lad, come sit by me here," the Lord of the Castle said in deep voice. And when the boy had climbed the dais and stood beside him, the man said nothing for a moment, but saluted the progress of his young apprentice by a silent inclining of his great, black-bearded head.

At last, "Look into this book," he said, touching the vellum on his lap. "Canst read the words?"

"Aye, father."

"Art easy enough in the Latin?"

"Aye, father."

"Then read this."

The man ran his thick forefinger under words inked in a light brown calligraphy, while Julian pronounced them out loud:

"Amen dico vobis: Quamdiu fecistis uni ex his fratribus meis minimis, mihi fecistis."

Julian's father said, "What does our Savior Jesus here teach us, my son?"

And Julian said, "Even as we serve the least of his brothers, we serve him, father, Christ our Lord and Heaven's King."

10.
THE EDUCATION OF THE SAINT IN MATTERS COMPLETELY HIS OWN

Julian was alert and obedient in all his youthful lessons. No one found a fault in him. All who taught him loved him, for that he seemed so much to love the learning. Wherever he went in the castle, he was sunlight and laughter and gentle favor, and *"Proficit sapientia,"* said the priest one day to the lord regarding the lord's son: "'He increases,' as saith St. Luke of the young Christ, 'in wisdom and stature and in favor with God and man.'"

So. Even so.

But Julian's deepest longing, his own intensest longing, was to grow ever more expert in the use of weapons. From infancy his toys had been swords, shields, little axes, a hauberk. After these there were added a bow and arrows, a spear, even a small working crossbow and several bolts to shoot from it. Daily, as his bone and muscle developed, Julian trained in the bailey under the grim, watchful guidance of men for whom the art of war was as familiar as breathing. They taught him balance, the swift cut and the several thrusts of his sword; they rehearsed with him the deceptive feint, a spinning parry, the effect of sudden, astonishing stillness; by rough demonstrations—which sometimes left the lordling giddy and bleeding—they made his body know the values of absolutely every movement he made, hand, head, torso, foot, and the glancing of his eye; they showed him why a single step to the right, when it should have been to the left, might straightway initiate a long defeat.

Veterans bellowed and roared when they engaged in mock battles. Julian at twelve and thirteen, despite their urgings to do the same, held his tongue. He flew into combat like a horrid thing, ghostly, inhuman, for that he descended in a perfect silence, his brown eyes wide, his lips retracted, his teeth—so said the young soldiers that scattered before him—rimmed with blood. Under sunlight the lad's skin would burn and blister and peel, giving him the red-mottled, flaking appearance of some severe disease. When he rode his charger topspeed, or else ran swiftly afoot, his red hair streamed backward and his forehead blazed, so that his attack seemed the advent of some terrible angel from the fires of heaven.

A swooping, six-winged seraph was Julian at war.

All of a sudden in a late spring dawning, Julian, rising from bed and reaching for his yew bow, heard the *peet-tweedle* of a lark, ascending the air outside his window. One of the wooden shutters stood open on an angle, showing a vertical strip of lavender sky. He had seen nothing; but by the cry alone, Julian imagined the flight of the bird, its speed and direction. Instantly, without a thought, he notched an arrow on his bowstring, turned, shot into airy nothingness, and only then saw the bird cross the sky in busy flight—just before the tip of the arrow entered its breast, transfixing it.

Julian's heart stopped. His scalp tingled at the thing that he had done—nay, at the thing that he *could do!* He felt the smarting of the bowstring on his fingerpads; he heard fluttering as the lark went falling down; he held his breath—he held his breath in a passion of unrealized delight, until there came the faint thump of the corpse on the ground below, and then did the young lad split his face in grinning. He grinned at the walls, grinned at the basin on the floor as if it were a bright companion, grinned most ravishingly upon his strong yew bow, this engine so immediate to his impulse that even thought needn't intervene.

Julian, child, at such a tender age: oh, the thing that you can do!

From his tenth birthday onward, Julian attended the hunts of his father. Whomever else the lord invited into his forests, there ever went among the men the shadow of his son. He drew no attention to himself, did Julian, neither by boastings nor by misadventures. Instead, he watched with a hungry eye. He restrained his desires in order first to train the raw gift Heaven had given him—and yet, desires blazed in the brains behind his eyes!

So ravenous was Julian for the chase, the strike, the sight of a dying prey; so deeply, so physically did his yearning tremble within his bowels, that it seemed it must be a sinful thing, withal, and he kept it a secret, unconfessed. He rode to the hunt affecting a casual attitude, maintaining his mother's mildness of expression: a shadow, was Julian; a mere darkening of sunlight when everyone turned to watch the falcon stoop.

But his learning was prodigious.

And let it here be recorded that the teachers he most attended to were not the huntsmen, but the beasts, both the chasers and the chased.

Where his father depended on dogs to find a deer's spoor, on lymers to drive the beast from hiding, on greyhounds to chase it and bring it to bay, Julian *became* the spirit of every such dog. He longed to be the solitary hunter. Therefore he acquired the hounds' abilities: distinguishing the scent of any quarry; reading their scats to know their diets, their health and their endurance; in the depth and the shape of their tracks discovering their weight and their speed and the years of their age. Julian could nose out deer on the wind and wild boar at fifty yards. He knew the rotting odor of wolves' exhalations, the dusty smell of small-eyed bear, the leaf-moldering coat of the aurochs, the vinegar piss of fox—and even the more timid creatures of the forest he could locate by the sound of them: hares, badgers, squirrels, martens, otters.

Where his father depended on hawks to hunt a flying quarry, Julian schooled himself *by* himself to outreach even the hawk's dramatic flight. His eye was the falcon's, interpreting grey shadow in grey cloud: ducks, cranes, geese, swan, small birds swift on the wing. And his arm was godlike, for by a preternatural discipline, practicing day after day and year after year, the youth increased the snap of his arms and the strength of his back until he could shoot a crossbow as quickly and as surely as another man shot the lighter wooden bow. He fashioned his own bolts, since others manufactured bolts for the armies in volume, roughly, using leather fins where Julian used feathers. He built his own bow in layers of wood and horn and sinew, a trigger of his own devising. At fifteen Julian could send his crossbow's bolt farther than half a thousand yards straight up through the grey clouds to pierce a pale tern in passage there.

11.
THE KNIGHTING OF SAINT JULIAN

On September twenty-nine, the day of his sixteenth birthday, Julian was knighted on a platform in an open field some distance from the castle wall. Flourishes of trumpets announced the occasion. Pavilions filled the eastern reaches of the field, heraldic colors, banners displaying dragons, wyverns, lions, fishes, harps. Bristles of weapons sprouted under their canopies. And for every grand pavilion there was a knight that had come to joust and to fight mock battles afterward.

Peasants and nobles pressed toward the platform. People plain and people liveried caused a very carnival of colors. The weather had the sharp savor of autumn, the sky a glorious blue with puffs of pure white cloud, great trees embordering the field itself in a pageantry of yellows, oranges, and fire-burst vermilions.

Ah, Julian! Ah, my Chevalier!

And why would Julian *not* take joy in this, his knighting's day, and in this, the great gathering all in his name—yea, and in this: that the King himself had come and was sitting attendance under purple and golden awnings in the center of the platform? What a boon for the candidate! With what public luster the royal smile would cause the young knight's name to shine!

And indeed, when Julian himself appeared on the road that led from the castle, neither riding nor walking in a knightly party, but flanked by his mother only, and the priest; when these three parted the crowds by their coming and Julian, last of all at the platform, ascended it (the lean young man a dazzle of white, his silk shirt white, his trunks and tunic and ermine robe all lily-white); and finally when Julian, his hair in flames, his eyes wide set, stepped lightly onto the carpet of the platform—why, then His Majesty the King did not wait to be approached, did not wait for obeisance, no! But the King rose up himself and moved to Julian and crushed Julian's snow-clothes in a regal embrace, then kissed him and led him to the place where his father stood, waiting with freshly hammered armor.

Why would the beautiful Julian *not* take joy in such glory as this? But he did not.

And it was precisely then, in the moment when the King exalted him, that people began to remark the strange detachment in the young man's manner. He did not flush with gratitude for the King's kiss, nor with pride, nor yet with modesty or even surprise. He remained as grave and pale as a marble column. He did not return the King's exceptional embrace! What was this? Whenever had anyone, lord or porter, ignored the love of the King? *This* King especially? But Julian seemed so lost in thought that his mind had abandoned his body. The young man's eyes stared fixedly downward, fixedly at nothing the people could see. And he must have bitten his lip: a line of blood ran into the soft rust of his chin-whiskers—

And so knots of people began to talk. They studied their beloved Julian, and they thought they understood:

"Seestow, Tom? Seest how devoutly the young lord creeps to his knighting?"

"Pious in all his preparations."

"Humble he is."

"And mortified!"

"Cold to a king an' warm to the poor! This one shan't forget the darling hearts that fed and dressed and raised him up."

"Look ye at the downcast eye! 'Fore God, he is a faithful one!"

"Fasted a fortnight, I ween by the pallor of those cheeks."

"Serves Heaven's King first, all others second."

"But wouldee *look* at those eyes? Blind to the world's bright treasure! They see nought but the Spirit of God and the sorrows of our Lord."

"More than that iron pot his father lifts over his head, 'tis the helmet of *salvation* for our good lad!"

Then one of the chambermaids said, "He did-na sleep in his bed last night."

"Och," said Tom: "then he slept on the humid soil, I trow."

"On straw's more likely," one of the sons of the nobles said, leering: "and a pretty muff to keep the cold parts warm."

"Nay!" the Almoner spoke for the first time: "Nay, but he did not sleep at all, neither in bed nor else in company. He lay face-down, rather, on the chapel floor. Wakeful. Keeping vigil. Purifying his soul."

"When, man?" demanded the high-born youth. "When did he get to the chapel? At what hour?"

The Almoner said, "I don't know that. 'Twas after midnight I found him there—" The gaunt Almoner paused, then spoke in a kind of wonderment: "for I had heard a wailing in the night. I heard some soul howling for mercy in the pure-dark chapel. I went to see, and my torch revealed my lordling, belly-flat on stones, his arms stretched out in the form of a cross—"

The young man snapped his fingers and said, "Yes: and could he have been there the day long too, the day and the night together?"

And the Almoner, in his pipet's voice: "Nay, he was not in the chapel at eventide. 'Twas only his sword, lying on the altar, which the priest had come to bless."

Then six or seven sons of the nobility shook their heads, baffled: "Then where was Julian yesterday? We sought him and saw no sign of him, not at the banquets, not at the games, though the games and the day were all in his honor."

"Fasting," said the brewer, "just as I thought."

"An anchorite," said the sauce cook, "secluding himself to meditate upon five wounds and a crown of thorns. . . ."

Nay, nay, but here is the truth of it:

Early in the morning of the day before his knighting, even before the dawning, Julian had arisen from bed and crept down to the chapel, where he laid his great sword on the altar, then had slipped out the postern gate into the mists of the new-mown fields. He carried his yew bow and arrows, his crossbow and bolts, and a sling for the stones he would find on the way. For he went to kill. For he had awoken in darkness with the vision of a mighty stag rampant guardant, a most tawny and magnificent beast gazing straight at the sleeper—and the bulk of the stag and its near proximity had caused such a sweet twisting in his bowels that Julian straightway determined to find the creature and to kill it. Therefore he rose and dressed and went forth hunting and to hunt.

In greylight, just at the outside edge of his father's forests, Julian noticed an intenser stillness in the midst of all the morning's stillnesses. Though he could not see it, he sensed the presence of a living concentration. Swiftly he notched an arrow, drew it to his ear, and shot it: not at any target, but down the airways of impulse and instinct. The hunter was as silent as starlight. The arrow alone made noise. Its feathers hissed a warning, but too softly and too late. The lovely *thunk* of its bite in flesh brought Julian to life so brightly, so abruptly, he seemed to wake from some primeval slumber—already flying toward his prey, full of the knowledge of death. Yes! Christ, yes! And Julian found in the underbrush the loose form of a wolf. And the discovery that his arrow had pierced through the right eye into its bestial brain—that the shaft of the arrow seemed to *be* the sightline of the dead wolf—drove a roar of laughter into Julian's torso. The hunter shook with a soundless delight, though none of it showed in his face. He was, to all the world, as solemn as the priest who drinks from a silver chalice.

Solemnly, then, he entered the forest, wherein all ways seemed suddenly his for the passing.

And with a wordless jubilation, with mindless persistence and a terrible precision, Julian went a-hunting.

Every living thing before him he shot and killed. Every rustle in the autumn leaves he probed with the tip of an arrow. Even tiny creatures, hiding in fright, the bites of his arrows dispatched. Birds flitting among the branches he stunned with the stones released from his sling. He caught rabbits—so quickly dead in a terrified leap, that they could not know when their corpses hit ground again. Weasels, slippery as worms, he cracked at the backbone. Otters: even as they dived in deep streams his bolts followed and found them and brought them lifeless to the surface.

The easy, tireless motion of this engine, his body, astonished Julian. It was as if the hunter stood outside himself, watching with awe the things he could do. For he never failed. He did not shoot, but that he hit. He did not hit, but that he killed. And he did not kill but killing increased both will and the skill for killing more. Greater hosts of animals perished in the forest than had ever perished before, except in fire. Blood made a mud where Julian walked. Carcasses marked the trail behind him, since he left the dead in postures where they fell.

By noon he had slaughtered the bears of the forest. All of them. And the wild boars, and the bison, and every fox that ran stinking in fear. Pigs too, and the villagers' cattle grazing on acorns. He wiped out the wild cats, shot badgers through the soil, struck down the red hind and the fallow deer and the roe.

And if so much carnage could produce an outcry—animal horror, creation's grief and the Maker's lamentation—Julian did not hear it. *Thunk!* And again, *thunk* in living hides, and the merry *zzzing* of arrows scoring the air; his godlike reach; the useless bleatings of dying beasts, the pulsing fountains of fresh blood: these caused in his strong heart hymns of gladness. And so he did not stop, nor could he stop, for he had not yet in daylight seen the stag he'd seen in darkness, the stag rampant in his morning's dreaming.

As the sun lowered into afternoon, Julian strode the

treeless fields, by means of his crossbow dropping eagles, hawks, the traveling geese, herons, ducks, and the mute high-flying swan. He made a rain of feathered creatures, raglike in the air, bouncing when they hit the ground and crying out at impact, yea, though they were dead.

His mouth had gone dry; his throat swallowed convulsively. The hunter had begun to moan in a growing frustration. For the sun was setting and he wanted, but he had not seen, that tawny stag!

All at once Julian turned and ran toward foothills northeast of the castle's lands. It was the choice of his foot, not of his mind. Soon he was ascending the lower slopes, sweating, racing the sun. Over their shoulders he dashed, over their succeeding summits—until suddenly the hunter was standing at the high edge of a hidden valley, panting, staring down upon a scene irenic, almost an Eden. Lo, how pure the grassy hummocks, the buzzing shadows, the shining pools and ancient trees still summer-lush and green. 'Twas a minute; 'twas two and ten minutes solidly that Julian stood transfixed by the sight, his spirit stirred to a genuine reverence; for the valley was populated by a great herd of grazing deer, groups and families of the perfectest deer, unto whom Julian could not help but give his adoration.

The young man's face grew warm with smiling. His shoulders folded devoutly forward, making a greater cavern of his chest.

So many harts and hinds, so proud and so unblemished! As blameless as on the seventh day! Oh, how tender in his nostrils was their scent, the various breathings of does and brockets and yearlings, the huffing breath of bucks, the earth-odor ascending from their flanks!

Julian sighed. His sigh was soft, but not altogether soundless, and a hundred creatures swung their faces upward, questioning; twice one hundred ears all twitched to listen; and in that instant the valley was absolutely quiet.

And in that instant too, as if resolving the questions below him, the hunter began to shoot. His bolts and arrows fell like a hail among the deer.

Julian didn't breathe. He didn't so much as open his mouth. He attended to his task with swift efficiency, both giddy and expressionless, like sunlight touching every beast, their heads and their necks and their breasts, with his bright darts, killing them, killing them, filling the valley with his slaughter, murdering every deer below until there were but three left living, three deer standing in a plowing of earth-brown bodies, three in a band together: a fawn whose muzzle dripped its mother's milk; the fawn's mother, a doe of particular grace; and a stag, grandly antlered.

Julian placed the front curve of his crossbow down against the ground, the crosspiece vertical to his kneecap; he bent and hooked the bowstring to an iron hook on his belt; then, with a bunching of the powerful muscles in his back, he raised himself and the bowstring up, bending the bow itself until the string had reached the end of the stock, where he slipped the string over its trigger hitch. With conscious control, then, the hunter had armed his weapon. Now he lifted it, laid a bolt in the groove of the stock, aimed, and shot the young fawn through an artery in its neck.

In a flash he had re-armed the bow and had shot a second time, driving this bolt with marvelous force through the ribs and into the heart of the doe, so that both mother and child stumbled and struck the ground together. And the third bolt was in the air before the stag, the last remaining beast in the valley, could bugle wrath or else surprise.

Unerring, that third bolt! As fast as thought. And yet so taut was Julian's perceiving that he followed the bolt as if he rode it: he watched as the point of it touched the forehead of the stag precisely in its center, watched as it bored through bone and sank halfway into the skull. And blood burst from the wound, yes—

But the stag did not, like every other quarry, fall. The stag did not die.

With great brown eyes it stared straight back at Julian and began to walk across the valley floor, its head still holding high that magnificent rack of antlers.

The stag said, *Julian.*

Julian could not move. He was paralyzed by the marvel: an animal mortally wounded, yet walking, coming, climbing the valley wall toward him at the top of it.

The stag said, *Julian!* And, ominously: *Juuuuuu-lian!*

Julian was shaking now. He could not hear the stag's tread, the clatter of its hooves on scrabble rock.

But he said, "What?"

And the stag said, *Juuuuuu-lian, thou art cursed.*

Suddenly, just as it arrived on a level with the hunter, the creature reared up on its hind hooves and dashed its fore-hooves across the young man's sight. The great stag, dread-fully rampant, cried: *As thou hast taken the lives of the forest, so shalt thou kill thy mother dead!*

Down came the stag, striking rock and causing the round valley to ring as from the throat of a bell.

Again it rose up. And again it cried: *And as thou hast mur-dered me, my son, so shalt thou murder thy father and thy lord!*

Immediately the stag lost form and purchase, and fell down dead. The blood at its forehead was scabrous, and al-ready the small flies were drinking from the cups of its open eyes.

It was on the following morning that the priest found Julian stretched face-down on the flagstones of the chapel, his sword untouched on the altar.

"Stir yourself, Julian," the priest said, touching the back of his head; but Julian was awake. Julian had not slept at all that night. "Rise and wash. It is your birthday, my little lord, and the day of your knighting."

And so Julian rose and washed; and his mother brought the pure-white vestments, and the three of them walked out to the field all full of folk, the good priest bearing Julian's sword.

Amid flourishes of trumpets Julian ascended the plat-form, where he was met and kissed by the generous King, who led him to his father and a table covered with gleam-ing, freshly beaten armor.

The King, then, and his father—with other knights attending—armed Julian in a corselet of doublewoven mail: "Which no lance," said his father proudly, "nor any javelin can pierce."

They shod him with boots of the same double mesh, girded golden spurs on, and hung a shield around his neck. It was his father alone who placed upon his head a helmet gleaming with many precious stones, saying, "Which no sword can pierce or mar, my son." He was given a spear of ash tipped with iron. The sword was now brought forward, and all the colorful crowds sank into a watchful silence as Julian kissed the hilt of it—in the hollow of which was a holy relic encased—and sheathed it in the scabbard at his side.

Then Julian's father approached him face to face. The broad-chested, bearded senior suddenly delivered unto the junior an open-handed whack of such force that the young man reeled backward and fell to his rump. This was the *colee*. And as Julian struggled in all his armor to stand again, the Lord of the Castle bellowed, "Be thou brave and upright, Knight, that God may love thee—and remember! Remember that thou springst from a race that never can be false!"

It was the *remember, remember!* which the *colee* was meant to fix in the young knight's mind for as long as he should live.

When Julian had indeed found his foot and was standing again before his father, his hair an autumn flame of leaves, he replied: "So shall I do, so shall I be, an' the Lord our Christ be help for me."

Again the long trumps shattered the air with a fanfare composed for this moment alone; the crowds raised glad cheers of honor; knights hastened back to their pavilions in order to arm themselves and their massive chargers for the joust; and as Julian himself had received from his father the gift of an Iberian war-horse, swift and fearless, muscled and beautiful, he was himself the first prepared to enter the lists.

The King of the Land and the Lord of the Castle, brothers in purpose and in history, took seats on the platform with their wives, all four in the shadow of canopies, chewing cloves and preparing to enjoy the splendor of knights thundering toward each other and splintering lances in the shocks of their collisions.

And then, at one point during the revelries in the name of Julian, Knight, when no one noticed his motion, the King bent toward his counselor's ear, solemnly whispering an extended speech which contained such words as "War" and "East" and "Saracens." After all, the King had come as his own herald, therefore, requesting in person the help of his most noble *cavaliere.*

Thus, on the first day of the sixteenth year of his age, did Julian enter into his knighthood.

12.
THE SMITH'S BOY

November was "Blood Month," the season when domestic animals were slaughtered and smoked or salted: meat for the rest of the year. Feed was too scarce to keep most cattle alive and thriving through the spare months of winter. The plowman's oxen must be maintained, of course; the best of the breed-stock must likewise survive on good oats and corn—some cows too, and some goats for milk and whey and butter and cheese. Chickens, geese and ducks all were able to live on a little. But the rest of the livestock, sheep, swine, cattle, were knocked in the head or else hung up and nicked at the sides of their necks and drained of their blood.

And wild game was brought in from the lord's forests to be dressed and preserved in the castle larders: venison, wild pork, bear fat, the great strips of bison meat.

Ah, but by this particular November, the villagers' herds had been much diminished. And the sky was perpetually overcast, as if to hide its face. And a sense of desolation had seized every soul dependent upon the castle's administration and upon this lord; for the game, the wild game—yea, *all* the fatness of the forests . . .

The blacksmith of the castle—whose forge and whose bed were attached to the stables—shoed the lord's horses whenever he was asked; in preparation for the harvest, he ground the scythes of the lord; he sharpened the sheep shears in spring, and axes and swords at any time. And in exchange for these labors, the smith received several privileges of his own, one of which was that castle plowmen plowed his private fields. A second such privilege was that the smith might freely gather wood in the lord's forests, wood to make charcoal for the fires of his forge, wood as well to warm his bones.

Accordingly, in early October the smith sent his boy with a low cart to gather fallen wood and any ready charcoal he could find. No ox to pull this cart, of course: the lad pushed it out of the village and over a straight path through the fields northward, whistling as he went. He was a raw-boned boy of extended stridings, an orphan whom the smith befriended, an obedient fellow, withal, and content with his life's position; for though he may not have possessed the wit ever to become a blacksmith himself, he was beloved of one, and he made his pallet by his master's bed.

Now, then, as this lad came into view of the forest, he ceased his whistling and listened, for he heard a hard humming among the trees before him, sourceless, as wide as the verges of field and forest, as rich as monksong. He ceased his whistling, but did not cease his striding. Rather, he pushed forward with an open-mouthed watchfulness. Several strides, and suddenly he gagged and snapped his mouth shut, for the wind had brought from the forest an odor so thick it seemed to color the air, a sweet and sultry putrefaction.

The lad strode forward in order to find the wood the smith had sent him for—but in several strides more the right wheel of the cart bumped on something, and the carcass of a wolf rolled out of the long grass, an arrow wagging in its hollow eye.

Gaze ye at me, sir? the boy thought with a shiver. *Nay, but the dead don't see!* He stepped on the shaft of the arrow and snapped it in two, and still continued into the forest, for hadn't his master asked it of him?

And then, as his sight adjusted to the darkness, he saw what was making so universal a humming, for he was surrounded by a shifting, living, coal-black cloud of—and the hellish whine of—ten million flies. The lad could scarcely breathe in an air so loaded with the exhalations of death. And everywhere he turned and everywhere looked there were the signs of a mighty slaughter: bodies grotesque and broken, bodies bloated, bodies burst, bodies eyeless and pouring forth from their entrails masses of wet white maggots.

Jesus, sweet heart, pity me! Pity me!

Now, finally, the long-legged lad turned around. He left the cart right where it was and began with a terrible caution to creep back the way that he had come.

Sprites, begone! Ye hosts of that old serpent the Devil, let me be!

For here was an extermination so great that the people would surely have heard it, if it *could* be heard. Here was a slaughter which required a host of hunters, and these the people would have seen, if the hunters had been solid flesh and *could* be seen. But no one saw! And no one heard! And none but the smith's boy knew what ruin had been visited upon the people. . . .

"The Devil," he cried, bursting through the wooden door into the smithy. "The Devil is walking the earth! The Devil and all his angels!"

Now, the lad had been mute until this moment. His eyes had never known trouble. But here he came with such an articulate and horrified cry, that the smith was immediately convinced: indeed, the Devil must be abroad, and surely the young lad had encountered him, or whence had this miracle come, that the dumb began to speak?

So the smith, his own eyes white with fear, hastily gathered a small army—some grooms, to whom he gave sharpened hooks; peasants, plowmen with mattocks and rakes and whips of their own; the priest, carrying consecrated host, two visiting monks—and led the lot in the way he had sent his boy that morning. That boy, however, did not join the smith and his warriors, for he had set himself to counting the castle's store of nails and would not quit until the task was done.

But nowhere in the fields and nowhere in the forest did the smith and his brave companions meet the Devil. None doubted that the enemy, that dragon, had been here, infecting the earth and the air; but clearly, he had also departed, leaving death as the sign of his magnificent hatreds. For nothing—absolutely *no* thing—could be found alive, neither a sparrow nor the tiny vole. Rather, black flies and a wasting death had fallen upon the lord's forest and his hills and his valleys too, and these had been turned into a barrens so grave as to swallow up a thousand mattocks and ten thousand swords—and the smith knew that he stood in the midst of mystery and spectacular wickedness.

And so this troop returned to the castle in a heavy silence, the first to realize what desolations must attend the winter to come.

By November all game was gone, none fresh and none salted.

One visiting knight, a boisterous fool who thought himself a hunter of superior skill, announced that he would bring meat and break the famine here. Scorning the word of the "lewèd," as he called such people as the smith was, this knight and several servants clattered out the castle gate and rode to a morning's hunt. But when he blew his ivory horn, his dogs would only circle and whine. And the falcon would not leave his fist. In the evening that knight returned with nothing but a sepulchral prophecy: "Nay, and there shall not run new game in those forests till twenty Aprils have washed their roots."

And so it was that this particular Blood Month passed with very little bleeding: domestic animals had also been lost on the day the wild beasts died; and some had been butchered early to take the place of duck and venison; and much that had been already preserved was carried off with warriors to war. There was scarcely a tenth of the original herds left to be slaughtered and smoked, to feed the castle's dependencies through the winter.

So people made supplication of St. Michael the Archangel that he come with his angelic hosts and protect them, lest the dragon return to oppress the people themselves, by sitting upon their chests at night and by devouring infants the instant they slipped from their mothers' wombs.

And of the smith's boy too—for that he learned to peer into human souls, and know the complexities of the present, and was, therefore, a miracle among them—the people made supplication. Mothers begged blessings for their children and for themselves, and the lad complied by pressing the palm of his hand against their foreheads, causing the weaker women to weep.

13.
THE SAINT AND THE WIMPLE

On the morning of December twenty-third, Julian woke to the favor of heaven: snow, descending like mercy from a windless sky.

While still in bed, the young knight heard soft brushings on the oiled skins that closed his winter windows. He arose, removed the skins and stretched his bare arms into cold weather. His breath issued vaporous rags upon the air. Snowflakes touched the light hairs on the back of his hand—each flake perfectly woven, six-pointed, the lace of the angels—and Julian felt like crying, *Deo gratias!* He raised his eyes with thanksgivings unto the Creator, and:

Oh, Lord, how lovely is your snow: snow as white as absolution on the bailey grounds; snow in rounded mounds on the merlons at the top of his father's tower; snows to bank the grey-black river, snows to keep it sharply bound as, serpent-like, it wound through pure-white fields unto the horizon.

So quiet, so cool the morning, Julian dressed in a robe of camlet and boots of a high black leather; he slung a quiver of arrows over his back, hooked his yew bow to that, then went down the interior stairs, down the stairs of the forebuilding, and out the porch door to make first tracks in the pristine snow, to walk in pleasant solitude.

He strode toward the great tower, admiring its fresh stones through a dimensioned air, an air made solid by the snowfall. He entered the tower through an oaken, iron-banded door and climbed a circular stairway past two vaulted stories to the top. As he went, he fingered his breast and felt the pendant that lay between his robe and his tunic, hanging from a silver chain.

Julian's father was gone from the castle. He had been absent, in fact, for seventy-nine days, he and his knights having obeyed the call to arms which their young king had issued everywhere throughout his kingdom:

Ride eastward with me to my cousin, king who rules extremest east, whose borders the infidels are storming!

Customarily, wars were only planned in winter, quite late in the winter, and fought in summertime; but the infidel abused all good customs and offended against the wisdom of the ancestors.

Therefore, a mere five days after his knighting, Julian had kissed his father farewell, then watched the complex arranging and the dusty departing of the castle's war-party. For the lord and every knight in his retinue traveled to battle with a squire and three chargers, with clothing to last six months and victuals to last for three. Carts, therefore, and wagons were driven and drawn along, bearing flour, wine, the last of the salted pork and smoked beef, adzes, axes, augers, slings. Each warrior brought on the back of a pack horse his personal gear: hauberk, chain mail, shield, greaves, a helmet, sword, lance, and a knife; the archers their bows, and every man his tent.

Julian had climbed then, too, to the top of his father's tower and watched between the merlons as this slow train went clanking and crunching and yelling away, raising around itself an enormous cloud of dust. The dust concealed the travelers, and finally the cloud alone was left, like an aerial curtain, blowing lightly southward.

The cloud was a bare, brief remembrance of the passage of his father. Soon it vanished and Julian came down from the tower as the solitary knight of the castle.

There was, however, a remembrance more durable than that cloud and closer to his heart: the silver pendant his father had pressed into his hand while they were kissing, a filigreed silver cross and the murmured words:

Manage defenses while I am gone, both horse and the breast-work on the wall. Watch to the west. Be ready to break the painter. And by this pendant I pledge thee, my son, to return for the Christmas fortnight, to celebrate the Babe's nativity, thou and thy mother and I.

Julian gazed from the top of the same tower now, eastward over the new-fallen snow. The Christmas fortnight would begin on December the twenty-fourth. Tomorrow. At some time during the morrow, then, he should see his father riding hither, dividing the white fields, his merry pennant above him, his great charger causing the earth to tremble, his manly grin splitting his moustaches and his beard with white teeth and bright laughter.

Please, God: tomorrow!

For they had heard no word from the wars, not in all these seventy-nine mornings. And if his father was dead, then he . . . then he, Julian, would be—

"Christ!" Julian cried, drawing backward from the tower's crenellation. "Christ, I cannot think such things!" He whirled around, leaped for the steps, and rushed down them as fast as he could go, since thinking the unthinkable could cause it to happen. . . .

Out the tower, next, into the bailey, stomping the fresh snow, casting his memory backward, filling his head with the good past, *refusing* a darker future thereby:

— How his father's black moustaches would rime with the ice of his breathing on stark winter days, and his nose go red, and his great chest glad in the cold.

— How his father would ride a mighty charger through explosions of snow straight at him, Julian, and would at the very last chance lean down and grab the boy's whole arm and sweep him high in the air, and Julian *soaring* as the horse dashed by, then landing plump at his father's back, laughing, laughing and waving to his mother who stood on the doorstep watching, covering her eyes in a game of fear, and giggling.

— How his father once led him to a snow-hole under a clutter of fallen trees in the forest; how the two of them crept all soundlessly to its lung-colored entrance, and his father gestured *Listen,* breathing forth flags of a mighty steam; and the boy made all his motion stop; and for a moment the winter woods were still; then lo!—there was a stirring under snow, and next a mewing; Julian heard the infant mewing and knew he was bending over a den with a she-bear and her cubs inside; and his father grinned and formed the words *Lazare, veni foras,* which was a solemn joke, meaning that life comes out of the graves after all, and spring will follow winter.

"Veni foras," Julian said now, stomping over these latter snows on the bailey ground. He raised his right arm. "Lazarus," he yelled in honor of his father's wisdom, "Come forth!"—and suddenly, astoundingly, clouds east of the castle began to part, and the morning sun burst forth, and Julian was forced to squint against the dazzle of sunlight on the snow.

He took three steps blindly, rubbing his eyes with his knuckles.

When he looked up, his vision was distorted; nevertheless, he noticed white wings across the yard. Julian saw a pair of swan's wings wavering over a high garden hedge at the back of the bailey. Immediately he notched an arrow on the string of his yew bow, aimed, and shot. *Zzzing*—the arrow ripped air and pierced the hedge a handsbreadth from

the top, where the body of the swan must be. And a cry
went up.

What? Christ!—'twas a *human* cry?

Yes, and after that a series of short, astonished sobs.

Julian picked up his feet and raced toward the hedge,
wanting to shout, *'Twas the famine on my mind,* and knowing
at once it was a lie. He tried to leap over the tough old
hedge. It bent beneath his weight. He tore the flesh of his
arms and legs, left patches of camlet on the thorns behind
him, then found no swan on the other side, but his mother
in a flowing white wimple, curled tightly on the snow, her
knees to her forehead, weeping.

"Mother!"

Julian dropped down beside her, unwound the wimple
from her chin in order to free the woman, perhaps to comfort her; but when the wimple was pulled away, he saw his
arrow caught mid-shaft in the coil of her thick blonde hair,
and on its iron head some blood, and along his mother's
temple a line of bleeding drops.

The woman was whispering, "Julian? Is that you? Thank
God you came to help me—"

But Julian was himself groaning now. He had folded his
arms over the great horror now scouring his heart; he was
rocking back and forth on his knees, and hearing the curse
of the dying stag not as the murmurous words of a dream,
but rather as the clear bugling of a living creature and a
prophet.

How *easy* the act! How near to him this sin most
damnable!

O Christ! Christ Jesus, bind my heart!

So then it was not the son, but the mother who rose to comfort the other. She drew him to her bosom and crooned this perfume into his ear: "All's well, my child. Everything is well, and I am well, and harm has not been done today. No need to cry, no need to cry, my darling child."

14.
CHRISTMAS AND THE MUMMER'S CAROL

Julian's father did not return that next day, December the twenty-fourth.

Every house in the villages, every parish church in the lord's demesne, and the castle chapel too, and all the rooms in the castle itself were merrily decked with holm and ivy and bay and whatsoever the season afforded to be green.

The yule log was brought into the great hall on the day before Christmas, exactly as if the lord *had* returned to preside over festivities there. It was a twelve-foot length of tree-trunk, kindled to burn continually through the next twelve days. Julian, the son of the castle lord, had seen to that.

On that same day, Christmas Eve, villagers and tenants and every laborer brought to the castle gifts of bread, a thin hen or two, ale which they had brewed themselves.

Then, on the Day of the Nativity of our Lord Jesus, after the Christ Mass and its spiritual jubilation, all the folk came back again to the castle and sat at trestle tables in the great hall, enjoying a feast of the foods they'd brought yesterday, now prepared as savory dishes by the lord's own cooks, now enriched by some small scraps of fowl-meat (this being the winter deprived of the finer roasts of venison or beef), and finally concluded with puddings and beers. There flowed a river of beer in the great hall then, as much as any villein was able to hold, for on this holy night even the poorest could drink in the lord's hall till the dawn of the following day.

But no knight came for the joy of this feast. Not a single one.

Nor did the lord attend his own celebrations. Empty was the chair that stood between the chairs of the castle's lady and her son. And though the lady smiled with grace on every guest beneath the dais, her son did not. His brow was pale and filled with thinking. His lips were drawn thin, his eyes bent downward. He did not eat.

Oh, how heavily the pendant weighed round Julian's neck! Not because his father had not kept the pledge of it; but rather because he, Julian, was unworthy of any pledge his father might make to him.

On December twenty-six Julian's mother asked him to fulfill the Christmas role of the Lord of the Castle. She asked with mildness; too, she would have taken his hand in hers and stroked it, except that, for the last three days, her touch had caused her son to shudder.

"Wouldst thou, Julian, my pretty boy? Thou shalt make an handsome lord."

Julian nodded. He would bow to take his father's place.

And so he dressed in green cheer on this day and the next, distributing gifts to noble families attached to the castle, jewels, wardrobes consisting of tunics, surcoats, mantles; to the lordlings who companioned him he gave swords, to their sisters palfreys, to their mothers gold and silver cups, necklaces, girdles studded with precious stones. But all this he did with only the ghostliest of smiles. He was ever bowed, as the people believed, in pious meditations. Of course they would never hold his solemnity against the young man; for hadn't he, ever since his knighting, shown a special sanctity in all his ways? Surely, the cross of Christ had, like a long sword, pierced the heart of the lord's only son, whose bones must one day become relics deserving reverence.

Mummers came on the twenty-seventh. The castle staff gathered to watch their maskings and antics. The staff roared with laughter, beat their knees and begged relief. Julian sat in his father's chair, presiding over the show with a sober nobility. In the end he offered trifles and drinks to the mummers as thanksgiving for their mirth.

Then, just before they departed into the winter's cold, one of the mummers—and she the prettiest girl-child dressed in a fawn-soft jerkin—turned to face the Christmas lord and curtsied and began to sing for him a carol. The child's voice was as pure as birdsong. She opened her mouth and the music that flew therefrom, the song that soared to the ceilings of the great hall, silenced every heart that had been so noisy before. Laughter ceased. The caroler fluttered her eyelids as she reached the higher notes, almost dreamlike in expression. The rest of the mummers sang a choral refrain to the girl-child's verses; and when near its ending the carol took a melancholy turn, many an eye blinked tears.

What did the Christmas lord do under the spell of such a

carol? Well, but who had thought to watch *him* when the song had drawn all eyes to the poor, be-jerkinned singer? (And how could she keep warm in such thin dress?) No, none had watched him. The Almoner once whispered this strange notion: that at some moment during the eternal-seeming carol the Christmas lord had slipped from his throne, had approached the girl-child softly, and then had bowed on one knee down before her. But only once did the Almoner whisper the notion, for it felt much more as a fancy within him than as a fact.

Much likelier is that the Christmas lord in his glad green raiment sat and listened and showed no mood nor fleeting emotion at all.

Finally, so charmed were all the people who heard the carol, that when the bird-notes died in the hall, and silence again prevailed, the entire band of mummers seemed suddenly to have vanished, as if the song itself had carried them up the chimneys and away like so much smoke on the wind.

And, as I am pledged to record for your benefit each detail I myself have been able to uncover, here are four verses of the carol sung that third day of Christmas under the temporary lordship of the young Sir Julian:

> Jesus was born with hair
> With needle teeth
> A milk-blue breath
> Four paws walking and aware:
> *A natal song we sing for thee;*
> *In terra canunt angeli.*

Mary his mother licked
All lovingly
His rheumy eye
With a doting tongue and quick:
And lullabies we croon for thee;
In terra canunt angeli.

Flesh of the flesh of beasts
Creation's ward
That was its Lord
Born to host and meat our feasts:
Astonished hymns and litanies
In terra canunt angeli.

Cub of Creation, go
Break from thy den
Run among men
Cross the crust of our hunted snows—
And prove what sort of beasts we be.
In terra canunt angeli,
Et lamentantur archangeli.

15.

THE SAINT AND THE BATTLE-AX

December twenty-eight was Childermas—the Mass for the
children of Bethlehem whom King Herod had killed in

order to kill the Christ; it was the Feast of the Holy Inno-
cents, martyrs in the morning of their lives.

The priest hanged red cloths both from the altar and
from the pulpit in the chapel; and before he sang the Mass,
he hanged a red stole round the back of his neck, kissing
it first.

As soon as the Mass was finished, all the children ran
screaming from the chapel, and after them ran the younger
adults carrying willow switches, and with these some
grandmothers too, all preparing to give the children whip-
pings and buffets and playful beatings. By noon the bailey
was a boil of color and rushing bodies and hootings and
laughter. Ah, such boisterous, busy gaiety! For this was the
game of the day, to make a pretence of punishment and so to
make the children mindful of children who suffered truly at
the hand of wickedness; and this, too, was the purpose and
the yearning of the game, to grant those more hard-bitten
elders a way to say, *I love thee, lass,* by an inversion, as it
were: by means of a knock on her noggin.

"Lances!"

A voice in the distance was crying: "Lances longer by a
foot!"

The games in the bailey did not diminish. None of those
glad hearts could hear the cry. But one watching them
from the top of the great tower, *he* heard, and he rushed
to the far side of the tower and peered through the crenellation, and immediately set up a cry of his own: "Father!
Oh, my *Father!*"

Riding one charger at breakneck speed, a second one gal-loping freely behind, came Julian's father, the Lord of the Castle, across the white fields, crying, "Ho, smith! Smith! Canst hear me, smith? Lances, sir, longer by a foot! Five hundred bolts—!"

Julian raced down winding stairs, burst out below, and ran to the gatehouse. With his lean strength he shifted the bars from their iron catches, pulled the great doors open, and leaped aside as his father thundered into the bailey.

The games stopped. A moment passed, and then the great congregation burst into shouts and clappings of wel-come: "Welcome home!"

The Lord of the Castle lifted his right hand in receipt of their love; he nodded splendidly; but he did not check his horses, which continued at that headlong gallop across the bailey, around the great hall, and down to the stables.

Julian in green came sprinting behind.

And by the time he reached his father, that man had al-ready swung down from the saddle, and was at the side of his second beast, touching the weapons and all his armor there, shouting, "This for sharpening, smith! This for beating out! This for the repair of its seams. Smith! Smith, dost hear me?"

The crunch of Julian's foot brought his father around, frowning: "Well, where hastow . . ."

The man blinked, squinted, his brow be-grimed, his great beard clotted with sweat and wild riding. Then, sud-denly, he smiled, and sunrise broke from those magnificent teeth.

"Ah, my son, of course it would be you!"

Julian's father spread his arms and gathered the younger man to his breast, an embrace of filth and tenderness. He kissed him—

—And Julian felt a blaze of shame to sweep his cheeks. How could this be?—that the love of his father had become a scalding thing? Well, but the love of his father was oblivious of Julian's truer self. The one whom his father was embracing could never equal the one whom his father *thought* he was embracing, and Julian suffered the difference all prively within himself alone.

"They fight aground." His father drew back and began immediately to talk: "They fight afoot with hails of arrows, careless of dying, *rabid* men, Julian. Reasonless. But we, could we keep good order and attack as a single man, we, I say, could triumph. I *know* this, for I have seen its opposite."

Suddenly two more mounted knights came clattering around the great hall, their horses stamping and blowing great plumes of steam. By the stables they dismounted. They clapped Julian on his back, grinning, and then began to remove their weapons from the backs of their pack horses.

"God's *bones!*" cried Julian's father, "where *is* my good smith?"

Julian said, "It's Childermas, father."

"It's what?"

"Childermas. Men fear to work on such an unlucky day."

"Ah, yes, yes, and no one will marry today," said his father. "Childermas, and I knew it not."

The broad-shouldered, black-bearded lord gazed at his son. He put forth a hand and laid it on Julian's shoulder.

"Pardon me, my young sir, please," he said. "I could not keep my pledge to thee." Truly, the wide grey eyes of his father lay upon Julian, seeking forgiveness, while Julian's heart was filled with nothing *but* forgiveness; forgiveness swelled to bursting within him. "I have come home late," his father said, "and early must I leave. As soon as new weapons are made."

Genuine humility in both men—and the hunger that his father had revealed, hunger for the dear forgiveness and the love of his son—changed every hesitation in Julian, and now he longed for his father's touch, and he said, "Yes, Father." He said, "In me is such forgiveness for thee." And he threw his arms around his father's neck, and his father said, "However far I must go from thee, never shall I *not* love thee, oh, my gentle Julian."

Then three more knights arrived and, counting his father, that made six. Others would be coming, every one of his surviving knights, "For all the western lords are going home to fashion another sort of weaponry."

Then the Lord of the Castle in loud and jolly tones declared: "If the smith considers the day unlucky, I'll hone the irons myself. Knights, bring your equipment piece by piece to me!"

Julian's father entered the smithy and found, to his everlasting glee, that the smith's boy had already kindled the charcoal and was standing with bellows, waiting to work; and when the lord himself bent down above the anvil to beat rucked metal smooth again, that long-legged servant brought every necessary tool just as it was required, and he whistled while he did.

That was an excellent day, that Childermas.

Word went forth that the lord had turned himself into a smith. People came down to watch and to wonder at his skill. Children cheered his hammer strokes.

The Lady of the Castle came by, wearing the rough tunic of a servant, serving him and many people a warm mulled wine. And when the smith himself came by, *crept* by all full of fear, the lord called for a samite robe and, roaring with laughter, gave it to the smith to wear.

"'Tis well! And all is well!" he roared. "For this is the Day of Exchangings!"

But next he told the smith of the weapons he wanted ere he must leave the castle again. "I have persuaded the king," said the Castle Lord, "to change his tactic. 'No more shall ye draw your sword yourself to fight,' I said, 'but ye shall sit on a high place, surrounded by heralds, sending commands down to the battle as ye see the need. Nor shall your knights dismount to fight! We shall meet the infidel with speed and force, all as one in an ordered shock-attack—and longer lances shall pierce his heart before his sword can enter ours.' Longer lances, therefore, my smith, tipped by an alloy I shall show thee; and narrower shields and,"—and so forth, spoke the lord.

Oh, what a memorable day was that Childermas!—even to the end of it, though the ending would not, by two souls, be remembered in joy.

After a banquet of broiled fish and bean soups for the knights in clean clothes and for their ladies, glad at the homecoming, and after these had departed to their various places, the lord and his son sat alone on the dais, drinking a wine so mulled it twitched in their noses.

"Father," said Julian, "let me go back to the battle with you."

The bigger man sat silently a while, pursing his lips.

Finally he said, "Thou'rt lightly built, lad."

"But I have an eye of swift precision."

"Arrows."

"Aye! Arrows and bolts."

"Hast not been listening, Julian? 'Tis lances we go to fight with after all—a heavier lance, in fact, meant to be gripped underhand and parallel the charger's body. Thou art lightly built, lad."

"But I am strong at heart."

"Aye! 'Tis my own heart beats in thee. But thine arm is nearer thy mother's."

"Father, fie! There's nothing womanish in me!"

"Except thy mind, son. 'Tis the mind of thy mother. Any knight would covet her mind."

Julian's father chuckled deeply in his beard.

Julian drew a long swallow of wine from his cup, then set the cup down and muttered, "Ye have not said No."

"I have not said Yes either, for who would see to the defense of my castle while I am gone? Who would keep guard of thy mother?"

Julian considered this duty a moment. It was not puny.

Nor was it make-work. It must be done, and it could require a young man's courage. Rightly, he should at this point have ceased the debate and bowed obedience to his father's word. But he took more swallows of wine. And emotions in him were like a horse already running and hard to halt; besides, there was greater glory in a war, and life was more honorable when death was near.

Therefore Julian said with some heat: "Father, I can wield your lances! I can swing your heaviest weapon! Let me come with you!"

"This is a war most brutal, sir," said his father as man to man: "and the worse for one as yet unhardened and inexperienced."

"I have fought! I have slaughtered."

"I know not when. Oh, release me, Julian. Let me go to my lady this evening. Then grant me a day to think on thy request—"

But Julian, trembling, had already jumped up, knocking his chair to the side. Again, he jumped to the top of the table, where he turned to face the wall behind them, crying, "An' is it *proofs* ye seek, my lord? Must I *prove* the strength of mine arm for you?"

"What? Julian, what—?"

The young man stood tiptoe at the edge of the table and canted forward. He stretched out his right arm and caught his lean long body between the wall and the table.

"Then shall I," he cried with a manic hilarity, "*astonish* you by my strength!"

With his left hand, Julian reached for the handle of the great battle-ax which hanged on iron hooks fixed in the oaken frame of the wall.

His father cocked his head backward to see what Julian was doing above him; the lord threw back his chair till the crown of his head leaned against the wall.

"One-armed, sir! With one good arm I fetch you your battle-ax!"

But as soon as Julian took hold of the butt of its handle, that massive weapon broke from its hooks, its blade singing, its sharp edge beginning to swing on a slow arc downward. Julian didn't let go the handle. Off his balance, so close to falling himself, he could not let go of the handle's butt, which therefore became a fulcrum around which the mighty ax-head turned; and down it turned: in a great rotation downward to the white neck of his father, exposed as to the executioner.

Julian screamed in his heart.

He gathered himself, his sinew and all his force, finally to pitch the ax handle a bare six inches to the left, and the blade cut through his father's ear and through his father's hanging hair and through the post of the chair, then bit the wooden floor and stood on that hard bite, humming.

The Lord of the Castle did not move, but whispered, *"In nomine Patris!"*

And Julian was still screaming, but inside himself, all soundlessly, staring at the shear cut of his father's hair and the side of his head exposed, and the pinna of his father's ear cut in half and blossoming blood. Julian's mouth was wide open, his lean frame caught between table and wall, his throat working a terrible gag. He was a chalky infant again. There were no words left in him, save these:

As thou hast murdered me, my son,
so shalt thou murder thy father.

Like smoke are the laws of God!—unable to bind the heart, and blown apart by mere human breathing!

O Christ, how thin is the glaze 'twixt love and brutality. A little heat only, and kissing is killing instantly.

How, then, can we save ourselves from the cunning of our own deepest cravings?

16.
THE FIRST DEPARTURE

In the dark hours before the dawning of December the twenty-ninth, while the entire castle lay in a winter's sleep and a bitter wind howled and there was neither a moon nor a lodestar by which to pick a path, Julian gathered his weapons, his armor, some clothing and a little food, then departed the castle by the postern gate, riding the same Iberian horse his father had given him ninety days ago for gladness at his knighting.

He rode forth in a perfect solitude.

He bowed his head. He hunched his narrow shoulders against the enmity of the wind. With fingers like knots, he clasped to his throat the robe which the wind kept grabbing and snapping, seeking to rip it away and render the young knight naked and cold in the universe. But by a mindless stamina the rider prevailed, guiding his blind Iberian south by southwest.

There was no alternative to this, that he must be clean cut off from his parents. For Julian loved them both, above all things else in the world; and yet he believed the curse: were he good or were he evil, his hand would conclude by killing his mother and his father—unless he left them, immediately and forever.

THE THIRD PART

———⊰∞∞∞⊱———

SIN

17.

THE ALMONER

Sources are silent regarding the next several years of the young knight's life. "Julian," the baptismal name of one well-born, well-beloved and capable; "Julian," the son of a lord most noble, heir to his castle and all its vast demesne— this Julian vanished from public discussions, vanished like a dead man from the pages of the chroniclers.

To be sure, there was a season of furious talk and speculation. But it was all founded on air and this single fact, that the knight was here in the evening and gone by the morning, and no better word ever returned to the castle with comfort or else explanations.

"Murder," the cottar-men declared over stone jars of ale.

"Elijah's chariot," whispered their women. "Fire hath borne him up to Heaven—fire and the whirlwind."

Moreover, the river that winter went mad. And none was such a fool as to think this convulsion of nature a mere coincidence, for as falcons reflect their master's commands, so do wind and the storms of heaven reflect the mind of Almighty God.

Maids gazed dreadfully down from the northern windows of the castle, searching the roaring waters below. They saw not a living soul. Nor did the ferryman stand duty now. The

river would kill him. It had already torn the painter-cable
from its moorings. Mighty was the river. Wider, it was,
than ever a maid remembered before. A silent, speeding fell
of branches and brush and nodding logs: it was ripping the
life from its shores. Corpses of every kind of distant creature
rode the waters by. Why not (the maids did never ask), why
not the body of their bonnie lord?

Aye, but Candlemas came with its plowing again, and the
peasants bent to the planting of oats and beans, barley and
vetches, as every year past had required of them, as every
year future would demand until the end of the world. Speculation grew tired of itself and ceased. The name "Julian"
passed from the lips of day-laboring people. By Mayday the
young were turning their attentions to dalliance, while their
elders were turning *them* into a finer sort of gossip than
death and mysteries.

The Lord of the Castle and his Lady (and the Almoner, too,
could any have read his thoughts) continued to grieve and to
wander the hallways of their perplexity as if these were tunnels underground: for their son had dissolved; his body had
changed to air, his soul into a dew. He had been swallowed
by the night. And though they begged news of him often
and everywhere, of passing travelers both here at home and
far abroad, no one knew anything of Julian, and none could
answer, "I've seen him there," or else, "He perished here."

The Almoner. Aye, and I must speak of the Almoner. For, growing ever more gaunt than his beneficiaries, that one stole into the chapel and spent his midnights praying for the boy whose piety he had held in the palm of his own hand, and had helped to train. Like a tender whistling wind his supplications sailed to Heaven, lovely and longing and murmuring "Julian."

While all the world went forward through the greening spring into busy summer, the castle interior became a cavern of shadow and melancholy. The lord governed his people in a kind of vacancy. As honorable as ever before were all his judgments, but since they came, it seemed, from so remote a distance, from the far countries of sorrow and isolation, these same judgments now carried the holy force of the very Stones of Moses. How deeply the people revered this suffering lord of theirs.

And servants heard their mistress singing in the middle of the night, singing behind the door of the room where her lost son once slept, but singing to none but herself in a delicate, beautiful and terrible French:

> *"Chanterai por mon coraige*
> *Que je vuil reconforter,*
> *Qu'avecques mon grant domaige*
> *Ne quier morir n'afoler;*
> *Quant de la terre sauvage*
> *Ne voi mais nul retorner,*
> *Ou cil est qui rassoaige*
> *Mes maus quant j'en oi parler. . . ."*

"I will sing," she sang on the winds of her sighing. "I will sing to cheer my heart, afraid I may die of grief or else go mad, when I can hear no herald returning from that wild reach where he remains. . . ."

Her golden hair soon suffered shocks of grey, while by Lammas—the first day of August, when her husband went out to oversee the reaping of his fields by gangs of villeins—his beard and all *his* raven hair had turned as white as snow.

And this, such hopeless preoccupation—what can it do but cause a rot in the first defenses of a lord and his castle and all his lands?

18.
THE RED KNIGHT

Now, it happened in those days that a new tale began to be told throughout the Christian kingdoms: songs, their refrains crude and uncrafted, for that they were the boasts of fighting men who had survived the fields of bloody mud and had come home again; men who had heard the tales from more distant warriors who said they had themselves *seen* the worthy that had inspired the tales in the first place, had "seen him bloody red," as they said, everyone. For the tale and the song and the lusty refrain all extolled the same man. A knight. "A red knight," they told it as it had been told to them: "lean and tall, some seven feet tall, whose shoulders fold in upon themselves as an archangel's wings do fold."

This dauntless knight could fly.

And perhaps had fought in Jerusalem.

And perhaps had fought on the blue ices of the north.

And who knows but that he had stood in the bows of boats on the wind-driven seas:

The world-rim-walker, he!

For, as the tales were annually refreshed, becoming ever the richer for detail, they revealed a knight that did not fight as any other knight these battle-toughened warriors had ever seen.

The Red Knight cast off his greaves! His legs were long and lithe. He wore close to his head a mail coif, not the iron pot helmet of every other knight, and a leather corselet in place of the forty-pound hauberk of chain mail. His was a light, one-handed shield of wicker, fitted with an iron boss. And his horse was no charger of massy strength and size: a shining Arabian, swift and mobile, which the Red Knight rode by the mere nudgings of his knees. Aye, aye!—but what the man gave away of the body's protection he gained a hundredfold in agility.

He flew! He needed no war saddle with its high, encircling cantle, no double girth to secure it. No spurs. No weight! He took to the field with a lightsome lance, a sword as sharp as a lover's eye-beam, a quiver of arrows of various weights—and three bows: a recurved Turkish bow, worn at his shoulder for shooting while riding; a crossbow hooked to the left side of his Arabian; and hooked to the right, a long-bow carefully cut and shaven from a staff of yew full seven feet long.

But here was one of the greatest wonders of these tales: that the eye of this knight was faster than arrows. That he read the enemies' postures even as they were first notching their arrows. That he saw the flight of an arrow already in an archer's intent, in an archer's *mind!*

Therefore, "The Red Knight," as the brutish warriors told the tale: "he rides alone. He canters wide of our foremost columns, knights in a shock-line, footmen and bowmen close behind. And ever at his own delight, the Red Knight flies at the flanks of the enemy, biting, stinging, troubling them as the falcon's stoop terrifies whole flocks of sheep."

"He flies," sang the songs, "in a ruby silence, his brown eyes wide and as wild as a stallion's.

"His face is a fire, for intensity kindles the blood in it.

"But his face is a *ravaging* fire, for the bright sun burns its delicate pallor; the sunlight blisters his skin; then he, like the serpent, sheds one skin for another, but in patches!"

"His head is a *flame* of fire," sang the songs in an inhuman adoration, "for as he rides his black Arabian wings to the attack, his great red beard and his cardinal hair stream backward like flames from a torch. His forehead blazes! His bared teeth flash—and when he swoops down on the enemy, he is the descent of some terrible angel: a six-winged seraph at war! Red, he is! Blood-red is this knight!"

Blood-red, too, were his ambitions. This, together with

the slender man's fierce and brooding silences, made him a forbidding figure and friendless, withal—though ever the more fascinating to the tender at home. For, though they spoke *of* him with a proprietary pride, none of the fighting men had ever spoken *to* him. For the Red Knight could, with a persistent spray of fifty-one arrows, kill fifty-one of the foe-men dead in their saddles. And when an army of infidels broke in the battle and fled for their lives, the Red Knight would fly beyond them all; would whirl about, dismounting; and would, by a swift succession of bolts from his crossbow and arrows from his longbow, drop the lot of them, empurpling the fields with the pennants and the flags of their running blood.

19.
A FINISHING ADVANCE

In time the tales of the Red Knight changed, growing less crude, less boastful, and infinitely more articulate. Tales first told at fairs and at boards of beer now moved into rooms more hushed; and that which had been lewèd now turned Latinate: for the bearers of his tales had also changed. No longer the footmen and the bowmen of foreign wars, 'twere churchmen now who carried the Red Knight's glory through Christian kingdoms.

"He has attached himself to a marcher lord in the extreme southwest, to a Christian king whose kingdom is bordered by the Saracen!"

So said clerics one to another as they met in Rome and then again as they returned to their scattered appointments. So said priests from their various pulpits:

"And the king has received the Red Knight because he came with no attachments, neither servants to pay, nor family to enlarge, nor traditions to keep, nor any other mouth but his own to fill. He wants nothing—nothing but what his lean and lengthy corpus requires. On the other hand, the king has received him for what the Red Knight *does* bring, too: his native abilities. The man is a brilliant strategist, which the king has sorely needed for more than a score of years, because twice yearly the Saracen Caliph south of him has plundered his kingdom, carrying booty away, as well as the bodies of living children to serve as slaves for the godless!

"And the Lord our God through Jesus Christ *(cui est gloria in saecula saeculorum, amen)* has also received our Red Knight for the sake of humble worship and obedience and all his pieties. For he lives like a poor man. He leads a chaste and decent life, never debasing himself with frivolity, ever attending to the state of all mortal flesh: *'Memento mori,'* the good knight seems ever to keep as a frontlet between his eyes: *'Thou art dust, and to dust thou shalt return.'*

"And this is trustworthy surely, a true saying indeed: that Christ Jesus takes the highest delight in our valorous Red Knight; for when he leads his armies south to war, exercising full authority in the name of his king, the marcher lord, he never goes but that bishops go with him. And priests for the saying of the Mass. And monks with crosses held high in their arms.

"*Deo gloria!* How can such holiness ever by evil be defeated? During his armies' marches, Mass is sung on Sundays and on every feast day of the year. And always the monks chant psalms and canticles. And after every battle the clergy chant Gradual Psalms for the fallen, even as others rush out onto the battlefield with Last Rites for the wounded and the dying.

"No one does not admire this leader; and here is the proof of this: that every churchman who follows the Red Knight's armies, though he need not enter the fighting, will nonetheless share all the hardships of the lowest of the footmen. Though some of us love our luxury, the Red Knight inspires monks to the truth of their vows again.

"Ah, God, is there a bolder sanctity than this? There shall be miracles next! And after them, *si quidem permiserit Deus,* a new Saint in our Heaven."

Here is a story:

Men in the ranks wore clothing of light wool and linen. So did the knight that led them. His frugality commanded theirs. And if this were not enough, he made his will an explicit order: every man coming must muster and march with no superfluous thing. And if the command itself were not enough . . .

Well! Once a great landowner arrived aglittering, his cloak, his smock, his belt—his very arms and hair and the curls of his beard—all studded with jewels. Knights that took note of that one's arrival divided into groups, some marveling at such a lustrous wealth, and some giggling, and some laughing outright. But the Red Knight's rage broke forth like fire: "Wretch that thou art!" he cried like another Jeremiah. "Is it not enough that thou shalt die on the battlefield? Must thou also give thy soul's ransom to the infidel?" And he caused the rich man to swallow every precious stone that first had adorned him. "Let them cut thy belly like a pig's for all thy wealth and thine every heavenly glory."

Discipline prevailed here, under the Red Knight's prudence, as nowhere else under Christian crosses, nor under the horns of the pagan, nor under the book of Mohammed.

Memento mori! seemed—as discipline itself did seem—to be a freeing principle for this captain, verily *releasing* him to fight like a demon of terrible calm.

"A Mass before we fight! Those who know that they shall die are *best* for killing Caliphs!"

And then it happened that a traveling Cardinal—the day before he entered a ferryman's barge to cross the waters of a wide, unkindly river—spent his evening in conversation with a priest. This priest served the castle known as the "Point of Crossing" in that country. Between Vespers and Compline the two men sat in the first chairs of a stone chapel, eating several sorts of breads and drinking a flagon of unconsecrated wine.

"In gratitude for your hospitality," the Cardinal announced (though likelier than gratitude was that he loved to talk), "I'll tell thee, brother, the round unvarnished tale of a military marvel.

"A marvel!" he repeated, leaning forward and poking a thick finger into the priest's shoulder.

Neither of these clerics noticed, in the dark corner at the back of the chapel, a gaunt Almoner also listening, his head bowed down. Nor did they, at the end of the Cardinal's story, hear him softly sing a trembling *Te Deum:*

"For thou hast answered the prayers of my craving!" the Almoner wept.

Hear, then, the Cardinal's "unvarnished tale" in full:

After five or seven years of fighting back and forth across the borders—after years, too, of building watchposts at every small advance—the Red Knight deemed it an acceptable time to make a finishing advance: the hammer's attack and the ring of the anvil. He sent, therefore, covert requests to knights he knew, archers with whom he had fought, men of the strictest discipline, warriors in whom there was not a vainglorious bone. Unto his call and unto his honor they came: each with horses and food and carts, equipment, armor, weapons and brutal, unbendable wills. Thus the Red Knight gathered the greatest force he'd ever yet assembled.

Late in the spring he and his forces began to march straight toward the heart of the Caliph's land. Long was the ride and arduous was the route—but not unknown, for the Red Knight had traveled the course alone, under cover of the drizzling winter.

For seven weeks in that shivering season—himself for seven weeks a midnight creature and soundless as the owl on her wing—the Red Knight had sought and then had measured the works which the Caliph had commanded for the defense of his administrative city. These proved all to be centered upon two strongholds newly built of mortar and dressed stone on the south banks of a great, west-flowing river. Clearly, the Caliph had determined by such fortifications to make this river the final line against intruders. As he crept passed the strongholds and farther south of the river, even toward the Caliph's city, the Red Knight's nostrils began to sting with a certain scent, and he knew it for the spoor of fear. Why, 'tis a leader aware of *weaknesses* that anticipates a fallback to the very doors of his dwelling. Designing, devising strategies for his army's advance, the spying knight now bound himself to remember this acrid odor of Moorish fear, for it would, come the spring, sharpen his mind and encourage his heart.

Then, but two nights' journey from the city itself and caught by the sunrise in a wide and well-chewed grassland, the Red Knight slipped behind the stone fencing of an abandoned sheepfold. He pillowed his head on a fallen rock. He laid his weapons lengthwise down the sides of his thighs, then watched. And listened. But soon he could not help it, but that he fell asleep.

Almost immediately bright noontide arrived, and the knight, unmoving, was wide awake. And the causes of his wakefulness were of two separate natures. The first: 'twere voices of a band of Saracen warriors just outside the sheepfold on its northernmost side. By the yawning tones of their talking, the knight determined that they were preparing to eat something and then to rest in the thin shade.

The nature of the second alarm was closer and more frightening: 'twas the sight of a small Moorish shepherd, here, in the same sheepfold, squatting against the opposite wall and staring straight back at the knight. Several sheep, overgrown with wool, lay on either side of the shepherd. The beasts chewed mindlessly. Neither of the two men moved. And in that moment of violent uncertainties, the knight tried to assess this little, unwarlike Saracen: his beard as thin as a wisp of tow; his eyes dark and moist and steadfast and large; his hands upon his knees. Ah, the hands! There was nought but a single finger left on either one— but *which* finger was impossible to tell, for the hands were ravaged. This little shepherd, the Red Knight reasoned, could scarcely attack him. But he could surely call out and rouse the warriors. Aye, but he hadn't yet, had he? And the knight knew not how long the shepherd had been squatting there, watching him as he slept. And if it *were* a good long time, didn't that argue a merciful heart?—that *this* Moor, anyway, might keep the Christian's secret and let him live another day?

And all this assessment happened in a flash, for the knight was as taut as a bowstring.

Then the shepherd began to raise his right arm, drawing its paw toward his mouth; and so it was that in one smooth motion the Red Knight lifted his lance and drove its point straight through the shepherd's throat into his neckbone.

The sheep on either side of the small man continued chewing. Their woolly bodies pillowed the shepherd's body, so that it did not slump; but the feet slipped out one after the other, toeless; and the torso descended to a sitting position. And then all was still beneath the noonday sun. All, except for some coughing among the Saracen warriors, was very still.

That escape took place in the winter, "And is not," the Cardinal assured the priest, "the military marvel I have promised you. Nay, *that* was accomplished in late spring and in the summer!"

So, then: in the warmer and the drier months, the Red Knight, goat-footed, led his excellent army through thick forests and the dangers of wild beasts. Over bare rocks of no seeming footholds he led them, then down their deep defiles; over plains with no cover from the sun or the enemy. Nor was the Red Knight's march a secret. He *wanted* it known that by switches and degrees his final goal was the great west-flowing river at a point between the two strongholds which the Caliph had built.

"Let," he said in the hearing of several bishops, "the foeman send his best to meet our worst."

As the Christian armies traveled southward, the Caliph's men worried their flanks and harassed the rear guard, often trying to sever the baggage train from its fighting forces. Once these Saracens watched from rocks above a narrow gorge while the army moved slowly by below. The Moors were prepared to drop boulders down just between the rear guard and the Christian wagons. But swifter and more clever than these was the Red Knight himself, silent as tree-bark, invisible as Azazel. He was determined to see his army all the way to that river, to lead the warriors all intact and in their strength. And hadn't he already conned the enemies' ways and their pathways together? Therefore was this single champion waiting among the high rocks even before the Caliph's men had arrived to cut in half his war-train below. So then it was not boulders, but bodies, by the hand of a single Christian knight, that dropped into the gorge.

And then 'twas from the Holy Book the strategy was taken and laid to catch a Caliph and all his dominion:

Just before his great host reached the river, the Red Knight ordered a halt in open fields. There they camped for three days, in sight of the Saracens manning their two strongholds, but out of an arrow's range. The enemy was therefore forced to witness as the Christians worshipped and built fresh barges. Every morning a Mass was said, every afternoon a Vespers chanted, and all day long new barges builded. There was an absolute fast on the first day; on the second and the third days porridge was sent—and bread and beans and thin beer—to every fighter and every supporter. No meat, no fish, no wine, however; not for any man all three days.

On the morning of the fourth day, the Red Knight's armies struck camp and divided into two parts, one marching along the north side of the river, the other being ferried across. Barges rowed and tilled, barges poled by knights in full war panoply; barges fluttering pennants from upright lances, flashing sunlight from a thousand polished surfaces, helmets, scabbards; barges heaped with forests of weapons and harvests of foodstuffs; barges of high sides and scowling appearances—one hundred barges, in slow procession, sailed all up and down the river.

Strategy!

The lean knight's calculation and all his godlike confidence!—for he had smelled the Moorish fear, and hadn't he made a savor of it?

"The Israelite armies of Joshua, circling Jericho in an inhuman silence for five long days, and six . . ."

"Holiness," announced the Cardinal. "'Twas holiness broke the spirits of the infidel! For those whom the Caliph had sent to save him by mortal war and sacrifice—why, they were panicked instead. They rushed from their strongholds waving their hands, weeping and wailing and begging mercy.

"Aye, but the Red Knight knows no mercy for the despisers of the Christ! He himself with a sweep of arrows from that longbow laid the first row low, every man transfixed at the neck, so goes the story, so goes the history that I have been told. His archers, next, imitated him. His knights rode in and took possessions of the strongholds.

"And then from thence, at our Red Knight's command, a great fire spread out, swallowing every green and living thing, laying waste the Caliph's land and terrifying all the peasants upon whom the Caliph depended—for no man nor any woman remembered so close an incursion before.

"In fine, the presence of the Red Knight at their doorstep

shattered the faith of the Moors. And today they are like dogs in caves. And their wealth has been distributed among Christian coffers. I bear a piece of it myself, today!

"And as soon as he learned of this Red Knight's most marvelous triumph, the Pope wrote in the plurals of the kings: *'Vestra exaltatio, nostra est laetitia!'*

"'What is the Red Knight's name?' asked the Pope in mine own hearing, 'that we might send our message to him?'

"But no one knew—nay, and no one had ever known—another name than the one he received when first he emerged, the color of blood and his own complexion and his hair: Red.

"Therefore: *'Ad Rufo charissimo filio,'* wrote the Pope in the flourish of his own hand: 'Your triumph is our joy!'

"And now," said the Cardinal, wiping the wine and the spittle from his lips with a linen he kept in the cuff of his sleeve, "now the Red Knight fights no more. The marcher lord has elevated him by giving him lands the Caliph once held, and a castle too—aye, and a wife, blameless and beautiful, a niece of the king himself."

The Cardinal rose. He began to walk toward the doorway at the back of the chapel, but suddenly paused and turned and lifted the forefinger of his right hand. Then in a moist, mellow chant the red ecclesiastic began to sing a curious sort of Compline:

> "He paces his green fields these days,
> Rides forth his bright and sable horse,
> Then fiercely sets a febrile gaze
> On lands beyond the lands he forced.

His long hair torn by vagrant winds,
Unresting, restless Knight! O Lord,
That knowest well thy servants' minds,
What further tasks must he perform?"

Then that large man turned surely toward the doors and strode through them, the castle's priest close at his heels:

"They say of this Lord Rufus, so called by the Pope," the Cardinal said as he went, "that having been so suddenly stunned by peace and bound by matters domestic, he is trying to read the twenty books of the Etymologies of Isidore of Seville. Ha ha! Wouldn't books—any books, but *these* especially—be heavier sailing than the march to the heart of the Caliph?"

And so it was that the two clerics passed not ten feet from where the Almoner stood in his corner of darkness. And then it was the full *Te Deum Laudamus* that this threadbare, colorless soul allowed himself all softly to sing, for his heart was voluble with gladness, for he had learned the place of his lordling's abiding:

"To thee all angels cry aloud:
The heavens and all the powers therein. . . ."

20.
THE RESTLESS, THE UNRESTING SOUL

Early one morning, after a long night of sleeplessness, Julian watched the first grey light of dawn with such a howling emptiness of heart, with such a fiery hunger in the bowels, that he took his bows, his bolts and all his arrows, and went forth hunting and to hunt.

In reverence for her peace of mind, however, he first stopped by the bedside of his wife, to tell her what it was he meant to do.

This woman, Julian's wife of a full three years now, was filled with worry on her husband's behalf. She loved him more than her uncle the king had loved him—for though the man had been useful to the king, unto her he was the full rounding of life itself. She did not mind his silences. She was herself no garrulous woman, but prudent, rather, in all she said and did. Theirs was a castle of reduced means, modest, unwalled and ungarrisoned, fed by a few fields, by several milch cows and goats and flocks, and by one magnificent forest which, uncut and uncultivated, seemed primeval in its age. Herein, Julian's wife was as much cook as she was a lady, he as much plowman as a lord. And each had vowed to the other—he for the ascesis, she for love—that this was enough.

And in terms of plain wealth and possessions, her husband had not lied to her: the low castle was *more* than enough, in that it was anything at all for a man who had lived so long with nothing at all.

Moreover, on their wedding night he had confirmed his vow by granting her two tokens of its truth. The first was a pendant. Though he had never told her anything regarding his personal heritage, he did show her this single link to his past, explaining that his father had given it to him five days after his knighting, and that, by the grace of God, both his father and his mother were likely to be living still, a mighty lord and a high-born lady, rich in lands, possessions and glory throughout Christian kingdoms to the north. The pendant was in the shape of a cross, on the back of which she found the words inscribed: *Miseracordia Dei.* He swore that he had never shown this token to any other living being, never until now and to her, as proof that she would be the family of his future even as these good persons had been the family of his past.

And the second token of his willing attachment to her and to this humble existence was his name. Julian.

Ah, what a tender gift! she thought: *the name of his infancy and his baptizing, the thing his mother uttered when he was a suckling at her breast.*

None but she was given to know it. None but she was granted to invoke the dearer heart within the martial, grim, unreadable exterior of the Red Knight. "Julian," the root and the bloom of the man together. Ah, Julian.

No: regarding possessions particularly, her husband had not lied to her. But regarding the agitations of his spirit, perhaps he had lied as well to himself. It was *not* enough.

The man could plow his furrows straight the daylong, himself unresting, exhausting his oxen. He could plow with his plowmen field after field and day after day, his delicate flesh growing scabrous under the sunlight. . . .

But he could not sit two minutes together. She watched him. But it took no *close* watchings to know.

He scarcely slept.

He read while pacing—or else, while pacing he listened to her as she read to him.

When he asked her to sing, she sang; and he patted his knee for a verse and a refrain or two; but then leaped up and away, as if the rhythms were chains too tight for him. She took the song into her own heart, then, and loosed him by her silences.

The man ate porridge and vegetables. Gruel and soup and thin beer. No meat for him, though he showed no offense in others' meals of animal flesh. No wine. Nothing of eastern spices. Therefore, though she could feed him, she could not awaken his palate nor delight him with savory morsels.

In candlelight on certain evenings, her husband would watch as she wound her long auburn hair into coils about her head. She had no mirror, doing all by touch. The finger of candle-flame trembled on the table before her, causing the shades in their bedroom to dance. She would glance up to him, this unquiet pillar of darkness at her shoulder; and sometimes, as ghostly as cloud in moonlight, she would witness some blessed memory gliding through his eyes, and he was gazing at her particularly! Ah, what clemency then came to her husband's face!—and so to her heart as well. Affection; contentment; small tuggings at the corners of the dear man's mouth. How lovely was her Julian then! How like himself when first they married! Her hands would pause, therefore, in the ocean of her burnished hair, and her soul would cry unto Christ, *Let that memory last! Whatever has eased him a little, let it surface and utter its name, and keep my husband easy a little longer.*

Ah, but the midnight cloud is soundless and, in want of a moon, invisible; for Julian would suddenly notice the fixity of his wife's dark eyes so eagerly upon him, then he would blink and breathe, and the memory would inevitably dissolve into the well of his sorrows, and she would bow her head in misery for that she had driven goodness into hiding again; and what these sorrows were he never did tell her, and so she could not bear the burden with him. Well, she *could,* but he knew it not.

Rare were these moments of swift revelation.

More commonly, the man was impenetrable. Wheels were turning behind his pale forehead, wheels *within* wheels working, but all to no avail. When the two of them sat and ate and spoke together, he would lift his eyes most kindly to her, and she would return his gaze—only to grow lost in the spinning complexity of his desperation. Perhaps, of his wanhope.

As the seasons of the fourth year of their marriage ground more heavily and more slowly round, the woman came more and more to worry for her husband. Where was the sane one, her simplest "Julian" undivided? Where was the tender one who had appeared at the soft calling of his Christian name when once he'd granted her to know it and to use it: *Julian?*

But how, if she knew not the cause of his torments, could she comfort him? How salve the hidden anguish? How save his better part? Nay, but only Christ can read the hearts of the sorrowful.

Soon Julian's wife was lighting candles. Soon she was bearing two slender, sacred tapers into the oratory— scarcely a room in that modest house, no more than an alcove at the top of the stairs that led from their bedroom into the hall. Soon she was a nunnish figure, kneeling on a little fold-stool, the candles in sconces on either side of her: and there she prayed. Julian's wife prayed one phrase from the Mass, that phrase compulsively, over and over and louder each time she prayed it: *"Dona, Domine,"* she begged of Heaven, *"ei requiem."* And then she added to that shorter phrase this longer one: *"Agnus Dei, dona Julio meo requiem sempiternam."*

The first prayer begged the Lamb of God for the thing most needful to her husband's soul: rest. "Grant him rest, O Lord."

And the second . . .

Well, but let me prepare for the weight and the effect of that second, more measureless petition.

On the afternoon of the seventh day of the Lenten fast, Julian came home from the fields a full two hours before the dark. He had not scraped or polished his iron-shod plow; he had not removed it from the field; no, the man had not even spoken to the villagers that had been planting the furrows behind him. He came home glowering, a great storm behind his eyes.

For one of his oxen had shied from something—some sly
vermin, some vole at its snout, as Julian guessed—and then
had broken the yoke and snapped the traces, and straightway had gone snorting and galloping through beanfields
freshly sown. Julian whooped and gave chase, barking commands the beast ignored: *Graceless, mindless brute!* Then, just
as he drew near, reaching for the ox's ears, that ox whirled
round and gave him such a kick that he, Julian, suddenly
ceased.

Ceased running: collapsed to the ground and lay on his
back the tenth of an eternal hour.

Ceased the work of the day by furious determination even
before he rose to his feet again.

Ceased, could the present state of his mind now govern
the rest of him, his duties altogether: his farming, his ad-
ministrations, his lordship, the terrible schooling of his soul
in domestic quietude.

Aye, and so it was that Julian himself began to break the
yoke and to snap the traces. He took hold; he leaped to his
feet, nearly buckling under the strike the ox had given his
thigh; but, far from disregarding the pain, he leaped up *feeding* on it, and turned and strode back to the castle mute for
the storming within him.

When by the great front door he entered the hall, Julian
heard his wife's voice echoing everywhere around him:
"Dona Julio meo," she was keening her second and heavier
prayer, *"requiem sempiternam!"* It named her husband by
name, begging a rest that had no end: "Grant *Julio meo,"* she
wailed, *"eternal* rest!"

The man stood stockstill. Never had he heard such a thing from her lips before. These words (did she know it? could she mean it?) came not from the ordinary Mass, but rather from the Mass for the Dead.

Julian withdrew again through the door of his house and closed it softly and went on his injured leg, step-stepping to the stables.

What depths? What meanings and anxieties was his wife expressing with such a petition as this? For the supplication was ambiguous. It might be the lesser prayer that begs a blessed change in his life, thus: *Calm his restless spirit, O Lamb of God.* Or else it might be the graver prayer that begs the peace that can *follow* life, that begs an end altogether to his troublous life—as if his affliction, verily, *was* to live, and life alone were more than he could bear; as if her tenderness suffered with him, and her own tormented compassion could conceive of nothing more easeful for her beloved than the mansions waiting above. Again: nothing more easeful—however hard *her* sacrifice of solitude—than death.

For he knew her love. And he knew that her spirit was shaped in service. This woman would never wish his death for *her* release.

Ah, Christ! But he would set her free! *He* would! He longed to explain to her his spirit's restlessness, indeed!—if only he himself could understand it! But he couldn't. No, he could not understand. Worse: restlessness turned his every present benefaction into iron anchors winched to his ankles. Worse and worse: he, Julian (but how could he *be* so wretched?), considered these blessings of the Almighty God as so many treacheries binding him down. Oh, how could his wife, her very *goodness,* be blamed as the shackle and weight that kept him from running? Flying the broad fields? Soaring the sky?

"Ahhhh!" roared Julian, spittle damping his beard. "Ahhh-*ha!*" he roared, clapping his hands together and terrifying the horses.

The horses? Indeed: he was in the stables still.

And when he saw what his roaring had done—when he saw the whites of the animals' eyes now rolling in terror—the soul of the man split in twain, one part exulting in the power of his hands, the other part despising the milk-fed fear of the horses, the *meekness* to which it testified.

"Sheepish, the lot of you!" Julian boomed, then laughed an unsatisfying laugh at the joke. "Timorous, obsequious, wretched *dogs!*"

Not enough! It was not enough.

So he picked up a shovel and with the flat of it struck the wooden sides of a stall. "Ha! Ah-ha!" he bellowed, whacking the split boards, stall after stall. The horses reared and whinnied and bit at their tethers. The storm was in the stables now. Horse-heads were black clouds above him.

Next, Julian smelled the scent of animal panic, and it drove him to greater extremes; for while he was nourished by strikes to his body, these brutes were fainting at the bare music of threat!

Ah, Julian, thou art the thunder, and these canst transect by thy lightning!

He cocked the shovel behind him, tightening his arms

and his back for a swing, a mighty swing at the head of a horse which would drop it dead to the ground . . .

But *Agnus Dei,* he heard as if he stood in the hall of his house, *Dona Julio meo requiem sempiternam.*

For his wife was praying on his behalf. And did he hear it here because the holy angels had taken to praying too? And with what would God answer this prayer for the peace of his soul?—with eternal rest, the sleep that is eternal?

O God! O holy and almighty God! O Jesus Christ upon thy solitary cross: What does the soul of poor Julian *want?*—when nothing, nothing satisfies?

Julian turned and looked outside the stables and saw some light appearing. Both the evening and the night had passed away. He saw the grey emergence of dawn. He smelled the moistures of the morning. He laid the shovel down.

For his heart was howling an inarticulate emptiness; and the hunger of his bowels felt like a fire. And the man was certain that he could no longer contain these wolves of the wilderness. Therefore he went inside his house by the lower door and dressed himself and gathered his weapons and prepared to go hunting.

But before he left, he stopped at the bedside of his wife. He gazed down upon her small, dark form a while, then knelt and leaned and kissed her until she sighed and awoke.

"Thou art faithful," he whispered to her, and in that instant believed the sense of what he said. He laid the print of his finger upon her two lips, and there he felt such softness of flesh, such a mobile warmth, that another sort of storm began to shake his soul. "Uncomplaining," he whispered, nearly in tears. "Ah, woman, thou hast been my firmament and the foundations under my feet. What would I do if I could not trust in thee? What would a poor man do?"

In this manner did Julian express his love for his wife. Too, it seemed to him that he had hinted somewhat at the change he felt must quickly come into their lives.

Then, abruptly, he stood up, saying, "I go a-hunting."

And he left.

21.
CONCERNING THE WIFE OF THE SAINT

Neither does she have a name—none that I could find even in my most persistent researches: Julian's gentle lady, I mean; she whom I sought and chased and wooed (as it were) down a warren of historical tunnels. Well, and you, my more durable reader, shall already have noted that none but the Saint has been named thus far. And I assure you that the rest of his tale cannot be different from the former part: only Julian's name will be remembered and recorded. Julian's, that is, and one other's.

Ah, but this one, this particular woman: how I have longed to call her by name! For it is not a false figure, to say that I have danced with her. A teller of such tales as this must learn its characters not by fact and analysis only, for then he could neither know their hearts nor grant them life. But if he can dance with one, that character may willingly *grant* him her heart; and having that, he has the means for granting her life in return, in the realm of his tale. I have danced with Julian's wife. I have the means to bring her to life. But I cannot call her name. Her life must therefore be bound to the tale and to the husband that knows how to name her.

For without that precious, most personal word, I cannot take the delicate woman's life and make it *mine.*

And as concerning *your* reception of this tale: O dear my reader, I fear that her namelessness might reduce the woman to a mere type in your mind. But I will show you how fully fleshed she is. And I entreat you to love her even as I do, on account of the sacred solemnity and the ineffable grace of this woman's suffering: for Julian's wife is like another woman who walks unnamed through a story which is named for the man she loves. She is like Jephthah's daughter, who chose to bewail her virginity for two months on the mountains, after which she returned to her father and bad him do what he had sworn to do. For *I have opened my mouth unto the Lord,* her father said. Jephthah had vowed a treacherous vow: just before he entered a battle, he swore that, should God give him victory, he would thank the Lord by sacrificing the first one who came out to greet him. Indeed, the Lord made Jephthah victorious. And who was first—with timbrels and gladness—to meet him at home? Jephthah said to his daughter, *I have opened my mouth unto the Lord, and I cannot go back,* and he did what he had sworn to do: he sacrificed her life and her name forever.

There is no more magnificent a suffering than this: to suffer willingly; to suffer in the full knowledge of one's

innocence; to suffer because of the sin of another, and yet to
do so for love of that other.

From the beginning this woman loved by serving. And
since it was a genuine love, it was genuine service as well,
and she took joy in the joy that it gave.

Likewise, she knew work ere she was twelve years old,
and hard work too. For her father, the youngest brother to
the king, was rich neither in servants nor in sons, and therefore his daughter became, among other things, the keeper of
his vineyard. She labored with a hoe and with a pruning
blade five years and six, with harvesters and with the tread-
ers, and in the end was altogether her own vintner, for she
learned well from her teachers, the monks. The king himself
took notice of his brother's daughter's produce, and so it was
that he remembered her when he sought to express his gratitude to the Red Knight.

By the eighteenth year of her age, the woman's complexion had grown richly dark, as dark as a Barbary maid's; yet
she had a smile that curled tightly into her cheeks, revealing
but two of her front teeth. And the nail of the first finger on
her right hand was slightly rippled—and this Julian sometimes ran his own nail over, making a mutual vibration. And
she laughed with something like a squealing in her nose, and
during the first year of their marriage, each time her husband
heard that little music, he jumped up, his frame filled with
something like astonishment; and next he, Julian, would
move toward her and look into her face; and she knew that he

saw the sheen of tears that her laughing caused, but that *he* could not tell what caused them, whether it might be some hurt that he had given her. So then the husband would go down on his knees wherever the two of them happened to be, down on his knees asking wordlessly what she was feeling; and she would straightway kneel down too, directly in front of him, her blood grown warm with so much loving; and then she would place the flat of one hand upon his breast and the flat of the other upon her own, and she would let spill the words of her gladness and all her hunger:

"O that thou wouldst kiss me with the kisses of thy mouth," she murmured, sending her breath as a warm milk over his eyes and his nostrils, "for thy love is sweeter than wine."

And she knew what her words would accomplish. For then her darling would gather her into his arms, and bear her to some private place, and lay her gently down, and grant her the kisses she had requested; and her warrior (she knew by his breathing) would almost die from the suffocation of his own increasing love. Then inevitably, by a brutish touch, Julian would find the ties and the fastenings with which she kept her clothing close to her body; and he would begin to undo these; but she was more complicit than he knew, for she herself now slowly unsheathed her shoulders, *she* stripped the cloth from her legs, she revealed her chilly torso all bare beneath his seeing. *O my dear!* he would not say, for the water had left his mouth; but *O my dear!* she heard in her heart, watching her husband steadfastly as he kneeled above her, allowing his eyes to brush each part of her tenderer self: her temples, her eyelashes, her chin; her breasts ascending under his sight, her girlish breasts, their nipples as solemn as two small peas; her stomach, brown as a wheatfield; her thighs, by a handsbreadth separated; and that central pelt protecting her womanhood which, when the deer-eyed Julian gazed upon it, shivered, spilling honey. Immediately she raised her hands to the back of his neck. Swiftly she drew him down, his mouth and whiskers down to her throat. "Look not upon me," she murmured, "for I am swarthy, for the sun it was first looked upon me, long, with a changing heat."

And so it was by kissing, then, that her husband sought that tenderest part. And so she invited him inside herself, and when he accepted, and when he arrived, his nautical presence drove such joy through her that she laughed: such loving as this caused Julian's wife to make that high sweet squealing in her nose—and so Julian raised up his head and roared with laughter too; and she, so softly that she knew not whether she had spoken at all, said:

Oh, linger within me, my love!

This was the plea of her laughing, yes! But then it became the plea of her weeping. For as the marriage grew older, her husband grew ever more restless; then she, whose love never did diminish, suffered the loss of joy.

Oh, linger within me this night, my love! she wept in the fourth year of their marriage, when the thing was done and Julian made motion to withdraw: *Grant me one night when nothing divides us. For I have begun to fear the mornings and thy terrible awakenings. . . .*

22.
GUESTS, AND A GRATEFUL HEART

From the beginning, Julian's wife had loved by serving, nor did the urge to service depart her, however consumed she was with fear for her husband.

What else might account for the woman's response to strangers knocking at her door when she was alone, in the evening of the very day that Julian had gone out hunting?

Supper had already been laid on the trestle table in the hall, food enough for the lord at his return and for the lady too—food, and yet no meat, since she was hoping he would bring fresh venison home. And perhaps his pleasure in the kill might persuade him also to partake.

Servants were gone for the night. There were neither beds nor rooms for servants in this simplest of castles.

And suddenly an enormous knocking sounded from the oaken door: *Boom! Boom! Boom!*

Julian himself would have come by the lower door, set close to the stables. And the servants of her relatives would have sung out her name or her lord's, the Red Knight.

This *boom-booming* betokened a stranger, and one of a powerful arm.

Nevertheless, Julian's wife drew a light robe over her shoulders, caught hold of a lantern, and walked swiftly to the door. She lifted the bar from its brackets; then, holding the lantern high above her head, she pulled the great door inward.

Standing outside—now several steps away from her—were two figures, a woman and a knight, she with a palfrey, he with a charger, the two of them altogether alone, both of them threadbare and lacking baggage.

It was the man, surely, that had beaten on her door.

The strangers stood silently a while; and as this silence extended, Julian's wife felt some apprehension, for the knight had a powerful bearing and strength in his arm.

"Is it peace?" she ventured. "Do you come in peace?"

The woman, then, lowered her woolen hood and un-wound her wimple, presenting her face and her head in the open.

"In peace," she said softly. "And in need, child. And in love."

She spoke with a gentle, constricted courtesy. In the light of her lantern, Julian's wife saw a woman older than her frame, for she was willow-like, slender as a summer reed, her shoulders bent like folded wings. Her eyes contained great skies of kindness; her hair was rich and thick and grey, falling in a great rope down her spine. This guest smiled, and Julian's wife felt the warmth of it.

Almost at once the knight bowed with a difficult humility. He was strong, truly; but he was trembling too, and when he spoke through his massive beard, his voice broke: "May we," he said. He swallowed: "May we see the lord of this place?"

"You may indeed," said Julian's wife, "when he returns and *can* be seen."

The knight narrowed his eye and scrutinized her. "Spoken with authority," he murmured, frowning. "Art not a servant here?"

"A servant, aye. And a wife besides."

He drew a swift breath. "Why, then thou art . . ."

"My lord's lady."

"Ahhh!" The knight suddenly stepped forward, reached and caught her hand in his own large hand and kissed it. He raised his face and turned away, making harsh barking sounds in his throat.

The knight's lady then spoke: "'When he returns and can be seen,'" she repeated the phrase with some urgency: "Surely he comes quickly? He can't have gone to war, can he? For Christ hath settled a great peace upon the land—"

"And we," the knight took up the urgency, "have heard of the Red Knight, that he loves the soil now, even as *his* father loved a harvest more than a conquest."

"Nay," said Julian's wife almost in a whisper, lowering the lantern-light the better to see these faces before her: "Neither to war nor else to the plow. My husband's gone a-hunting."

"O praise God!" the knight roared in explosive delight.

"But how," she said to the knight, "do you know what my husband's father loves?" And to his lady: "And why do you weep?"

The knight, whose wild hair and whose divided beard were both a snow, said, "I know my own soul very well." Then, shaking his head, "but I think I have never known my son's . . ."

"Your *son?*" Julian's wife made a squeak of the word. "What are you saying to me?"

The woman stepped forward and took the lantern from the hands of her gentle hostess and set it on the ground outside the doorway. She turned and laid her hands on the shoulders of the younger woman, softly answering: "This, child, is what he says to you: that he is the father of your husband. And I am the one who gave him birth."

"But you are too poor to be the parents he told me of. Why?—" Her voice had withered almost to a dust: "Why should I believe you?"

"Because we know his truer name," she said.

"His name?"

"Aye, the name that calls his soul."

"You know my husband's name?"

The older woman fairly sang, "Aye, for I was the first to hear it, and I spoke it the day of his birth. Daughter," she said, "your husband's name is *Julian.*"

Two words stung the eyes of Julian's swarthy wife: that maternal *daughter,* granting her place in the woman's heart, and *Julian,* now in the mouth of another. She began to sob. She could not speak. So the lady embraced her, saying, "Hush, hush," and the knight behind them punctuated his own moist emotions with blustering, explanatory phrases: "The Almoner, you know!" He blew his nose. "And my castle, you know! 'Twas burned to the ground."

His bluster and the lady's high-born sympathies caused Julian's wife straightway to love them both.

"Oh, my lord and my lady," she cried, wiping the tears, "come in!" She stepped inside the hall. "There's a supper already prepared. Oh, how can I thank you for traveling hither? Please do come in." She flew back out the door and snatched up the lantern: "I'll take your horses down to the stables," she cried. "I'll brush them. Surely your love and my love together will grant my husband rest, and peace to his turbulent heart. Go in!"

23.
AN EDEN, INDEED

Julian traveled soundlessly through the pastel mists of the morning. He blacked a path behind him, for his passage crushed the dew and bent the grass-blades down.

He did not question himself. He did not consider the thing he intended to do. In the manner of animals Julian went hunting animals, all his attentions narrowed to this present purpose: alert and nervous were the beams of his searching eyes; as taut as drumskins, his listening ears; quivering, his nostrils; his muscles easy, his bones bird-hollow, the tips of his fingers raw to the wind. Here, right *here* was the primal impulse of the hunter's hunting: at these crossings of his person with the rest of creation. Altogether the hunter, he! Altogether thoughtless.

And tireless.

As always before in his extremest contests, Julian felt a lovely, limitless strength now pouring like wine into his limbs. At a dead run he leaped the hedges. Like a deer he bounded the planted fields, his face filled with the wind of his going, his heart as the falcon released from her jesses.

Arrows and bolts rattled like pinions at his back. Ursine was the power in his torso, feral his teeth, and like flame the red hair streaming behind him.

Julian, flying, drew breath and roared at the ancient forest before him: *"Etiam venio cito!"*

And (how ravishing the dialogue!) *Cito* the forest sang back at him: *Citium, citissime!*

"Surely," Julian bugled his return to the hunt, "I am coming quickly!" And immediately the forest in a single voice, a yapping declarative voice, answered, *Quickly!* And Julian saw a great wolf dashing left and right at the edge of the forest, barking in Latin: *Quick!* and *quicker!* and *quickest!*

Christ, what sacred invitations!

Sprinting still, Julian twitched an arrow from his back, notched it on his bowstring, and drew the full shaft to his ear.

Lo: then the wolf stopped broadside to the hunter, turned its face to profile, and stood still.

Julian slowed to a halt as well, relaxing his bowstring in wonder:

For now the wolf's eye closed, the mouth opened, the chaps drew back in a marvelous grinning yawn, and the tongue lolled out in a lazy loop.

In that peculiar instant, Julian knew as a dogmatic certainty that he had a choice. Action sped forward on instinct alone; but when that action paused, thought flowed in.

For look how the wolf was leaning its thorax down, clawing the ground in front of itself, and stretching its ribs luxuriantly apart. Wasn't the hunted opening the very cage of its heart to the hunter?

Sacred invitations, indeed! Here was creation as at the beginning! Eden unafraid and he, who was in the image of God, granted the garden again! Oh, yes! Yes! And with a vaulting delight, Julian was pleased as Adam to take dominion!

Fixed, therefore, like a pillar at the edge of the forest, he raised his bow. He sighted down his arrow, then calmly released the bowstring.

That shaft! That tooth! That slender minister of death ripped so freely through the air, so precisely for the heart of its quarry, that Julian had already returned to racing and was peering into the forest for a further prey—when, instead of the fleshy *thunk,* he heard the sounds of little clatterings.

Why, the wolf had risen to its four feet! Julian's arrow had shattered on a stone where the ribs had been. And still the wolf stood like a carving in the same place.

In a twinkling Julian notched a second arrow and shot, but the wolf moved mere inches aside, and the arrow missed. In the same way, Julian's prey slipped his third arrow and his fourth. Suddenly the hunter was breathless and covered with an acid sweat. He bent to arm his crossbow; he rose and saw that the wolf had vanished.

Julian was trembling. Sweat tormented his eyes. But he did as he had ever done before, binding himself by an aweful discipline. He made a thin line of his mouth. He concentrated upon the smooth machinery of murder. With persistence, then, and terrible intent, he entered the forest to shoot and to kill—

And, by God, *failed* at killing.

These woods were an Eden, indeed! At every level the timbers teemed with life: small beasts burrowing; the low beasts, those smooth long-bodied beasts, slithering through muds and sliding into streams of water; the tusked beasts racing stiff-legged under patchy sunlight, their tails erect, their children dashing all giddily behind them; the nobler beasts cutting the middle air at the level of a hunter's eye, returning him stare for stare, their dappled offspring learning to leap; small fowl flitting at the lower branches; the aerial royalty, lords and ladies of the grace-blue sky, circling on their motionless wings; creatures high and low, so densely whirling before the hunter's iron points; creatures everywhere calling their calls in an air dimensioned by their motion—and yet Julian could not with any weapon, nor with all his cunning, craft and strategies, kill a single one of them.

He cocked the bow. He aimed, and he shot. And he missed.

Aye: among a myriad of myriads he cocked the crossbow. But how does one aim, when absolutely *everywhere* is a target? Aiming becomes a meaningless comma before the shot. And each single shot finds the one dark spot where the blithering creatures are *not!*

So Julian, making a furious kiss of his lips and thumbing the sweat from his eyes, broke forth like the storm of heaven: he released bolts as swiftly as drops in a sheeting rain. He clouded the forest! He made it thick with swarms of his arrows—for how could lightning strike and not strike *something?* But this storm *did* strike nothing. And this hunter missed everything.

When he paused to catch his breath—when even the last shaft shot had rattled to stillness—Julian saw that all his missiles, *all* the stings of his magnificent wrath, were sinking into the rich fertility of the forest floor, worms and insects chewing them, scats and pods and petals falling on his weaponry as on any other twig and hollow log.

"Ahhh-*HA!*" roared Julian in a glee of frustration. He clapped his hands, but none was startled, not one animal frightened. And curiously, *because* of his failing, the hunter redoubled his efforts. It was as if he meant to prove the impossibility of it all, for then his enemy might be grand, and grander than all creation!

The more he missed, the more violently did he continue to shoot.

Rabbits ran past him as courageous as boars. Weasels sat up like long-bodied maidens. Otters flashed wet faces full of laughter.

He would choke upon his emotion; the man would cough, and arrows already aimed fell loose from his bow. Crossbow bolts, shot with savage accuracy, puffed like dust against the hides of bears and bison. His arrows felt like straws of wheat—and finally, in the blood-streaks of the evening, Julian broke from the forest like a madman, weaponless, shaking his fists at the heavens.

He turned dizzily in the center of a treeless field; he lifted his arms as in praise, and he howled, *"Filios vester!"*

"Your children!" he screamed.

For, flashing like vermilion in the light of the sunset, there wheeled above him eagles and the greater hawks, royal and untouchable.

"*Filios vester interficiam in morte!*" Julian promised the circling birds, while crossing himself to warrant the pledge: "I go to get a hammer and a dagger! Then I shall set my face toward the high rock where you leave your children in nests of sticks on shelves of stone!

"No more my yew bow!" Julian howled. He brought his looking down to earth and began cantering over the grassy fields toward his castle. "No more the crossbow!" he wailed. "I'll be there come the morning, and with a knife and a hammer I shall kill your children dead!"

24.
THE SAINT, THE HAMMER, AND THE DAGGER

He is a ravening lion, the Julian now returning in a starry darkness to his castle: hungry is his blood tooth and unsatisfied. Sweat rains his face. The filth and the salt of it sting his eyes, which pour forth their cleansing water; but Julian drives his knuckles into the sockets, and the stinging gives way to blind fire.

He stumbles toward the lower door of his abode, passing the stables.

It is killing on his mind. It is the will to kill he has brought home with him. He wants a hammer and a blade for the closer, more personal work of his imaginings, and for the keeping of his manic pledge: *"Filios vester interficiam in morte!"* Between the fields and the stables, that pledge has entered the spheres of virtue. It seems to Julian that there shall be righteousness in finally finishing the promise of his heart.

But, though that heart is of a single intent, his burning eyes are suddenly distracted by a light. Before he enters the door of the castle, yellow beams of a watery light draw Julian's attention backward.

Why is there light in the stables?

He turns in to them. When he squints the bright beams vanish, for they were in his own seeing, and he descries the shape of a hanging lantern; and that were odd enough, but odder still are the two horses lit by the glow of it, shut within a single stall. To know these, Julian puts forth his hands and strokes them and finds one to be the charger of a knight and the other a palfrey with its mane in bow knots as 'twere a gift for a woman! And both had been ridden that evening!

It seems he hears his wife's voice, bodiless, murmuring, *Oh, linger, my love.*

A sweat more sour than that of physical labor springs at the roots of Julian's hair. Oily sweat, it seeks his eyes and his teeth and his tongue; and the long tendrils of his hair, as he twists his head around and leaps for the castle doorway now, snap and spray as if he were leviathan rising from the sea.

Bounding through the lower door into the dark interior of the buttery, his inhalations seething through clenched teeth; sweeping soundlessly through the great hall, smelling therein trenchers empty of food, touching the rims of two wine cups drained of wine; sailing up the staircase as deft and dark and soft as the owl, and only *then* knowing that he has snatched from the board below the haft of a cutting knife and the handle of a good stone jug; standing, standing—fixed in the stance of a watchman standing—just outside the door of the sollar wherein he shares the bed with his wife, Julian's senses scream in a bleeding acuity, for they receive each small stimulus as needles and brilliance and pain.

The door stands open.

The air from the room bears whiffs of leather, tincture of metal, the muzzy smells of sleeping.

All of Julian is slick with his sweat now; and the table tools in either hand slide like grease in his fingers.

Nay, but there are two asleep in there!

And one of them blows his breath through the whistling hairs of a briar beard—that one on the right of the bed. And the other sighs as his wife will sigh, for the utter love of sleeping. That one is on the left.

The hunter will enter the den of his prey. And all will happen as if in a flood of light. For scent and sound are Julian's illuminations now; and though his eyes are jellies of fire, he knows the distances; he knows the postures, that both of these sleepers lie on their backs; he knows by the air at their lips how the throat of the woman descends from her chin, how the brow of the man is a hill above.

Now then: with a cry of high accomplishment and praise to the Eternal, Julian takes two mighty strides and flies to the bed, above the bed, down onto the bed precisely between the sleepers; and as he lands, his left hand stabs the throat of the lady, his right hand strikes the brow of the man.

Neither one of his murders falters. It is with accuracy, with conviction and strength that he delivers the simultaneous blows. There are no screams from the dead. Julian lies in perfect stillness between them, still clutching the haft and the handle of his two weapons, his heart still galloping as if it were the charger racing still at breakneck speeds, now that the battlefield is razed and all the dead are down.

A long sigh passes through the lips of the man beneath him. The queerest bubbling gurgle occurs in the throat of the woman.

Warm fluid begins to wash the hunter now, washes his fingers first and then his hands and the lower parts of his arms. Julian feels a deep gratitude for the cleansing flow— and for the quietness of its coming. His forehead bent upon the coverlet, he feels another sort of water flooding from his eyes, and he wonders what these tears betoken.

Morning rain, the gentle thought occurs to him, and he desires fully to enter that thought and to abide there a while, submerged in its peace.

But it is not the morning light that illumines the sollar and all its furniture now. This light has sprawling, wavering shadows. It flickers.

Julian lifts his head and looks backward toward the light. Two lights, in fact: the flames of two white tapers in the slender hands of his wife, who has entered the bedroom behind him.

There are sticks and strings of straw clinging to her hair. Her nightgown, too, is dusty and straw-bestrewn.

She says, "I came to your cry, Julian. I heard you cry out. What is the matter?"

But Julian cannot answer her.

He has been granted his sight again. In the candlelight, his mouth utterly stopped, he turns and raises himself to his elbows and forces his clear eyes to view the murders he has accomplished.

On the left is the face of his mother, as white as powder and lovely; and her hair is pulled back and bound in grey voluminous skeins for sleeping. There stands in the base of her throat the black haft of the cutting knife, for the blade ran though and through that tender place, down to her neckbone, cracking it. Her blood has washed her breasts and her shoulders and one of the arms of her son.

On the right is the face of his father, framed by snow white hair and a soft white bib of a beard, both of these growths divided by a central line, and all of it thickened by his own blood now. The dead man's right hand rests at the side of his head, the forefinger curled and pointing toward his ear. Julian must place the stone jar elsewhere on the coverlet in order to reach his own hand, washed in the blood of his father, up to his father's white hair; must open his sticky fingers to move the hair aside; must lower his own gaze, then, to see the old man's ear, half the pinna cut away. And that is the lesser wound, the greater somewhere in the old man's brain.

Behind him, Julian's wife whispers miserably, "I waited

for you in the stables. I called to you. Didn't you hear me? Julian, Julian, you ran away and left me there."

Ah, dear reader, I am more sorry than I can say. But I have been enjoined to tell the truth.

But didn't we know it had to come to this? O Christ, the Crucified!—didn't we know?

25.
THE SECOND DEPARTURE

At some point that night Julian's wife set one of her tapers in a small wall-sconce and stepped forward and sought to comfort her husband. He had not moved. He was kneeling lowly between his parents, his hands upon their mouths. She leaned lightly down behind him and stroked the back of his neck.

At that tender caress, he shot his head and his shoulders so quickly, so mightily forward that he cracked his skull on the headboard.

"Go away," he hissed. There was a violent constraint in his voice. "Don't touch me. Leave!"

The woman could not have known that the ache he'd caused in his head was infinitely less painful than the fire her touch had caused in his flesh.

Nevertheless, she obeyed. She went away. She closed the bedroom door and in the light of a single taper descended the stairs. Then she took a seat at the table in the great hall, listening to her husband's sorrow; for he burst into tears, and his explosive sobbings filled the house.

Julian's wife fixed her taper to the tabletop by means of a little warm wax.

Again in that night, the door above her opened, and there was silence in the household about the space of half an hour. But after that Julian set himself to a difficult labor, and she knew him now: she knew that he would refuse her help, and therefore she did not offer to help him.

Julian bore his parents one by one downstairs upon his back—his father as weighty as God's own glory, his mother hardening at the joints, her hair a dry hay.

For the rest of the night, even until the dawning, she sat in candlelight and listened as her husband digged in the earth: one hole. Two holes. His breath whoofed as he worked. And sometimes it broke into howling.

Her taper burned down to a blunt inch, surrounded, as it were, by its clothing all cast off.

By morning, when Julian came to her where she sat in the great hall, she saw that his flesh was everywhere blotched and cankered.

And because there seemed a supplication in his countenance, she asked in her gentlest, most compliant voice, "What can I do for thee?"

"Bring the priest," he whispered hoarsely. *Hoarsely,* for that he had beaten his throat! At some hour in the night, he had crushed his throat, and it would not grow well again. "They lie each beside their separate graves," he whispered. "'Twould be a kindness if you saw to their Christian committals and paid for a Requiem Mass. And let me go. That, too. For I shan't be home when the priest is here."

"I can do two of those," she whispered, looking with longing upon her husband, who would not look at her.

"Three!" he croaked. He was wearing a thin tunic and leathern breeches, but no hat and no shoes on his feet, no weapon, no scrip. He had chopped his hair with a knife. His skull was patchy and scabrous.

His appearance broke her heart. "I love thee, Julian," she said.

"Nay, woman," he retorted with formality: "You torment me, rather."

"I do not mean to."

"But you love me, and you mean for me to know it as a consolation, but it is your *love* that burns me like the fires of hell."

"Well, then I shall cease to tell you of it."

"That too would come of your loving," he croaked as harshly as a corbie. "That too would give me mortal wounds."

"O Julian!" she cried out. "Then what is left?"

"Nothing," he said, and she gasped at that word as if slapped.

But his face was weighted with a terrible sadness, too. And he said more softly, "It is because you *are* love, my beloved, that you can do nothing to ease me. Every gesture of love must tear my flesh as if with hooks, for I know I do not deserve your love. Oh, woman, 'tis what *I* am! Love in any form can do nothing but scourge me with the whip-knots of my sin! Release me, please. Oh, let me go."

She said nothing. Her eyes spilled tears she did not wipe; and neither did she sob.

"This," Julian said, still softly, "would be your fate, should I stay and live with you: ever to weep and to lament. Nay, the evil of my leaving is better than the evil of mine abiding. For the more you love me, _____" (here Julian must have called his wife by name), "the greater the pain in our household, and the greater the woe for us both. And if you should cease to love me—oh, how terribly our attachment would bedevil you then! But if you can hate me, hate will set you free. Hate me for leaving," he said. "I am leaving."

And he left.

26.
SAINT JULIAN'S WIFE:
BEWAILING HER SOLITUDE

I cannot hate him. I cannot kill him in my bosom, for he has caused a lasting love in me.

At night on my bed I seek him whom my soul must love. I seek him, but I find him not.

I am sleeping, surely. Surely, I am in my bed, and sleeping. But my heart remains awake.

Suddenly, someone knocks. Listen! It's the voice of my Julian, calling, *Open the door! Open to me, my darling!* For my head is wet with dew, and my locks shake down the drops of the night!

For one witless moment, I am resentful. I think to myself, *I've put off my coat; how shall I put it on again?* And I think, *I have already washed my feet; how shall I defile them?*

But then I see the hand of my Julian through the hole of the door, and my heart sings with love for him. How swiftly I rise! How swiftly I run barefoot to the door! My fingers touch its handle with sweet-smelling oils. I throw open the door— but my beloved has left. He is gone. Oh, didn't my soul burn when he called to me? Am I waking? Am I sleeping still?

I dash out, crying his name in the night; but he gives me no answer. I run barefoot to the villages, calling his name. I run in a gown which tears when I stumble. I run in a rain which veils my face with my own wet hair. I run until the watchmen stop me and strike me and wound me. They strip me of all my honor. They leave me like a madwoman, naked in the grass.

I charge you, women and watchmen, servants and all! If you find my Julian, my beloved, tell him that I am sick with love.

THE FOURTH PART

⸻ ∞ ⸻

SORROWS

27.

THE RED KNIGHT:
HIS CONSUMMATION

In those days it came to pass that the Red Knight whom priests and bishops had begun to call "Rufus" vanished from the face of the earth. No one encountered him, north to the sea, west to the sea, east to the infidel, south again to the sea—or southwest, where he had himself defeated the great Caliph and his armies, and had settled down to dwell with a wife in a modest castle. No one bore report of him. Not in months. No, not in years.

But one of such courage: How could he be killed?

And one of such foresight, intellect and canny strategy: How could he even be *found* by a killer to be killed?

Surely the Red Knight had not been killed. As proof, the people pointed to peace. There were no wars. Neither footmen nor horsemen were dying those days.

And one of such honor and self-control; one of such a sunlit righteousness; one who worshipped none other god but the Lord God and his Son first, the Christ who was born of the Virgin: How could such a one grow sick and die? Why, this servant of the Heavenly King had lived but half his life! God would not let his holy one see corruption! Neither would he allow the Red Knight to die out of due time, a dishonorable death: alone, unhousled, unattended.

"Therefore, the chariot!" declared people of vigorous devotion. Elijah himself, they swore on the rood, had descended in a chariot of fire with horses of fire, to part the Red Knight from the rest of this ruinous world. And Elijah had taken him up, living still, on a whirlwind into Heaven.

"See how God loves us?" the villagers said, plowmen and cottars alike. Nor did their priests disagree. "See how it is that God gives us saints to warm our winters and to lighten our darkness? The Red Knight is battling Lucipher now, and the myriad spirits that seek to ensnare us and pull us by ropes to perdition."

Adieu, mon chevalier!

Ora pro nobis.

28.
THE TORMENTS OF SAINT JULIAN: IN SPIRALS OF DESPAIR

But Julian lived.

And year by year despised himself for living.

His hair had long ago grown out again, a dirty mass of wires and dirt-clots. The sour bush of his beard hid the lower part of his face. And when he entered innocent villages, he visored his eyes with his hand lest anyone should look upon him. It was not that he sought to conceal his identity, for that was lost. None of the Julians that he had been remained in his outward appearance. No, he covered himself, rather, because human eyes disturbed him. For if someone should spy out the truth in him, that someone must run away in horror and revulsion—and the revulsion of God's simple servants is a purer form of judgment. And precisely because Julian deserved the judgment, he straight-way must suffer this human rejection as cinders and heat from the furnaces of hell.

Julian had no excuses. He was guilty. There was no justi-fication for the things he had done. Nor could he plead ig-norance. Nay, he had known, and therefore was Julian guilty. And guilt rendered him altogether too foul for human com-munion. He was monstrous among the villagers.

But he was forced to move among them nonetheless. To beg. To gather scraps, to eat, and so to keep his soul still a tenant of his body a while.

His head bent low, one hand extended through folds in his robe, not a word to further the beggary, just that hand, open and upturned and empty: so did Julian crouch on muddy corners outside houses of wattle and daub—and he waited. This is how he spent his days, now: waiting, and yet not waiting at all, since a wait assumes an end to waiting, something still to come. This, more precisely, is how he spent the daylight hours: empty of self-conscious thought; his mind a wordless, unfurnished place, a wilder-ness; his eyes bent down on nothing at all, and his stom-ach resigned to starvation.

Scraps. A mere crust was all he needed and all he hoped for than he deserved to get!

Therefore when, one morning after Mass, a fine lady approached him and placed a small, uncut loaf of blackbread in his hand, Julian began to shake.

This lady wore a surcoat trimmed in sable and a gown of sendal so well-woven it seemed a liquid covering. She drew her pretty breaths through a round bag filled with sweet fennel, lavender, mint, pennyroyal. Her face she had painted white, her cheeks pink. One servant went before her, a basket on his back; another followed after. The latter blew on a merry whistle-stick as his lady reached into the basket of the former and took out the little loaf.

"The peace of Christ upon thy soul," she said as she bent from high nobility to base poverty and placed the loaf in Julian's outstretched hand. But he did not return unto the woman thanks. Nor did he withdraw the loaf into his robe. Rather, he began to shake with a rabid violence.

A wave of wretchedness had seized his limbs because this was a loaf! A whole loaf, much too much for his deserving, and therefore an accusing thing. So dervish was his shaking that he dropped the loaf into the dust. But then his stomach was screaming, and the man split in two: hunger howled in his abdomen and drove his right hand forward; but guilt restrained that clawlike hand a bare three inches from the food. In that posture the beggar shook and strained and made a marvelous fool of himself.

"Tom!" snapped the lady. "Take it up and give it to someone more grateful for getting my gifts!"

Tom ceased tweedling on his stick and jumped down with such a loud clump that those who had ignored his whistling, together with this lady's charity, now turned and began to watch.

But before Tom could grab his lady's loaf again, the beggar snatched it up and tucked it into his robes.

"Thief!" the lady screamed. She began to curse him.

But lo: her cursing was a consolation to Julian, and now he thanked her indeed. With genuine feeling he began to bow before her.

She shrieked: "He scorns me! Defies me! This animal taunts me!"

Julian grew all the more grateful. Removing his woolen cap and bowing his forehead down upon the ground, he murmured, "It is right and proper. Strike me, strike me with your hatreds."

The villagers pressed closer to this little play. The lady's servants looked left and right, uncertain of the loyalties of the vulgar. And when a sound of loathing seemed to rise from the crowd, Tom scrambled a little distance away from the beggar and found a stone and threw it at him.

The stone caught Julian on his very crown, causing sparks of light to shower past his eyes. He raised his head. He nodded slowly. He smiled beamingly, and he began to weep. Tears sprang from his eyes and ran to the tip of his nose. He felt in the dust beside himself and found the stone that had hit him and raised it up to the servant, Tom, who was shifting his weight from foot to foot and watching him.

"Tibi gratias ago," Julian said to the servant. Then he saw, standing behind that benefactor, a girl-child, golden-haired and weeping too, the same as he, and he smiled more kindly, repeating the sentiment: *"Tibi gratias ago."*

"What, brute? What, thou sullen beast?" Tom snarled, flashing glances at the villagers near him. "What callst me in thy yaa-yaa tongue?"

"Why," said Julian with humble feeling, lifting the stone yet higher between them, "I gave you thanks."

"Thanks, animal? Thanks to me?" Tom glanced at his lady, who was demonstrating interest in nothing just now, daubing her nostrils with the bag of crushed fragrances. But her indifference seemed suddenly to make a man of Tom, who flew into a pretty rage, bellowing: "Thanks for what?"

Julian, calm for the propriety of all these things, whispered, "For the stone. I thank you for the touch of your stone."

"Yow!" the servant roared. He ran straight to Julian and, grabbing him by the hair, began to beat him, face and throat and body. Even when the beggar slumped senseless into the dust, Tom continued to kick him with square-toed boots.

"Tom," his lady called, glancing backward over her shoulder.

He paused, panting. "My lady?"

"Forget my bread and I shall forget *thy* bread this even."

Julian woke in the heat of the afternoon. Flies buzzed about him, treading his wounds and drinking tears at the corners of his eyes. He heard the rolling of wagon's wheels above him; he felt a mud beneath him. He did not open his eyes, but it seemed to him that he had been dragged outside the village and left in a ditch.

Then, the chilly winds of the dusk descending, Julian lay in the mists between sleeping and waking, seeking which way to go.

Easeful death.

Oh, how death would set him free!

For hell could not be worse than this. This: not the beatings nor the stonings nor the hurt they gave his body; but rather the mortified conviction that beatings and stonings were proper indeed. Julian despised himself. No spiritual armor remained, nor anything of righteousness to protect his soul from the pains of punishment. The fist and the foot of his assailant in the village, why, those were the limbs of God! The loathing in his lady's face, that was the loathing with which the King of Heaven looked upon him now. Could hell be worse than this?

Then Julian heard a gentle breathing somewhere beside him.

The sound of it—aye, and the scent of it too—caught him as a hook catches the fish: it dragged him back from the mists to the shores of his infinite pain.

Julian opened his eyes under the golden columns of an evening sky. He looked upward and saw the face of a child gazing down upon him. Her hair was a nimbus of gold, tangled with the sunset colors; her eyes as green as the evening, her mouth a coral shell. Who could this be?

"You came back," she trilled, a sweet, melodious voice. She gazed on Julian with pity, without fear, without the hint of condemnation. "I took you for dead, truly," she said. "And sad I was for it. And sorry, too, for what my village did to you—"

Ah! This was the girl-child that had watched his degradations.

"But I prayed to our Mother for your life. Over there. Against that rock," she sang softly, nodding, folding her hands to show him: "and you did, you see? You came back."

Julian blinked, striving to keep his vision steadfast.

The child suddenly came forward on all fours and leaned her smiling face directly above his own. Ringlets and tendrils of her sunset hair fell like curtains around them both, causing Julian to think of the canopies that hung over high altars in the bishops' cathedrals.

He did not speak.

But she of the sea-green eyes brought her playful face lower and closer to his, giggling, showing a row of tiny teeth. "I brought you a biscuit," she announced, "sweeter than any blackbread. An' would you a taste of my biscuit, sir?"

But just then the ends of her sun-down hair brushed Julian's brow, then his temple, his cheek; and where her hair touched, vines of fire sprouted and flourished. Roots of fire drove down into his brains and blazoned there the sentence: *Discedite a me maledictus!*

Julian yipped and jerked. He swung a fist. He almost struck the beautiful child—but she had thrown herself backward, shrieking a sharper terror. Julian tore at his face with finger-claws. The poor girl rose up and ran toward her village, wailing.

And so Julian fought desperately to hold his tongue, not to howl the damage done to his soul: for it was kindness that inflicted the greatest pain. It was goodness and innocence that cut the moorings of himself and sent him like a small boat loose on the rolling billows of this endless sea: *Depart from me, thou cursed!—in ignem aeternum!*

Yea, and were eternal hell a horror worse than this hell, where beauty tormented and mercy destroyed, then Julian must and must and ought to die. Why shouldn't he be permitted to make a payment equal to his wickedness? And as his suffering here but terrorized children, surely Christ would let him die:

"Kill me, Jesus!" beating his breast, rolling in the ditch: "Crucify me a worser crucifixion than thine!"

But even as his better self begged Heaven for death, his stomach commanded the hand that reached into the mud beside himself, where there was buried a little honeyed biscuit.

Julian rose up and limped away from the place of the child, away from the village of his abasement, and down the midnight highway, chewing the delicate cake as he went. Life drove him forward still. Hunger belied his holiest prayer. He could imagine no conclusions to his wandering: Julian walked the world in spirals of despair.

29.
THE TORMENTS OF SAINT JULIAN:
SOLITARY IN THE WINTER'S COLD

Perversely, Julian continued to enter villages wherever he went. In spite of the shame, *because* of the shame, he moved through the habitations of the peasants. On the daylit lane he was the cankered stranger, eyes cast down, a verminous robe clutched tightly at his throat. At night among the shuttered houses he was the revenant dressed in death-clouts and dusty from the grave—him whom children and criminals feared the same. In the green evenings, weary Julian sat on gravestones and listened as men and women sang Christian hymns in the church hard by.

After wakeful nights he would hear the churchbells ringing daybreak for the festivals of the saints. At any hour he heard the same bells toll news of life and of death, of local birthings and the dyings of kinfolk and the return of knights at arms from skirmishes abroad, or else from joustings where they earned a martial glory. Ah, the warm knit of human community! Wherever a farmer was working in his fields, he learned as soon as his wife what changes had occurred in his parish, for each heard the pealing both at once.

And when the bells began to toll alarm, all feet save Julian's ran to the village to converge at the stone church itself: a fortress, if people were under attack; a storehouse of buckets, if fire had broken out; a courthouse where the lord of the land sat judgment upon his villeins; a prison for the treacherous, the dangerous, the unfamiliar.

On icy winter nights the Wanderer would notice firelight in the thatched cottages that lined the roads he traveled. He saw orange light under the eaves and flickers of yellow flame through chinks in the walls; for a wall was composed of willow sticks and a muddy daub, and though it resisted the frigid wind, it cracked in winters and pulled apart. Julian paused, blowing frost clouds into black air. He stood under the stars and thought of the family that slept within those walls: human scent, contented breathing, flesh enclosed by flesh to keep each other warm. Julian tried by memory and imagination to enter the cottage; but memory failed him, and his imaginings were altogether bleak: the vision would not come. In a rush of needfulness, then, he stepped forward and rose on tiptoe and applied his eye to the brightest chink—and so he saw. Aye, on the dirt floor—aye, and on pallets around the central hearth where little flames still licked its logs—lay five figures of the peasant family, slumbering: between two children an ancient shrunken grandmother; and the mother on her stomach, her right arm flung across the chest of a third child, a pretty boy beside her. The farmer's pallet was empty, causing Julian a quick fright, for the man might be returning. . . . Nay, but there was the farmer, lying among his cattle at the far end of the room, his mouth wide open, his mind oblivious. So tears beclouded Julian's seeing, for that the sight was homely and plain and good: benches and stools, a chest, two iron pots on iron hooks, wooden bowls on wooden shelves with wooden cups and spoons, linen towels, a table, a beautiful woolen blanket with colors for no purpose but to delight a peasant's heart.

Ah, God, to be a peasant! A cottar. A villein burdened by the week's work and fees. A poor man asleep by the flank of his ox. . . .

As he withdrew his eye from the chink and was once again solitary in the winter's cold, it occurred to Julian that he might begin again.

He walked. He lifted his eyes and saw the stars—and saw, by means of them, the starry sparkling that once had adorned his father's midnight hair, the lord's black beard.

Perhaps he, Julian, might use the new year to make sober preparations to begin again. Hum. And then the spring, and after that the summer, aye. Perhaps he might have something to offer at the harvest market, when the old year's accountings were closed and new books about to be opened. Hum.

30.

THE TORMENTS OF SAINT JULIAN: TEMPTED TO A FURTHER PRIDE

On the first Monday after the Epiphany, Julian watched the plow-races of freemen, each man trying to cover more land than his neighbor, because as much as he plowed in daylight, even so much could he sow alone that year. There was much shouting and laughing and pretty girls waving their arms in glad encouragement.

Julian watched as the "fool-plow" was hauled through the villages, saw groups of boisterous plowmen begging pennies at the doors of every cottage. Their leader the boys called "Bessy," one dressed as an old woman with a bull's tail under his gown. If pennies were refused, "Bessy" commanded his team to plow up the ground at the pinch-penny's door. And thick-shouldered women threw back their heads and roared at the joke.

Perhaps he, too, might one day do that. Julian might one day return and laugh as well. This, only this: he must bring an offering, some something worthy to someone else.

On Ash Wednesday the Wanderer watched as the stone and steepled churches—the signal building for every parish, built on its highest hill—were veiled in black. He saw the cross and all the images shrouded.

On Good Friday the cross was unveiled and set on the steps before the altar. Parishioners came forward to kiss it, kneeling, bowing low—"creeping to the cross," as plain folk put it. Then the cross—burdened by the lips of the devout, by their sins and their supplications for salvation—was removed and buried in some secret place within the wall of the church. Its burial vault was surrounded by candles, a wide avenue, a liquid pool of candlelight.

On Holy Saturday all of the lights and all of the candles and all of the fires in the parish were extinguished, and the Wanderer went away.

On Easter Sunday morning, all alone in a green wood by a fast and frigid stream, Julian began, as he had planned, to make preparations for beginning again. He stripped himself and entered the stream and washed his skeletal body; and by its cold he quenched the fires that burned within him.

Next he washed his robe and spread it out on willow bushes to dry.

While his clothing rolled in fresh breezes, Julian flaked one stone upon a harder stone, fashioning for himself a sharp instrument. Thus he passed the Easter of his beginnings.

In the days and the weeks that followed Julian wandered boggier waters and sought stout reeds hollowed from the year before. A good number of such reeds he cut and carried away. In a private place he cut them again, into lengths of two spans each, then split them at their tips.

He gathered various plant gums and cooked them in water and a little sour wine. He collected lampblack by burning a smoky oil under a metal basin, then with the edge of a feather brushing the soot produced there into a shell. These he mixed and sealed in wax-covered pots.

Throughout the summer the poor man practiced. He had to convince himself of his skills before he might sell them to another.

And then came the harvest, and joy to the peasants.

And then came the market that followed the harvest; and

Julian, mute with excitement and fear, barefooted, his poor robe washed to a translucence, bore his small offering in a leathern sheet to the churchyard where others were building their booths and piling their produce and hanging their handiwork out for the bartering.

On grass in the churchyard Julian spread the leathern sheet, arranged his tools, heated and thinned his inks with a little water, then sat and quietly murmured his offering to people passing by: he would write a peasant's chosen words on any material a peasant might bring: names on clay, records on planed wood, poems on stray pieces of parchment.

He sighed as he waited. He swallowed often, his heart wrung dry with this great longing to belong again.

And indeed: within the hour a certain man and woman passed by Julian's patch more than once, perhaps three times. Soon he spied them some little distance away, with bowed heads talking to one another. But it was the woman held the greater portion of the conversation. The man tugged at his chin-whiskers. He shrugged great shoulders. He sighed—then all at once the woman swept away from him and struck straight out for Julian like a longship on the sea. Her approach struck sparks in Julian's vision—indeed, oppressed him with a morbid fright, as if a hawk were about to hit. He dropped his looking and could not lift it up again.

The toes of two slippers stepped on his sheet, and then those of two boots.

Julian croaked through his ruined throat: "Speak it, and I shall write it down."

"Well, Gerd?" The woman's voice was like a switch on horseflesh: "Well? Well?"

The man dropped a leather belt on the sheet by Julian's tools, by the circlet of ink and his reeds. But then he said nothing. And Julian waited in silence.

Everywhere else in the churchyard noise unfurled like pennants in a stiff wind. Rhythms stretched and snapped and chattered. Children ran thither and yon; women inspected foodstuffs, men the dry goods; hussies gossiped; minstrels strummed and strolled and sang; vendors pushed carts and cried their wares. Bright garments whirled in sunlight. Whistles chirped. Leather bladders farted. Teeth flashed in laughter. And the air was fresh, and the sky high blue, and Julian's ears were caverns for the noises, his nostrils tingling with aromas. Only his looking was narrow and low, attending only to the belt which the peasant Gerd had dropped upon his sheet.

Finally the woman, with a stamp of her slipper, snapped, "Write thee this, thou scribbler. Write: 'On this, the Feast Day of St. Michael—'"

Julian laid the belt flat, stretched it between the palms of his feet, reached for a reed, dipped the split end in ink, and swiftly began to inscribe the letters: *On this, the Feast Day of St. Michael—*

"'Gerd the plowman,'" recited the woman faster than Julian could draw the letters. But he would remember. He would not forget. And she said: "'The husband of Bertrada—'"

Gerd the plowman, Julian turned the letters carefully upon his material, then he stopped. Facing groundward he murmured, "But 'tis a belt."

"Hold thy tongue!" The woman stamped her foot again. Her ankles were huge above the slippers, engorged with a purple bloodwork. "Dost question thy betters, scribbler?"

Gerd, wrote Julian, *the husband of Bertrada*—

"'Hath purchased,'" she fairly shrieked with laughter, beating her thick hands together, "'his freedom of his glorious Lord Charles—'"

Hath purchased—Ah, but then this was a document meant to be indelible!

Julian stopped again. It had to be right! So he gathered courage and murmured again, "But soon 'twill wear away. Too soon for the saving—"

"Fool!" The slippered foot stamped but an inch from Julian's fingers. "Gerd'll cut thy lettering into the leather forever!"

Hath purchased his freedom of his glorious Lord Charles, Julian inscribed the leather slowly, with grand flourishes for that the sense of the thing was so important, almost causing Julian to weep: the mute plowman above him was free!

The wife snatched the belt up. The freeman dropped a copper coin on the leather sheet. Then both of them, while the scribbler lifted his eyes to watch, went walking away: he stoutly, she with massive wobblings behind.

Julian allowed the spasm of a smile within himself. For he had accomplished something. He had lent letters to the freedom of a quiet man. Nay, 'twas more than a smile: he suffered a surge of gratitude, and he almost uttered the name of the Lord.

Thus, he surmised, *my beginning again.* A toehold in community might soon become a foothold, and then a step.

(Ah, Julian! Julian, you will break my heart! Such trust is perilous, Julian!)

But glad he was as any harvest youth when a young woman suddenly moved from the milling crowd in his direction, smiling, holding forth a lovely piece of parchment which never yet had been written upon nor ever scraped to receive new words. He kept his seeing raised this time. He allowed her smile a lodging in his bosom.

Her eyes were bright, her skin an ivory white, unpowdered and unblemished. The samite mantle upon her shoulders announced the woman to be high-born and noble. Her swift strides were taken in confidence—and that smile on her face was a gift, those flashing eyes were radiant gifts for Julian alone. Oh, how his breast bucked at her searching eyebeams.

"A love letter!" the woman sang as she approached. "A letter to my true love, sir, and make your hand extravagant to write it!"

Her beautiful feet seemed to leave the ground. She floated, then she descended and sat by the place where Julian was sitting, his brains in a clamor: I am here. Here I am, in the midst of human happiness.

As the gentlewoman settled herself—her hair a cloud of acacia, her breath a vapor of orient spices—Julian scrambled to his knees and grabbed a reed, preparing to dip it in the ink. He glanced up. Tiny sunlight was cupped in the curves of her black lashes. Julian gasped. He could scarcely tolerate this nearness to joy.

Ah, God, is it now? And shall it surely be?

"'O blythe beloved!'" The lady's voice was a deep, mysterious chime. "'O blythe beloved,'" she said.

But the parchment. Julian reached for the fresh parchment in her left hand.

Instead—astoundingly!—she offered him her empty right hand, and he took it; and, reverting thoughtlessly to the Julian of his nobler years, he drew the lady's hand to his lips, preparing to kiss the back of it, raising his eyes as he did. . . .

All at once Julian saw the woman with terrible clarity. Below her smile the white column of her throat was altogether too comely and familiar. And at the base of that Julian recognized the delicate indentation of his earliest, most innocent memories. Tender love now bloomed in him. Already he was making a point of his forefinger, reaching to touch that pulsing, ivory hollow. But it was a small boy's finger! Ah, but as he brought his finger closer, the woman's shoulders curved gently inward, making a cave of her chest and her reception. And what if he did poke his finger into her throat? Would it drive into the flesh? Would blood spring forth?

Julian was panting. He was making mewing sounds behind his lips. The woman lifted her eyebrows and uttered something like a question, but he was hearing ballads sung and the giggling of a little boy—

"GET AWAY!" Julian roared in horror. "GET AWAY FROM ME!"

The lady frowned, cocking her head engagingly to one side.

Julian drove his heels into the sod and kicked himself backward. His foot shot out and whacked the circlet of ink. The ink flew up and blacked the lady's samite mantle. She put her hand there, patting her breast, and it blacked her fingertips too.

But she wasn't scolding him! Her gaze did not accuse him. She merely turned sad eyes upon the wretched Julian, and it seemed that the ink was darkening her person with grief.

Why didn't she scream?

Hate me! Curse me! Bite and tear me with your teeth!

Julian was standing on unstable legs, turning. Beside this lady he saw another, equally as dark with maternal sorrow, equally long-suffering—and next to her, another; and next to her, another: not one of them his mother! But yet all of them were his mother, surely. For when he murdered the primal woman, he had murdered every woman, everywhere.

The marketplace was crowded and quiet and watchful.

Lo, and there was the man whose belt he had inscribed, the stolid villein, a villein no longer: that man had his father's raven hair! Nay, but every man in the churchyard bore the loving look which his father had sent him, beckoning: *Canst read, lad?*

Aye, father.

Art easy enough in the Latin then?

Aye, father.

Then read this and give me the sense of it: "Quamdiu fecisti—"

And Julian threw his hands to his ears and shrieked: "Inasmuch as ye have done it unto one of the least of these my brethren—"

Oh, how multiplied were the murders of his parents. Once these two had been all the world to the little boy and the fullness of his community. Now they were the world again; and in every community where mothers and fathers dwelt, Julian's bloodlusty rage had gathered a host of sisters and brothers for his dead progenitors: every woman a lady of caven shoulders who had kissed and cuddled and sung to him; every man a noble lord of intelligence and strength who had raised him up to sense and to righteousness.

"—unto one of the least of these my brethren, thou hast done it unto me."

And so it was that Julian left that village, and all villages else, running. He was done with the species. Never again would he wander past human habitations, for they tempted him to further pride and greater torments at the fall.

For how could he look on anyone any more? The eyes of this murderer made murders wherever they turned. His tremendous guilt had grown at last too heavy to bear. Therefore, Julian determined to find some solitary, barren place and to kill himself and so to rid the world of such corruption as he had become in it.

Justice must have her conclusions. Only then would common things be righted, and ordinary things made well again.

31.
A MASS FOR THE DEAD:
THE WHOLE CREATION GROANETH

Through savage regions Julian went. He did not know his direction, save that it took him nowhere near the cultivations of humankind, not ever where men had tamed wild beasts and the wilderness. This man so darkly marked, around whom every land was the blasted Land of Nod; this sinewed man, lean as a willow switch and bearded like the willow tree; this fugitive condemned to death: he kept himself to rock and the high defiles, to marshes that stank with moody exhalations, and to the uninhabited hills.

He did not eat. He did not drink.

His tongue swelled and stuck to the roof of his mouth.

And all this was right.

Pustules on his face broke and burned in the bitter wind; they leaked a liquid corruption that scabbed at the roots of his beard. The calluses on the soles of his feet cracked and bled, so that he left blood-prints on the stony shelves behind him. But he walked. He kept on walking, never resting, for all these things were just and proper to the condition of his sinful soul. Julian walked both day and night, blindly forward, ceaselessly somewhere, seeking a solitary tarn, a pool of green water into which salts and deadly minerals had leached.

Blow, thou bitter wind! Tear the robe from the thin man's back! Make him labor, in shame, to cover his nakedness!

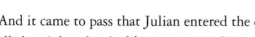

And it came to pass that Julian entered the darkest night of all the nights that had been appointed him for life. And he knew it was to be such a night, for a voice came to him from the thickening shadows, saying: *Et factum est silentium in caelo, quasi media hora.*

It seemed to Julian that the words had come in a night-jar's nasal cry. The grey bird of monstrous coal-black eyes, flying on a soundless wing, had called: "And there was silence in heaven about the space of half an hour."

And the bird spoke truly: for the silence immediately descended as heavy as heaves of the ocean. Julian—walking, walking—could feel the weight of this tremendous silence. It was as though he had been swallowed by the cave where the eight men sleep, yea, though there were sheets of stars above him! For the God whose word was as constant as earth and sky had ceased to speak. Christ!—such cosmic stillness causes the innermost ear to roar.

Julian walked; and it seemed to him in the Absence of God that every step diminished him. His chin was upon his breastbone. His hair fell like a raining around his face. His breath blew out in whistles shrill as shrieks—and these may have been the expirations of his spirit. *By this night's end, I shall have become a nothing in a nowhere.*

But suddenly the silence was broken. A massive bear not far ahead rose up on two legs and drooped her shoulders and thrust her great head forward and made her mouth enormous by jutting her ragged lips. The she-bear set up such a loud lamentation that all the creatures where Julian was stirred and woke.

What was the creature saying? Perhaps: *The hunter cometh.* Or perhaps it was a *Dies Irae.*

Packs of wolves on the high ridges where they roamed heard the bellow of the she-bear. They shivered and gathered and paced and barked all softly among themselves, restless, watchful. Then, at some common signal, they swung their heads Heavenward, and the wolves howled unto God such mournfulness that they melted the firmament and swallowed the stars with weeping: *Requiem aeternam dona eis Domine.*

After the wolves, the aurochs huffed and grunted a more private grief. And after the aurochs, the owls: *Recordare, Jesu pie.* And after the owls, all the small deer, sobbing in unhappy holes.

And so it was all that long night, as far as he walked upon his bleeding feet, that a doleful music followed Julian. None complained. But one after the other, breed by breed, the beasts were weeping his passage as they would weep for blight and sadness and drought and mortal scarcity.

And Julian, compulsively, wordlessly: *I am sorry. I am sorry.*

Sound surrounded him. Sound kept him ever at its center. The mournful sound drowned all thought, and he could wish he were in that cosmic silence again.

Julian, mutely: *O Bear of Lamentations, I am sorry! O Howling Wolves—*

The man moved in the animals' Mass as if he moved in an

army marching—except that every creature remained in its lair, its nest and den. 'Twas only the music moving, mouth to mouth and place to place. And the mobile Mass was itself a cathedral of vaulting sound, an airy cathedral advancing. For carrion birds took wing and caught the wolves' *Kyrie,* then circled the murderer, growling above him: *Eleison.*

At his passage ground squirrels jabbered, wrens set up a fervent chit, serpents whispered: *Libera animus!*

Insects cricked. Their myriad tickings, like a wind-blown shifting of sands, hissed a sibilant *Sanctus.*

And Julian walking, placing his wet feet down: *O ye on whom I tread, I am sorry. . . .*

Birds murmured in every tree the man approached.

Foxes barked in the darkness. Weasels seethed. The woodcock drummed a wooden *Agnus Dei*—

And the priest of all was a stag, a silhouette rampant in the distance, bugling like a trumpet. And it seemed to Julian, forced to look toward the sound, that the stag was chanting suffrages:

Oremus pro parentibus nostris absentibus—

"Our absent parents!" Nay, but this suffrage was more than a creature's cry. It was a thing of stupendous weight. It came down as if it were a great sheet knit at the four corners, enclosing every kind of four-footed beast and wild beasts and creeping things and fowls of the air; and these were the animals' parents, but more than their parents; these were brothers and sisters, families, children: all their dead kin. Within the sheet was the whole communion whom Julian had killed with his weapons and craft, and with his canny strategies.

And when the stag's chanted invitation ended—and when the sheet was taken up again into Heaven—then it seemed that every living creature, both near and far, responded. Every beast on the face of the earth, young and old, creeping and digging and soaring, joined its voice with all the others' in a universal chorus: *Salvos fac servos tuos, Deus nostrus, sperantes in te!*

"O God, our God, save thy servants that trust in thee!"

And this put word to the nightlong revelation which Julian had been experiencing. It told the truth he must have known, but the words of which he never had heard till now.

Julian, in a torment of remorse: *The animals are servants of God no less than the angels. Whom have I killed? In gladness, them that trusted in him.*

That grand chorus of the creatures of God—and the sense with which it pounded him—broke the soul of Julian into a fine ceramic dust, and all the rest of him turned to ash.

I am sorry, he strove to cry. But he could not make his thick tongue work. It was dry as a shard of clay. *Children of the great Creator, I am ashamed of all my killings and the pleasure I took in them.*

But how can animals mourning their dead interpret the stains on a small man's face? Penitence lodged in Julian's chest; contrition lay prisoned within the bars of his ribs and languished there.

32.

REPENTANCE:
SO TO FAIL THYSELF THAT
NOTHING IS LEFT BUT MERCY

Morning dawns a pewter grey. Julian is standing up, is standing still. Finally the man has ceased his walking—and when the grey sky affords him sight, he understands why: his feet have come to the edge of a precipice. One more step would pitch him, headlong, some several furlongs down. What, then, does this mean? That merest instinct has preserved his pitiful life?

Clouds shut him off from the whole horizon of the heavens. No bird dashes underneath the cloud. Not a creature creeps these shelves or calls in the distance. Animals have left him alone, as has all humanity, since he fled them both. Julian is the single dark figure in an endless sweep of grey, the only body here on high, on barren rock where dead grasses shiver in the fissures.

He has come to the end. For he has—even as he prayed he might—found the destination of all his present desire.

Far down, at the base of this precipice, Julian sees a pool of water as still and as grey as the sky. He pulls the woolen hood back from his head. He unties the cincture at his waist, throws open his filthy robe, and drops it on the stone around his feet.

He will jump, now, and drown himself. He will remove this corruption from earth and from Heaven. He will pay the price for his awful life. Hell is just, and Julian seeks nothing but justice now—by his punishment to make all things right again.

So he inches to the broken lip of the ledge. The palm of his foot crumbles the edge and breaks loose a little gravel, which falls into the void like a handful of bird's eggs—and catches at Julian's sight. The gravel fixes his eyes, if not his interest, and he allows the point of his seeing likewise to fall down and down as the pieces converge above the pool—and look! Look down! There is another figure floating in that pool, indistinct to be sure, but staring back at him!

Julian is startled to a truer interest now. The gravel plinks the water.

Who is that? Who is that man as naked as he is, waiting below?

Nay! But Julian shall not have a witness to his suicide and to the assurance of his falling to hell after all! This theft of his privacy maddens him, and Julian rushes to his right, where the cliff gives way to a narrow decline of scree. Downward he is sliding now; slowing himself by his heels and his elbows, down; scoring his backside a thousand times, down; accepting the cuts as the first of his scourgings, forefeelings of the hell to which he is already plunging: and, down! But by the time he reaches the bottom, Julian has pitched head forward, striking his brow on rock and stunning himself a while.

But I will it. I will it. I shall by suicide bind my soul to the doorposts of perdition.

When sight and his senses return, he glances immediately toward the pool and finds it a green sheet of water. Behold: there is no man in it. No one swims that water. It is as still as crystal, for nothing can live in such a tarn.

Therefore Julian stands up and stoops down. He seeks a stone for his right hand, and another for his left. Then clutching these weights, the naked man struggles to a limestone projection, a sort of platform by the water. He must lay one stone down on the step in order to climb it. But he manages. And then, holding death in either hand, Julian approaches the edge of his low elevation. He looks down, and sees that man again, that witness gazing up at him—

Jesus! Oh, Jesus! Why will you close every door to me? I cannot, I cannot, I cannot, I cannot, I can, not—

For the man in the water is his father: the same lines at his eyes; the same bloody wound in his forehead; pure white hair, a white beard, white the hairs on his caven chest and, by a white path down his belly, pure white his pubis too: the body exactly that Julian had years ago borne down to burial but did not bury.

And this is the question that stops poor Julian absolutely: How could he kill his father a second time? For to destroy the image that stares up from the water; to enter that water, replacing the image with his own person, and by drowning himself to banish eternally all that his sire has left on the earth—that would *surely* be to kill his father for the second time. Here is the thing that Julian cannot do. It is proscribed even for him to take his own life. Too many lives abide in his.

And therefore are all doors closed to Julian now. And forever. And therefore he sits down on his low platform and moans in a wretched, wordless desolation. For there is no moisture left in the man. All his parts are dry. And his tongue is a clog at the back of his throat. But this is the sense of his moaning, for this is absolutely the only word given unto Julian truly to say:

Peccavi. Peccavi. Peccavi.

The word defines him. It is his name. It is his one true thing: *I have sinned.*

The channel of all his communications can carry just that single grain of sand, for Julian is as narrow as the central pinch of an hourglass. There is nothing left of his life and all his history, except this one word:

Peccavi.

And then a voice—very thin, altogether birdlike—answers: "Aye, thou hast."

Julian is a dry stick on limestone. He cannot look up.

But it was a human voice he heard, not of his imaginings, and not his own voice, either. Julian surrenders to the mortification: for he finds himself in someone else's company. Someone's eyes are upon him now, and he is known.

Again the high, piping voice utters words quite easily: "My lordling, let me speak for thee. Ah, let the confessions of King David be also thine: *Domine, averte faciem tuam a peccatis meis.*"

All at once a cool hand scoops under the back of Julian's neck. "Here." Julian's head is tilted upward. "Drink this," and the hole of a leathern bottle pours forth a cool stream of water into his mouth.

He drinks.

And straightway his tongue is loosed.

And as the birdlike voice recited in Latin, "O Lord, hide thy face from my sins," so Julian, also in Latin, responds: "And blot out all mine iniquities."

That utterance releases all the locks in him. Julian squints upward. There is a man standing in the pool beside his stony platform, a wiry fellow, but solidly fleshed, as Julian can tell by the waves he makes in the water. The face is gaunt, completely unaccommodated, steadfast in looking. It is a threadbare man dressed all in black.

"Ah," murmurs Julian, "'tis thou."

And: "Indeed, my lordling, my sweet heart, Julian," the Almoner warbles in loveliest birdsong, "'tis I." He leans closer. He tips the leathern bottle and floods Julian with another drink.

"Julian," he said. My skinny tutor has called me, "Julian."

After all these years of a nameless solitude, the Almoner has snatched Julian back to something like his youth again, to that ancient chapel and the charities. And this is a kind of beginning. *I am Julian!* The water rushing into his mouth goes down to the dust that was his soul and makes a pretty mud of it; water courses through his desiccated limbs; and water softens his joints and breaks forth from his eyes, and Julian is crying with the great, sucking sobs of a child, his mouth and his eyes wide open.

"Create in me," the Almoner sings, "a clean heart, O God."

And Julian: "Renew a right spirit within me!"

With uncommon strength, the Almoner lifts Julian's torso to a sitting position. He reaches for Julian's throat and

takes hold of the pendant swinging there and lifts it up to
Julian's eyes.

"Seest thou?" he says. "Remembrest thou? Canst read the
legend thy father etched in it?"

Julian reads between the hiccups of his sobs: "*Misericordia
Dei*. The mercy of God."

"Lordling," the Almoner sings dovelike now: "Heavenly
mercy never left thee. Here it hath lain"—placing the flat of
his hand upon Julian's caven chest—"and here it lieth still
above thine heart, waiting, waiting for thee so to fail thyself
that nothing is left but mercy."

Where his teacher's hand is applied to his breast, Julian
feels a great heat spreading. It is the heat of a painful and radiant longing. So urgent grows the heat, that Julian starts
to pant.

"But what shall I do?" he says. He begs this. It is the very
supplication which has tormented him all these latter years;
aye, but this time he begs and does not answer it himself.
For now he knows he has no answer, and so his begging is
pure.

Julian heaves his wounded body to its knees. He places
his hands together. Face to face with the Almoner, he is the
supplicant, pleading: "But what shall I do? How shall I live
my miserable life?"

The Almoner removes the thin black robe from his back
and whirls it over both their heads, then settles it on Julian's
shoulders alone and closes it with an iron brooch at his
throat.

He takes hold of Julian's hands, and one by one he kisses the tips of the fingers, singing, "Ten servants to join the hosts of Heaven."

Once more he reaches to the pendant swinging behind the black drape, and with his nail taps it so smartly that it rings, *Misericordes!* The cross and the legend and the silver disk all seem, like bells of the empyrean, to ring in pretty syllables:

Beati misericordes! Quoniam ipsi misericordiam consequentur.

The Almoner bows and allows a smile to wreathe his hollow cheeks, then ascends from the pool, himself raining rivers of water. He walks away. He walks directly toward the grey face of the precipice down which Julian had thrown himself—and as he goes, he utters the words that the heavens themselves have just declared:

"Blessed are the merciful, for they shall obtain mercy."

The Almoner walks through the stone wall. Julian blinks and immediately remembers that his Confessor, stripped of the robe, was nonetheless not naked, but clothed in light. And where he passed through the wall a moment ago, there is now a portal. And the sunshine on the other side has a greenish cast.

THE FIFTH PART

———— ∞∞∞ ————

SAINTHOOD

33.
NOT A HOLE, NOR A NEST, NOR A HOME

The last journey which Julian accomplished—this one also on foot, from the pool in which he had seen his father to the banks of another water altogether—took him, in the strength of the Almoner's robe, but a single day. The stone portal in the precipice gave forth on a green field with hedges closed against foraging cattle. Tender shoots were greening the good land—and the whole scene, once Julian had stepped into it, seemed to receive him with whispers of a personal welcome. It was familiar to him. The scent, the breezes, the slant of morning sunlight, the angles and corners of the hedges—all this fit memories formed in his milk teeth and in his soft bones. . . .

Aye. Julian recognized the place. It was a field near the foothills of his father's old demesne. It lay under the hills northeast of the castle, under the loftier ledges where a younger Julian used to hunt.

The older Julian bent down and cupped blossoms of daffodils tenderly in his hands, and one by one he greeted them: "God mercy thee," to a yellow trump, "God speed thee," to another. Thus he began to salute each natural thing in its springtime freshness: "God give thee grace!" to trees and the gangs of leaves unfolding on their branches;

ever "God be with thee" to pebbles in the furrows and the
bean sprouts shading them above.

And having reacquainted himself with the lesser citizens,
he climbed a stile to the top of the hedge and gazed out
across the lands his father once had governed and sighed and
descended and set his face to the southwest and so com-
menced his final journey, marveling that all his wanderings
had done no more than bring him home again.

When he was a boy, Julian had been a greyhound: his red
hair flying like flames behind, himself racing the regions in
less than a morning. Now, however, the sun was swifter
than he, and the day far shorter than it used to be. Julian
walked. Julian took stock of the pieces of self left unto him
and giggled a string of moist "tee-hees."

Arms as narrow as hoe-handles, hands like shovels attached to the ends of them.

A spine bent round and down, both shoulders fallen inward, as if Julian were carrying a load against his anterior
portions. Ah, but 'twas only the hollows there: hunger, and
his mother's own caven frame.

Tee-hee! Tee-hee! Oh, how pale and bunched and meatless
were the legs that forked from the hem of his dusky robe!
Julian had become a hobbler. His backside was as stringy as
goat-gristle.

Therefore it was evening before he came to that open
place all bordered by oak where his father had governed the
most glorious jousts in the kingdom. Through diminishing
light and weakening eyes, Julian sought the platform which
he had himself ascended for his knighting, upon which he

had received that remarkable clout to his head from his father's hand. Julian looked to see the shadows of the young king and the Lord of the Castle sitting side by side, both of them chewing cloves and conferring together. But there was no platform in the field. Julian found only the charred stumps of post-wood, the blackened ends of the great planks and a sooted scent intolerable. Knightly clashings left no echo. The field had forgotten and gone to weed. Inhospitable.

As Julian hurried across, thorns and thistles scored his skin as high as his thighs. But he did not notice these. He could think of nothing but what the destruction of the jousting platform signaled regarding the greater destructions ahead of him.

Julian hastened toward a swollen, empurpled sky. The sun was done for the day; it had seen the sights this old pilgrim approached and had sunk below the earth, leaving behind a twilight of bruises.

Against that gloaming, then, and walking forward still, Julian seemed to see the ascent of a jagged, skeletal thing: poor, chopped posts and beams arising black.

Ah, then this was lost as well.

Ah, God, what grief it must be to the choir of his eyeless ancestors; for here was nothing but coal-black timbers against a violet sky. His father's castle had been put to the torch, and its lead-lined roof had melted in a rain of fiery drops, and all its trusses had collapsed, and its walls had crashed down upon its floors, and all things lay in stinking hills of char.

Christ: the floor that had taken the footfall of his mother was an airy vacancy now. Humps and rubble were the kitchens, the stables, the barracks, the granaries; yea, and the chapel was an enclosure of stones, a high-built sheepfold open unto the heavens.

And there, on his right-hand side—solitary, lofty, abandoned—stood the great tower his father had built; but its few windows were sockets in a skull's head, and the whole was a hollowness with neither stairs nor landings nor ceilings nor a roof: a stone pipe in which the wind blew mournful music.

Ah, my father: this is thine inheritance and all thy legacy now.

Stars began to emerge. The night was drawing all its blankets down. A light breeze, embittered by cinders, blew hither from the heavy ruin. It scorched the tender cavities of Julian's nose. It tugged at his hair and his beard, and seemed to darken the moon as with a veil. Julian grew chilly. He tightened his threadbare robe—and by that gesture loosed within himself this thought: *And all thy legacy left on earth . . . oh, Father, it is I.*

"Haloo? Haloo! A hand if you will!"

Here was a rough command from the mass of the castle, the rough-edged accent of a northman.

Julian saw no one in the night.

"Darst not duck, Man! Darst not hide, Knape! I see thee where thou standest! And now I will a ride!"

Julian tried to follow the sound. He walked through the cluttered shadows, tilting his head one way and the other.

He called, "Where are you?"

"Right where my two feet strike the earth!"

"What do you seek?"

"Hast ears? Hast not heard my belling? A ferryman!"

"Aye, a ferryman. Why?"

It was Julian's notion to find the fellow by means of his mouth, since but one of them seemed willing to move. Therefore he said, "Why?"

"*Why?* Why, to ferry me!"

"Ferry you whither?"

"God save the wretch from wretchdom! Across the *water!*"

"Aye. The water. And which cross of the water?"

"Art an *ass,* man? To the opposite side! As once I was ferried to *this* side!"

"Aye, aye, 'tis a perfect ass I am. But it is *your* ass I am for the night," said Julian approaching a stout man who was robed in the great pelt of a bear, carrying an ax and a shield, wearing a scabbard and a small leather srip. "For I have come to help you, if I can," he said. "Follow me. I think I remember this place."

And so Julian led the northman on a path of potsherds and nails. Over the ruins of the northwest wall they climbed, then steeply downward to a channel hewn in bedrock and filled with river water, for it gave access to the river itself.

"I've grown loath of your southern ways," the northman blustered as they went, "your jack-a-dandy manners, lisping fops and foppish fighters! Time to live the hardier life again! Time to pick a proper wife—"

"Here," Julian said by the side of the stone-cut channel. "Here is where the ferrymen kept their boats protected."

"Boats? What boats, Tulk? Seestow *boats?*"

Aye, the demolitions of his father's estates had the completeness of some insatiable vengeance: everything useful had been stolen, every combustible thing had been burned. There were no boats in the ferryman's channel, and none on blocks.

"What," said the northman, drawing his weapon, "will I do with thee now?"

"But I have not done with you, yet," Julian answered pleasantly, "and the sign of our success is above us. See?" Julian gestured to the moon now shedding a purer light. "It is that we *can* see. Let me have this a while."

At his own word Julian plucked the sword from the stout man's hand, walked upward of the channel until he had crossed again the crumbled timbers of the wall. There he began to slash through a patch of low thickets. He cut himself a thorny trail to the center, then bent and took hold of an iron ring and lifted a door set flatly on a frame of stones. "'Twas meant to be hidden," Julian sang out. He threw back the door. Cold air, a moist air rushed out at him, and he called back to his passenger: "A flow well, kept for sieges!" *A pretty room, kept for secrets, too.*

Julian went down several steps and entered and felt blindly around himself. Soon he brought forth from the cellar a small coracle—a round wicker-work boat that was covered with hides—then its paddle, and finally a clay jar full of the oil which was meant for the lamps of the little room.

These things he carried down to the channel, grinning: "My lord," he fairly cackled, "your longboat!"

Then, with thanksgivings unto God, Julian rubbed oil all over the out-facing leather of the coracle until it gleamed in moonlight. This he plopped into the channel, crying, "Come, sir. For everything is ready!"

As light as a petal the round hull lay on the water. Julian held it while the heavy northman shifted his bulk into it; then he too—scarcely adding to the weight—stepped inside and, kneeling, plied his paddle to the water.

Swiftly they were out of safety. The river's currents seized them and spun them, and Julian bent his back and arms to break their spinning and next to paddle across the mighty flow. Silent as his mother was, exultant as his father, Julian strove at the task, dashing water, pulling deep, glaring at the black horizon of trees that passed on the farther side, for the river was bearing them southwestward, but *crossing,* by God!—crossing, since they were in the belly of the flood and the only good to come of this must be their safe arrival at the northeastern bank.

This Julian knew by the sweat and the manner of the northman: that he was kin to the blonde berserkers that had burned his father's castle down, for they had left their scent in the burning. A pagan race, a raping, untrammeled breed, whom his grandfather had with bloody glee subjected. But his father had put faith in conversions. He might, therefore, have accepted one or two who, after their baptisms, had asked to serve as border guards.

Thus my traveler acts as if he owns both sides of the river and all the water too.

But Julian felt no need to speak the thing he knew.

And that he and the northman accomplished a crossing at all that night; that they walked dry-shod on the other side, parting under an endless field of stars; that Julian had kept his pledge to another human being—all these things he considered no less than signs of the grace of God. For he was aware of the obstacles. For there had not been strength in his body even so much as to *walk* the distance, let alone to paddle it. Nevertheless, his shoulders and his arms endured. His back stayed rigid. His eye did not fail him. And he felt nought but kindness toward the northman. For which:

Soli Deo gloria.

34.
THE LABORS OF SAINT JULIAN

And so it was that Julian found a blameless task with which to fill his days—use for his body and service for his soul.

He became a ferryman.

At first he paddled the small coracle to and fro; but only for a single season would the river remember its milder mood. This would not last. Besides, word soon spread abroad that an old man could be counted on—in darkness as in daylight—to answer the call of travelers at the river's edge. That bend in the river became a Point of Crossing again. Therefore the frequency of his to-ings and fro-ings increased, as did the size of the groups that required his service. And though Julian was willing to make as many crossings as there were people in a party, the people themselves grew impatient and complained.

Therefore he built himself a boat with oarlocks and thwarts capable of holding five people besides himself—though five and their baggage could constitute a tremendous weight, and the time of their crossing tripled.

Aye, and yet God's grace persisted. There continued to grow good strength in his arms and in the long extensions of his body. He was granted the power to row a troubled water; to row, as it were, whole populations over the river. And when autumnal winds tore leaves like flocks from the shivering trees, and when southward or groundward went every meek thing of the earth, even then Julian's arm was not diminished, nor could the fussiest churchman accuse his crossing as clumsy or hesitant—so long as that cleric would sit on his hams and not rise up like Christ in the back of the boat.

It was of fresh-cut timber that Julian had built his boat. Likewise, of living willow did he construct a little hut; for the winter season, its freezings, its blizzards and its thawings, caused such furious weathers, such floodings and such durable glooms, that no traveler would call his name for a crossing in winter's bitterest weeks, and he himself required the shelter to survive.

There was no shelter otherwise, nor materials with which to build, as all was a wreckage now, and 'twas nothing that was not ruined. The northmen had made of the great tower a mighty flue for their bloodier conflagrations; its round interior showered soot, its roofless top invited ravens, and the rubble at its bottom had become a habitation of rats. Julian blessed the rats with individual blessings ("God mercy thee," "God speed thee, groundling") and left their homes alone.

Once, early in his return, he had gone to inspect the chapel, for there might have been some salvage there. But when he had gained the doorway, he could not take another step forward. For not only had its roof been consumed, but its flagstone floor had also been subjected to the pounding of such massive weights that it had fallen into the rooms below. All the sepulchers of Julian's forebears had been exposed and likewise smashed. The great stone cross lay akimbo in a burial box. Leg-bones and skulls and the separated dice of finger-bones lay scattered among the broken stones: an inglorious desecration, a bloodline abolished, that bloodline for which he, Julian, was the last living representative: And what of dignity could he return to these? And how could he, a ferryman and a pauper, honor them by his existence?

But an old dog was pawing through the charnel pits; a mouse was gnawing candlewax in a sconce; spiders tweedled the gauzy air; and bats clung everywhere to the higher walls, streaking the stones with their acid shit. It was a busy chapel after all, nor could Julian dispossess a single one of its inhabitants. Therefore, he blessed them with *"Benedico,"* and left them to their ancient abode.

For himself he built of his willows a hut of daub and wattle. He thatched it, enclosing space enough for one man only, too low for standing erect, a stool for sitting, a central hearth, a few shelves on one side for provisions, and on the other side a straw pallet and blankets for sleeping.

Over the years Julian wove a long rope, thick and much too stiff to be turned into loops. And fortunate it was that he did, for as the rope approached the length he needed, he recognized within himself a wasting and a weakening. The man was old. His life had been long and difficult.

When the thing was finally done, Julian wove one end of the rope to iron hooks in bedrock on his southeastern side of the river. The other end he lashed to the stern of his boat, then pushed off into the river. This crossing was one of his most exhausting, for the rope was a mighty drag in the current, and the current kept driving Julian upstream along his own southeastern banks. He had to fight free of land and strike back over the water in a great returning arc, dragging his vinous anchor against the current. In the days of his father, servants had made a train of boats, then handed the rope from man to man: it never caught the water. And Julian had tried carrying first a lighter cord across, this attached to the heavier rope, which was the painter to be; but once *that* was far enough into the river to pull with the weight of its current, the smaller cord snapped, the painter snaked free, and Julian was forced to start all over again.

And again; and yet again: until one night it seemed to him he saw the great form of a she-bear swimming the river, the painter in her mouth. Immediately he rowed to the far side where, finding nothing but the end of his rope, he attached it to hooks in iron girdles round the trunks of oaks. And so it was done.

Thereafter Julian locked his legs beneath a thwart and pulled the boat hand over hand across. In this manner he could brave the river in the dead of night and never lose his way.

These, then, are the labors of the elder Julian: at the calling of his name, whether "Julian!" or else "Ferryman!" he carried every sort of person over the waters.

He ferried sweating messengers, both of landed lords and of the church, men in too much haste to seek their comfort.

Impoverished knights he bore with their weaponry across, their big-boned chargers swimming behind and easing the pull of the ferryman.

Minstrels passed his way.

Mummers.

Physicians escaping the rages of one lord, hoping to find the favor of another.

Poor clerics, since those of higher office and larger demesnes had money for barges more handsome than Julian's.

People. Stonemasons to places where kings were building. Fugitives. Scholars. Wanderers. The least of these. All. He never turned a soul away. He served.

And so Julian received now and again a coin from the purses of generous strangers. And so he grew content withal, capable of keeping his wild hair brushed and his poor bones covered and his stomach fed on barley bread.

35.
SEE HOW IT IS THAT GOD MAKES SAINTS

Winter, now. The first black hours of February the twelfth. An ice-storm shrieks outside poor Julian's hut. It rattles the walls. Ice-rain whirls in the smoke-hole, causing his hearth-fire to redden, to snap and sparkle. Then suddenly the storm sucks air out of the hut and sparks swarm like bees upward into the night—and Julian, that old man, is on watch: for the hellish wind might tear thatch from his roof, or else some lingering spark might set it afire. Sparks strike his own flesh and he rubs the pain in his arms, sharp as bee-stings.

Julian!

Whence such a violent storming? Here is a riddle, indeed. For the evening of the eleventh—no more than four hours ago—had closed the day with a wondrous clarity. And at the door of his hut, Julian had paused in the windless cold and lifted his eyes to a sky of ten million crystals. His lips breathed ragged ghosts of thanksgivings into the air.

The night was well. All manner of thing was well. Therefore, having received the benedictions of the tranquil heavens, Julian bowed down and crawled inside the hut and banked his fire and opened his pallet and covered himself and fell asleep—

—and then was shocked awake by a thunderclap.

And now he crouches in the midst of an elemental riot. For lightning does indeed flash above the smoke-hole, and the ice-rain is fixed in that flash, and then the thunder punches Julian's chest, and he coughs. Where is his robe? It had been his blanket. He finds it knotted behind himself. He loosens it and pulls it around his shoulders and ties it with leather ties at his throat.

Julian! Julian!

Sleet sweeps the earth. Sleet in a high wind strakes the hut, encasing its northwest side in a crackling mantle of ice. The river is shattered; it surely is. Julian knows that the wind has thrown its surface into a jubilation of waves and whitecaps—which, too, the lightning freezes with its flashes.

Julian prays aloud: *"Illumina, quaesumus, Domine, tenebras nostras!"*

Julian prays: "Lighten our darkness, O Lord we beseech thee, and by thy great mercy defend us from every treachery of this night."

Juuuu-lian!

What? What was that?

A faint cry in the night, extending the first syllable of his name to a thrilling length: *Juuuuuuuuuuu-lian!*

Immediately Julian becomes alert to things more distant than sparks or the condition of his thatched roof. He tunes his hearing to that far-away call.

But, *CRACK!*

Ha!—but delicate listening redoubles the thunder when it comes: *CRACK!* Julian grabs his head and groans. "How can an addled man listen, O Lord?"

Juuuuuuuu-lian!

There it is again! And he *can* hear it, and can recognize it too, for 'tis his name in the form of asking. And hasn't he heard that particular supplication innumerable times before? Aye, but never on such a night as this!

Christ in thy mercy: Who can want passage tonight?

Nevertheless, Julian crawls to the door and cracks it open; and though the wind would drive its panel full-force inward, yet Julian holds it against his shoulder and calls: "Here I am."

Marvelously, he too is heard. And he is answered: "Julian! Come and help me over!"

Ah, how miserable must that pilgrim be, to consider this storm a lesser misery than his own.

Suddenly the entire night swells electric white: lightning grants a flash of seeing, and there on the far shore stands a solitary figure—ah!

Thunder follows and puts out the light. The wind shrieks. The hearth-flames are torn sideways from their coals. Julian leaps outside and shuts his little door. The ice-rain rakes his face. It makes whips of his long hair, which lash him about the neck and shoulders. But he clutches his robe at the throat and at his bowels, and bends his head into the weather, and begins to descend to the channel of water for this reason alone: that there is a traveler in need.

"Juuuu-lian!"

"I am coming. I will be there soon, my brother, soon!"

His boat is rocking madly in the channel. The river leaps and stampedes like terrified horses. Julian steps into the boat and unties it and swiftly grabs the painter above, balancing the whole by the bending of his knees. He sits. He locks his calloused legs beneath a thwart and then begins to pull himself out of the safety of the channel and into the turbulent darkness beyond.

"Juuuuu-lian!"

"Count, brother! Count my handstrokes with me! Count with me my coming unto you."

Hand over hand, then, Julian cries the count: "Eighteen! Nineteen! Twenty!" Hand over hand, and only the long rope knows the way. All else is howling darkness and misdirection. "Forty-two, sir! Forty-three!" The river's current wants to tear Julian westward, seaward. But his fingers clutch the rope, his arms maintain a steadfast rhythm, and he drags his prancing boat toward the lonely figure. Ice is in his hair, hard at the ends of it, a sucking cold at his crown, whence his heat is leaving him. Ice makes iron his beard. And his robe is cloying with the cold.

Do not pause! 'Tis the going that keeps me steadfast now. But if I pause once, I may pause for the rest of the night.

"Eighty-nine! Ninety!"

But the going is so exhausting that soon the breathless ferryman is thinking fiercely: *May pause for the rest of my life!*

Then the sky is sundered by lightning, and Julian discovers that he has just arrived at the other side, at a low stone bank upon which stands the pilgrim, murmuring with more than supplication, with something like familiarity: "Julian."

Still shouting in order to be heard, Julian makes his invitation: "Come then, friend. Step inside while I balance it."

The man is wiry. There is no meat on him, belly or thigh. His neck is a spindle. Nonetheless, when he steps into Julian's boat, the stern of it sinks down treacherously.

"Sir!" cries Julian. "For God's sake, sit, or we shall be swamped!"

The thin man does not sit. But he moves amidships and squats there. The bow comes down—but so does the boat entirely, and the river claps its waves above the sides of it.

And now that his rider is so near unto himself, Julian sees him in smaller detail: eyes dark and moist, enlarged with diseases; a ruined face in which the beard is but wisps; his bony body ravaged, his hands so consumed that there is but a single finger left on either one.

Meselle, Julian thinks to himself. A leper.

And a passenger too, unto whom the ferryman has sworn his service. For that reason and for this, that the man is in the greatest need, Julian begins to pull for the other shore. Ah, but the leper's remarkable weight and the boat's deep draft almost break the ferryman's arms, as if he were dragging a tree through the waters, many-branched and thick with leaves.

Hand over hand. No counting now since exertion requires his every breath. And he squints into the icy rain, and he grits his teeth as 'twere a knife between them, and he fights against a tormenting wind and through the imperious current: he could die. No crossing was ever more dangerous than this one. Julian's hands are completely without feeling. His calves at the edge of the thwart are bloodless.

But it is service that he has chosen. In his hand-over-handing is all the purpose of Julian's life, and without it he would not be.

Therefore, from whence does an old servant draw strength for so difficult an endeavor? Why, from the groanings of his passenger. From the sounds of the pilgrim's misery. For the drowning weight of the leper is precisely the measure of Julian's service: this ferryman, frozen and cramping, shall not fail to keep his promise.

And finally tonight—*Soli Deo gloria*—the servant succeeds. Trembling uncontrollably, Julian draws his flooded vessel into its channel. He stands up. He falls to sitting again, and laughs.

"Oh, my two pegs are bloated and blue," he confides to his passenger. "Grant me three blinks to rub them and I shall rise again."

In that little moment, however, lightning scores the sky like a brilliant scribbling; and Julian, grinning at the pilgrim, exchanges laughter for solemnity; for, even before the thunder follows, he has the whole of this squatting man imprinted on his inner vision: the cheeks have been eaten through; the palms of his wretched hands are pure white; pustules and boils all over his visible skin are red and running; and despite such destruction of his flesh, Julian can see that *this* flesh is deeply brown, a foreign complexion.

The pilgrim is a Moor.

The leper is a Saracen.

And when Julian peers into the pilgrim's black eyes, which remain unwinking and watchful, he seems to see a thousand Saracens reflected, generations and individuals, the fathers and the mothers of this, their son.

But Julian has called him "brother" and "friend," and for no other reason than that the poor man is in gravest need, Julian manages to stand, despite spasms in his legs. He steps up from the boat to the stone rim of the channel and reaches back for one of the leper's hands. And though the boat is rocking wildly, the Moorish leper grabs and returns his grip with an astonishing strength in that single remaining finger, so that Julian could not release him even if he wanted to. He pulls, then, his passenger almost bodily to shore and, having brought him to the land, he says, "The peace of the Lord be with you, sir."

Julian would relax his grip, but the leper's finger is a hawk's claw and holds.

"Julian," the ruined traveler says, "I have come alone and undefended. For pity's sake, grant me the space of your house a while."

Now, both men are rimed in ice and shivering fearfully. In Julian's hut there is room for one man comfortably; a second must press them both to the walls. And this one exhales the breath of corruption.

Nevertheless, Julian neither withdraws from him nor explains the conditions.

He says, "Come."

Then he leads the lesser man. Nay, he *bears* him, for the other can scarcely move but in painful jumps, toadlike. Yet Julian carries the marvelous weight as a spiritual thing, for it seems to be the gravity of sorrow and sickness and isolation in the man.

At the hut he reaches down and opens the doorway. The leper lets go his hold and bows and crawls in first. When Julian follows he is astonished to find the hearth-fire burning with a bright, homely flame.

How—?

The Moor now squats against the wall and gazes at Julian, his black eyes as wide as hallways. "I am wet," he whispers. "I am so very cold. Julian, grant me thy robe to cover me and make me dry again."

Straightway Julian shrugs out of his robe while his guest removes his own few scraps, revealing a dark nakedness thick with scabs and an amber fluid, all his vitality leaking out. Julian hands him the robe, and when the other has drawn it around his shoulders, only the host is naked now.

"Brother," Julian murmurs, "do I know you?"

The Saracen speaks again: "Julian, I am thirsty. For the love of God, give me something to drink."

There is a skin of water hanging from a hook. Julian

slings it down and bites out the plug and spits that aside. He leans forward and lifts the neck of the waterskin to the leper's lips. Greedily the sick man drinks, water squirting from chew-holes in his cheeks. He drinks the entire bottle gone. There is none left in the hut. But the water that ran from his cheeks: it has landed crimson in the dust, and Julian would swear that it smells like wine.

How quiet the night is now! How completely solitary is this house in all the universe. Has the storm exhausted itself? Will the morning come clear and blue?

"I know you," Julian murmurs most softly. "You are a shepherd."

"Julian, I am hungry. Give me something to eat."

Aye, and this is possible. For Julian has one loaf of barley bread left to his home. This he pulls from warming in the ashes. His own poor stomach lurches at the crackling brown crust. At the bare *sight* of this food his mouth is flooded.

But he hands it to his companion, who takes the loaf between his mittenish hands and stuffs it whole into his mouth and chews, and must cover his cheeks in order to swallow. But the mash that breaks through: to Julian's nostrils it has the savor of meat.

"Julian, I am so weary. Grant me thy pallet for sleeping on."

"Ah."

And Julian presses himself as hard as he can against the wall, so that the pallet lies free. Tremblingly the leper crawls to it. He falls sideways, crying out for the pain, then rolls over onto his back and the robe falls like two curtains open on either side of him. He lifts his ruined arms and says unto Julian, "Come. Help me over. Lay thy body here on mine."

Julian moves to comply. He approaches the leper on his hands and his knees. He starts to straddle the ruptured body of his guest, then notices at the base of his throat a little wound the size of a button.

"Oh, Shepherd!" Julian groans in a sudden anguish: "Forgive me, for I think that I murdered you once."

"Nay, not once," the Moor responds. "Thou hast murdered me often, hast slain me again and again and a thousand times again. Come, now: lay thy face upon my face, thy limbs upon my limbs, and skin on skin till all is touching. Come."

Julian does. There is authority in the command. Therefore Julian does not think to argue or refuse, but obeys. He places the whole of himself as a blanket and a mirror and a comfort upon his dying guest, for he has warmth to give this coldness, and muscle to give this desiccation, and a fine northern flesh to give this diseased, this dark and slippery skin.

Suddenly the leper throws Julian's rich robe around them both and embraces the ferryman's torso in arms of an increasing strength.

"What?" Julian cries in surprise. "You wish to hold me hard to the ground?"

"Nay, but to take you from it!"

The leper's embrace grows tighter and tighter, until it feels to Julian that iron bands are crushing his ribs and driving the life from his lungs. He cannot breathe.

Christ!

No—he cannot even keep the breath within himself. The Saracen's pressure drives out all his air and all his thought. Prayer alone is left within him:

Jesus Christ, have mercy upon me!

Immediately upon this supplication, the leper's hair shoots out like a bright bristle of arrows from his skull. Every hair is a beam of light, and all together are such a radiance that Julian's hut is flooded with sunlight.

And now they—the two of them wrapped in that robe together—are rising from the pallet.

No longer do they lie on the earth. But Julian's companion is the engine now. He is lifting them upright, though their feet do not touch ground. Nay, they are breaking through the thatch of the hut. Julian gasps. He returns the embrace for safety and affection and a wild delight. For everything is changing. The flesh of his guest is suddenly smooth. His spine is true and strong. His breast has expanded to reap the wind as does the eagle's.

For he is no leper now, but a man of unspeakable beauty, a blaze of ascendant light.

And the sky is a scoured blue to receive them.

For Julian has found his ferryman, who takes them airborne, soaring past the treetops and the ashy castle and the river, arising higher than the fields and the countryside and the forests and this kingdom and all the kingdoms of the earth.

There is a middle moment when Julian sees the bones of his body, his flesh gone wraithlike, so to be borne by the sun of morning. And in that light Julian, glancing down, is able to see all the places where once he walked the earth, and this he knows in an instant of mortal relief: all his life's laboring was only wrestling. He burned out his little time in wrestling—first with God, and second with himself. But the fight he is leaving behind. Pure Julian: he is flying now, borne up on eagles' wings.

And then, approaching the round empyrean, the golden man, the very flight of the flying Julian, begins to sing. He is the clapper, while all the cosmos is his silver bell. He tolls a death and a birth in the universe of his authority, and all his song is *Julian!*

Julian is his glorious chorus.

And Julian's soul is laughing now, as booming and boisterous as the thunder.

And the Lord's embrace is his golden rope. . . .

For so it was that our Lord Jesus Christ did himself bear to Heaven the soul of the steadfast Julian, Saint and Hospitaller.

EPILOGUE

AT THE TALE'S
CONCLUSION

36.
SUCH LIGHTNESS OF HEART
AS SHAMELESSLY MAY CONTRADICT
ITSELF

And whether I ought write more than I have already written, well: I am not convinced of the need. From first to last Saint Julian's tale is a wholeness. Moreover, from its first telling even down to this one, it contains the entireties of countless generations, for each generation has polished the previous telling and each has added the characteristics of its own age. The tale is alive, and always the same, and ever changing, too. Such tales *are* their fullness. They need no further comment. They are, in fact, by comment reduced from something a hearer may experience wholly and personally, into something the hearer may only consider by mental applications. Analysis. Cold homily. Abstractions, interpretations: truths as collectible and as dry as pebbles. And then such tales, lacking animus, were dead indeed.

Nay, a tale needs only (as I now, at its conclusion, do desire for this Saint's Tale) to be released into the hearts of its hearers, where it shall abide as your own experience until one of you, or else one of your children, is moved to tell the tale again, unchanged from this my telling, and yet, like sunrise, ever new.

Oh, dear my listener: you need not examine this thing so much as dance with it—and, if you will, enter in and make it your habitation a while.

It is what I have done, and the doing has sustained me.

And yet, despite my arguments to the contrary, a small thing nags at me even now. I have laid my pen down and walked away from my lectern. I have returned to my ministries, gravely conscious of the shortness of the life still left to me, yet grateful that there is life at all—especially now that the task is finished, the tale is told, and my stride is that much lighter for the lightening of my load. Yes, and doesn't my heart at baptisms now sing with such good pleasure, that the people *must* twitch to the noise in the baptistry? Well, and if they don't, the infants surely do, for they screw open their Mandarin eyes and peer up into the face of their ancient baptizer. And every funeral being almost my own, I utter earth and ashes and dust upon the departed with a barely concealed delight, for I seem to be sending myself unto Heaven, and the nearer that journey to me, the more darling it seems, until it is with tears that I cry, "In the hope of the resurrection to eternal life!" Some of my people have murmured that their minor cleric is bereaved by every departure now. But I know my soul, and it is gladness that washes every casket now, for here goes my sister, one step ahead of me, and there calls my brother backward, "You, Pastor! Are you next?" *Next,* my spirit answers, *when my Christ shall call me. Till then, ask Julian if*

he may come partway, to ferry me the crystal water the rest of the way to Heaven!

Ah, and you see how an old mind might, in its jubilations, become distracted?

For I meant to say that every time I have laid my pen down and turned from my lectern to the joy of the life just now described, a little thing nags me. And I keep picking at the thing—the person, really—seeking some deciphering after all.

'Tis the Smith's boy.

Even to the end I could neither find nor fancy a finish to his thread in the tale. It wants tacking in again. As farther I went in telling of Julian, I kept looking for that long-legged servant to walk into the picture again and perhaps to find for me, as he did for Julian's father, precisely the tools that needed finding. I thought perhaps that by some miracle he would be present at the castle even in its final destructions, greeting the son of his old, departed lord and serving the servant, Julian.

But in all the years that Julian dwelt there, ferrying his thousand folks across, not once did the Smith's boy appear again. And so I considered that perhaps this raveled thread would hang out forever from the weave of the tale, perplexing me.

But yesterday it was, on the occasion of my birthday, that a reason was vouchsafed me for why the thread should dangle so: 'tis I.

The Smith's boy *did,* after all, accompany Julian even when the Saint was a ferryman. He did serve that servant until service itself was no longer required, and both of them were set free.

For I am the Smith's boy. I wept at the sights of his terrible slaughters. I read his mind. When he crossed the river's waters, I heard the hymns of his heart. And I it is who knows the other name that is named in the telling of this tale: Jesus, the Christ, the Son of the living God.

Door of Hope Dolls, 1901 to 1949

These dolls were made in Shanghai and Canton, China, at a Protestant mission called the Door of Hope, established to rescue and educate destitute children and slave girls.

At the Door of Hope Mission, the girls were taught needlework, embroidery, knitting, and other skills used to make doll clothing. A girl working five days a week could complete one doll a month. The smooth wood was not painted or varnished. The hair, eyes, and lips were painted. A few of the dolls had fancy buns or flowers carved into their heads. Most have hands with rounded palms and separate thumbs, although some have been found with cloth stub hands. Cloth bodies were stuffed with raw cotton donated to the mission by local textile factories. The elaborate handmade costumes are exact copies of clothing worn by the Chinese people. Dolls were unmarked or labeled "Made in China."

DOOR OF HOPE GRANDMOTHER

11" Door of Hope Chinese grandmother. Intricately carved wood, with facial detail, with silk outfit and headpiece (open at back but covering ears and exposing the back of head, which depicts a bun and thinning hair), and carved wooden arms. Significant fading to front of jacket.

.... $2,300-$2,500

DOOR OF HOPE BRIDEGROOM
11 1/2" Door of Hope bridegroom. Intricately carved wood with elaborate plum silk outfit and hat with carved wooden arms. Fine original condition.
.... **$2,000-$2,400**

DOOR OF HOPE MOURNER
11 1/2" Door of Hope Chinese male mourner. Intricately carved wood with fancy muslin and burlap clothing, including hat, and carved wooden arms. Fine original condition. ....$2,500-$2,700

Wooden Dolls

A. Schoenhut & Co., founded 1872

Located in Philadelphia, Albert Schoenhut came from a family of German toy makers. He came to the United States at the age of 17, and at 22 established his own toy factory. Schoenhut's first toy was a piano. The Humpty Dumpty Circus, introduced in 1903, probably included Schoenhut's first attempt at doll making. At about this time, Schoenhut introduced the Chinaman, Hobo, Negro Dude, Farmer, Milkmaid, and Max and Moritz. Rolly-Dollys were patented in 1908. In 1909, Schoenhut filed a patent application for his swivel, spring-jointed dolls, but the patent was not granted until 1911.

After Albert Schoenhut's death in 1912, his six sons took over: Harry, Gustav, Theodore, Albert Jr., William, and Otto. The new directors introduced an infant doll with curved limbs in 1913. The dolly faced all-wooden dolls produced in 1915 had rounded eyes, advertised as "imitation glass" (as opposed to intaglio eyes), and mohair wigs. A series of 19" tall older boy dolls, called "Manikins," commonly dressed as athletes, was also introduced in 1915.

Walking dolls, jointed at the shoulder and hip only, were introduced in 1919. Cloth-bodied mama dolls and a less expensive line of dolls with elastic joints were marketed in 1924.

SCHOENHUT DOLLY FACE

15" **Schoenhut dolly face.** Carved wood with molded and painted teeth, blonde mohair wig (replaced) on a jointed wood body. Painted eyes and finely feathered eyebrows and has been redressed. Some paint crazing on cheeks. .... $700-$900

Wooden Dolls

SCHOENHUT MAMA
16" Schoenhut "mama" doll. Blonde mohair wig and blue painted eyes on a cloth body with wood hands and "mama" cry box, wearing new striped romper. Light crazing, original paint, skullcap is original, but mohair has been attached. Crier is in working condition. .... **$500-$700**

Other Dolls

Peddler Dolls

During the late 18th and early 19th centuries, peddler dolls were popular fashion accessories. Frequently created to exhibit a woman's artistic talents, a peddler doll depicted a traveling vendor and served as a decorating accent, sometimes placed under a glass dome in a prominent location.

Itinerant traders traveled over Europe and the United States, but it was the English peddler doll for which there seemed a special fascination. Women traveled about the countryside selling needles, pins, and other small articles. These women were called "Notion Nannies," and were familiar figures in English country districts. The weathered and wrinkled dolls made to resemble these travelers were made of cloth, leather, wood, papier-mâché, wax, cork, china, dried apples, and even breadcrumbs. The bodies were usually wooden or cloth-covered wire. The Notion Nannies—with traditional red cape, calico dress gathered to expose a black quilted slip, white apron, and black silk bonnet over a white-laced "mob" cap—were a particular favorite.

Although the majority of vintage peddler dolls were homemade, C. H. White of Portsmouth, England, advertised commercially made dolls. The marbleized paper-cover base and "C. H. White/Milton/Portsmouth" label allows for easy identification.

PEDDLER DOLL

10" wax peddler doll with wares. A wonderfully presented peddler in good condition with an incredible assortment of miniatures. Most pieces appear to be original. Large split at forehead continuing down through eye. The damage has little effect on this wonderful example of an early peddler doll.

.... **$4,000–$5,000**

Glossary of Doll Terms

Applied Ears: Ears that are molded separately and affixed to the head.

Appropriately Dressed: Clothing that fits the time period and doll style.

Ball-Jointed Body: Doll body of wood and composition, jointed at shoulder, elbows, wrists, hip, and knees, allowing movement.

Bébé: French dolly-faced doll.

Bébé Tout en Bois: Doll all of wood.

Bent-Limb Baby Body: Five-piece baby body of composition with curved arms and legs, jointed at shoulder and hip.

Bisque: Unglazed porcelain.

Blown Glass Eyes: Hollow eyes of blue, brown, or gray.

Breather Dolls: Dolls with pierced or open nostrils.

Brevete: French marking indicating a registered patent.

Bte: Patent registered.

Caracul: Lambs skin used to make wigs. (Also spelled karakul.)

Character Doll: Dolls molded to look lifelike; may be infants, children, or adults.

Child Doll: Typical dolly-face dolls.

China: Glazed porcelain.

Composition: A wood-based material.

Crazing: Fine lines that develop on the painted surface of composition.

D.E.P.: A claim to registration.

Dolly Face: Typical child doll face.

D.R.G.M.: German marking indicating a registered design.

Feathered Brows: Eyebrows painted with many tiny strokes.

Five-Piece Body: Body composed of torso, arms, and legs.

Fixed Eyes: Eyes set in a stationary position.

Flange Neck: Doll's neck with ridge and holes at the base for sewing onto a cloth body.

Flirty Eyes: Eyes that move from side to side when head is moved.

Flocked Hair: A coating of short fibers glued to a doll's head to represent hair.

Ges (Gesch): German marking indicating a registered design.

Googly Eyes: Large, round eyes looking to the side.

Gutta-percha: A pinkish-white rubbery, hard, fibrous substance once used to make dolls, bodies, and parts.

Hard Plastic: Material used after 1948. It is very hard with excellent impressions and good color.

Glossary of Doll Terms

Hina-Ningyo: Japanese festival doll.

Huminals: Figures having both human and animal characteristics.

Ichimatsu: Japanese play doll.

Intaglio Eyes: Sunken, rather than cut, eyes that are then painted.

Kabuto: Japanese warrior or helmet for a Japanese warrior.

Kid Body: Doll body made of leather.

Lady Doll: Doll with adult face and body proportions.

Magic Skin: A rubbery material used for dolls. They age poorly, becoming dark and deteriorating as the surface turns soft and sticky.

Mask Face: A stiff face that covers only the front of a doll's head.

Mohair Wig: Wig made from very fine goat's hair.

Mold Number: Impressed or embossed number that indicates a particular design.

Open Mouth: Lips parted with opening cut into the bisque. Teeth usually show.

Open/Closed Mouth: Molded mouth appears open, but no opening is cut into the bisque.

Painted Bisque: Paint that is not baked into body; brighter in color, but can be rubbed off.

Painted Eyes: Flat or rounded painted eyes.

Paperweight Eyes: Blown glass eyes with an added crystal to the top, resulting in a look with depth and great realism.

Papier-mâché: Material made of paper pulp and glue.

Pate: Covering for the opening in a doll head. May be made of cardboard, cork, or plaster.

Peppering: Tiny black specks in the slip of many older bisque or china dolls.

Personality Doll: Doll molded and fashioned to resemble a famous person.

Pierced Ears: Holes in a doll's ear lobes. Hole goes all the way through the lobe.

Pierced-in Ears: Hole for earring passing through doll's earlobe and straight into doll's head.

Pouty: Closed-mouth doll with a solemn or petulant expression.

Pug or Pugged Nose: Small, button, slightly turned-up nose.

Queue: Asian hairstyle of a single plait.

Regional Costume: A traditional costume worn in a specific region or country.

Reproduction: A doll produced from a mold taken from an existing doll.

Rub: A spot where the color has worn away.

Sakura-Ningyo: Traditional Japanese cherry doll.

S.G.D.G.: Registered but without government guarantee.

Shoulder Head: Head and shoulder in one piece.

Shoulder Plate: Shoulder portion with socket for head.

Socket Head: Head with neck that fits into a shoulder plate or the opening of a body.

Solid-dome: Head with no crown opening. May have painted hair or wear a wig.

Stationary Eyes: Glass eyes that do not sleep; also known as staring eyes.

Stockinette: Soft jersey fabric used for dolls.

Toddler Body: A short, chubby body of a toddler; often with diagonal joints at hips.

Turned Head: Shoulder head with head slightly turned.

Vinyl: Material used after 1950.

Walker Body: Head moves from side to side when legs are made to walk.

Watermelon Mouth: A closed, smiling mouth, usually with a single line.

Weighted Eyes: Sleep eyes that operated by means of a weight attached to a wire frame holding the eyes.

This is a Parragon Publishing Book
This edition published in 2004

Parragon Publishing
Queen Street House
4 Queen Street
Bath BA1 1HE, UK

ISBN: 0-75255-523-5

Printed in China

Note

Cup measurements in this book are for American cups. This book also uses imperial and metric measurements.
Follow the same units of measurement throughout; do not mix imperial and metric.
All spoon measurements are level: teaspoons are assumed to be 5 ml and tablespoons are assumed to be 15 ml.
Unless otherwise stated, milk is assumed to be whole milk, eggs and individual vegetables
such as potatoes are medium, and pepper is freshly ground black pepper.

Recipes using uncooked eggs should be
avoided by infants, the elderly, pregnant women, convalescents, and anyone
suffering from an illness.

COOKSHELF

Mediterranean

Anne White

p

Contents

Introduction

Anyone who has spent even the briefest amount of time along the Mediterranean can not come away without a lasting recollection of the wonderful aromas and flavors of the region. "Robust" and "intense" are just two of the appropriate adjectives to describe the range of dishes you will find from coastal Spain through France, Italy, Greece, Turkey, and along North Africa.

Most of the region's best-known dishes are, in essence, simple fare produced for generations from plentiful home-grown or local ingredients. To capture the true sun-kissed flavors of the region, it is important to seek out the best-quality produce. All the recipes in this book are simple and easy to prepare, but because most are so simple, they rely on ripe, flavor-filled ingredients for their character.

OLIVE OIL

Olive oils vary in color from almost emerald green to the palest yellow, with flavors that range from peppery and spicy to very mild. There are even olive oils with a hint of chocolate.

If you are used to cooking with other vegetable oils, such as sunflower or corn, olive oil can be an acquired taste, and the only way to find the oils you like the most is to taste many. Olive oils are available in different grades. Extra-virgin is produced from the first pressing, so it has the fullest flavor and, consequently, is the most expensive. Save this to use in salad dressings and with uncooked ingredients, where heat doesn't diminish the flavor. For cooking, choose an oil simply labeled as "olive oil."

Much is made of the healthy qualities of the Mediterranean diet, because olive oil contains so little saturated fat, the type of fat possibly linked to heart disease. But remember, it is still a fat, so it should be used sparingly.

TOMATOES

Sun-ripened, juicy tomatoes are synonymous with Mediterranean food, giving flavor to both cooked and uncooked dishes. When you can only buy flavorless hot-house tomatoes, a good-quality canned variety is a better option for cooked dishes.

Italian plum tomatoes are a good choice for most Mediterranean dishes, but the larger tomatoes and small cherry tomatoes are also ideal for many recipes. When you are buying tomatoes, look for smooth, undamaged skins and textures that feel just soft when you squeeze lightly.

Try preserving tomatoes in Oven-Dried Tomatoes (see page 174) to use in the colder months. When you have a large quantity of tomatoes lacking in flavor, use them for recipes such as Slow-Cooked Tomato Sauce (see page 192) or Ratatouille (see page 134), both of which freeze well and have other ingredients that compensate for the weak tomato flavor.

GARLIC

Garlic is the all-important flavoring in many Mediterranean dishes, and it is also used both cooked and uncooked. Raw garlic can be too strong for some people, but when cooked slowly its flavor softens and whole cloves become meltingly soft and deliciously sweet.

Do not buy garlic bulbs that have sprouted because that is a sign that they are old and may taste bitter. The best garlic has compact cloves and tight-fitting skin. Don't store it in the refrigerator—it keeps best at room temperature in a dark location.

Roasted Garlic Delicious smeared on broiled chicken pieces or steaks, or on toasted bread. Put a whole bulb of unpeeled garlic in a piece of foil, large enough to enclose it, and drizzle with olive oil. Roast in a preheated oven at 375°F/190°C for 40 minutes, or until the cloves are very soft when pierced with a knife. Squeeze the cloves out of their papery skins.

EGGPLANTS

Eggplants, with their deep-purple skins, also symbolize Mediterranean cooking to many people—they are an essential ingredient to the French and Italians.

Most recipes specify sprinkling cut pieces of eggplant with salt and letting the pieces stand for about 30 minutes before using. This simple technique draws out moisture to prevent the flesh from becoming soggy and helps to eliminate bitterness, which is a characteristic of older eggplants. After they have drained, rinse them well to remove the excess salt. If the eggplant slices are going to be baked or fried, pat them dry with paper towels first.

At the height of summer, Mediterranean market stalls are piled high with miniature varieties of eggplants with pale yellow or almost white skins. Local chefs use these to make attractive appetizers or edible garnishes. Only buy eggplants that feel smooth and firm. Size doesn't affect the flavor, but remember that the thicker an eggplant is, the more seeds it is likely to contain. Eggplants have a natural affinity for tomatoes, so you'll often find the two ingredients combined in Mediterranean dishes.

SEAFOOD

With the teeming waters of the Mediterranean, it is not surprising fish and shellfish feature regularly in the local diets. Bouillabaisse, the classic French seafood stew that is a feast in a bowl, is an example of the wonderful use made of the daily catches. But the dish is an expensive feast, so instead enjoy the flavor with the scaled-down version of Seafood Stew (see page 100), or Mediterranean Fish Soup (see page 98).

Whether you are buying fresh fish or shellfish, the golden rule is the same—only buy the freshest available and cook it on the same day. Fresh fish should have clear, shiny eyes and red gills. When you pick up a whole fish, it should be firm, not floppy. If it droops, it has been out of the water for more than a day and should be left on the fish counter.

Cut pieces of fish, such as swordfish or tuna steaks, should have a clear, clean looking surface. White fish, such as sea bass, should have a pearllike color.

Fish should not smell "fishy." Instead, it should have a fresh, almost sweet aroma, as if it has come out of the water only a few hours before.

Remember that shellfish, such as mussels, oysters, and clams, should actually be alive when you buy them. You can tell they are fresh if their shells are closed. Shrimp, on the other hand, are usually frozen before they are shipped.

As a general rule, the less time you cook seafood the better the flavor and texture will be.

FRESH HERBS

If you drive along the Mediterranean coast at the height of summer, you will find the air is scented with rosemary, basil, cilantro, dill, oregano, sage, flat-leaved parsley, and thyme growing in profusion. Winter stews and casseroles use dried herbs, but only the freshest, fullest-flavored herbs will do for the summer dishes and salads. The obvious solution if you plan to do a lot of Mediterranean cooking is to grow your own, so you always have a supply. Even a single pot of various herbs growing on your window sill will make a difference to your cooking.

When you are buying fresh herbs, reject any that do not look fresh and vibrant; limp, dull-looking herbs without their full aroma will not add anything to your dish. Be sure to sniff the herbs before you buy, because greenhouse-grown herbs can look marvelous but lack the essential flavor.

Basil Where would Italian cooks be without this fragrant herb? It has an affinity for tomatoes and is often included in pasta dishes and soups. It is difficult to preserve successfully, so if you have too much, freeze large quantities of Pesto Sauce (see page 124) or Pistou sauce (see page 28). Do not freeze the leaves because they will turn black and loose their aroma. Instead, layer them with sea salt in a nonmetallic, tightly covered container and store for up to 3 months. The leaves can then be added to cooked dishes.

Cilantro Also popular in Asian cooking, this herb has a distinctive taste. It is used in many Turkish, Moroccan, and Greek recipes. Be careful when you are buying because it looks similar to flat-leaf parsley and often the only way to tell them apart is to taste a leaf. Use in soups and with seafood recipes and pickles.

Dill This feathery green herb with its distinctive flavor goes well with all seafood and tomato dishes, and is particularly used in Greek cooking.

Parsley Mediterranean cooks favor the flat-leaf variety of this all-purpose herb, sometimes referred to as Italian parsley. Use generously in salads and as a garnish. Always use fresh or frozen, and avoid dried.

Marjoram The Greeks consider this the "joy of the mountains" and it features in the islands' cuisines. It is good with pork and poultry dishes.

Oregano Also known as wild marjoram, this pungent herb should be used sparingly. It dries well, and is good added to casseroles and pizza toppings. Try it with tomato, zucchini, and eggplant dishes.

Rosemary Strongly flavored, this shrub herb should be very young if used in uncooked dishes. It's a natural partner to lamb. Throw branches onto barbecue coals to add an authentic aroma, or use twigs as skewers.

Sage Popular both fresh and dried in Italian cooking, sage has a pronounced flavor and a little goes a long way. Good for boiling with beans and for flavoring broiled poultry, the purple-leaf variety also makes an attractive garnish.

Thyme The small leaves are good for flavoring tomatoes, stews, and broiled meats. Thyme also goes well with olives.

Herbes de Provence Use an abundance of summer herbs to make this classic French combination. Dry equal amounts of fennel seeds, lavender flowers, marjoram, rosemary, sage, summer savory, and thyme. Put into an airtight container and store for up to 6 months. Herbes de Provence is traditionally used to flavor cooked poultry, meat, and vegetable dishes, especially during the winter. It is also good in cooked pasta sauces and pizza toppings.

Snacks & Appetizers

One of the most enjoyable aspects of Mediterranean cuisines is the emphasis on snacks and simple dishes that are served at almost any time of the day. The Spanish, for example, are renowned for their tapas, and the Greeks, Turks, and Moroccans enjoy nothing more than sitting down at a table filled with a selection of appetizers, called meze.

The recipes in this chapter are easy to prepare and always popular because they are so full of flavor. They are also the type of food to enjoy at relaxed, social occasions, and recipes such as Hummus, Taramasalata, Tapenade, Eggplant Spread, and Aioli instantly capture the atmosphere of easy-going, sunny Mediterranean meals.

When it's a hot day and you don't want to spend time in a steaming kitchen, where better to look for inspiration than the Mediterranean? For no-cook recipes, try the Gazpacho, Garlic & Almond Soup, or Ceviche, along with any of the mouthwatering dips listed above. And what can possibly beat prosciutto with melon and figs on a hot day? If you want a sophisticated start for a meal, but again don't want to cook, try Crab & Celery Root Remoulade. Serve it with a chilled bottle of Provençal rosé and your dinner will be off to a marvelous start.

Hummus

Makes about scant 3 cups

INGREDIENTS

7 oz/200 g dried garbanzo beans	1 tbsp lemon juice, or to taste	TO GARNISH
2 large garlic cloves	salt and pepper	extra-virgin olive oil
7 tbsp extra-virgin olive oil		paprika
2½ tbsp tahini		fresh cilantro

1 Place the garbanzo beans in a large bowl. Pour in at least twice the volume of cold water to garbanzo beans and let stand for 12 hours until they double in size.

2 Drain the garbanzo beans. Put them in a large flameproof casserole or pot and add twice the volume of water to the garbanzo beans. Bring to a boil and boil hard for 10 minutes, skimming the surface.

3 Lower the heat and let simmer for 1 hour, skimming the surface if necessary, or until the garbanzo beans are tender. Meanwhile, cut the garlic cloves in half, remove the pale green or white cores, and coarsely chop. Set aside.

4 Drain the garbanzo beans, reserving 4 tablespoons of the cooking liquid. Put the olive oil, garlic, tahini, and lemon juice in a food processor and blend until a smooth paste forms.

5 Add the garbanzo beans and blend gently until they are finely ground but the hummus is still slightly textured. Add a little of the reserved cooking liquid if the mixture is too thick. Season with salt and pepper to taste.

6 Transfer to a bowl, cover with plastic wrap, and chill until ready to serve. To serve, drizzle with some olive oil, sprinkle a little paprika over the surface, and garnish with fresh cilantro.

Taramasalata with Pita Wedges

Makes about 2 cups

INGREDIENTS

8 oz/225 g smoked cod's roe
1 small onion, finely chopped
1 garlic clove
2 oz fresh white bread
    without crusts
finely grated rind of 1 lemon

4 tbsp lemon juice, plus extra
    to taste, if desired
²/₃ cup extra-virgin olive oil
6 tbsp hot water
salt and pepper

hollowed-out tomatoes, to serve
fresh flat-leaf parsley sprigs,
    to garnish

PITA WEDGES
2 pita breads
olive oil, for brushing

1 Remove the skin from the smoked cod's roe. Put the roe and onion in a food processor and process until well blended and smooth. Add the garlic and process again.

2 Break the bread into the food processor, then add the lemon rind and 4 tablespoons of the lemon juice. Process again until the bread is well incorporated.

3 With the motor running, gradually add the olive oil through the feed tube, as if making a mayonnaise. When all the oil is incorporated, add the hot water and process again. Add salt and pepper to taste, plus extra lemon juice if desired. Spoon into a bowl, cover with plastic wrap, and chill until ready to serve.

4 To make the pita wedges, using a serrated knife, cut the pita breads in half through the center. Cut each half into 6–8 wedges, depending on the size. Place

on a cookie sheet and brush the inside surfaces of the wedges with olive oil.

5 Bake in a preheated oven at 350°F/180°C for 20 minutes. Place on wire racks to cool.

6 Spoon the taramasalata into the tomato shells, garnish with parsley, and serve with the pita wedges for dipping.

Tzatziki

Makes about 3 1/3 cups

INGREDIENTS

2 large cucumbers	3 garlic cloves, crushed	TO SERVE
2½ cups Greek Strained Yogurt	1 tbsp finely chopped fresh dill	1 tbsp sesame seeds
(see page 182), or plain	1 tbsp extra-virgin olive oil	cayenne pepper
thick yogurt	salt and pepper	fresh dill sprigs (optional)

1 Using the coarse side of a grater, grate the cucumbers into a bowl lined with an absorbent, perforated kitchen cloth. Pull up the corners of the cloth to make a tight bundle and squeeze very hard to extract all the moisture (see Cook's Tip).

2 Put the cucumbers in a bowl and stir in the yogurt, garlic, dill, olive oil, and salt and pepper to taste. Cover with plastic wrap and chill for at least 3 hours for the flavors to blend.

3 When ready to serve, remove the dip from the refrigerator and stir. Taste the mixture and adjust the seasoning if necessary.

4 Put the sesame seeds in a small, ungreased skillet and dry-cook them over medium heat until they turn golden and start to give off their aroma. Immediately pour them out of the pan onto the tzatziki—where they will sizzle.

5 Dip the tip of a dry pastry brush into some cayenne pepper. Tap a light sprinkling of cayenne all over the tzatziki. Garnish with fresh dill, if desired, and serve.

COOK'S TIP

It is essential to squeeze all the moisture out of the cucumbers in Step 1, or the dip will be watery and will separate.

COOK'S TIP

The ungarnished tzatziki will keep, covered, for up to 3 days in the refrigerator.

Eggplant Spread

Makes about 1¾ cups

INGREDIENTS

2 large eggplants
1 tomato
1 garlic clove, chopped
4 tbsp extra-virgin olive oil
2 tbsp lemon juice

2 tbsp pine nuts, lightly toasted
2 scallions, finely chopped
salt and pepper

TO GARNISH
ground cumin
2 tbsp finely chopped fresh
   flat-leaf parsley

1 Using a fork or metal skewer, pierce the eggplants all over. Place them on a cookie sheet in a preheated oven at 450°F/230°C and roast for 20–25 minutes until they are very soft.

2 Use a folded dish towel to remove the eggplants from the cookie sheet and set aside to cool.

3 Place the tomato in a heatproof bowl, pour boiling water over to cover, and let stand for 30 seconds. Drain, then plunge into cold water to prevent it from cooking. Skin the tomato, then cut in half, and scoop out the seeds with a teaspoon. Finely dice the flesh and set aside.

4 Cut the eggplants in half lengthwise. Scoop out the flesh with a spoon and transfer to a food processor. Add the garlic, olive oil, lemon juice, pine nuts, and salt and pepper to taste. Process until smooth.

5 Spoon the mixture into a bowl and stir through the scallions and diced tomato.

Cover and chill for 30 minutes before serving.

6 Garnish the dip with a pinch of ground cumin and the finely chopped parsley, then serve.

VARIATION

Add 2–4 tablespoons of tahini, to taste, in step 4.

Tapenade

Each makes about 1¼ cups

INGREDIENTS

BLACK OLIVE TAPENADE

9 oz/250 g black Niçoise olives in brine, rinsed and pitted

1 large garlic clove

2 tbsp walnut pieces

4 canned anchovy fillets, drained

about ½ cup extra-virgin olive oil

lemon juice, to taste

pepper

GREEN OLIVE TAPENADE

9 oz/250 g green olives in brine, rinsed and pitted

4 canned anchovy fillets, drained

4 tbsp blanched almonds

1 tbsp bottled capers in brine or vinegar, drained

about ½ cup extra-virgin olive oil

½–1 tbsp finely grated orange rind

pepper

CROUTES

thin slices of day-old baguette

olive oil

fresh flat-leaf parsley sprigs, finely chopped, to garnish

1 To make the black olive tapenade, put the olives, garlic, walnut pieces, and anchovies in a food processor and process until blended.

2 With the motor running, slowly add the olive oil through the feed tube, as if making mayonnaise. Add lemon juice and pepper to taste. Transfer to a bowl, cover with plastic wrap, and chill until required.

3 To make the green olive tapenade, put the olives, anchovies, almonds, and capers in a food processor and process until blended.

4 With the motor running, slowly add the olive oil through the feed tube, as if making mayonnaise. Add orange rind, and pepper to taste. Transfer to a bowl, cover with plastic wrap, and chill until required.

5 Serve the tapenade on croûtes. Toast the slices of bread on both sides until crisp. Brush one side of each slice with a little olive oil while it is still hot, so the oil is absorbed.

6 Spread the croûtes with the tapenade of your choice and garnish with parsley to serve.

Bagna Cauda

Serves 4–6

INGREDIENTS

1¾oz/50 g canned anchovy fillets
in oil

2 garlic cloves

5 tbsp olive oil

6 tbsp butter

TO SERVE
red and green bell peppers

zucchini

carrots

small broccoli florets

1 Begin by preparing the vegetables for dipping. Cut the bell peppers in half, remove the cores and seeds and slice into ¼-inch/5 mm strips. Cut the zucchini and carrots into ¼ inch/5 mm strips. Place the pieces in a plastic bag and chill until required.

2 Drain the anchovy fillets, reserving 5 tablespoons of the oil. Then chop the anchovies and garlic. Put the anchovy oil and olive oil in a pan with the butter over high heat and stir until the butter melts.

3 Lower the heat to medium and add the garlic. Stir for 2 minutes, without letting it burn. Add the anchovies and allow them to simmer for about 10 minutes, stirring frequently, until they dissolve and turn the mixture into a thin paste.

4 Transfer the dip to a bagna cauda or fondue burner to keep it hot while you are eating. Serve with a platter of the prepared bell peppers, zucchini, carrots, and broccoli for dipping.

VARIATION

This full-flavored dip has a natural affinity for the sun-kissed vegetables from the Mediterranean, but you can serve it with any selection you like.
Other suggestions include blanched white or green asparagus spears, blanched baby artichokes, blanched green beans, and cauliflower florets.

Iced Gazpacho

Serves 4–6

INGREDIENTS

2 ripe red bell peppers
1 cucumber
14 oz/400 g large, juicy
    tomatoes, skinned, deseeded,
    and coarsely chopped
4 tbsp olive oil
2 tbsp sherry vinegar
salt and pepper

GARLIC CROUTONS
2 tbsp olive oil
1 garlic clove, halved
2 slices bread, crusts removed,
    cut into ¼ inch/5 mm cubes
sea salt

TO GARNISH
diced green bell pepper
diced red bell pepper
finely diced deseeded cucumber
chopped scallions
ice cubes

1 Cut the bell peppers in half and remove the cores and seeds, then coarsely chop. Peel the cucumber, cut it in half lengthwise, then cut into quarters. Remove the seeds with a teaspoon, then coarsely chop the flesh.

2 Put the bell peppers, cucumber, tomatoes, olive oil, and vinegar in a food processor and process until smooth. Season with salt and pepper to taste. Transfer to a bowl, cover, and chill for at least 4 hours.

3 Meanwhile, make the garlic croûtons. Heat the oil in a skillet over medium-high heat. Add the garlic and cook, stirring, for 2 minutes to flavor the oil.

4 Remove and discard the garlic. Add the diced bread and cook until golden on all sides. Drain well on crumpled paper towels and sprinkle with sea salt. Store in an airtight container if not using at once.

5 To serve, place each of the vegetable garnishes in bowls for guests to add to their soup. Taste the soup and adjust the seasoning if necessary. Put ice cubes into soup bowls and ladle the soup on top. Serve at once.

Chilled Garlic & Almond Soup

Serves 4–6

INGREDIENTS

14 oz/400 g day-old French
    bread, sliced
4 large garlic cloves
3–4 tbsp sherry vinegar
6 tbsp extra-virgin olive oil

8 oz/225 g ground almonds
4 cups water, chilled
sea salt and pepper

TO GARNISH
seedless white grapes, chilled
    and sliced
pepper
extra-virgin olive oil

1 Tear the bread into small pieces and put in a bowl. Pour over enough cold water to cover and soak for 10–15 minutes. Using your hands, squeeze the bread dry. Transfer the moist bread to a food processor.

2 Cut the garlic cloves in half lengthwise and use the tip of a knife to remove the pale green or white cores. Add to the food processor with 3 tablespoons of the sherry vinegar and 1 cup of the water, and process until blended. Add the oil and ground almonds and blend.

3 With the motor running, slowly pour in the remaining water until a smooth soup forms. Add extra sherry vinegar to taste, and season with salt and pepper. Transfer to a bowl, cover, and chill the soup for at least 4 hours.

4 To serve, adjust the seasoning. Ladle into bowls and float grape slices on top. Garnish each with a sprinkling of pepper and a swirl of olive oil. Serve while still very cold.

COOK'S TIP

Instead of grapes, serve with Garlic Croûtons and diced vegetables (see the Gazpacho recipe on page 20). For garlic lovers, cook thin slices of garlic in olive oil until golden brown, then sprinkle over to add a crunchy contrast to the soup. Alternatively, sprinkle with a dusting of paprika or very finely chopped fresh parsley just before serving.

Avgolemono

Serves 4–6

INGREDIENTS

5 cups homemade chicken stock
3½ oz/100 g dried orzo, or other
    small pasta shapes
2 large eggs

4 tbsp lemon juice
salt and pepper
fresh flat-leaf parsley, finely
    chopped, to garnish

1 Pour the stock into a flameproof casserole or heavy-bottomed pot and bring to a boil. Sprinkle in the orzo, return to a boil, and cook for 8–10 minutes, or according to packet instructions, until the pasta is tender but not too soft.

2 Whisk the eggs in a bowl for at least 30 seconds. Add the lemon juice and continue whisking for another 30 seconds.

3 Reduce the heat under the pot of stock and orzo until the stock is not boiling.

4 Very slowly add 4–5 tablespoons of the hot (not boiling) stock to the lemon and egg mixture, whisking constantly. Slowly add another 1 cup of the stock, whisking to prevent the eggs from curdling.

5 Slowly pour the lemon and egg mixture into the pan, whisking until the soup thickens slightly. Do not allow it to boil. Season with salt and pepper.

6 Spoon the soup into warmed soup bowls and sprinkle with chopped flat-leaf parsley. Serve at once.

VARIATION

To make a more substantial soup, add 2 cups finely chopped, cooked, skinless chicken meat. This version uses orzo, a small pasta shape that looks like barley grains, but you can substitute long-grain rice.

Roasted Bell Pepper & Tomato Soup with Dill

Serves 6–8

INGREDIENTS

2 lb 4 oz/1 kg juicy plum
   tomatoes, halved
2 large red bell peppers, cored,
   deseeded, and halved
1 onion, quartered

3 sprigs fresh dill, tied together,
   plus a little extra to garnish
1 thin piece of orange rind
juice of 1 orange
2½ cups vegetable stock

salt and pepper
1–1½ tbsp red wine vinegar
Mediterranean Bread (see page
   198), to serve

1 Place the tomatoes and peppers on a cookie sheet, cut-sides up to catch the juices. Add the onion quarters. Place in a preheated oven at 450°F/230°C and roast for 20–25 minutes until the vegetables just start to char on the edges.

2 As the vegetables become charred, transfer them to a large, flameproof casserole or stockpot. Add the dill, orange rind and juice, stock, and salt and pepper to taste. Bring to a boil.

3 Lower the heat, partially cover, and simmer for 25 minutes. Remove the bundle of dill. Transfer the rest of the ingredients to a food mill (see Cook's Tip) and puree. Alternatively, process in a food processor and work though a strainer.

4 Return the soup to the rinsed casserole or stockpot and reheat. Stir in the vinegar and adjust the seasoning with salt and pepper, if necessary. Ladle into bowls and garnish with extra dill. Serve hot, with slices of Mediterranean Bread (see page 198).

COOK'S TIP

A food mill, or mouli-legume as it is called in France, is ideal for pureeing vegetable soups and sauces because it removes the skin and seeds in the process.

Pistou

Serves 6–8

INGREDIENTS

2 young carrots	10 cups vegetable stock or water	PISTOU SAUCE
2 potatoes	1 bouquet garni of 2 sprigs fresh	1½ cups fresh basil leaves
7 oz/200 g fresh peas in	parsley and 1 bay leaf tied in	1 garlic clove
their shells	a 3 inch/7.5 cm piece of celery	5 tbsp fruity extra-virgin olive oil
7 oz/200 g thin green beans	3 oz/85 g dried small soup pasta	salt and pepper
5½ oz/150 g young zucchini	1 large tomato, skinned,	
2 tbsp olive oil	deseeded, and chopped	
1 garlic clove, crushed	or diced	
1 large onion, finely chopped	pared Parmesan cheese, to serve	

1 To make the pistou sauce, put the basil leaves, garlic, and olive oil in a food processor and process until well blended. Season with salt and pepper to taste. Transfer to a bowl, cover, and chill until required.

2 Peel the carrots and cut them in half lengthwise, then slice. Peel the potatoes and cut into quarters lengthwise, then slice. Set aside until required.

3 Shell the peas. Trim the ends from the beans and cut them into 1 inch/2.5 cm pieces. Cut the zucchini in half lengthwise, then slice.

4 Heat the oil in a large pot or flameproof casserole. Add the garlic and cook for 2 minutes, stirring. Add the onion and continue cooking for 2 minutes until soft. Add the carrots and potatoes and stir for about 30 seconds.

5 Pour in the stock and bring to a boil. Lower the heat, partially cover, and simmer for 8 minutes, until the vegetables are starting to become tender.

6 Stir in the peas, beans, zucchini, bouquet garni, and pasta. Season and cook for 4 minutes, or until the vegetables and pasta are tender. Stir in the pistou sauce and serve with Parmesan.

Prosciutto with Fruit

Serves 4

INGREDIENTS

1 cantaloupe or honeydew melon	12 wafer-thin slices prosciutto	pepper
4 ripe fresh figs (optional)	olive oil, to drizzle	fresh parsley sprigs, to garnish

1 Cut the melon in half lengthwise. Using a spoon, scoop out the seeds and discard them. Cut each half into 8 thin wedges. Using a paring knife, cut the rind off each slice.

2 Cut the stems off the figs, if using, but do not peel them. Stand the figs upright with the pointed end upward. Cut each into quarters without cutting all the way through. Open them out into attractive "flowers."

3 Arrange 3–4 slices of prosciutto on individual serving plates and top with the melon slices and fig "flowers," if using. Alternatively, arrange the melon slices on the plates and completely cover with the prosciutto; add the fig "flowers," if using.

4 Drizzle with olive oil, then grind a little pepper over the top. Garnish with parsley and serve at once.

COOK'S TIP

For an attractive presentation, you can also prepare all the ingredients on one large serving platter and let guests help themselves.

VARIATION

For a Spanish flavor, replace the prosciutto with Serrano ham, which also has a lightly salty flavor but is rarely cut as finely.

Chorizo & Garbanzo Bean Tapas

Serves 4

INGREDIENTS

7 tbsp olive oil	1 small Spanish onion,	salt and pepper
about 2 tbsp sherry vinegar	chopped finely	finely chopped fresh oregano or
9 oz/250 g fresh chorizo sausage,	14 oz/400 g canned garbanzo	flat-leaf parsley, to garnish
in one piece	beans	chunks of fresh bread, to serve

1 Place 6 tablespoons of the olive oil and 2 tablespoons of the vinegar in a bowl and whisk together. Taste and add a little more sherry vinegar, if desired. Season with salt and pepper and set aside.

2 Using a small, sharp knife, remove the casing from the chorizo sausage. Cut the meat into ¼ inch/5 mm thick slices, then cut each slice into half-moon shapes.

3 Heat the remaining olive oil in a small skillet over medium-high heat. Add the onion and cook for 2–3 minutes, stirring. Add the chorizo sausage and cook for 3 minutes, or until the sausage is cooked through.

4 Using a slotted spoon, remove the sausage and onion and drain on crumpled paper towels. Transfer to the bowl with the dressing while still hot and stir together.

5 Empty the garbanzo beans into a colander and rinse well under running water; shake off the excess water. Add to the bowl with the other ingredients and stir them all together. Let cool.

6 Just before serving, adjust the seasoning, then spoon the salad into a serving bowl, and sprinkle with chopped herbs. Serve with chunks of fresh bread.

Dolmas

Makes 25–30

INGREDIENTS

8 oz/225 g packet grape leaves
preserved in brine, about
40 in total
⅔ cup olive oil
4 tbsp lemon juice
1¼ cups water
lemon wedges, to serve

FILLING
generous ½ cup long-grain rice,
not basmati
1½ cups water
⅓ cup currants
2¼ oz/60 g pine nuts, chopped
2 scallions, very finely chopped

4 tbsp very finely chopped
fresh parsley
1 tbsp each of very finely
chopped fresh cilantro
and dill
1 tbsp finely chopped fresh dill
finely grated zest of ½ lemon
salt and pepper

1 Rinse the grape leaves and place them in a heatproof bowl. Pour over enough boiling water to cover and soak for 5 minutes. Drain well.

2 Meanwhile, place the rice and water in a pan with a pinch of salt and bring to a boil. Lower the heat, cover, and simmer for 10–12 minutes, or until all the liquid is absorbed. Drain the rice and let cool.

3 Stir the currants, pine nuts, scallions, herbs, and lemon zest into the cooled rice. Season well with salt and pepper.

4 Line the bottom of a large skillet with 3 or 4 of the thickest grape leaves, or any that are torn.

5 Put a grape leaf on the counter, vein-side upward, pointed end facing away from you. Put a small, compact roll of the stuffing at the bottom of the leaf. Fold

up the bottom end of the leaf over the filling.

6 Fold in each side to overlap in the center. Roll up the leaf around the filling. Squeeze lightly in your hand. Continue this process with the remaining grape leaves.

7 Place the leaf rolls in a single layer in the pan, seam-side down. Combine the olive oil, lemon juice, and water, and pour into the pan.

8 Fit a heatproof plate over the rolls and cover the pan. Simmer for 30 minutes. Remove from the heat and let the stuffed grape leaves cool in the liquid. Serve chilled with lemon wedges.

Broiled Sardines

Serves 4–6

INGREDIENTS

12 sardines	DRESSING	1 small, fresh, red chile, deseeded
olive oil	⅔ cup extra-virgin olive oil	and finely chopped
fresh flat-leaf parsley sprigs,	finely grated rind of 1 large	1 large garlic clove, finely
to garnish	lemon	chopped
lemon wedges, to serve	4 tbsp lemon juice, or to taste	salt and pepper
	4 shallots, thinly sliced	

1 To make the dressing, place all the ingredients in a screw-top jar, season with salt and pepper, then shake until blended. Pour into a nonmetallic baking dish that is large enough to hold the sardines in a single layer. Set aside.

2 To prepare the sardines, chop off the heads and make a slit all along the length of each belly. Pull out the insides, rinse the fish inside and out with cold water, and pat dry with paper towels.

3 Line the broiler pan with foil, shiny side up. Brush the foil with a little olive oil to prevent the sardines from sticking. Arrange the sardines on the foil in a single layer and brush with a little of the dressing. Broil under a preheated broiler for about 90 seconds.

4 Turn the fish over, brush with a little more dressing, and continue to broil for another 90 seconds, or until they are cooked through and flake easily.

5 Transfer the fish to the dish with the dressing. Spoon the dressing over the fish and cool completely. Cover and chill for at least 2 hours to allow the flavors to blend together.

6 Transfer the sardines to a serving platter and garnish with parsley. Serve with lemon wedges for squeezing over.

Ceviche

Serves 4

INGREDIENTS

8 fresh, cleaned scallops
16 large shrimp in shells
2 sea bass fillets, about 5½
    oz/150 g each, skinned
1 large lemon

1 lime
1 red onion, thinly sliced
½ red chile, deseeded and
    finely chopped
2–4 tbsp extra-virgin olive oil

TO SERVE
salad leaves
lime or lemon wedges
pepper

1 Rinse the scallops under cold running water. Cut the scallop coral free from the flesh. Slice the flesh into 2 or 3 horizontal slices each, depending on the size. Place in a nonmetallic bowl with the corals.

2 Cut the heads off the shrimp, then peel off the shells. Using a small, sharp knife, make a thin slice all along the back of the shrimp. Use the tip of the knife to remove the thin black vein. Add to the scallops.

3 Cut the sea bass into thin slices across the grain and add to the shellfish.

4 Firmly roll the lemon and lime backward and forward on a work counter. Cut the lemon in half and squeeze the juice over the fish. Repeat with the lime.

5 Gently stir, to coat the seafood well in the citrus juices, then cover, and chill for 2 hours, or until the seafood becomes opaque, but do not leave for longer because the seafood will become too soft.

6 Using a slotted spoon, transfer the seafood to a bowl. Add the onion, chile, and olive oil and gently stir together. Let stand for 5 minutes.

7 Spoon onto individual plates and serve with salad leaves, lemon or lime wedges, and black pepper.

Crab & Celery Root Remoulade

Serves 4

INGREDIENTS

1½ tsp lemon juice
1 tsp salt
1 lb/450 g celery root
1½ tbsp Dijon mustard
1 large egg yolk

⅔ cup extra-virgin olive oil
2 tsp white wine vinegar
2 tbsp capers in brine, rinsed
10½ oz/300 g fresh crab meat

radicchio leaves, rinsed and
    dried, to serve
fresh dill or parsley sprigs,
    to garnish

1 Put the lemon juice and salt in a bowl of water. Using the shredding disk of a food processor or a hand grater, shred the celery root. Put the celery root in the bowl of acidulated water as it is grated, to prevent it from discoloring.

2 To make the sauce, beat the mustard and egg yolk together in a bowl. Gradually whisk in the olive oil, drop by drop, until a mayonnaise forms (see Cook's Tip). Stir in the vinegar.

3 Drain the celery root and pat dry with paper towels. Add it to the mayonnaise, stirring to coat well. Cover and chill.

4 About 20 minutes before serving, remove the remoulade from the refrigerator so it can come to room temperature. Stir in the capers and crab meat.

5 Line a platter or bowl with radicchio leaves and spoon the remoulade mixture on top. Garnish with dill or parsley and serve.

COOK'S TIP

If the sauce begins to curdle, beat another egg yolk in a bowl, then slowly beat in the sauce to rectify. Continue to add the remaining oil.

Greek Salad

Serves 4

INGREDIENTS

9 oz/250 g feta cheese	2 large, juicy tomatoes	salt and pepper
9 oz/250 g cucumber	1 tsp honey	fresh or dried oregano, to garnish
9 oz/250 g Greek kalamata olives	4 tbsp extra-virgin olive oil	pita bread, to serve
1 red onion or 4 scallions	½ lemon	

---

1 Drain the feta cheese if it is packed in brine. Place it on a cutting board and carefully cut it into ½ inch/1 cm cubes. Transfer to a salad bowl.

2 Cut the cucumber in half lengthwise and use a teaspoon to scoop out the seeds. Cut the flesh into ½ inch/1 cm slices. Add to the bowl with the feta cheese.

3 Pit the olives with an olive or cherry pitter and add them to the salad bowl. Slice the red onion (or finely chop the white and green parts of the scallions) and add to the salad bowl.

4 Cut each tomato into quarters and scoop out the seeds with a teaspoon. Cut the flesh into bite-size pieces and add to the bowl.

5 Using your hands, gently toss all the ingredients together. Stir the honey into the olive oil (see Cook's Tip), add to the salad, and squeeze in lemon juice to taste. Season with pepper and a little salt, if wished. Cover and chill until required.

6 Garnish the salad with the oregano and serve it with pita bread.

COOK'S TIP

The small amount of honey helps to bring out the full flavor of the tomatoes.

Baked Goat Cheese Salad

Serves 4

INGREDIENTS

9 oz/250 g mixed salad leaves, such as arugula and endive

DRESSING
6 tbsp extra-virgin olive oil
3 tbsp red wine vinegar
½ tsp sugar

½ tsp Dijon mustard
salt and pepper

CROUTES
12 slices French bread
extra-virgin olive oil, for brushing

12 thin slices of Provençal goat-cheese, such as Picodon
fresh herbs, such as rosemary, thyme, or oregano, finely chopped

extra French bread, to serve

1 To prepare the salad, rinse the leaves under cold water and pat dry with a dish towel. Wrap in paper towels and put in a plastic bag. Seal tightly and chill until required.

2 To make the dressing, place all the ingredients in a screw-top jar and shake until well blended. Season with salt and pepper to taste and shake again. Set aside while preparing the croûtes.

3 To make the croûtes, toast the slices of bread on both sides until they are crisp. Brush a little olive oil on one side of each slice while still hot, so the oil is absorbed.

4 Place the croûtes on a cookie sheet and top each with a slice of cheese. Sprinkle the herbs over the cheese and drizzle with olive oil. Bake in a preheated oven at 350°F/180°C for 5 minutes.

5 While the croûtes are in the oven, place the salad leaves in a bowl. Shake the dressing again, pour it over the leaves, and toss together. Equally divide the salad between 4 plates.

6 Transfer the hot croûtes to the salads. Serve at once with extra slices of French bread.

Orange & Fennel Salad

Serves 4

INGREDIENTS

4 large oranges
1 large bulb fennel
2 tsp fennel seeds

2 tbsp extra-virgin olive oil
freshly squeezed orange juice,
   to taste

finely chopped fresh parsley,
   to garnish

1 Using a small, serrated knife, remove the zest and pith from one orange, cutting carefully from the top to the bottom of the orange so it retains its shape. Work over a bowl to catch the orange juices.

2 Peel the remaining oranges the same way, reserving all the juices. Cut the oranges horizontally into ¼ inch/5 mm slices and arrange in an attractive serving bowl; reserve the juices for later.

3 Put the fennel bulb on a cutting board and cut off the fronds. Cut the bulb in

half lengthwise and then into quarters. Cut crosswise into very thin slices. Immediately transfer to the bowl with the oranges. Toss with a little of the reserved orange juice to prevent browning.

4 Sprinkle the fennel seeds evenly over the oranges and fennel.

5 Place the olive oil in a small bowl and whisk in the rest of the reserved orange juice, plus extra fresh orange juice to taste. Pour over the oranges and fennel and toss gently. Cover with plastic wrap and chill until ready to serve.

6 Just before serving, remove from the refrigerator and sprinkle with parsley. Serve chilled.

VARIATION

Replace the fennel with a finely sliced onion or a large bunch of scallions, finely chopped. This version is from Spain, where orange-colored oranges would be used, but in Sicily the dish is made with blood-red oranges.

Spanish Tortilla

Serves 6–8

INGREDIENTS

½ cup olive oil	1 large onion, sliced	6 large eggs
1 lb 5 oz/600 g potatoes, sliced	1 large garlic clove, crushed	salt and pepper

1 Heat a 10 inch/600 g skillet, preferably nonstick, over high heat. Pour in the oil and heat. Lower the heat, add the potatoes, onion, and garlic and cook for 15–20 minutes, stirring frequently, until the potatoes are tender.

2 Beat the eggs together in a large bowl and season generously with salt and pepper. Using a slotted spoon, transfer the potatoes and onion to the bowl of eggs. Pour the excess oil left in the skillet into a heatproof pitcher, then scrape off the crusty bits from the bottom of the pan.

3 Reheat the pan. Add about 2 tablespoons of the oil reserved in the pitcher. Pour in the potato mixture, smoothing the vegetables into an even layer. Cook for about 5 minutes, shaking the pan occasionally, or until the bottom is set.

4 Shake the pan and use a spatula to loosen the edges of the tortilla. Place a large plate face down over the pan. Carefully invert the tortilla onto the plate.

5 If you are not using a nonstick pan, add 1 tablespoon of the reserved oil to the pan and swirl around. Gently slide the tortilla back into the pan, cooked-side up. Use the spatula to "tuck down" the edges. Continue cooking over medium heat for 3–5 minutes until set.

6 Remove the pan from the heat and slide the tortilla onto a serving plate. Let it cool for at least 5 minutes before cutting. Serve hot, warm, or at room temperature with salad.

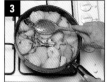

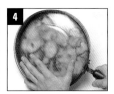

Spinach, Onion & Herb Frittata

Serves 6–8

INGREDIENTS

4 tbsp olive oil

6 scallions, sliced

9 oz/250 g young spinach leaves,
   any coarse stems removed,
   rinsed

6 large eggs

3 tbsp finely chopped mixed
   fresh herbs, such as flat-leaf
   parsley, thyme, and cilantro

2 tbsp freshly grated Parmesan
   cheese, plus extra for
   garnishing

salt and pepper

fresh parsley sprigs, to garnish

1 Heat a 10 inch/25 cm skillet, preferably nonstick with a flameproof handle, over medium heat. Add the oil and heat. Add the scallions and cook for about 2 minutes. Add the spinach with only the water clinging to its leaves and cook until it wilts.

2 Beat the eggs together in a large bowl and season generously with salt and pepper. Using a slotted spoon, transfer the spinach and onions to the bowl of eggs and stir in the herbs. Pour the excess oil left in the

skillet into a heatproof pitcher, then scrape off the crusty bits from the bottom of the pan.

3 Reheat the pan. Add 2 tablespoons of the reserved oil. Pour in the egg mixture, smoothing it into an even layer. Cook for 6 minutes, shaking the pan occasionally, or until the bottom is set when you lift up the edge with a spatula.

4 Sprinkle the top of the frittata with the Parmesan. Place the pan below a preheated broiler and

cook for about 3 minutes, or until the excess liquid is set and the cheese is golden.

5 Remove the pan from the heat and slide the tortilla onto a serving plate. Let cool for at least 5 minutes before cutting and garnishing with extra Parmesan and parsley. Serve the frittata slices hot, warm, or at room temperature.

Piperade

Serves 4–6

INGREDIENTS

2 tbsp olive oil
1 large onion, finely chopped
1 large red bell pepper, cored,
    deseeded, and sliced
1 large yellow bell pepper, cored,
    deseeded, and sliced

1 large green bell pepper
8 large eggs
salt and pepper
2 tomatoes, deseeded and
    chopped

2 tbsp finely chopped fresh flat-
    leaf parsley
4–6 slices thick country-style
    bread, toasted, to serve
fresh flat-leaf parsley sprigs,
    to garnish

1 Heat the olive oil in a skillet over a medium-high heat. Add the onion and peppers, lower the heat, and cook slowly for approximately 15–20 minutes until they are soft.

2 Meanwhile, place the eggs in a mixing bowl and whisk until well blended. Season with salt and pepper to taste. Set aside.

3 When the peppers are soft, pour the eggs into the pan and cook, stirring constantly, over very low heat until they are almost set but still creamy. Remove the pan from the heat.

4 Stir in the chopped tomatoes and chopped parsley. Adjust the seasoning, if necessary. Place the pieces of toast on individual plates and spoon the eggs and vegetables on top. Garnish with sprigs of parsley and serve at once.

COOK'S TIP

To make this dish more substantial, serve with thickly cut slices of Serrano ham from Spain or prosciutto from Italy. The salty taste of both contrasts well with the sweetness of the bell peppers.

Lemon Risotto

Serves 4

INGREDIENTS

2–3 lemons
2 tbsp olive oil
2 shallots, finely chopped
1½ cups risotto rice
⅓ cup dry white vermouth

4 cups vegetable or chicken
    stock, simmering
1 tbsp very finely chopped fresh
    flat-leaf parsley
2 tbsp butter

freshly pared Parmesan cheese,
    and avocado slices, to serve

TO GARNISH
thin strips of pared lemon zest
fresh parsley sprigs

1 Finely grate the zest from 2 lemons. Firmly roll the zestless lemons backward and forward on a board, then squeeze a scant ½ cup juice. If you don't have enough juice, squeeze another lemon. Set the grated zest and juice aside.

2 Heat the olive oil in a heavy-bottomed skillet. Add the shallots and cook, stirring, for about 3 minutes until soft. Add the rice and stir until all the grains are thoroughly coated.

3 Stir in the vermouth and let it bubble until it evaporates. Lower the heat to medium-low. Add the lemon juice and a ladleful of simmering stock. Stir together, then let simmer, only stirring occasionally, until all the liquid is absorbed into the rice.

4 Add another ladleful of stock and stir, then simmer until absorbed. Continue adding stock in this way, allowing it to be absorbed after each addition, until all the stock has been used and the risotto is creamy, with several tablespoons of liquid floating on the surface.

5 Stir in the lemon zest and parsley. Add the butter, cover, remove from the heat, and let stand for 5 minutes. Stir well and then garnish with lemon strips and parsley. Serve with Parmesan cheese and avocado slices.

Pissaladière

Serves 6–8

INGREDIENTS

about 6 tbsp olive oil

3 large garlic cloves, crushed

2 lb 4 oz/1 kg onions, thinly
sliced

3–4 tbsp Black Olive Tapenade
(see page 16)

1¾ oz/50 g canned anchovy

fillets in oil, drained and
halved lengthwise

12 black olives, such as Niçoise,
or Flavored Olives
(see page 172), pitted

finely chopped fresh flat-leaf
parsley, to garnish

PIE SHELL

1¼ cups all-purpose flour

pinch of salt

6 tbsp butter, diced

2–3 tbsp ice-cold water

1 To make the pie dough, put the flour and salt in a bowl and stir. With your fingertips, rub the butter into the flour until fine crumbs form. Add 2 tablespoons of the water to make a dough. Only add the extra water if necessary. Lightly knead the dough, then shape into a ball, wrap in plastic wrap, and chill for at least 1 hour.

2 Heat the oil in a large skillet with a tight-fitting lid. Add the garlic and stir for 2 minutes. Add the onions and stir to coat in oil. Then turn the heat down to its lowest setting.

3 Dip a piece of baking parchment, large enough to fit over the top of the pan, in water. Shake off the excess and press it onto the onions. Cover with the lid and cook for 45 minutes, or until the onions are tender.

4 Meanwhile, roll out the dough on a lightly floured counter and use to line an 8 inch/20 cm tart pan with a removable bottom. Prick all over and line with baking parchment and baking beans. Chill for 10 minutes.

5 Bake the lined pie shell on a hot cookie sheet in a preheated oven at 425°F/ 220°C for 15 minutes. Remove the paper and bake for another 5 minutes. Lower the oven to 350°F/180°C.

6 Spread the olive paste over the baked pie shell. Fill the shell with the onions. Arrange the anchovy fillets in a lattice pattern and scatter the olives over the top.

7 Bake for 25–30 minutes. Stand for 10 minutes before removing from the pan. Scatter with the chopped parsley and serve.

Spanakopittas

Serves 4

INGREDIENTS

2 tbsp olive oil

6 scallions, chopped

9 oz/250 g fresh young spinach
leaves, tough stems removed,
rinsed

¼ cup long-grain rice (not
basmati), boiled until tender,
and drained

4 tbsp chopped fresh dill

4 tbsp chopped fresh parsley

4 tbsp pine nuts

2 tbsp raisins

2¼ oz/60 g feta cheese, drained
if necessary, and cubed

1 whole nutmeg

pinch of cayenne pepper (optional)

40 sheets phyllo pastry

generous 1 cup melted butter

pepper

1 Heat the oil in a pan, add the scallions, and cook for about 2 minutes. Add the spinach, with just the water clinging to the leaves, and cook, stirring, until the leaves wilt. Squeeze excess moisture out of the spinach, using a wooden spoon.

2 Stir in the rice, herbs, pine nuts, raisins, and feta cheese. Grate in one-quarter of the nutmeg, and add black and cayenne peppers to taste.

3 Leave the phyllo sheets in a stack. Cut forty 6 inch/15 cm squares. Remove 8 slices and cut into eight 4 inch/10 cm circles. Rewrap the unused sheets and cover the squares and circles with a damp dish towel.

4 Brush a 4 inch/10 cm tart pan with a removable bottom with butter. Place in one square of phyllo and brush with more butter. Repeat with 7 more sheets. Do not push the phyllo into the ridges.

5 Spoon in one-quarter of the filling and smooth the surface. Top with a phyllo circle and brush with butter. Repeat with another phyllo circle. Fold the over-hanging phyllo over the top and brush with butter. Make 3 more pies.

6 Put the pies on a cookie sheet and bake in a preheated oven at 350°F/180°C for 20–25 minutes until crisp and golden. Let stand for 5 minutes before removing from the cookie sheet.

Tuna & Tomato Boreks

Makes about 18 boreks

INGREDIENTS

about 18 sheets phyllo pastry,
    each 15 x 6 inches/45 x 15 cm,
    defrosted if frozen
vegetable oil, for shallow cooking
sea salt, to garnish
lemon wedges, to serve

FILLING
2 hard-cooked eggs, shelled
    and finely chopped
7 oz/200 g canned tuna in brine,
    drained
1 tbsp chopped fresh dill

1 tomato, skinned, deseeded, and
    very finely chopped
¼ tsp cayenne pepper
salt and pepper

1 To make the filling, put the eggs in a bowl with the tuna and dill. Mash the mixture until blended.

2 Stir in the tomato, taking care not to break it up too much. Season with the cayenne and salt and pepper to taste. Set aside.

3 Place one sheet of phyllo pastry on a counter with a short side nearest to you; keep the remaining sheets covered with a damp dish towel.

Arrange about 1 tablespoon of the filling in a line along the short side, about ½ inch/2.5 cm in from the end and 1 inch/2.5 cm in from both long sides.

4 Make one tight roll to enclose the filling, then fold in both long sides for the length of the phyllo. Continue rolling up to the end. Use a little vegetable oil to seal the end. Repeat to make 17 more rolls, or until all the filling has been used.

5 Heat 1 inch/2.5 cm oil in a skillet to 350–375°F/180–190°C, or until a cube of day-old bread browns in 30 seconds. Cook 2–3 boreks at a time, until they are golden brown all over. Drain well on crumpled paper towels and sprinkle with sea salt. Serve hot or at room temperature with lemon wedges.

Pizza Biancas with Zucchini

Makes two 9 inch/23 cm pizzas

INGREDIENTS

scant 3 cups all-purpose
   flour, plus extra for rolling
   and dusting
1 envelope active dry yeast
1 tsp salt

1 tbsp extra-virgin olive oil, plus
   extra for greasing

TOPPING
2 zucchini
10½ oz/300 g buffalo mozzarella
1½–2 tbsp finely chopped fresh
   rosemary, or ½ tbsp dried

1 To make the crust, heat 1 cup water in a microwave oven on HIGH for1 minute, or until it reads 125°F/52°C on an instant-read thermometer.

2 Stir the flour, yeast, and salt together and make a well in the center. Stir in most of the water with the olive oil to make a dough. Add the remaining water, if necessary, to form a soft dough.

3 Turn out onto a lightly floured counter and knead for about 10 minutes, until smooth but still soft.

Wash the bowl and lightly coat with olive oil. Shape the dough into a ball, put it in the bowl, and turn the dough over so it is coated. Cover and let rest until doubled in size.

4 Turn the dough out onto a lightly floured counter. Quickly knead a few times, then cover with the upturned bowl, and let rest for 10 minutes.

5 Meanwhile, using a vegetable peeler, cut long, thin strips of zucchini. Drain and dice the mozzarella.

6 Divide the dough in half and shape each half into a ball. Cover one ball and roll out the other one into a 9 inch/23 cm circle. Place the circle on a lightly floured cookie sheet.

7 Scatter half the mozzarella over the bottom. Add half the zucchini strips and sprinkle with half the rosemary. Repeat with the remaining dough.

8 Bake in a preheated oven at 425°F/220°C for 15 minutes, or until crispy.

Pan Bagna

Serves 4

INGREDIENTS

16 inch/40 cm long loaf of
    country bread, thicker than
    a French baguette
fruity extra-virgin olive oil
Black or Green Olive Tapenade
    (see page 16), optional

FILLING
2 eggs
1¾ oz/50 g anchovy fillets in oil
about 3 oz/85 g Flavored Olives
    of your choice (see page 172)

lettuce or arugula leaves, rinsed
    and patted dry
about 4 plum tomatoes, sliced
7 oz/200 g canned tuna in brine,
    well drained and flaked

1 To make the filling, start by hard-cooking the eggs. Bring a pan of water to a boil. Add the eggs and return the water to a boil, then continue boiling for 12 minutes. Drain and immediately plunge into a bowl of ice-cold water to stop the cooking.

2 Shell the cooked eggs and cut into slices. Drain the anchovy fillets well, then cut them in half lengthwise if large. Pit the olives and slice in half. Set aside.

3 Using a serrated knife, slice the loaf in half lengthwise. Remove about ½ inch/1 cm of the crumb from the two pieces, leaving a border all around.

4 Generously brush both halves with the olive oil. Spread with tapenade, if you like a strong, robust flavor. Arrange a layer of lettuce or arugula leaves on the bottom half.

5 Add layers of hard-cooked egg slices, tomato slices, olives, anchovies, and tuna,

sprinkling with olive oil and adding lettuce or arugula leaves between the layers. Make the filling as thick as you like.

6 Place the other bread half on top and press down firmly. Wrap tightly in plastic wrap and place on a board or plate that will fit in your refrigerator. Weigh down and chill for several hours. To serve, slice into 4 equal portions, tying with string to secure in place, if desired.

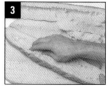

Olive Cake

Makes 12–15 slices

INGREDIENTS

9 oz/250 g pitted black or green
olives, or a mixture of both
2 cups plus 2 tbsp self-rising
flour

4 large eggs
1 tbsp superfine sugar
½ cup milk
½ cup olive oil

butter, for greasing
salt and pepper

1 Lightly butter an 8 inch/
20 cm cake pan, 2 inches/
5 cm deep. Line the bottom
with a piece of baking
parchment cut to fit. Put the
olives in a small bowl. Toss
them in the 2 tablespoonfuls
of measured flour.

2 Break the eggs into a
bowl and whisk lightly.
Stir in the sugar and season
with salt and pepper to taste.
Stir in the milk and olive oil.

3 Sift the remaining flour
into the bowl of egg
mixture, add the coated
olives, and stir together.

Spoon the mixture into the
prepared pan and smooth the
surface level.

4 Bake in a preheated
oven at 400°F/200°C for
45 minutes. Lower the oven
temperature to 325°F/160°C
and continue baking for
about 15 minutes, until the
cake is risen, golden, and
coming away from the sides
of the pan.

5 Remove from the oven
and let cool in the pan on
a wire rack for 20 minutes.
Remove from the pan, peel
off the lining paper, and let

cool completely. Store in an
airtight container.

COOK'S TIP

*Serve this with Black
Olive Tapenade (see
page 16) for spreading,
or as part of an antipasti
platter with a selection
of cooked meats.*

Entrées

The seemingly endless variety of fish and shellfish from Mediterranean waters means Mediterranean cooks can rely on freshly caught ingredients in the best condition. Mouthwatering dishes combining shellfish and fish are a specialty and the Seafood Stew is a classic example. For a taste of heartier Mediterranean flavors, try Seared Tuna with Anchovy & Orange Butter, or pan-fried red mullet wrapped in grape leaves. Few dishes can be easier to prepare than Mediterranean Monkfish, where the sweet white fish is paired with cherry tomatoes and pesto sauce.

The Italians love their tender veal—Vitello Tonnato is a divine combination of veal and tuna—while the Greeks, Turks, and Moroccans always cook lamb, broiled with herbs. Pork is often turned into hearty dishes, transforming the most inexpensive cuts into succulent meals, such as Country Pork with Onions. Mediterranean winters can be as cold and fierce as the summers are hot, so comforting winter casseroles are also called for. When you need a one-pot dinner to take the chill off a gray winter day, try Traditional Provençal Daube, Moroccan Chicken Couscous, or Basque Pork & Beans.

Traditional Provençal Daube

Serves 4

INGREDIENTS

1 lb 9 oz/700 g boneless lean
stewing beef, such as leg, cut
into 2 inch/5 cm pieces
1½ cups full-bodied dry red wine
2 tbsp olive oil
4 large garlic cloves, crushed
4 shallots, thinly sliced
9 oz/250 g unsmoked bacon

5–6 tbsp all-purpose flour
9 oz/250 g large chestnut
mushrooms, sliced
14 oz/400 g canned chopped
tomatoes
1 large bouquet garni of 1 bay
leaf, 2 sprigs dried thyme,
and 2 sprigs fresh parsley,
tied in a 3 inch/7.5 cm piece
of celery

2 inch/5 cm strip dried orange
rind (see page 176), optional
2 cups beef stock
1¾ oz/50 g canned anchovy fillets
in oil
2 tbsp capers in brine, drained
2 tbsp red wine vinegar
2 tbsp finely chopped fresh
parsley
salt and pepper

1 Place the stewing beef in a nonmetallic bowl with the wine, olive oil, half the garlic, and the shallots. Cover and marinate for at least 4 hours, stirring occasionally.

2 Meanwhile, place the bacon pieces in a pan of water, bring to a boil, and simmer for 10 minutes. Drain.

3 Place 4 tablespoons of the flour in a bowl and stir in about 2 tablespoons of water to make a thick paste. Cover and set aside.

4 Strain the marinated beef, reserving the marinade. Pat the beef dry and toss in seasoned flour.

5 Arrange a layer of bacon, mushrooms, and tomatoes in a large flameproof casserole, then add a layer of beef. Continue layering until all of the ingredients are used, tucking in the bouquet garni, and orange rind if using.

6 Pour in the beef stock and reserved marinade. Spread the flour paste around the rim of the casserole. Press on the lid, sealing tightly.

7 Cook in a preheated oven at 325°F/160°C for 2½ hours. Drain the anchovies, then pound with the capers and remaining garlic.

8 Remove the casserole, break the seal, and stir in the mashed anchovies, vinegar, and parsley. Re-cover and continue cooking for another 1–1½ hours until the meat is tender. Adjust the seasoning and serve.

Vitello Tonnato

Serves 6–8

INGREDIENTS

1 boned and rolled piece of
    veal leg, about 2 lb/900 g
    boned weight
olive oil
salt and pepper

TUNA MAYONNAISE
5½ oz/150 g canned tuna in
    olive oil
2 large eggs
about 3 tbsp lemon juice
olive oil

TO GARNISH
8 black olives, pitted and halved
1 tbsp capers in brine, rinsed
    and drained
finely chopped fresh flat-leaf
    parsley
lemon wedges

1 Rub the veal all over with oil and pepper and place in a roasting pan. Cover the pan with a piece of aluminum foil if there isn't any fat on the meat, then roast in a preheated oven at 450°F/230°C for 10 minutes. Lower the heat to 350°F/180°C and continue roasting for 1 hour for medium, or 1¼ hours if you prefer your veal well done. Set the veal aside and let cool completely, reserving any juices in the roasting pan.

2 Meanwhile, drain the tuna, reserving the oil. Blend the eggs in a food processor with 1 teaspoon of the lemon juice and a pinch of salt. Add enough olive oil to the tuna oil to make up to 1¼ cups.

3 With the motor running, add the oil to the eggs, drop by drop, until a thin mayonnaise forms. Add the tuna and process until smooth. Blend in lemon juice to taste. Check and adjust the seasoning.

4 Slice the cool meat very thinly. Add any juices to the reserved pan juices. Gradually whisk the veal juices into the tuna mayonnaise, to obtain a thin, pouring consistency.

5 Layer the veal slices with the sauce on a platter, ending with a layer of sauce. Cover and chill overnight. Garnish with olives, capers, and a light sprinkling of chopped parsley. Arrange lemon wedges around the edge and serve.

Veal Chops with Salsa Verde

Serves 4

INGREDIENTS

4 veal chops, such as loin chops,
about 8 oz/225 g each and
¾ inch/2 cm thick
garlic-flavored olive oil,
for brushing
salt and pepper
fresh basil or oregano leaves,
to garnish

SALSA VERDE
2 oz/60 g fresh flat-leaf parsley
3 canned anchovy fillets in
oil, drained
½ tbsp capers in brine, rinsed
and drained
1 shallot, finely chopped

1 garlic clove, halved, green core
removed and chopped
1 tbsp lemon juice, or to taste
6 large fresh basil leaves, or
¾ tsp freeze-dried
2 sprigs fresh oregano, or
½ tsp dried
½ cup extra-virgin olive oil

1 To make the salsa verde, put all the ingredients, except the olive oil, in a blender or food processor and process until they are chopped and blended.

2 With the motor running, add the oil through the top of feed tube and quickly blend until thickened. Add pepper to taste. Transfer to a bowl, cover, and chill.

3 Brush the veal chops with the garlic-flavored

olive oil and season them with salt and pepper. Place under a preheated broiler and cook for about 3 minutes. Turn over, brush with more oil, and broil for another 2 minutes until cooked. Use the tip of a knife to test they are cooked.

4 Transfer the chops to individual plates and spoon a little of the chilled salsa verde beside them. Garnish the chops with fresh oregano or basil and serve

with the remaining salsa verde, passed separately.

COOK'S TIP

The salsa verde will keep for up to 2 days in a covered container in the refrigerator. It is also delicious served with broiled red mullet. Or use it to replace the pesto sauce in Mediterranean Monkfish (see page 108).

Osso Bucco with Citrus Zest

Serves 6

INGREDIENTS

1–2 tbsp all-purpose flour	9 oz/250 g onions, very finely	finely grated zest of
6 meaty slices osso bucco	chopped	1 large lemon
(veal shins)	9 oz/250 g carrots, finely diced	finely grated zest of
2 lb 4 oz/1 kg fresh tomatoes,	1 cup dry white wine	1 orange
skinned, deseeded, and diced,	1 cup veal stock	2 tbsp finely chopped fresh
or 1 lb 12 oz/800 g canned	6 large basil leaves, torn	flat-leaf parsley
chopped tomatoes	1 large garlic clove, very	salt and pepper
1–2 tbsp olive oil	finely chopped	

1 Put the flour in a plastic bag and season with salt and pepper. Add the osso bucco, a couple of pieces at a time, and shake until well coated. Remove and shake off the excess flour. Continue until all the pieces are coated.

2 If using canned tomatoes, put them in a strainer and let them drain.

3 Heat 1 tablespoon of the oil in a large, flameproof casserole. Add the osso bucco and cook for 10 minutes on each side until well browned. Remove from the pan.

4 Add 1–2 teaspoons oil to the casserole if necessary. Add the onions and cook for about 5 minutes, stirring, until soft. Stir in the carrots and continue cooking until they become soft.

5 Add the tomatoes, wine, stock, and basil and return the osso bucco to the pan. Bring to a boil, then lower the heat, and simmer for 1 hour, covered. Check that the meat is tender with the tip of a knife. If not, continue cooking for 10 minutes and test again.

6 When the meat is tender, sprinkle with the garlic and lemon and orange zest, re-cover, and cook for another 10 minutes.

7 Adjust the seasoning if necessary. Sprinkle with the parsley and serve.

Spanish Chicken with Garlic

Serves 4

INGREDIENTS

2–3 tbsp all-purpose flour
cayenne pepper
4 chicken quarters or other joints, patted dry

about 4 tbsp olive oil
20 large garlic cloves, each halved and green core removed
1 large bay leaf

2 cups chicken stock
4 tbsp dry white wine
chopped fresh parsley, to garnish
salt and pepper

1 Put about 2 tablespoons of the flour in a bag and season to taste with cayenne pepper and salt and pepper. Add a chicken piece and shake until it is lightly coated with the flour, shaking off the excess. Repeat with the remaining pieces, adding more flour and seasoning, if necessary.

2 Heat 3 tablespoons of the olive oil in a large skillet. Add the garlic cloves and cook for about 2 minutes, stirring, to flavor the oil. Remove the garlic with a slotted spoon and set aside.

3 Add the chicken pieces to the pan, skin-side down, and then cook for about 5 minutes, or until the skin is golden brown. Turn and cook for another 5 minutes, adding 1–2 tablespoons oil if necessary.

4 Return the garlic to the pan. Add the bay leaf, chicken stock, and wine and bring to a boil. Lower the heat, cover, and simmer for 25 minutes, or until the chicken is tender and the garlic cloves are very soft.

5 Using a slotted spoon, transfer the chicken to a serving platter and keep warm. Bring the cooking liquid to a boil, with the garlic, and boil until reduced to about 1 cup plus 2 tablespoons. Adjust the seasoning.

6 Spoon the sauce over the chicken pieces and scatter the garlic cloves around. Garnish with chopped parsley and serve.

COOK'S TIP

The cooked garlic cloves are delicious mashed and smeared on the chicken pieces.

Moroccan Chicken Couscous

Serves 4–6

INGREDIENTS

about 3 tbsp olive oil

8 chicken pieces with bones, such
    as quarters, breasts, and legs

2 large onions, chopped

2 large garlic cloves, crushed

1 inch/2.5 cm piece fresh root
    ginger, peeled and finely
    chopped

5½ oz/150 g dried garbanzo
    beans, soaked overnight
    and drained

4 large carrots, cut into
    thick chunks

large pinch of saffron threads,
    dissolved in 2 tbsp
    boiling water

finely grated zest of 2 lemons

2 red bell peppers, cored,
    deseeded, and sliced

2 large zucchini, cut into chunks

2 tomatoes, cored, deseeded,
    and chopped

3½ oz/100 g dried apricots,
    chopped

½ tsp ground cumin

½ tsp ground coriander

½ tsp cayenne pepper, or to taste

2½ cups water

1 tbsp butter

3¼ cups instant couscous

salt and pepper

harissa, to serve (optional)

1 Heat 3 tablespoons of the oil in a large, flameproof casserole. Pat the chicken dry with paper towels, add to the oil, skin-side down, and cook for 5 minutes, until crisp and brown. Remove from the pan and set aside.

2 Add the onions to the pan, with a little oil, if necessary. Cook for 5 minutes, then add the garlic and ginger, and cook for 2 minutes, stirring occasionally.

3 Return the chicken to the casserole. Add the garbanzo beans, carrots, saffron, and lemon zest. Pour in enough water to cover by 1 inch/2.5 cm. Bring to a boil.

4 Lower the heat, cover, and simmer for 45 minutes, or until the garbanzo beans are tender. Add the bell peppers, zucchini, tomatoes, dried apricots, cumin, coriander, cayenne pepper, and salt and pepper to taste. Re-cover and simmer for 15 minutes.

5 Meanwhile, bring the water to a boil. Stir in ½ teaspoon salt and the butter. Sprinkle in the couscous. Cover the pan tightly, remove from the heat, and let stand for 10 minutes.

6 Fluff the couscous with a fork. Taste and adjust the seasoning of the stew. Spoon the couscous into individual bowls and serve the stew and harissa, if using, separately.

Provençal Barbecued Lamb

Serves 4–6

INGREDIENTS

1 leg of lamb, about 3 lb 5 oz/
    1.5 kg, boned
about 1 quantity Black Olive
    Tapenade (see page 16)
olive oil, for brushing

fresh rosemary and thyme sprigs,
    to garnish

MARINADE
1 bottle full-bodied red wine

2 large garlic cloves, chopped
2 tbsp extra-virgin olive oil
large handful fresh rosemary
    sprigs
fresh thyme sprigs

1 Place the boned lamb on a cutting board. Holding the knife almost flat, slice horizontally into the pocket left by the leg bone, taking care not to cut all the way through, so the boned meat can be opened out flat, like a book.

2 Place the lamb in a large, nonmetallic bowl and add all the marinade ingredients. Cover with plastic wrap and marinate for at least 6 hours, but preferably up to 24 hours, turning the meat over several times.

3 When ready to cook, remove the lamb from the marinade and pat dry. Lay the lamb flat and thread 2 or 3 long metal skewers through the flesh, so that the meat remains flat while it cooks. Spread the tapenade all over the lamb on both sides.

4 Brush the barbecue rack with oil. Place the lamb on the rack about 4 inches/ 10 cm above hot coals and cook for 5 minutes. Turn the meat over, and continue cooking for about 5 minutes longer. Turn twice more at 5-minute intervals, brushing

with extra tapenade. Raise the rack to 6 inches/15 cm if the meat starts to look charred—it should be medium cooked after 20–25 minutes.

5 Remove the lamb from the heat and let rest for 10 minutes before carving into thin slices and serving, garnished with rosemary and thyme sprigs.

Lamb Skewers on Rosemary

Makes 4

INGREDIENTS

1 lb 2 oz/500 g boneless leg of lamb	depending on the size	MARINADE
4 long, thick branches fresh rosemary	12 large garlic cloves, peeled olive oil	2 tbsp olive oil
1 or 2 red bell peppers,	Spiced Pilau with Saffron (see page 196), to serve	2 tbsp dry white wine
		½ tsp ground cumin
		1 sprig fresh oregano, chopped

1 At least 4 hours before cooking, cut the lamb into 2 inch/5 cm cubes. Mix all the marinade ingredients together in a bowl. Add the lamb cubes, stir well to coat, and marinate for at least 4 hours, or up to 12 hours.

2 An hour before cooking, put the rosemary branches in a bowl of cold water and let soak.

3 Slice the tops off the bell peppers, cut the bell peppers in half, quarter them, and remove the cores and seeds. Cut the halves into 2 inch/5 cm pieces.

4 Bring a small pan of water to a boil and blanch the pepper pieces and garlic cloves for 1 minute. Drain and refresh under cold water. Pat dry and set aside.

5 Remove the rosemary from the water and pat dry. To make the skewers, remove the rosemary needles from about the first 1½ inches/4 cm of the branches so that you have "handles" to turn them over with while broiling.

6 Thread alternate pieces of lamb, garlic, and red bell pepper pieces onto the 4 rosemary skewers; the meat

should be tender enough to push the sprig through it, but, if not, use a metal skewer to poke a hole in the center of each cube.

7 Lightly oil the broiler rack. Place the skewers on the rack about 5 inches/13 cm under a preheated hot broiler and broil for 10–12 minutes, brushing with any leftover marinade or olive oil and turning, until the meat is cooked. Serve with the pilau.

Cypriot Lamb with Orzo

Serves 6

INGREDIENTS

2 large garlic cloves	4 sprigs fresh thyme	9 oz/250 g orzo pasta (see
1 unboned shoulder of lamb	4 sprigs fresh parsley	Cook's Tip)
1 lb 12 oz/800 g canned	1 bay leaf	salt and pepper
chopped tomatoes	½ cup water	fresh thyme sprigs, to garnish

1 Cut the garlic cloves in half and remove the green cores, then slice the garlic thinly. Using the tip of a sharp knife, make slits all over the lamb shoulder, then insert the garlic slices into the slits.

2 Pour the tomatoes and their juices into a roasting pan large enough to hold the lamb shoulder. Add the thyme, parsley, and bay leaf. Place the lamb on top, skin-side up, and cover the dish tightly with a sheet of foil, shiny side down. Scrunch the foil all around the edge so that none of the juices escape during cooking.

3 Put in a preheated oven at 325°F/160°C and cook for 3 ½–4 hours, until the lamb is tender and the tomatoes are reduced to a thick sauce.

4 Remove the lamb from the roasting pan and set aside. Using a large metal spoon, skim off as much fat from the surface of the tomato sauce as possible.

5 Add the water and orzo to the tomatoes, stirring so the grains are submerged. Add a little extra water if the sauce seems too thick. Season to taste with salt and pepper. Return the lamb to the roasting pan.

6 Re-cover the roasting pan and return to the oven for 15 minutes, or until the orzo is tender. Remove the bay leaf. Let the lamb rest for 10 minutes, then slice, and serve with the orzo in tomato juice, garnished with fresh thyme sprigs.

COOK'S TIP

Orzo is a small pasta shape that looks like barley grains.

Basque Pork & Beans

Serves 4–6

INGREDIENTS

7 oz/200 g dried cannellini beans,
    soaked overnight
olive oil
1 lb 5 oz/600 g boneless leg
    of pork, cut into 2 inch/
    5 cm chunks

1 large onion, sliced
3 large garlic cloves, crushed
14 oz/400 g canned chopped
    tomatoes
2 green bell peppers, cored,
    deseeded, and sliced

finely grated zest of
    1 large orange
salt and pepper
finely chopped fresh parsley,
    to garnish

1 Drain the cannellini beans and put in a large pan with fresh water to cover. Bring to a boil and boil rapidly for 10 minutes. Lower the heat and simmer for 20 minutes. Drain the beans and set aside.

2 Add enough oil to cover the bottom of a skillet in a very thin layer. Heat the oil over medium heat, add a few pieces of the pork, and cook on all sides until brown. Repeat with the remaining pork and set aside.

3 Add 1 tablespoon oil to the skillet, if necessary, then add the onion, and cook for 3 minutes. Stir in the garlic and cook for another 2 minutes. Return the browned pork to the pan.

4 Add the tomatoes to the pan and bring to a boil. Lower the heat, stir in the bell pepper slices, orange zest, the drained beans, and salt and pepper to taste.

5 Transfer the contents of the pan to a casserole.

6 Cover the casserole and cook in a preheated oven at 350°F/180°C for 45 minutes, until the beans and pork are tender. Sprinkle with chopped parsley and then serve.

VARIATION

Any leftover beans and bell peppers can be used in a pasta sauce. Add some sliced and fried chorizo sausage for a spicier dish.

Country Pork with Onions

Serves 4

INGREDIENTS

2 large pork shanks
2 large garlic cloves, sliced
3 tbsp olive oil
2 carrots, finely chopped
2 celery stalks, strings removed
    and finely chopped

1 large onion, finely chopped
2 sprigs fresh thyme, broken
    into pieces
2 sprigs fresh rosemary, broken
    into pieces
1 large bay leaf

1 cup dry white wine
1 cup water
20 pickling onions
pepper
fresh flat-leaf parsley, roughly
    chopped, to garnish

1 Using the tip of a sharp knife, make slits all over the pork shanks and insert the garlic slices.

2 Heat 1 tablespoon of the oil in a flameproof casserole over medium heat. Add the carrots, celery, and onion. Cook, stirring, for about 10 minutes.

3 Place the pork shanks on top of the vegetables. Scatter the thyme and rosemary over the meat. Add the bay leaf, wine, and water, and season with pepper.

4 Bring to a boil, then remove from the heat. Cover tightly and cook in a preheated oven at 325°F/ 160°C for 3½ hours, or until the meat is very tender.

5 Meanwhile, put the pickling onions in a bowl, pour boiling water over them, and let stand for 1 minute. Drain, then slip off all their skins. Heat the remaining oil in a large skillet. Add the onions, partially cover, and cook over low heat for 15 minutes, shaking the pan occasionally.

Cook until the onions are just starting to turn golden.

6 When the pork shanks are tender, add the onions and continue to cook for another 15 minutes. Remove the pork and onions and keep warm.

7 Using a large metal spoon, skim off as much fat as possible from the surface of the cooking liquid. Strain the cooking liquid into a bowl, pressing down lightly to extract the flavor; reserve the strained vegetables in the strainer. Adjust the seasoning.

8 Cut the meat from the pork shanks, if desired. Arrange on a serving platter with the onions and strained vegetables. Spoon the sauce over the meat and vegetables. Garnish with parsley.

Maltese Rabbit with Fennel

Serves 4

INGREDIENTS

5 tbsp olive oil

2 large fennel bulbs, trimmed and sliced

2 carrots, diced

1 large garlic clove, crushed

1 tbsp fennel seeds

about 4 tbsp all-purpose flour

2 wild rabbits, jointed

1 cup dry white wine

1 cup water

1 bouquet garni of 2 sprigs flat-leaf parsley, 1 sprig rosemary, and 1 bay leaf, tied in a 3 inch/7.5 cm piece of celery

salt and pepper

thick, crusty bread, to serve

TO GARNISH

fresh flat-leaf parsley or cilantro, finely chopped

fresh rosemary sprigs

1 Heat 3 tablespoons of the olive oil over medium heat in a large, flameproof casserole. Add the fennel and carrots and cook for 5 minutes, stirring occasionally. Stir in the garlic and fennel seeds and continue to cook for 2 more minutes, or until the fennel is just tender. Remove the fennel and carrots from the casserole and set aside.

2 Put 4 tablespoons flour in a plastic bag and season. Add 2 rabbit pieces and shake to coat lightly, then shake off any excess flour. Continue until all the pieces of rabbit are coated, adding more flour to the bag if necessary.

3 Add the remaining oil to the casserole. Cook the rabbit pieces for about 5 minutes on each side until golden brown, working in batches. Remove the rabbit from the casserole.

4 Pour in the wine and simmer over heat, stirring to scrape up all the bits from the bottom. Return the rabbit pieces, fennel, and carrots to the casserole and pour in the water. Add the bouquet garni and salt and pepper to taste.

5 Bring to a boil. Lower the heat, cover, and simmer for about 1¼ hours, until the rabbit is tender.

6 Discard the bouquet garni. Garnish with herbs and serve straight from the casserole with lots of bread to mop up the juices.

Pickled Tuna

Serves 4

INGREDIENTS

4 large tuna steaks, each about
  8 oz/225 g and ¾ inch/
  2 cm thick
1 cup olive oil
2 large red onions, thinly sliced
2 carrots, thinly sliced

2 large bay leaves, torn
1 garlic clove, very finely chopped
1 cup white wine vinegar or
  sherry vinegar
½ tsp dried chili flakes, or to
  taste, crushed

1 tbsp coriander seeds, lightly
  crushed
salt and pepper
finely chopped fresh parsley,
  to garnish

1 Rinse and pat the tuna steaks dry with paper towels. Heat 4 tablespoons of the oil in a large skillet, preferably nonstick.

2 Add the tuna steaks to the pan and cook for 2 minutes over a medium-high heat. Turn the steaks and continue to cook for another 2 minutes, until browned and medium cooked, or for 4 minutes for well done. Remove the tuna from the pan and drain well on paper towels. Set aside.

3 Heat the remaining oil in the pan, then add the onions and cook for 8 minutes, stirring frequently, until soft but not brown. Stir in the carrots, bay leaves, garlic, vinegar, chili flakes, and salt and pepper to taste, and cook for 10 minutes, or until the carrots are tender. Stir in the coriander seeds 1 minute before the end of cooking time.

4 When the tuna steaks are cool enough to be handled easily, remove any skin and bones from them.

Break each of the steaks into 4 or 5 large chunks.

5 Put the fish pieces in a nonmetallic bowl and pour the hot onion mixture over them. Very gently mix together, taking care not to break up the fish pieces.

6 Leave until completely cool, then cover, and chill for at least 24 hours. The fish will stay fresh in the refrigerator for up to 5 days. To serve, sprinkle with parsley and serve at room temperature.

Seared Tuna with Anchovy & Orange Butter

Serves 4

INGREDIENTS

olive oil
4 thick tuna steaks, each about
   8 oz/225 g and ¾ inch/
   2 cm thick

ANCHOVY AND ORANGE BUTTER
8 anchovy fillets in oil, drained
4 scallions, finely chopped
1 tbsp finely grated orange rind
8 tbsp unsalted butter, softened
¼ tsp lemon juice
pepper

TO GARNISH
fresh flat-leaf parsley sprigs
orange rind strips

1 To make the anchovy and orange butter, very finely chop the anchovies and put them in a bowl with the scallions, orange rind, and softened butter. Beat well until all the ingredients are blended together, seasoning with lemon juice and pepper to taste.

2 Place the flavored butter on a sheet of baking parchment and roll up into a log shape. Fold over the ends

and place in the freezer for 15 minutes to become firm.

3 To cook the tuna, heat a ridged skillet over high heat. Lightly brush the pan with olive oil, add the tuna steaks, in batches if necessary, and cook for 2 minutes. Turn the steaks over and cook for 2 minutes for rare, or up to 4 minutes for well done. Season to taste with pepper.

4 Transfer to a warm plate and put 2 thin slices of anchovy butter on each tuna steak. Garnish with parsley sprigs and orange rind and serve at once.

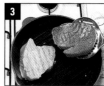

Mediterranean Fish Soup

Serves 4

INGREDIENTS

2 lb 4 oz/1 kg mixed fish, such as
sea bass, skate, red snapper,
rock fish, or any Mediterranean
fish you can find
2 tbsp olive oil
1 bulb fennel, trimmed
and chopped
2 shallots, chopped
2 garlic cloves, chopped
1 lb 5 oz/600 g vine-ripened
tomatoes, chopped

1 bouquet garni of 2 sprigs fresh
flat-leaf parsley, 2 sprigs
fresh thyme, and 1 bay leaf,
tied in a 3 inch/7.5 cm piece
of celery
pinch of saffron threads
3 cups Mediterranean Fish Stock
(see page 180), or good-
quality, ready-made chilled
fish stock
salt and pepper

French pastis or other anise-
flavored liqueur (optional)

TO SERVE
Rouille (see page 186)
1 loaf French bread, sliced
and toasted
4½ oz/125 g Swiss cheese, grated

1 To prepare the fish,
remove any skin and
bones and cut into pieces.

2 Heat the oil in a heavy-
bottomed pan. Add
the fennel and cook for
5 minutes. Stir frequently.
Add the shallots and garlic
and cook for about 5 minutes,
until the fennel is tender.

3 Stir in the mixed fish and
add the tomatoes,
bouquet garni, saffron
threads, fish stock, and salt
and pepper to taste.

4 Slowly bring almost to a
boil, stirring occasionally.
Lower the heat, partially
cover, and simmer for 30
minutes, stirring occasionally
to break up the tomatoes.
Skim the surface as necessary.

5 Remove the bouquet
garni. Process the soup in
a food processor, then work it
through a food mill into a
large bowl.

6 Return to the rinsed-out
pan and heat without
boiling. Adjust the seasoning.
Stir in a little pastis, if using.

7 Spread the rouille on the
toast and top with the
cheese. Place in each bowl
and ladle the hot soup over
the toast. Serve at once.

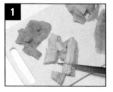

Seafood Stew

Serves 4–6

INGREDIENTS

8 oz/225 g clams

1 lb 9 oz/700 g mixed fish, such as
    sea bass, skate, red snapper,
    rock fish, or any Mediterranean
    fish you can find

12–18 tiger shrimp

about 3 tbsp olive oil

1 large onion, finely chopped

2 garlic cloves, very finely chopped

2 vine-ripened tomatoes, halved,
    deseeded, and chopped

3 cups Mediterranean Fish Stock
    (see page 180), or a good-
    quality, ready-made chilled
    fish stock

1 tbsp tomato paste

1 tsp fresh thyme leaves

pinch of saffron threads

pinch of sugar

salt and pepper

finely chopped fresh parsley,
    to garnish

1 Soak the clams in a bowl of lightly salted water for 30 minutes. Rinse them under cold running water and lightly scrub to remove any sand from the shells. Discard any broken clams or open clams that do not shut when firmly tapped with the back of a knife, because these will be unsafe to eat.

2 Prepare the fish as necessary, removing any skin and bones, then cut into bite-size chunks.

3 To prepare the shrimp, break off the heads. Peel off the shells, leaving the tails intact, if desired. Using a small knife, make a slit along the back of each and remove the thin, black vein. Set all the seafood aside.

4 Heat the oil in a large pan. Add the onion and cook for 5 minutes, stirring. Add the garlic and cook for about another 2 minutes, until the onion is soft but not brown.

5 Add the tomatoes, stock, tomato paste, thyme leaves, saffron threads, and sugar, then bring to a boil, stirring to dissolve the tomato paste. Lower the heat, cover, and simmer for 15 minutes. Adjust the seasoning.

6 Add the seafood and simmer until the clams open and the fish flakes easily. Discard the bouquet garni and any clams that do not open. Garnish and serve at once.

Salt Cod Fritters

Serves 6

INGREDIENTS

1 lb/450 g salt cod	1 onion, very finely chopped	1 tbsp capers in brine, drained
12 oz/450 g mealy baking	1 garlic clove, crushed	and finely chopped (optional)
potatoes	4 tbsp very finely chopped fresh	1 small egg, lightly beaten
1 tbsp olive oil, plus extra	parsley or cilantro	salt and pepper
for cooking		Aioli (see page 184), to serve

1 Break the salt cod into pieces and place in a bowl. Add enough water to cover and leave for 48 hours, changing the water 4 times.

2 Drain the salt cod, then cook in boiling water for 20–25 minutes, until tender. Drain, then remove all the skin and bones. Using a fork, flake the fish into fine pieces that still retain some texture.

3 Meanwhile, boil the potatoes in their skins until tender. Drain, peel, and mash the potatoes in a large bowl. Set aside.

4 Heat 1 tablespoon of the oil in a skillet. Add the onion and garlic and cook for 5 minutes, stirring, until tender but not brown. Remove with a slotted spoon and drain on paper towels.

5 Stir the salt cod, onion, and garlic into the mashed potatoes. Stir in the parsley or cilantro, and capers, if using. Season generously with pepper.

6 Stir in the beaten egg. Cover and chill for 30 minutes, then adjust the seasoning.

7 Heat 2 inches/5 cm of oil in a skillet to 350–375°F/ 180–190°C, or until a cube of bread browns in 30 seconds. Drop tablespoonfuls of the salt-cod mixture into the hot oil and cook for about 8 minutes, or until golden brown and set. Do not cook more than 6 at a time because the oil will become too cold and the fritters will become soggy. You will get about 18–20 fritters.

8 Drain the fritters on paper towels. Serve at once with aioli for dipping. Garnish with parsley.

Shrimp Skewers
with Tomato Salsa

Makes 8 skewers

INGREDIENTS

32 large tiger shrimp
olive oil, for brushing
Skordalia (see page 188) or Aioli
    (see page 184), to serve

MARINADE
½ cup extra-virgin olive oil
2 tbsp lemon juice
1 tsp finely chopped red chile

1 tsp balsamic vinegar
pepper

TOMATO SALSA
2 large, vine-ripened tomatoes,
    skinned, cored, deseeded,
    and chopped
4 scallions, white parts only, very
    finely chopped

1 red bell pepper, skinned,
    deseeded, and chopped
1 orange or yellow bell
    pepper, skinned, deseeded,
    and chopped
1 tbsp extra-virgin olive oil
2 tsp balsamic vinegar
4 sprigs fresh basil

1 To make the marinade, place all the ingredients in a nonmetallic bowl and whisk together. Set aside.

2 To prepare the shrimp, break off the heads. Peel off the shells, leaving the tails intact. Using a small knife, make a slit along the back and remove the thin, black vein. Add the shrimp to the marinade and stir until well coated. Cover and chill in the refrigerator for 15 minutes.

3 To make the salsa, put all the ingredients, except the basil, in a nonmetallic bowl and toss together. Season to taste with salt and pepper.

4 Thread 4 shrimp onto a metal skewer, bending each shrimp in half. Repeat with 7 more skewers.

Brush the ingredients with the marinade.

5 Brush a broiler rack with oil. Place the skewers on the rack, then position under a preheated hot broiler, about 3 inches/7.5 cm from the heat; cook for 1 minute. Turn the skewers over, brush again, and continue to cook for 1–1½ minutes, until the shrimp have turned pink and opaque.

6 Tear the basil leaves and toss with the salsa. Arrange each skewer on a plate with some salsa and garnish with parsley. Serve with skordalia or aioli dip.

Swordfish à la Maltaise

Serves 4

INGREDIENTS

1 tbsp fennel seeds

2 tbsp fruity extra-virgin olive
oil, plus extra for brushing
and drizzling

2 large onions, thinly sliced

1 small garlic clove, crushed

4 swordfish steaks, about
6 oz/175 g each

1 large lemon, cut in half

2 large, vine-ripened tomatoes,
finely chopped

4 sprigs fresh thyme

salt and pepper

1 Place the fennel seeds in a dry skillet over medium-high heat and toast, stirring, until they give off their aroma. Watch them carefully so that they do not burn. When roasted, immediately pour out of the pan onto a plate. Set this aside.

2 Heat 2 tablespoons of the olive oil in the pan. Add the onions and cook for 5 minutes, stirring occasionally. Add the garlic and continue cooking the onions until very soft and tender, but not brown. Remove from the heat.

3 Cut out four 12 inch/ 30 cm circles of baking parchment. Very lightly brush the center of each paper circle with olive oil. Equally divide the onions between the paper circles, flattening them out to about the size of the fish steaks.

4 Top the onions in each parcel with a swordfish steak. Squeeze lemon juice over the fish steaks and drizzle with a little olive oil. Scatter the tomatoes over the top, add a sprig of thyme to each, and season with salt and pepper to taste.

5 Fold the edges of the paper together, scrunching them tightly so that no cooking juices escape during cooking. Place on a cookie sheet and cook in a preheated oven at 400°F/ 200°C for 20 minutes.

6 To test if the fish is cooked, open one packet and pierce the flesh with a knife—it should flake easily. Serve the fish straight from the paper packets.

Mediterranean Monkfish

Serves 4

INGREDIENTS

1 lb 5 oz/600 g vine-ripened cherry tomatoes, a mixture of yellow and red, if available	2 monkfish fillets, about 12 oz/350 g each 8 tbsp Pesto Sauce (see page 124)	salt and pepper fresh basil sprigs, to garnish boiled new potatoes, to serve

1 Cut the tomatoes in half and scatter, cut-sides up, on the bottom of an oven-proof serving dish. Set aside.

2 Using your fingers, rub off the thin, gray membrane that covers the monkfish fillets.

3 If the skin has not been removed, place the fish skin-side down on a clean counter. Loosen enough skin at one end of the fillet so you can grip hold of it. Work from the front of the fillet to the back. Insert the knife, almost flat and, using a gentle sawing action, remove the skin. Rinse the fillets well and then dry them with paper towels.

4 Place the fillets on top of the tomatoes, tucking the thin ends under, if necessary (see Cook's Tip). Spread 4 tablespoons of the pesto sauce over each fillet and season with salt and pepper.

5 Cover the dish tightly with foil, shiny-side down. Place in a preheated oven at 450°F/230°C and roast for 16–18 minutes until the fish is cooked through, the flesh flakes easily, and the tomatoes are beginning to dissolve into a thick sauce.

6 Adjust the seasoning, if necessary. Garnish with basil sprigs and serve at once with boiled new potatoes.

COOK'S TIP

Monkfish fillets are often cut from the tail, which means one end is much thinner than the rest and prone to overcooking. If you can't get fillets that are the same thickness, fold the thin ends under for even cooking.

Wrapped Red Mullet with Stewed Bell Peppers & Fennel

Serves 4

INGREDIENTS

3 tbsp olive oil, plus extra
for rubbing
2 large red bell peppers, cored,
deseeded, and thinly sliced

2 large bulbs fennel, trimmed
and thinly sliced
1 large garlic clove, crushed
8 sprigs fresh thyme, plus extra
for garnishing

20–24 grape leaves in brine
1 lemon
4 red mullet, about 8 oz/225 g
each, scaled and gutted
salt and pepper

1 Heat the oil in a large skillet over medium-low heat. Add the bell peppers, fennel, garlic, and 4 sprigs of thyme, and stir together. Cook, stirring occasionally, for about 20 minutes, until the vegetables are cooked thoroughly and are very soft, but not browned.

2 Meanwhile, rinse the grape leaves under cold, running water and pat dry with paper towels. Cut 4 thin slices off the lemon, then cut each slice in half.

Finely grate the zest of half the lemon.

3 Stuff the mullet cavities with the lemon slices and remaining thyme sprigs. Rub a little olive oil on each fish and sprinkle with the lemon zest. Season with salt and pepper to taste.

4 Wrap 5 or 6 grape leaves around each mullet, depending on the size of the mullet, to enclose completely. Put the wrapped mullet on top of the fennel and bell

peppers. Cover the pan and cook over medium-low heat for 12–15 minutes, until the fish is cooked through and the flesh flakes easily when tested with the tip of a knife.

5 Transfer the cooked fish to individual plates and spoon the fennel and bell peppers alongside. Garnish with thyme sprigs and serve.

Moules Marinières

Serves 4

INGREDIENTS

4 lb 8 oz/2 kg live mussels
4 tbsp olive oil
4–6 large garlic cloves, halved
1 lb 12 oz/800 g canned
    chopped tomatoes

1¼ cups dry white wine
2 tbsp finely chopped fresh flat-
    leaf parsley, plus extra
    for garnishing

1 tbsp finely chopped
    fresh oregano
salt and pepper
French bread, to serve

1 Soak the mussels in a bowl of lightly salted water for 30 minutes. Rinse them under cold running water and lightly scrub to remove any sand from the shells. Using a small, sharp knife, remove the "beards" from the shells.

2 Discard any broken mussels or open mussels that do not shut when firmly tapped with the back of a knife. This indicates that they are dead and could cause food poisoning if eaten. Rinse the mussels again, then set aside in a colander.

3 Heat the olive oil in a large pan or pot over medium-high heat. Add the garlic and cook, stirring, for about 3 minutes to flavor the oil. Using a slotted spoon, remove the garlic from the pan.

4 Add the tomatoes and their juice, the wine, parsley, and oregano and bring to a boil, stirring. Lower the heat, cover, and simmer for 5 minutes to allow the flavors to blend.

5 Add the mussels, cover the pan, and simmer for 5–8 minutes, shaking the pan regularly, until the mussels open. Using a slotted spoon, transfer the mussels to serving bowls, discarding any that are not open.

6 Season the sauce with salt and pepper to taste. Ladle the sauce over the mussels, sprinkle with extra chopped parsley, and serve at once with plenty of French bread to mop up the delicious juices.

Seared Scallops with Champagne-Saffron Sauce

Serves 4

INGREDIENTS

generous pinch of saffron threads
about 4 tbsp unsalted butter
20 large scallops with the corals,
    each at least 1 inch/2.5 cm
    thick, shelled, juices reserved

4 tbsp dry champagne or
    sparkling wine
1¼ cups heavy cream
½ lemon
salt and pepper

fresh flat-leaf parsley sprigs,
    to garnish

1 Heat a large, dry skillet, preferably nonstick, over high heat. Add the saffron threads and toast just until they start to give off their aroma. Immediately pour onto a plate and set aside.

2 Melt half the butter in the pan. Add 10 scallops and cook for 2 minutes. Turn and cook for another 1½–2 minutes, until the scallops are just set and the flesh is opaque all the way through when you pierce one with a knife (see Cook's Tip).

3 Transfer the scallops to a hot dish, cover, and keep warm while cooking the rest in the same way, adding more butter as necessary.

4 Add the saffron to the cooking juices and pour in the champagne, cream, and any reserved scallop juices, stirring. Bring to a boil, then lower the heat slightly, and simmer for about 10 minutes, until the liquid is reduced to a consistency that coats the back of a spoon.

5 Add freshly squeezed lemon juice and salt and pepper to taste. Return the scallops to the pan and stir until just heated through. Transfer to 4 plates and garnish with parsley. Serve at once.

COOK'S TIP

If the scallops are thinner, only cook them for 1½ minutes on each side. Take great care not to overcook them.

Squid Salad

Serves 4–6

INGREDIENTS

2 lb small squid
½ cup lemon juice
¼ cup extra-virgin olive oil
1 oz/25 g fresh flat-leaf parsley
8 scallions

4 vine-ripened tomatoes,
    deseeded and chopped
salt and pepper

TO GARNISH
radicchio leaves

finely chopped red chiles
    (optional)
capers or black olives (optional)
fresh flat-leaf parsley,
    finely chopped

1 To prepare each squid, pull the head and all the insides out of the body sac. Cut the tentacles off the head and discard the head. Remove the beak from the center of the tentacles.

2 Pull out the thin, transparent quill that runs through the center of the body. Rinse the body sac under running cold water and, using your fingers, rub off the thin, gray membrane. Cut the squid body sacs into ½ inch/1 cm slices. Rinse the tentacle pieces and set aside with the body slices.

3 Put the lemon juice and olive oil in a large bowl and stir together. Very finely chop the parsley and add to the bowl. Finely chop the white parts of the scallions and add to the bowl with the tomatoes. Season with salt and pepper to taste.

4 Bring a pan of lightly salted water to a boil. Add all the squid and return to a boil.

5 As soon as the water returns to a boil, drain the squid. Add the squid to the bowl of dressing and

gently toss all the ingredients together to blend.

6 Let the squid cool completely, then cover the dish, and let marinate in the refrigerator for at least 6 hours, or preferably overnight.

7 Line a serving bowl with radicchio leaves. Add the chopped chiles, capers, or olives, to taste, if you are using them. Mound the squid salad on top of the radicchio leaves and sprinkle with finely chopped parsley. Serve very chilled.

Salade Niçoise

Serves 4–6

INGREDIENTS

3 large eggs

9 oz/250 g green beans, trimmed

9 oz/250 g small waxy potatoes, such as Charlottes, scrubbed and halved

1 large, sun-ripened tomato, cut into eighths

1 large tuna steak, about 12 oz/ 350 g and ¾ inch/2 cm thick, seared (see page 96)

½ cup Provençal-style Olives (see page 172), or plain black olives

1¾ oz/50 g canned anchovy fillets in oil, drained

1 tbsp chopped fresh parsley

GARLIC VINAIGRETTE

scant ½ cup extra-virgin olive oil

3 tbsp red or white wine vinegar

½ tsp sugar

½ tsp Dijon mustard

2 garlic cloves, crushed

salt and pepper

1 To make the vinaigrette, put all the ingredients in a screw-top jar and shake until blended. Season with salt and pepper to taste. Set aside.

2 Bring 3 pans of water to a boil. Add the eggs to one pan, bring back to a boil, then cook for 12 minutes. Drain immediately and run under cold running water to stop more cooking.

3 Put the beans and potatoes into separate pans of boiling water. Blanch the beans for 3 minutes, then drain, and immediately transfer to a large bowl. Shake the dressing and pour it over the beans.

4 Continue to cook the potatoes until they are tender, then drain, and add to the beans and dressing while they are still hot. Let the potatoes and beans cool in the dressing.

5 Add the tomato pieces to the vegetables in the dressing and toss together. Break the tuna into large chunks and gently toss together.

6 Shell the eggs and cut each into quarters lengthwise.

7 Mound the tuna and vegetables on a large serving platter. Arrange the hard-cooked egg quarters around the side. Scatter the olives over the salad, then arrange the anchovies in a lattice on top. Cover and chill.

8 About 15 minutes before serving, remove the salad from the refrigerator and let it come to room temperature. Sprinkle with parsley and spoon onto individual plates.

Lobster Salad

Serves 2

INGREDIENTS

2 raw lobster tails	LEMON-DILL MAYONNAISE	TO GARNISH
salt and pepper	1 large lemon	radicchio leaves
	1 large egg yolk	lemon wedges
	½ tsp Dijon mustard	fresh dill sprigs
	⅔ cup olive oil	
	1 tbsp chopped fresh dill	

1 To make the lemon-dill mayonnaise, finely grate the rind from the lemon and squeeze the juice. Beat the egg yolk in a small bowl with the mustard and 1 teaspoon of the lemon juice.

2 Using a balloon whisk or electric mixer, beat in the olive oil, drop by drop, until a thick mayonnaise forms. Stir in half the lemon rind and 1 tablespoon of the juice.

3 Season with salt and pepper, and add more lemon juice if desired. Stir in the dill and cover with plastic wrap. Chill until required.

4 Bring a large pan of salted water to a boil. Add the lobster tails and continue to cook for 6 minutes until the flesh is opaque and the shells are red. Drain immediately and let cool completely

5 Remove the lobster flesh from the shells and cut into bite-size pieces.

6 Arrange the radicchio leaves on individual plates and top with the lobster flesh. Place a spoonful of the lemon-dill mayonnaise on the side. Garnish with lemon wedges and dill sprigs and serve.

Pasta with Broccoli & Anchovy Sauce

Serves 4

INGREDIENTS

1 lb 2 oz/500 g broccoli
14 oz/400 g dried orecchiette
5 tbsp olive oil

2 large garlic cloves, crushed
1¾ oz/50 g canned anchovy
 fillets in oil, drained and
 finely chopped

2¼ oz/60 g Parmesan cheese
2¼ oz/60 g romano cheese
salt and pepper

1 Bring 2 pans of lightly salted water to a boil. Chop the broccoli florets and stems into small, bite-size pieces. Add the broccoli to one pan and cook until very tender. Drain and set aside.

2 Put the pasta in the other pan of boiling water and cook for 10–12 minutes, or according to the instructions on the packet, until al dente.

3 Meanwhile, heat the olive oil in a large pan over medium heat. Add the garlic and cook for 3 minutes, stirring, without letting it brown. Add the chopped anchovies to the oil and cook for 3 minutes, stirring and mashing with a wooden spoon to break them up. Finely grate the Parmesan and romano cheeses.

4 Drain the pasta, add to the pan of anchovies, and stir. Add the broccoli and stir to mix together well.

5 Add the grated Parmesan and romano cheeses to the pasta and stir constantly over medium-high heat, until the cheeses melt and the pasta and broccoli are coated.

6 Adjust the seasoning to taste—the anchovies and cheeses are salty, so you will only need to add pepper, if anything. Spoon into bowls or put out on plates and serve the pasta at once.

VARIATION

Add dried chili flakes to taste with the garlic in step 3, if you want. If you have difficulty in finding orecchiette, try using pasta bows instead.

Linguine with Pesto Sauce

Serves 4; makes about 1¼ cups sauce

INGREDIENTS

14 oz/400 g dried or fresh
    linguine
freshly grated Parmesan cheese,
    to serve (optional)

PESTO SAUCE
5½ oz/150 g Parmesan cheese
3 garlic cloves, or to taste
3 cups fresh basil leaves

5 tbsp pine nuts
⅔ cup fruity extra-virgin olive oil
salt and pepper

1 To make the pesto sauce, cut the rind off the Parmesan and finely grate the cheese. Set aside. Cut each garlic clove in half lengthwise and use the tip of a knife to lift out the green core, which can have a bitter flavor if the cloves are old. Coarsely chop the garlic.

2 Rinse the basil leaves and pat dry with paper towels. Put the basil in a food processor and add the pine nuts, grated cheese, chopped garlic, and olive oil. Process for about 30 seconds, just until well blended.

3 Add pepper and extra salt to taste, but cautiously—remember, the cheese is salty. Cover with plastic wrap and chill for up to 5 days.

4 Bring a large pan of water to a boil. Add ½ teaspoon salt and the linguine and cook according to the packet instructions. Drain well, reserving a few tablespoons of cooking water.

5 Return the linguine to the pan over low heat and stir in the sauce. Toss until well coated and the sauce is heated through. Stir in a couple of tablespoons of the reserved cooking water if the sauce seems too thick. Serve at once with grated Parmesan for sprinkling over the top, if desired.

VARIATIONS

Blanched almonds can be used instead of pine nuts. To make a creamy dip to serve with sliced zucchini and bell pepper strips, stir 4 tablespoons of the pesto sauce into 4 tablespoons of thick, plain yogurt.

Spaghetti with Corsican Clam Sauce

Serves 4

INGREDIENTS

14 oz/400 g dried or fresh
   spaghetti
salt and pepper

CORSICAN CLAM SAUCE
2 lb/900 g clams in their shells

4 tbsp olive oil
3 large garlic cloves, crushed
pinch of dried chili flakes
   (optional)
2 lb/900 g tomatoes, skinned and
   chopped, with juices reserved

2¼ oz/60 g Flavored Olives (see
   page 172) of your choice, or
   plain green or black olives,
   pitted and chopped
1 tbsp chopped fresh oregano,
   or ½ tsp dried

1 Soak the clams in a bowl of lightly salted water for 30 minutes. Rinse them under cold running water and lightly scrub to remove any sand from the shells.

2 Discard any broken clams or open clams that do not shut when firmly tapped with the back of a knife. This indicates that they are dead and could cause food poisoning if eaten. Soak the clams in a large bowl of water. Bring a large pan of lightly salted water to a boil.

3 Heat the oil in a skillet over medium heat. Add the garlic and chili flakes, if using, and cook, stirring, for about 2 minutes.

4 Stir in the tomatoes, olives, and oregano. Lower the heat and simmer, stirring frequently, until the tomatoes soften and start to break up. Cover and simmer for 10 minutes.

5 Meanwhile, cook the spaghetti in the pan of boiling water according to the instructions on the

packet, until cooked just al dente. Drain well, reserving about ½ cup of the cooking water. Keep the pasta warm.

6 Add the clams and reserved cooking liquid to the sauce and stir. Bring to a boil, stirring. Discard any clams that do not open, then transfer to a larger pan.

7 Add the pasta to the sauce and toss until well coated. Transfer the pasta to individual dishes. Serve immediately.

Pasta with Tuna & Lemon

Serves 4

INGREDIENTS

4 tbsp butter, diced
1¼ cups heavy cream
4 tbsp lemon juice
1 tbsp grated lemon rind
½ tsp anchovy extract

14 oz/400 g dried fusilli
7 oz/200 g canned tuna in olive
   oil, drained and flaked
salt and pepper

TO GARNISH
2 tbsp finely chopped
   fresh parsley
lemon zest, grated

1 Bring a large pan of lightly salted water to a boil. Melt the butter in a large skillet. Stir in the heavy cream and lemon juice and simmer, stirring, for about 2 minutes, until thickening.

2 Stir in the lemon rind and anchovy extract. Meanwhile, cook the pasta for 10–12 minutes or according to the instructions on the packet, until just al dente. Drain well.

3 Add the sauce to the pasta and toss until well coated. Add the tuna and gently toss until well blended but not too broken up.

4 Season to taste with salt and pepper. Transfer to a serving platter and garnish with the parsley and lemon zest. Grind some pepper over the dish before serving.

COOK'S TIP

As an alternative, use the thin, twist-shape pasta, casareccia, instead.

VARIATION

For a vegetarian version, omit the tuna and anchovy extract. Add 5½ oz/150 g pitted olives instead. For extra "kick" add a pinch of dried chili flakes to the sauce instead of the anchovy extract.

Vegetables & Side Salads

The fresh produce from the Mediterranean is some of the most luscious and flavorful in the world. Slowly ripened under the hot Mediterranean sun, eggplants, zucchini, bell peppers, and tomatoes look so marvelous you can almost taste them with your eyes.

With such full flavors, you'll find the vegetable dishes are not complicated. For a Mediterranean touch, serve globe artichokes with a classic Hollandaise sauce flavored with blood-orange juice. Or, for another simple recipe, savor Fava Beans with Feta & Lemon—delicious served hot or cold. Char-Grilled Vegetable Platter makes the most of fresh produce at its peak, while slow cook stews, such as the classic Ratatouille, enhance the flavors of vegetables that are starting to pass their prime.

Salads feature prominently in Mediterranean meals, and there can't be many dishes more typically Mediterranean than Roasted Bell Pepper Salad, or Mozzarella & Cherry Tomato Salad. Both have simple dressings and they make ideal accompaniments or appetizers. And, at any time of the year, it's difficult to beat Panzanella, the Italian salad based on leftover bread and made into a colorful medley with refreshing tomatoes, cucumbers, and bell peppers.

Char-Grilled Vegetable Platter

Serves 4–6

INGREDIENTS

4 lb 8 oz/2 kg mixed fresh
    vegetables, such as eggplants,
    endive, zucchini, fennel, bell
    peppers, scallions

garlic-flavored olive oil
salt and pepper

fresh basil leaves, to garnish

1 Prepare the vegetables as necessary. Trim the ends of the eggplants and cut into ¼ inch/5 mm slices. Cut each head of endive in half lengthwise.

2 Trim the ends from the zucchini and cut the zucchini into ¼ inch/5 mm slices. Remove the fronds from the fennel and slice thickly across the grain.

3 Cut the bell peppers into quarters, then remove the cores and seeds. Trim the top green parts of the scallions, and cut in half lengthwise if large.

4 As each vegetable is prepared, put it in a large bowl, drizzle with the garlic oil, and season lightly with salt and pepper. Using your hands, toss the vegetables together so they are lightly coated with oil; the vegetables should not be dripping in oil.

5 Heat a large, ridged cast-iron skillet over high heat. Lightly brush with oil. Add a batch of vegetables—enough to fit in the pan in a single layer. Cook the vegetables on one side over medium-high heat until they are starting to turn limp.

6 Brush the half-cooked vegetables with a little more oil, then turn them. Continue cooking until they are tender—the exact cooking times will depend on the age and thickness of the vegetables. Transfer to a large platter and repeat with the remaining vegetables.

7 While still hot, sprinkle the vegetables with salt and pepper. Garnish with basil leaves and serve.

Ratatouille

Serves 4

INGREDIENTS

1 large eggplant, about 10½ oz/300 g	1 lb 12 oz/800 g canned chopped tomatoes	tied in a 3 inch/7.5 cm piece of celery
5 tbsp olive oil	1 tsp sugar	salt and pepper
2 large onions, thinly sliced	1 bouquet garni of 2 sprigs fresh thyme, 2 large sprigs parsley, 1 sprig basil, and 1 bay leaf,	fresh basil leaves, to garnish
2 large garlic cloves, crushed		
4 zucchini, sliced		

1 Coarsely chop the eggplant, then place in a colander. Sprinkle with salt and let drain for 30 minutes. Rinse well; pat the pieces dry.

2 Heat the oil in a large, heavy-bottomed flameproof casserole over medium heat. Add the onions, lower the heat and cook, stirring frequently, for 10 minutes.

3 Add the garlic and continue to cook for 2 minutes until the onions are very tender, and just lightly browned.

4 Add the eggplant, zucchini, tomatoes and their juice, the sugar, bouquet garni, and salt and pepper to taste. Bring to a boil, then lower the heat to very low, cover, and simmer for 30 minutes.

5 Adjust the seasoning. Remove and discard the bouquet garni. Garnish the vegetable stew with basil leaves and serve.

COOK'S TIP

This is equally good served hot, at room temperature, or chilled. To make a vegetarian meal, serve it over cooked couscous (see page 80), or with Green Tabbouleh (see page 166).

Artichokes with Sauce Maltaise

Serves 4

INGREDIENTS

4 large globe artichokes	SAUCE MALTAISE	3 tbsp water
2 lemon slices	1 blood orange	3 egg yolks
	¾ cup butter	salt and pepper
	2–3 tbsp lemon juice	

1 To prepare the globe artichokes, bring lightly salted water to a boil in a pan large enough to hold the 4 artichokes upright. Add the lemon slices. Break off the stems and trim the bottoms of the artichokes so they are flat and will sit upright on a plate.

2 Put the artichokes in the pan and place a heatproof plate on top. Lower the heat and simmer for 20–25 minutes, until you can easily pull a leaf out.

3 Meanwhile, make the sauce. Finely grate the rind from the orange and squeeze 2 tablespoons orange juice. Put the butter in a pan over medium heat and melt, skimming the surface.

4 Put 2 tablespoons of the lemon juice, the water, and salt and pepper in a bowl set over a pan of simmering water, making sure the bottom of the bowl does not touch the water. Whisk until heated.

5 Whisk in the egg yolks, until blended and warmed through. Add the hot butter in a steady stream, whisking constantly until a thick, smooth sauce forms.

6 Stir in the orange rind and juice. Adjust the seasoning, adding extra lemon juice if necessary. Remove from the heat.

7 Drain the artichokes. Place each on a plate with a ramekin of the Sauce Maltaise.

COOK'S TIP

Pull out the leaves, starting with the outer layer; work inward, until you get to the inedible purple leaves. Dip the bottom of each leaf into the creamy sauce and scrape off the fleshy part with your teeth. Cut off the central core of leaves and the hairy choke to reveal the delicious bottom, that can be cut with a knife and fork.

Baked Eggplant Gratin

Serves 4–6

INGREDIENTS

1 large eggplant, about 1 lb 12 oz/800 g	3 oz/85 g Parmesan cheese	good-quality canned tomato sauce for pasta
salt	olive oil	salt and pepper
10½ oz/300 g mozzarella cheese	1 cup Slow-Cooked Tomato Sauce (see page 192), or	

1 Trim the ends from the eggplant and, using a sharp knife, cut it into ¼ inch/5 mm slices crosswise. Arrange the slices in a single layer on a large plate, sprinkle with salt, and set aside for 30 minutes to drain.

2 Meanwhile, drain and grate the mozzarella cheese and finely grate the Parmesan cheese. Set aside.

3 Rinse the eggplant slices and pat dry with paper towels. Lightly brush a cookie sheet with olive oil and arrange the eggplant slices in a single layer. Brush the tops with olive oil.

4 Roast in a preheated oven at 400°F/200°C for 5 minutes. Using tongs, turn the slices, then brush with a little more oil, and bake for another 5 minutes, or until the eggplant is cooked through and tender. Do not turn off the oven.

5 Spread 1 tablespoon olive oil over the bottom of a gratin dish or other ovenproof serving dish. Add a layer of eggplant slices, about a quarter of the tomato sauce, and top with a quarter of the mozzarella. Season to taste with salt and pepper.

6 Continue layering until all the ingredients are used, ending with a layer of sauce. Sprinkle the Parmesan over the top. Bake in the oven for 30 minutes until bubbling. Let stand for 5 minutes before serving.

Imam Bayildi

Serves 4

INGREDIENTS

2 eggplants, about 10½ oz/
    300 g each
5 tbsp olive oil
2 large onions, finely chopped
2 large garlic cloves, crushed
1 lb 12 oz/800 g canned
    chopped tomatoes

3 tbsp raisins
3 tbsp finely chopped fresh
    flat-leaf parsley
finely grated rind of
    ½ unwaxed lemon
2 tbsp lemon juice
½ tsp ground cinnamon

½ tsp ground cumin
pinch of cayenne pepper
salt and pepper
fresh flat-leaf parsley sprigs,
    to garnish

1 Cut each eggplant in half lengthwise. Using a knife, scoop out the flesh from each half, leaving a ¼ inch/5 mm shell all around. Set the shells aside.

2 Finely chop the eggplant flesh, place in a colander, sprinkle with salt, and let drain for 30 minutes. Rinse and pat dry.

3 Heat 3 tablespoons of the olive oil in a large skillet. Add the onions and cook, stirring frequently, over medium-high heat until softened. Add the garlic and continue cooking for another 2 minutes, stirring.

4 Add the tomatoes, eggplant flesh, raisins, parsley, lemon rind, lemon juice, cinnamon, cumin, and cayenne, then season with salt and pepper to taste. Simmer for 20 minutes, stirring occasionally, until the mixture has thickened.

5 Spoon the mixture into the eggplant shells, mounding it up slightly. Place the filled shells in an ovenproof dish and add the remaining olive oil.

6 Cover the dish with foil. Roast in a preheated oven at 350°F/180°C for 45–50 minutes until the eggplant shells are tender and the filling is hot. Serve hot, or let cool, then chill until required. Garnish with sprigs of parsley.

Sweet & Sour Zucchini

Serves 4-6

INGREDIENTS

1 lb 2 oz/500 g zucchini
3 tbsp olive oil
1 large garlic clove,
   finely chopped
3 tbsp red or white wine vinegar

3 tbsp water
6-8 anchovy fillets, canned
   or salted
3 tbsp pine nuts
1¼ oz/35 g raisins

salt and pepper
fresh flat-leaf parsley sprigs,
   to garnish

1 Trim the ends from the zucchini, then use a sharp knife to cut them into long, thin strips. Heat the oil in a large skillet over medium heat. Add the garlic and cook, stirring, for about 2 minutes.

2 Add the zucchini and cook, stirring, until they just start to turn brown. Add the vinegar and water, cover, and simmer for 10 minutes, stirring constantly.

3 Meanwhile, drain the anchovies if canned, or rinse if they are salted.

Coarsely chop, then use the back of a wooden spoon to mash them to a paste.

4 Stir the anchovies, pine nuts, and raisins into the pan. Increase the heat and stir until the zucchini are bathed in a thin sauce and are tender. Adjust the seasoning, remembering that the anchovies are very salty.

5 Either serve at once, or let cool completely and serve at room temperature garnished with fresh flat-leaf parsley sprigs.

VARIATION

Replace ordinary raisins with golden raisins. Add a little grated lemon or orange zest for zing.

Deep-Fried Zucchini

Serves 4

INGREDIENTS

5 tbsp cornstarch	⅔ cup water	fresh herb sprigs, such as basil,
1 tsp salt	2 lb/900 g zucchini	flat-leaf parsley, or sage,
pinch of cayenne pepper, or	vegetable oil, for cooking	to garnish
to taste	sea salt, to serve	

1 Sift the cornstarch, salt, and cayenne pepper into a large mixing bowl and make a well in the center. Pour in the water and beat until just blended to make a thin batter. The batter may have a few lumps but this does not matter. Set aside to rest for 20 minutes.

2 Meanwhile, cut the zucchini into ¼ inch/ 5 mm slices. Heat the oil in a deep skillet or deep-fat fryer to 375°F/190°C or until a cube of bread sizzles in 20 seconds.

3 Stir the batter. Working in batches, put some zucchini slices in the batter and stir around until coated. Using a slotted spoon, remove the slices from the batter, shaking off the excess.

4 Drop the coated zucchini slices into the hot fat and cook for about 45–60 seconds, or until just golden brown on each side. Immediately remove from the fat and drain well on crumpled paper towels. Sprinkle with sea salt and keep warm if not serving straight away.

5 Repeat this process with the remaining slices. You can serve them garnished with a variety of herbs, according to what is available.

COOK'S TIP

It is important to get the fat to the correct temperature, otherwise the cooked zucchini will be soggy.

VARIATION

Cook red onion rings coated with the batter.

Braised Fennel

Serves 4–6

INGREDIENTS

2 lemon slices

2 or 3 bulbs fennel, depending
on size

1½ tbsp olive oil

3 tbsp butter

4 sprigs fresh thyme, or
½ tbsp dried

¾ cup chicken or vegetable stock

1 cup freshly grated Parmesan
cheese

pepper

1 Bring a large pan of water to a boil and add the lemon slices. Trim the fennel bulbs and slice each one lengthwise. Put them in the boiling water, bring back to a boil, and simmer for about 8 minutes, until almost tender. Drain well.

2 Put the oil and butter in a flameproof casserole and melt over medium heat. Swirl the melted mixture around so that the bottom and sides of the casserole are well coated.

3 Add the fennel slices and stir until coated. Add the thyme and pepper to taste. Pour in the stock. Sprinkle the cheese over the top.

4 Bake in a preheated oven at 400°F/200°C for 25–30 minutes until the fennel has absorbed the stock and is tender, and the cheese has melted and become golden brown. Serve at once.

COOK'S TIP

This is an ideal way to serve older fennel bulbs.

Mixed Vegetables à la Grecque

Serves 4–6

INGREDIENTS

9 oz/250 g small pickling onions
9 oz/250 g mushrooms
9 oz/250 g zucchini
2 cups water
5 tbsp olive oil
2 tbsp lemon juice
2 strips lemon rind

2 large garlic cloves,
    thinly sliced
½ Spanish onion,
    finely chopped
1 bay leaf
15 black peppercorns,
    lightly crushed

10 coriander seeds,
    lightly crushed
pinch of dried oregano
finely chopped fresh flat-leaf
    parsley or cilantro, to garnish
focaccia, to serve

1 Heat a kettle of water until the water boils. Put the small onions in a heatproof bowl and pour boiling water over them to cover. Let stand for 2 minutes, then drain. Peel and set aside.

2 Trim the mushroom stems; cut the mushrooms into halves or quarters if they are large, or leave whole. Trim the ends from the zucchini, cut off strips of the peel for a decorative finish, then cut into ¼ inch/5 mm slices. Set both aside.

3 Put the water, olive oil, lemon juice and rind, garlic, Spanish onion, bay leaf, peppercorns, coriander seeds, and oregano in a pan over high heat and bring to a boil. Lower the heat and simmer for 15 minutes.

4 Add the small onions and continue to simmer for 5 minutes. Add the mushrooms and zucchini and simmer for another 2 minutes. Using a slotted spoon, transfer all the vegetables to a heatproof dish.

5 Turn up the heat to return the liquid to a boil, and boil until reduced to about 6 tablespoons. Pour over the vegetables and set aside to cool completely.

6 Cover the dish with plastic wrap and chill for at least 12 hours.

7 To serve, put the vegetables and cooking liquid in a serving dish and scatter the fresh herbs over them. Serve with chunks of focaccia bread.

Glazed Baby Onions

Serves 4–6

INGREDIENTS

1 lb 2 oz/500 g pearl onions
2 tbsp olive oil
2 large garlic cloves, crushed
1¼ cups vegetable or
   chicken stock

1 tbsp fresh thyme leaves
1 tbsp light brown sugar
2 tbsp red wine vinegar
about ½ tbsp best-quality
   balsamic vinegar

salt and pepper
fresh thyme sprigs, to garnish

1 Bring a kettle of water to a boil. Put the onions in a large heatproof bowl, pour over enough boiling water to cover, and let stand for 2 minutes. Drain well.

2 Using a small knife and your fingers, peel off the skins, which should slip off.

3 Heat the olive oil in a large skillet over medium-high heat. Add the onions and cook, stirring, for about 8 minutes until they are golden on all sides.

4 Add the garlic and cook for 2 minutes, stirring. Add the stock, thyme leaves, sugar, and red wine vinegar, stirring until the sugar has completely dissolved.

5 Bring to a boil, then lower the heat and simmer for 10 minutes, or until the onions are tender when you pierce them with the tip of a knife and the cooking liquid is reduced to a thick syrupy glaze.

6 Stir in ½ tablespoon balsamic vinegar. Season to taste with salt and pepper

and extra vinegar, if desired. Transfer to a serving dish and serve hot or cold, garnished with fresh thyme sprigs.

VARIATION

For extra texture, stir in 2 tablespoons toasted pine nuts just before serving. Do not add them earlier or they will become soft.

Spiced Lentils with Spinach

Serves 4–6

INGREDIENTS

2 tbsp olive oil
1 large onion, finely chopped
1 large garlic clove, crushed
½ tbsp ground cumin
½ tsp ground ginger
1¾ cups Puy lentils

about 2½ cups vegetable or
   chicken stock
3½ oz/100 g baby spinach leaves
2 tbsp fresh mint leaves
1 tbsp fresh cilantro leaves
1 tbsp fresh flat-leaf parsley

freshly squeezed lemon juice
salt and pepper
grated lemon zest, to garnish

1 Heat the olive oil in a large skillet over medium-high heat. Add the onion and cook for about 6 minutes. Stir in the garlic, cumin, and ginger and continue cooking, stirring occasionally, until the onion just starts to brown.

2 Stir in the lentils. Pour in enough stock to cover the lentils by 1 inch/2.5 cm and bring to a boil. Lower the heat and simmer for 20 minutes, or according to the package instructions, until the lentils are tender.

3 Meanwhile, thoroughly rinse the spinach leaves in several changes of cold water and shake dry. Finely chop the mint, cilantro, and parsley leaves.

4 If there isn't any stock left in the pan, add a little extra. Add the spinach and stir through until it just wilts. Stir in the mint, cilantro, and parsley. Adjust the seasoning, adding lemon juice and salt and pepper. Transfer to a serving bowl and serve, garnished with lemon zest.

COOK'S TIP

This recipe uses green lentils from Puy in France because they are good at keeping their shape even after long cooking. You can, however, also use orange or brown lentils, but it is necessary to watch them while they cook or they will quickly turn to a mush.

Borlotti Beans in Tomato Sauce

Serves 4–6

INGREDIENTS

1 lb 5 oz/600 g fresh borlotti
    beans, in shells
4 large leaves fresh sage, torn
1 tbsp olive oil

1 large onion, finely sliced
1¼ cups Slow-Cooked Tomato
    Sauce (see page 192), or
    good-quality canned tomato
    sauce for pasta

salt and pepper
extra shredded sage leaves,
    to garnish

1 Shell the borlotti beans. Bring a pan of water to a boil, add the beans and torn sage leaves, and simmer for about 12 minutes, or until tender. Drain and set aside.

2 Heat the oil in a large skillet over medium heat. Add the onion and cook, stirring occasionally, for about 5 minutes until the onion is soft but not brown. Add the cooked borlotti beans and the torn sage leaves, then stir in the tomato sauce.

3 Increase the heat and bring to a boil, stirring. Lower the heat, partially cover, and simmer for about 10 minutes, or until the sauce has slightly reduced.

4 Adjust the seasoning, transfer to a serving bowl and serve hot, garnished with fresh sage leaves.

VARIATION

If fresh borlotti beans are unavailable, use canned instead. Drain and rinse, then add with the sage and tomato sauce in step 2.

Fava Beans with Feta & Lemon

Serves 4–6

INGREDIENTS

1 lb 2 oz/500 g shelled fava
    beans
4 tbsp extra-virgin olive oil

1 tbsp lemon juice
1 tbsp finely chopped fresh dill,
    plus a little extra for
    garnishing

2¼ oz/60 g feta cheese, drained
    and diced
salt and pepper
lemon wedges, to serve

1 Bring a pan of water to a boil. Throw in the fava beans and cook for about 2 minutes until tender. Drain the beans well.

2 When the beans are cool enough to handle, remove and discard the outer skins, to reveal the bright green beans underneath (see Cook's Tip). Put the peeled beans in a serving bowl.

3 Stir together the olive oil and lemon juice, then season to taste with salt and pepper. Pour over the warm beans, add the dill, and stir together. Adjust the seasoning, if necessary.

4 If serving hot, toss with the feta cheese and sprinkle with extra dill. Alternatively, let cool, then chill until required. Remove from the refrigerator 10 minutes before serving, season, then sprinkle with the feta and extra dill. Serve with lemon wedges.

COOK'S TIP

It's worth using a good-quality olive oil, because it will make all the difference to the flavor of the finished dish.

COOK'S TIP

If you are lucky enough to have very young fava beans at the start of the season, it isn't necessary to remove the outer skin.

Mozzarella & Cherry Tomato Salad

Serves 4–6

INGREDIENTS

1 lb/450 g cherry tomatoes

4 scallions

½ cup extra-virgin olive oil

2 tbsp best-quality balsamic
 vinegar

7 oz/200 g buffalo mozzarella
 (see Cook's Tip), cut into cubes

½ oz/15 g fresh flat-leaf parsley

1 oz/25 g fresh basil leaves

salt and pepper

1 Using a sharp knife, cut the tomatoes in half and put in a large bowl. Trim the scallions and finely chop the green and white parts, then add to the bowl.

2 Pour in the olive oil and balsamic vinegar and use your hands to toss together. Season with salt and pepper, add the mozzarella, and toss again. Cover and chill the salad for 4 hours.

3 Remove from the refrigerator 10 minutes before serving. Finely chop the parsley and add to the salad. Tear the basil leaves over the salad and toss all the ingredients together again to mix well. Adjust the seasoning and serve.

COOK'S TIP

For the best flavor, buy buffalo mozzarella— mozzarella di bufala—rather than the factory-made cow's milk version. This salad would also look good made with bocconcini, which are small balls of mozzarella. Look for these in Italian delicatessens.

VARIATIONS

Replace the cherry tomatoes with Oven-Dried Tomatoes (see page 174), or drained sun-dried tomatoes soaked in oil.

To make this salad more substantial, stir in 14 oz/400 g cooked and cooled pasta shapes. When the pasta is al dente, drain well, toss with 1 tablespoon olive oil, and cool completely before adding to the tomatoes and mozzarella in step 2.

Roasted Bell Pepper Salad

Serves 4

INGREDIENTS

4–6 large, red, yellow, and/or
orange bell peppers
2 scallions, trimmed

LEMON-PARSLEY VINAIGRETTE
6 tbsp extra-virgin olive oil
1½ tbsp freshly squeezed
lemon juice

2 tbsp finely chopped fresh
flat-leaf parsley
salt and pepper

1 To make the dressing, put the oil, lemon juice, and parsley in a screw-top jar and shake until well blended. Add salt and pepper to taste. Set the dressing aside.

2 Slice the tops off the bell peppers, then cut the body of each into quarters or thirds, depending on the size. Remove the cores and seeds—the flatter the pieces are, the easier it is to cook them evenly.

3 Finely slice the scallions crosswise.

4 Place the bell pepper pieces on a broiler rack

under a preheated hot broiler and broil for about 10 minutes, or until the skins are charred and the flesh is just softened.

5 Using tongs, remove each piece as it is ready. Immediately place in a bowl and cover with plastic wrap. Set aside for 20 minutes to allow the steam to loosen the thin outer skins.

6 When they are cool, carefully use a small, sharp knife (or your fingers) to remove all of the skins from the bell peppers, then slice the bell pepper flesh into long, thin strips.

7 Arrange the bell pepper strips on a serving platter. Shake the dressing again, then pour over the salad. Scatter the scallions over the top. Serve at once with crusty bread, or cover and chill until required.

VARIATION

For a party, marinate small, cooked shrimp in the dressing and scatter them over the salad. Other ingredients you can add to the salad include capers, anchovies, pitted and sliced green or black olives, and finely grated lemon zest.

Stuffed Tomato Salad

Makes 4

INGREDIENTS

about 1½ oz/40 g cucumber, finely diced	5 scallions, trimmed and sliced	small handful of basil leaves, plus extra for garnishing
3 large eggs	12 oz/350 g canned tuna in olive oil, drained	salt and pepper
4 extra-large tomatoes, about 10½ oz/300 g each	1–2 tbsp mayonnaise	
	squeeze of lemon juice	

1 Put the cucumber in a plastic strainer, sprinkle with salt, and drain for about 30 minutes.

2 Meanwhile, bring a pan of water to a boil, add the eggs, and cook for 12 minutes. Drain and place under running cold water to stop the cooking process.

3 Shell the eggs and chop the yolks and whites separately. Rinse the cucumber and pat dry with paper towels.

4 Working with one tomato at a time, slice off the top and use a small spoon to scoop out the insides; reserve the insides. Drain the tomatoes upside-down on paper towels. Chop the reserved scooped-out insides and drain.

5 Put the chopped tomato in a bowl and add the chopped cucumber, sliced scallions, all the egg yolks, and most of the egg white. Reserve a little egg white to sprinkle over the tops. Flake in the tuna.

6 Add 1 tablespoon of the mayonnaise, the lemon juice, and salt and pepper to taste. Stir together and add a little more mayonnaise if the mixture is too thick. Tear in the basil leaves and stir together. Adjust the seasoning, if necessary.

7 Spoon the filling into the hollowed-out tomatoes. Sprinkle the tops with the reserved egg white. Cover with plastic wrap and chill until required, but not for more than 3 hours or the filling will become soggy. Garnish with basil leaves before serving.

Panzanella

Serves 4

INGREDIENTS

9 oz/250 g stale Herb Focaccia
    (see page 206) or ciabatta or
    French bread
4 large, vine-ripened tomatoes
extra-virgin olive oil

4 red, yellow, and/or orange
    bell peppers
3½ oz/100 g cucumber
1 large, red onion, finely chopped
8 canned anchovy fillets, drained
    and chopped

2 tbsp capers in brine, rinsed
    and patted dry
about 4 tbsp red wine vinegar
about 2 tbsp best-quality
    balsamic vinegar
salt and pepper
fresh basil leaves, to garnish

1 Cut the bread into 1 inch/2.5 cm cubes and place in a large bowl. Working over a plate to catch any juices, quarter the tomatoes; reserve the juices. Using a teaspoon, scoop out the cores and seeds, then finely chop the flesh. Add to the bread cubes.

2 Drizzle 5 tablespoons of olive oil over the mixture and toss with your hands until well coated. Pour in the reserved tomato juice and toss again. Cover and set aside for about 30 minutes.

3 Meanwhile, cut the bell peppers in half and remove the cores and seeds. Place on a broiler rack under a preheated hot broiler and broil for 10 minutes, or until the skins are charred and the flesh softened. Place in a plastic bag, seal, and set aside for 20 minutes to let the steam loosen the skins. Remove the skins, then finely chop the bell peppers.

4 Cut the cucumber in half lengthwise, then cut each half into 3 strips lengthwise. Using a teaspoon, scoop out

and discard the seeds. Dice the cucumber.

5 Add the onion, peppers, cucumber, anchovy fillets, and capers to the bread, and toss together. Sprinkle with the red wine and balsamic vinegars and season to taste with salt and pepper. Drizzle with extra olive oil or vinegar if necessary, but be cautious that the bread does not become too greasy or soggy. Sprinkle the fresh basil leaves over the salad and serve the dish at once.

Green Tabbouleh

Serves 4

INGREDIENTS

1¼ cups bulgar wheat	½ oz/15 g fresh flat-leaf parsley	about 2 tbsp garlic-flavored
7 oz/200 g cucumber	1 unwaxed lemon	olive oil
6 scallions		salt and pepper

1 Bring a kettle of water to a boil. Place the bulgar wheat in a heatproof bowl, pour 2½ cups boiling water over, and cover with an upturned plate. Set aside for at least 20 minutes until the wheat absorbs the water and becomes tender.

2 While the wheat is soaking, cut the cucumber in half lengthwise and then cut each half into 3 strips lengthwise. Using a teaspoon, scoop out and discard the seeds. Chop the cucumber strips into bite-size pieces. Put the cucumber pieces in a large serving bowl.

3 Trim the top of the green parts of each of the scallions, then cut each in half lengthwise. Finely chop and add to the cucumber.

4 Place the parsley on a cutting board and sprinkle with salt. Using a cook's knife, very finely chop both the leaves and stems. Add these to the bowl containing the cucumber and onions. Finely grate the lemon rind into the bowl.

5 When the bulgar wheat is cool enough to handle, either squeeze out any excess water with your hands or press out the water through a strainer. Add the bulgar wheat to the other ingredients in the bowl.

6 Cut the lemon in half and squeeze the juice of one half over the salad. Add 2 tablespoons of the garlic-flavored oil and stir all the ingredients together. Adjust the seasoning with salt and pepper to taste and extra lemon juice or oil if needed. Cover and chill the tabbouleh until required.

COOK'S TIP

Serve as a meze with dips such as Hummus (see page 8).

Radicchio & Bacon Salad

Serves 4

INGREDIENTS

1 lb 5 oz/600 g radicchio, 3 or 4 heads, depending on size
about 3 tbsp olive oil

1 large garlic clove, crushed
10½ oz/300 g bacon pieces
about 1 tbsp best-quality balsamic vinegar

salt and pepper
fresh basil leaves, to garnish

1 Remove enough of the outer leaves from the radicchio heads to line 4 individual plates. Cut the remaining radicchio across the grain into ¼ inch/5 mm slices.

2 Heat 3 tablespoons of oil in a large skillet over medium-high heat. Add the garlic clove and cook, stirring, for 2 minutes. Remove from the pan with a slotted spoon.

3 Add the bacon pieces and cook for about 5 minutes, or until they are cooked through and brown on the outside. Do not overcook.

4 Add the shredded radicchio to the pan and toss for about 30 seconds, just until it is heated through and starting to become limp but not long enough to become soggy (see Cook's Tip).

5 Add 1 tablespoon of the balsamic vinegar and toss again. Drizzle with extra oil or vinegar, if desired. Add salt and pepper to taste. Spoon the hot salad on to the radicchio-lined plates and garnish with fresh basil leaves. Serve at once.

COOK'S TIP

It is important not to overcook the radicchio in step 4 or it will become gray. Just warm it through.

Accompaniments

You'll find a collection of diverse recipes in this chapter. These are the recipes that help you add a Mediterranean flavor to any meal you serve. Use the Mediterranean Fish Stock, for example, when you want to make a soup with subtle, authentic flavoring, or make Flavored Olives, preserved in olive oil, to have at hand when friends stop by for a drink.

Wherever you live, the chances are that there will be a glut of tomatoes at some time. Try the Mediterranean trick of slow-roasting the tomatoes, then storing them in olive oil so that you can add their fresh flavor to pasta sauces and casseroles throughout the year. Or make large batches of Slow-Cooked Tomato Sauce and stock the freezer.

The breads in this chapter are flavored with some of the region's most distinctive flavorings – Herb Focaccia makes a good accompaniment to any meal; Olive Rolls have so much flavor that they can be munched on their own or made into delicious sandwiches; and Sesame Breadsticks, soft on the inside with a crisp exterior, disappear in a flash when served with one of the creamy dips.

Greeks, Cypriots, and Turks, in particular, enjoy thick, creamy yogurt with just about every meal of the day. In some parts of the world this is readily available in supermarkets, but if you can't get it, follow the recipe in this chapter for Greek Strained Yogurt.

Flavored Olives

Each fills a 2 cup preserving jar

INGREDIENTS

fresh herb sprigs, such as cilantro,
  flat-leaf parsley, or thyme,
  to serve

PROVENCAL-STYLE OLIVES
3 dried red chilies
1 tsp black peppercorns
10½ oz/300 g black Niçoise olives
  in brine
2 lemon slices
1 tsp black mustard seeds
1 tbsp garlic-flavored olive oil
fruity extra-virgin olive oil

CATALAN-STYLE OLIVES
½ grilled red or orange bell pepper
  (see page 164)
5½ oz/150 g black olives in brine
5½ oz/150 g green pimento-
  stuffed olives in brine
1 tbsp capers in brine, rinsed
pinch of dried chili flakes, or
  to taste
4 tbsp coarsely chopped fresh
  cilantro leaves
1 bay leaf
fruity extra-virgin olive oil

CRACKED GREEK-STYLE OLIVES
½ large lemon
10½ oz/300 g kalamata olives
  in brine
4 sprigs fresh thyme
1 shallot, very finely chopped
1 tbsp fennel seeds, lightly
  crushed
1 tsp dried dill
fruity extra-virgin olive oil

---

1 To make the Provençal-style olives, place the dried red chilies and black peppercorns in a mortar and lightly crush. Drain and rinse the olives, then pat dry with paper towels. Put all the ingredients in a 2 cup preserving jar, pouring over enough olive oil to cover.

2 Seal the jar and leave for at least 10 days before serving, shaking the jar daily.

3 To make the Catalan-style olives, finely chop the bell pepper. Drain and rinse both types of olives, then pat dry with paper towels. Put all the ingredients into a 2 cup preserving jar, pouring over enough olive oil to cover. Seal and marinate as described in step 2.

4 To make the cracked Greek-style olives, cut the lemon into 4 slices, then cut each slice into wedges. Drain and rinse the olives, then pat them dry with paper towels.

5 Slice each olive lengthwise on one side down to the stone. Put all the ingredients in a 2 cup preserving jar, pouring over olive oil to cover. Seal and marinate as in step 2.

Oven-Dried Tomatoes

Makes enough to fill a 1 cup preserving jar

INGREDIENTS

2 lb 4 oz/1 kg large, juicy,
   full-flavored tomatoes

sea salt
extra-virgin olive oil

1 Using a sharp knife, cut each of the tomatoes into quarters lengthwise.

2 Using a teaspoon, scoop out the seeds and discard. If the tomatoes are large, cut each quarter in half lengthwise again.

3 Sprinkle sea salt in a roasting pan and arrange the tomato slices, skin-side down, on top. Roast in a preheated oven at 250°F/ 120°C for 2½ hours, or until the edges are just starting to look charred and the flesh is dry but still pliable. The exact roasting time and yield will depend on the size and juiciness of the tomatoes.

Check the tomatoes at 30-minute intervals after 1½ hours.

4 Remove the dried tomatoes from the pan and leave to cool completely. Put into a 1 cup preserving jar and pour over enough olive oil to cover. Seal tightly and store in the refrigerator where they will keep for up to 2 weeks.

COOK'S TIP

Serve these oven-dried tomatoes with slices of buffalo mozzarella: drizzle with olive oil and sprinkle with coarsely ground black pepper and finely torn basil leaves. Add a few slices of oven-roasted tomatoes to the ingredients in Slow-Cooked Tomato Sauce (see page 192) while the ingredients are simmering for extra depth of flavor. Add thin slices of these tomatoes to Salade Niçoise (see page 118), or Roasted Bell Pepper Salad (see page 160).

Preserved Citrus

Preserved Lemons: makes enough to fill an 8 cup preserving jar

INGREDIENTS

PRESERVED LEMONS
4 large, thin-skinned, unwaxed
    lemons
about 4 lb 8 oz/2 kg table salt
4 bay leaves

DRIED ORANGE RIND
1 large, unwaxed, sweet orange

1 To make the preserved lemons, rinse the lemons with warm water, then pat dry with paper towels. Stand a lemon on its stem end, then cut it into quarters without cutting all the way through. Repeat for all the lemons.

2 Spread a ¼ inch/5 mm layer of salt on the bottom of an 8 cup preserving jar with a nonmetallic lid. Add one of the lemons, cut-side up, pressing to open out the quarters. Add a bay leaf and enough salt to cover completely. Repeat the process to make 3 more layers.

3 Using a wooden spoon, press down on the lemons to release their juice. Cover with a layer of salt. Seal the jar and set aside for at least a month, turning the jar upside-down every day.

4 Pull out a lemon quarter when required and rinse well. To use, follow the specific recipe instructions – some recipes use the flesh as well as the rind, while others only use the rind.

5 To make the dried orange rind, use a small, serrated knife to cut the rind from a large orange. Aim to make a single spiral, starting from the top and working your way to the bottom.

6 Thread a needle with thin thread and stitch it through the orange rind to make a loop from which to hang the rind. Hang the rind from a hook in your kitchen until it is dry. Store in an airtight jar and use as required.

Candied Citrus Peel

Makes 60–80 pieces

INGREDIENTS

1 large, unwaxed, thick-skinned orange	1 large, unwaxed, thick-skinned lime	4½ oz/125 g best-quality dark chocolate, chopped (optional)
1 large, unwaxed, thick-skinned lemon	3 cups superfine sugar	
	1¼ cups water	

1 Cut the orange into quarters lengthwise and squeeze the juice into a cup to drink, or use in another recipe. Cut each quarter in half lengthwise to make 8 pieces in all.

2 Cut the fruit and pith away from the zest. If any of the pith remains on the zest, lay the knife almost flat on the white side of the rind and gently "saw" backward and forward to slice it off because it will make the zest taste bitter.

3 Repeat with the lemon and lime, only cutting the lime into quarters. Cut each piece into 3 or 4 thin strips to make 60–80 strips in total. Place the strips in a pan of water and boil for 30 seconds. Drain.

4 Dissolve the sugar in the water in a pan over a medium heat, stirring. Increase the heat and bring to a boil, without stirring. When the syrup becomes clear, turn the heat to its lowest setting.

5 Add the citrus strips, using a wooden spoon to push them in without stirring. Simmer in the syrup for 30 minutes, without stirring. Turn off the heat and set aside for at least 6 hours until completely cool.

6 Line a cookie sheet with foil. Skim off the thin crust on top of the syrup without stirring. Remove the citrus strips, one by one, from the syrup, shaking off any excess. Place the strips on the foil to cool.

7 If you want to dip the candied peel in chocolate, melt the chocolate. Working with one piece of candied peel at a time, dip the peel halfway into the chocolate. Return to the foil and leave to dry. Store in an airtight container.

Mediterranean Fish Stock

Makes about 8 cups

INGREDIENTS

2 lb 4 oz/1 kg fish bones
and trimmings
at least 6½ pints water
pinch of salt
4 large tomatoes

2 large bulbs fennel
2 large garlic cloves
1 leek
1 bouquet garni of 2 sprigs fresh
flat-leaf parsley and 1 sprig

fresh thyme, tied in a
3 inch/7.5 cm piece celery
½ cup dry white wine

1 Rinse the fish bones and trimmings under running cold water, wiping off any blood. Place them in a large, flameproof casserole or stockpot and pour over the water. Add a pinch of salt and heat until almost boiling with bubbles just breaking the surface, but do not let the liquid come to a boil.

2 Using a large spoon, skim the surface. Lower the heat to the lowest setting and simmer the stock, uncovered, for 30 minutes, skimming the surface as necessary to remove scum.

3 Meanwhile, chop the tomatoes, fennel, and garlic. Slice the leek, then chop the slices, and rinse well in a bowl of cold water.

4 Strain the fish stock from the pot into a large bowl and discard the solids.

5 Return the stock to the washed-out casserole or stockpot and add the vegetables, bouquet garni, and wine. Slowly bring to a boil, skimming the surface with a spoon as necessary.

6 Lower the heat, partially cover the casserole, and simmer for another 30 minutes, or until reduced to about 8 cups. Strain the stock into a large bowl and let cool. Store in a refrigerator until required.

COOK'S TIP

This will keep in the refrigerator, covered, for 2 days.

Greek Strained Yogurt

Makes about 2 cups

INGREDIENTS

2 lb 4 oz/1 kg plain yogurt
½ tsp salt, or to taste

OPTIONAL TOPPINGS
fruity extra-virgin olive oil
orange-blossom or lavender-
    flavored honey
finely grated lemon rind

coriander seeds, crushed
powdered paprika
fresh mint or cilantro, very
    finely chopped

1 Place a 50 x 30 inch/ 125 x 75 cm piece of muslin in a pan, cover with water, and bring to a boil. Remove the pan from the heat and, using a wooden spoon, lift out the muslin. Wearing rubber gloves, wring the cloth dry.

2 Fold the cloth into a double layer and use it to line a colander or strainer set over a large bowl. Put the yogurt in a bowl and stir in the salt. Spoon the yogurt into the center of the cloth.

3 Tie the cloth so that it is suspended above the bowl. If your sink is deep enough, gather up the corners of the cloth and tie it to the faucet. If not, lay a broom handle across 2 chairs and put the bowl between the chairs. Tie the cloth to the broom handle. Remove the colander or strainer and leave the yogurt to drain into the bowl for at least 12 hours.

4 Transfer the thickened, drained yogurt to a nylon strainer sitting over a bowl. Cover lightly with plastic

wrap and refrigerate for another 24 hours until soft and creamy. This yogurt will keep, refrigerated, for up to 5 days.

5 To serve, taste and add extra salt if needed. Spoon the yogurt into a bowl and sprinkle with the topping of your choice, or a combination of toppings.

Aioli

Makes about 1½ cups

INGREDIENTS

4 large garlic cloves, or to taste
pinch of sea salt
2 large egg yolks
1¼ cups extra-virgin olive oil
1–2 tbsp lemon juice, to taste
1 tbsp fresh white breadcrumbs
salt and pepper

CRUDITÉS (TO SERVE)
a selection of raw vegetables,
    such as sliced red bell
    peppers, zucchini slices,
    whole scallions, and
    tomatoes cut into wedges

a selection of blanched and
    cooled vegetables, such as
    baby artichoke hearts,
    cauliflower or broccoli florets,
    or green beans

1 Finely chop the garlic on a cutting board. Add the salt to the garlic and use the tip and broad side of a knife to work the garlic and salt into a smooth paste.

2 Transfer the garlic paste to a food processor. Add the egg yolks and process until well blended, stopping to scrape down the side of the bowl with a rubber spatula, if necessary.

3 With the motor running, slowly pour the olive oil in a steady stream through the feed tube, processing until the mixture forms a thick mayonnaise.

4 Add 1 tablespoon of the lemon juice and the fresh breadcrumbs and quickly process again. Taste and add more lemon juice if necessary. Season to taste with salt and pepper.

5 Place the aioli in a bowl, cover, and chill until ready to serve. This will keep for up to 7 days in the refrigerator. To serve as a dip, place the bowl of aioli on a large platter and surround with a selection of crudités.

COOK'S TIP

The amount of garlic in a traditional Provençal aioli is a matter of personal taste. Local cooks use 2 cloves per person as a rule of thumb, but this version is slightly milder, although still bursting with flavor.

Rouille

Makes about 6 oz/175 g

INGREDIENTS

2¼ oz/60 g day-old, country-style, white bread	2 small red chiles	1 tbsp tomato paste
2 large garlic cloves	pinch of salt	cayenne pepper (optional)
	3 tbsp extra-virgin olive oil	pepper

1 Cut the crusts off the bread. Put the bread in a bowl, pour over water to cover, and let soak for 30 seconds, or until soft. Squeeze the bread dry, reserving 2 tablespoons of the soaking liquid.

2 Coarsely chop the garlic and chiles. Put them in a mortar with a pinch of salt and pound with a pestle until they form a paste.

3 Add the paste to the squeezed bread, then continue working in the mortar until the ingredients blend together. Transfer to a bowl and slowly add the olive oil, beating constantly. If you find the mixture beginning to separate, add a little of the reserved soaking liquid and continue beating.

4 Add the tomato paste and cayenne pepper to taste. Adjust seasoning. Spread on croûtes and use to float on the surface of seafood soup.

COOK'S TIP

If the sauce appears to be separating after it has stood for a while, stir in 1 tablespoon hot water. If it appears too thin to spread on croûtes, beat in a little extra soaked bread.

VARIATION

For a smoother version, use a small food processor. Put the squeezed bread and chopped garlic and chiles in the food processor and blend. Add the olive oil and tomato paste and blend again until smooth. Adjust the seasoning.

Skordalia

Makes about 12 oz/350 g

INGREDIENTS

2¼ oz/60 g day-old bread,
  in one piece
1¼ cups unblanched almonds

4–6 large garlic cloves,
  coarsely chopped
²⁄₃ cup extra-virgin olive oil
2 tbsp white wine vinegar

salt and pepper
fresh cilantro or flat-leaf parsley
  sprigs, to garnish

1 Cut the crusts off the bread and tear the bread into small pieces. Put in a bowl, pour over enough water to cover, and let soak for 10–15 minutes. Squeeze the bread dry with your hands and set aside.

2 To blanch the almonds, bring a kettle of water to a boil. Put the almonds in a heatproof bowl and pour over enough boiling water to just cover. Let stand for 30 seconds, then drain. The skins should slide off easily.

3 Transfer the almonds and garlic to a food processor and process until finely chopped. Add the squeezed bread and process again until they are well blended.

4 With the motor running, slowly add the olive oil through the feed tube in a steady stream until a thick paste forms. Add the vinegar and process again. Season with salt and pepper to taste.

5 Transfer to a bowl, cover, and chill until required. This will keep in the refrigerator for up to 4 days. To serve, garnish with the fresh herb sprigs.

VARIATIONS

Many versions of this rustic sauce exist. For variety, replace the bread with 4 tablespoons well-drained canned cannellini or fava beans. You can replace the white wine vinegar with freshly squeezed lemon juice.

Fresh Tomato Sauce

Makes enough to fill two 2 cup jars

INGREDIENTS

2 lb 4 oz/1 kg juicy plum
  tomatoes
4–6 tbsp extra-virgin olive oil

2 tsp sugar
3 tbsp finely torn fresh basil or
  flat-leaf parsley

salt and pepper
pasta shapes, such as fusilli or
  shells, to serve (optional)

1 Bring a kettle of water to a boil. Cut a small X in the top of each tomato and place in 1 or 2 heatproof bowls. Pour over the boiling water and let stand for 1 minute, then drain. Work in batches if necessary

2 Peel off the skins and discard, working over a strainer placed over a bowl to catch and strain the tomato juices. Quarter all the tomatoes and remove the seeds. Coarsely dice the flesh into bite-size pieces.

3 Put the tomatoes and their juice in a bowl. Add 4 tablespoons of the olive oil, with the sugar and reserved tomato juice. Season with salt and pepper to taste. Gently stir together, adding a little more olive oil if it is too thick. Let the sauce stand for at least 30 minutes before using.

4 When ready to serve, stir in the fresh herbs. Serve with cooked pasta shapes.

COOK'S TIPS

When tomatoes are not at their peak, Slow-Cooked Tomato Sauce (see page 192) is a better option than fresh.

If you make the sauce in advance, cover and chill for up to 3 days. Twenty minutes before serving, remove from the refrigerator to allow the sauce to come to room temperature. Stir in the herbs just before serving.

Slow-Cooked Tomato Sauce

Makes about 2½ cups

INGREDIENTS

2 sprigs fresh parsley

2 sprigs fresh thyme

1 bay leaf

3 inch/7.5 cm piece of celery

2 lb 4 oz/1 kg plum tomatoes

2 tbsp olive oil

1 large garlic clove, crushed

3½ oz/100 g shallots, chopped

1¼ cups full-bodied red wine

2 strips freshly pared lemon rind

½ tsp sugar

salt and pepper

1 To make the bouquet garni, use a piece of kitchen string to tie the sprigs of parsley and thyme and the bay leaf in the piece of celery. Set the herbs aside.

2 Coarsely chop the tomatoes—it isn't necessary to remove the skins or seeds because this sauce will be processed in a food mill, which will result in a smooth texture.

3 Heat the olive oil in a deep skillet or pan with a lid. Add the garlic and shallots and cook for about

3 minutes, stirring with a wooden spoon, until they have softened.

4 Add the tomatoes, wine, bouquet garni, lemon rind, sugar, and salt and pepper to taste. Bring to a boil, stirring. Lower the heat, partially cover, and simmer the sauce very gently for 1 hour, or until most of the liquid has evaporated.

5 Remove the pan from the heat and let the sauce cool slightly. Remove the bouquet garni and process the sauce, including the

lemon rind, through a food mill, working in batches if necessary.

6 Adjust the seasoning, if necessary, being generous with freshly ground black pepper. If not using the sauce at once, let cool, then cover, and keep refrigerated for up to three days.

Spinach & Herb Orzo

Serves 4

INGREDIENTS

1 tsp salt
9 oz/250 g dried orzo
7 oz/200 g baby spinach leaves
5½ oz/150 g arugula
1 oz/25 g fresh flat-leaf parsley
1 oz/25 g fresh cilantro leaves

4 scallions
2 tbsp extra-virgin olive oil
1 tbsp garlic-flavored olive oil
salt and pepper

TO SERVE
radicchio or other lettuce leaves
2¼ oz/60 g feta cheese, well
    drained and crumbled
    (optional)
lemon slices, to garnish

1 Bring 2 pans of water to a boil, and put 12 ice cubes in a bowl of cold water. Add the salt and orzo to one of the pans, return to a boil, and cook for 8–10 minutes, or according to packet instructions, until the pasta is tender but not too soft.

2 Meanwhile, remove the stems from the spinach if they are tough. Rinse the leaves in several changes of water to remove any dirt and grit. Coarsely chop the arugula, parsley, cilantro,

and the green parts of the scallions.

3 Put the spinach, arugula, parsley, cilantro, and scallions in the other pan of boiling water and blanch for 15 seconds. Drain and transfer to the iced water to preserve the color.

4 When the spinach, herbs, and scallions are cool, squeeze out all the excess water. Transfer to a small food processor and process. Add the olive oil and

garlic-flavored oil and process again, until the mixture is well blended.

5 Drain the orzo well and stir in the spinach mixture. Toss well and adjust the seasoning.

6 Line a serving platter with radicchio leaves and pile the orzo on top. Sprinkle with feta cheese, if desired, and garnish with lemon slices. Serve hot or let cool to room temperature.

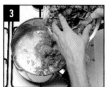

Spiced Pilau with Saffron

Serves 4–6

INGREDIENTS

large pinch of good-quality
   saffron threads
scant 2 cups water, boiling
1 tsp salt
6 tsp butter
2 tbsp olive oil

1 large onion, very finely
   chopped
3 tbsp pine nuts
1¾ cups long-grain rice
   (not basmati)
½ cup golden raisins or raisins

6 green cardamom pods, shells
   lightly cracked
6 cloves
salt and pepper
very finely chopped fresh cilantro
   or flat-leaf parsley, to garnish

1 Toast the saffron threads in a dry skillet over medium heat, stirring for 2 minutes, or until they give off their aroma. Immediately tip them onto a plate.

2 Pour the boiling water into a measuring pitcher, stir in the saffron and 1 teaspoon salt, and set aside for 30 minutes to infuse.

3 Melt the butter with the oil in a skillet over medium-high heat. Add the onion and cook for about 5 minutes, stirring, until it is soft.

4 Lower the heat, stir in the pine nuts, and cook for 2 minutes, stirring, until they just start to turn golden. Take care that they do not burn.

5 Stir in the rice, coating all the grains with oil. Stir for 1 minute, then add the golden raisins, cardamom pods, and cloves. Pour in the saffron-flavored water and bring to a boil. Lower the heat, cover, and simmer for 15 minutes without removing the lid.

6 Remove from the heat and let stand for 5 minutes without uncovering. Remove the lid and check that the rice is tender, all the liquid has been absorbed, and the surface has small indentations all over.

7 Use a fork to fluff up the rice. Adjust the seasoning, stir the herbs through, and serve.

Mediterranean Bread

Makes 1 loaf

INGREDIENTS

14 oz/400 g all-purpose flour,
plus extra for sprinkling
1 envelope active dry yeast
1 tsp salt
1 tbsp coriander seeds,
lightly crushed
2 tsp dried oregano

generous ¾ cup water, heated
to 125°F/52°C on an instant-
read thermometer
3 tbsp olive oil, plus extra
for greasing
5½ oz/150 g sun-dried tomatoes
in oil, drained, patted dry,
and chopped

2¾ oz/75 g feta cheese, drained,
patted dry, and cubed
3½ oz/100 g black olives, patted
dry, pitted, and sliced

1 Stir the flour, yeast, salt, coriander seeds, and oregano together and make a well in the center. Slowly add most of the water and the olive oil to make a dough. Gradually add the remaining water, if needed, drawing in all the flour.

2 Turn out onto a lightly floured counter and knead for 10 minutes, gradually kneading in the sun-dried tomatoes, cheese and olives. (The cheese will break up as you knead.) Wash out the bowl and lightly coat it with oil.

3 Shape the dough into a ball, put it in the bowl, and turn the dough over. Cover the bowl tightly and let the dough stand, until it doubles in volume.

4 Turn the dough out onto a lightly floured counter. Knead lightly, then shape into a ball. Place on a lightly floured cookie sheet. Cover and let rise, until it doubles in size again.

5 Lightly sprinkle the top with flour. Using a sharp knife, cut 3 shallow slashes in the top. Bake in an oven preheated to 450°F/230°C for 20 minutes. Lower the heat to 400°F/200°C and bake for 20 minutes longer, or until the loaf sounds hollow when you tap it on the bottom. Let cool completely. This bread keeps well for up to 3 days in an airtight container.

Sesame Breadsticks

Makes 32 sticks

INGREDIENTS

1¾ cups plus 2 tbsp unbleached
    strong white flour
1¾ cups plus 2 tbsp strong
    wholemeal flour
1 envelope active dry yeast

2 tsp salt
½ tsp sugar
2 cups water, heated to
    125°F/52°C on an instant-
    read thermometer

4 tbsp olive oil, plus extra
    for greasing
1 egg white, lightly beaten
sesame seeds, for sprinkling

1 Stir the flours, yeast, salt, and sugar together in a bowl and make a well in the center. Slowly stir in most of the water and the olive oil to make a dough. Gradually add the remaining water, if necessary, drawing in all the flour to the dough.

2 Turn out onto a lightly floured counter and knead for about 10 minutes until smooth. Wash the bowl and lightly coat with olive oil.

3 Shape the dough into a ball, put it in the bowl, and turn over so it is coated.

Cover tightly with a dish towel and leave the dough until it doubles in volume. Line a cookie sheet with baking parchment.

4 Turn out the dough onto a lightly floured counter and knead lightly. Divide into 2 equal pieces. Roll each piece into a 16 inch/40 cm rope and then cut into 8 equal pieces. Cut each piece in half to make 32 pieces in all.

5 Cover the dough you are not working with as you roll each piece into a thin 10 inch/25 cm rope, on a very

lightly floured counter. Carefully put the sticks on the cookie sheet.

6 Cover and let rise for 10 minutes. Brush with the egg white, then sprinkle thickly and evenly with sesame seeds. Bake in a preheated oven at 450°F/230°C for 10 minutes.

7 Brush again with egg white, and bake for another 5 minutes, or until golden brown and crisp. Cool on wire racks.

Olive Rolls

Makes 16 rolls

INGREDIENTS

4 oz/115 g olives in brine or
   oil, drained
6¼ cups unbleached strong white
   flour, plus extra for dusting
1½ tsp salt

1 envelope active dry yeast
scant 2 cups water, heated to
   125°F/52°C on an instant-
   read thermometer
2 tbsp fruity extra-virgin olive oil,
   plus extra for brushing

4 tbsp finely chopped fresh
   oregano, parsley, or thyme
   leaves, or 1 tbsp dried
   mixed herbs

1 Pit the olives with an olive or cherry pitter and finely chop. Pat off the excess brine or oil with paper towels. Set aside.

2 Stir the flour, salt, and yeast together in a bowl and make a well in the center. Slowly stir in most of the water and the olive oil to make a dough. Gradually add the remaining water, if necessary, drawing in all the flour to the dough.

3 Lightly knead in the olives and herbs. Turn out onto a lightly floured counter and knead for 10 minutes. Wash the bowl and lightly coat with oil.

4 Shape the dough into a ball, put it in the bowl, and turn over so it is coated. Cover tightly with a dish cloth and let rest until it doubles in volume. Dust a cookie sheet with flour.

5 Turn out the dough onto a lightly floured counter and knead lightly. Roll into 8 inch/20 cm ropes on a lightly floured counter.

6 Cut the dough into 16 even-size pieces. Shape each one into a ball and place on the prepared cookie sheet. Cover and let rise for 15 minutes.

7 Lightly brush the top of each roll with olive oil. Bake in a preheated oven at 425°F/220°C for 25–30 minutes, or until the rolls are golden brown. Cool on a wire rack.

Fougasse

Makes 2 large loaves

INGREDIENTS

6¼ cups unbleached strong white flour, plus extra for kneading and dusting	1 envelope active dry yeast 2 tsp salt 1 tsp sugar	2 cups water, heated to 125°F/52°C on an instant-read thermometer olive oil, for greasing

1 Stir the flour, yeast, salt, and sugar together in a bowl and make a well in the center. Slowly stir in most of the water to make a dough. Gradually add the remaining water, drawing in all the flour. If you need extra water, add it gradually one tablespoon at a time.

2 Turn out onto a lightly floured counter and knead for 10 minutes until smooth. Wash the bowl and lightly coat with olive oil. Shape the dough into a ball, put it in the bowl, and turn the dough over. Cover the bowl tightly with a dish cloth and leave until the dough doubles in volume.

3 Knock back the dough and turn out onto a lightly floured counter. Knead lightly, then cover with the upturned bowl, and let stand for 10 minutes.

4 Put a roasting pan of water in the bottom of the oven while it preheats to 450°F/230°C. Lightly flour a cookie sheet for the dough.

5 Divide the dough into 2 pieces, and roll each one into a 12 inch/30 cm oval, ½ inch/1 cm thick. Using a sharp knife, cut five 3 inch/7.5 cm slices on an angle in a herringbone pattern on each of the dough ovals. Cut all the way through the dough, using the tip of the knife to open the slits.

6 Spray the loaves with cold water. Bake for 20 minutes, turn upside-down, and continue baking for 5 minutes, until the loaves sound hollow when tapped on the bottom. Cool the bread on wire racks.

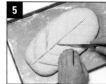

Herb Focaccia

Makes 1 loaf

INGREDIENTS

3½ cups unbleached strong white
  flour, plus extra for dusting
1 envelope active dry yeast
1½ tsp salt
½ tsp sugar

1¼ cups water, heated to
  125°F/52°C on an instant-
  read thermometer
3 tbsp good-quality fruity
  extra-virgin olive oil, plus
  extra for greasing

4 tbsp finely chopped fresh herbs
polenta or cornmeal, for
  sprinkling
coarse sea salt, for sprinkling

1 Stir the flour, yeast, salt, and sugar together in a bowl and make a well in the center. Slowly stir in most of the water and 2 tablespoons of the olive oil to make a dough. Gradually add the remaining water, if necessary, drawing in all the flour.

2 Turn out onto a lightly floured counter and knead. Transfer to a bowl and lightly knead in the herbs for 10 minutes, until soft but not sticky. Wash the bowl and lightly coat with olive oil.

3 Shape the dough into a ball, put it in the bowl, and turn the dough over. Cover tightly with a dish cloth and leave until the dough doubles in volume. Sprinkle polenta over a cookie sheet.

4 Turn the dough out onto a lightly floured counter and knead lightly. Cover with the upturned bowl and let stand for 10 minutes.

5 Roll and pat the dough into a 10 inch/25 cm circle, about ½ inch/1 cm

thick, and place on the prepared cookie sheet. Cover with a dish cloth and let rise for 15 minutes.

6 Using a lightly oiled finger, poke indentations all over the surface. Drizzle the remaining 1 tablespoon of olive oil over and sprinkle lightly with sea salt. Bake in a preheated oven at 450°F/230°C for 15 minutes, or until golden and the loaf sounds hollow when tapped on the bottom. Cool on a wire rack.

Sangria

Makes 8–10 glasses

INGREDIENTS

1 large orange
1 lemon
2 peaches

½ cup sugar, or to taste
4 cups full-bodied Spanish wine,
    such as Rioja

4 inch/10 cm piece of cucumber
ice cubes, to serve

1 Cut the orange into thin slices, then cut the slices into wedges. Place in a large ceramic or glass pitcher. Cut one long strip of rind from the lemon and add to the orange.

2 Slice right around the peaches, cutting down to the pits. Twist the halves in opposite directions, until the two halves come apart. Remove and discard the pits. Slice the peaches and add to the orange slices.

3 Add the sugar to the fruit and stir. Pour in the wine and stir until the sugar

dissolves. Taste and add more sugar or a squeeze or two of lemon juice to taste. Chill for at least an hour.

4 Meanwhile, dice the piece of cucumber or cut it into stick shapes.

5 When ready to serve, use a long-handled wooden spoon to stir and press the fruit against the side of the pitcher to extract some of the juice. Put the ice cubes into glasses and pour the chilled sangria over. Add some fruit from the pitcher to each glass, then add the cucumber. Serve at once.

VARIATIONS

Red wine is traditionally used in this popular drink, but you can use white wine as well. For a party, add a drop of brandy before you chill the sangria. Limes can also be used in this drink.

Desserts

Mediterranean fruits, like the region's vegetables, really benefit in terms of flavor from ripening under the intense sun. They are juicy and succulent, and a platter of simply prepared fruit can make the perfect end to a meal.

For simple recipes that don't adulterate the fruit's natural flavor, try ripe figs with a subtle orange-blossom cream, or Creamy Fruit Parfait, with peaches, apricots, and cherries, from the Greek island of Kythera. Or, when strawberries are just past their peak, serve Balsamic Strawberries with Mascarpone—the unlikely combination of ground pepper and balsamic vinegar will highlight any flavor there is left.

However, not all Mediterranean desserts are fruit-based. The Middle Eastern influence on Turkish and Moroccan cooking means very sweet desserts are enjoyed with small cups of strong, dark, espresso coffee. Few desserts can be sweeter than Baklava, thin layers of crisp phyllo pastry filled with spiced and sweetened chopped nuts and soaked in a sugar syrup. If you want something more comforting, there's a Creamy Rice Dessert from Greece, flavored with lemon.

The Italians are known for their excellent ice creams, so try the Lavender Ice Cream or Mint–Chocolate Gelato. When you are in a hurry, few desserts can be quicker than Italian Drowned Ice Cream—hot espresso poured over homemade vanilla ice cream.

Balsamic Strawberries with Mascarpone

Serves 4

INGREDIENTS

1 lb/450 g fresh strawberries	pepper	4–6 oz/115-175 g mascarpone
2–3 tbsp best-quality	fresh mint leaves, torn, plus extra	cheese
balsamic vinegar	to decorate (optional)	

1 Wipe the strawberries with a damp cloth, rather than rinsing them, so that they do not become soggy. Using a paring knife, cut off the green stalks at the top and use the knife's tip to remove the core.

2 Cut each strawberry in half lengthwise, or into quarters if large. Transfer the fruit to a bowl.

3 Add the vinegar, allowing ½ tablespoon per person. Add several twists of ground black pepper, then gently stir together. Cover the dish with plastic wrap and chill for up to 4 hours.

4 Just before serving, stir in torn mint leaves to taste. Spoon the mascarpone cheese into individual bowls and spoon the berries on top. Decorate with a few mint leaves, if desired. Sprinkle with extra pepper to taste.

VARIATION

Replace the mascarpone cheese with Vanilla Ice Cream (see page 228), or a premium commercial vanilla or strawberry ice cream.

COOK'S TIP

This is most enjoyable when it is made with the best-quality balsamic vinegar, one that has aged slowly and has turned thick and syrupy. Unfortunately, the genuine mixture is always expensive. Less expensive versions are artificially sweetened and colored with caramel, or taste of harsh vinegar.

Figs with Orange-Blossom Cream

Serves 4

INGREDIENTS

8 large fresh figs
4 large fresh fig leaves, if
    available, rinsed and dried

CREME FRAICHE (OPTIONAL)
2 tbsp buttermilk

1¼ cups heavy cream

ORANGE-BLOSSOM CREAM
½ cup crème fraîche, homemade
    (see left) or bought

about 4 tbsp orange-
    blossom water
1 tsp orange-blossom honey
finely grated rind of ½ orange
2 tbsp slivered almonds, to
    decorate (optional)

1 If you are making the
crème fraîche, begin at
least a day ahead. Put the
buttermilk in a preserving jar
or a jar with a screw top. Add
the cream, close securely, and
shake to blend. Let set at
warm room temperature for
6–8 hours, then refrigerate
for at least 8 hours and up to
4 days. It will develop a slight
tangy flavor. Lightly beat
before using.

2 To toast the almonds for
the decoration, place in a
dry skillet over medium heat
and stir until lightly browned.

Take care that they do not
burn. Immediately remove
the almonds from the pan.
Set aside.

3 To make the orange-
blossom cream, put the
crème fraîche in a small bowl
and stir in 4 tablespoons of
the orange-blossom water,
with the honey and orange
rind. Taste and add a little
extra orange-blossom water
if necessary.

4 To serve, cut the stems
off the figs. Do not peel
the figs, but stand them

upright with the pointed
ends upward. Cut each of
them into quarters without
cutting all the way through,
so you can open them out
into attractive "flowers."

5 If you are using fig
leaves, place one in the
center of each serving plate.
Arrange 2 figs on top of each
leaf, and spoon a small
amount of the orange-
flavored cream alongside
them. Sprinkle the cream
with the toasted slivered
almonds if desired, just
before serving.

Oranges in Spiced Caramel

Serves 4

INGREDIENTS

4 large, juicy oranges
4-6 tbsp shelled pistachio nuts,
   chopped, to decorate

SPICED CARAMEL
1¼ cups superfine sugar
5 black peppercorns, lightly
   crushed

4 cloves
1 green cardamom pod,
   lightly crushed
1¼ cups water

1 To make the spiced caramel, put the sugar, peppercorns, cloves, cardamom pod, and ⅔ cup of the water in a pan and stir to dissolve the sugar over medium heat. When the sugar has dissolved, turn up the heat, and boil, without stirring, until the syrup thickens and turns a deep caramel color. Use a wet pastry brush to brush the syrup down from the sides of the pan if necessary.

2 Very carefully, pour in another ⅔ cup water, standing back because it will splatter. Remove from the heat and, using a long-handled wooden spoon, stir until all the caramel has dissolved. Let cool.

3 Pare off the orange rind and pith, cutting carefully so that the oranges retain their shape. Leave the oranges whole, or, working over a bowl, cut into segments, cutting the flesh away from the membranes.

4 Pour over the caramel syrup with the spices and stir together. Cover and chill, until ready to serve. Serve the dessert in individual bowls with chopped pistachio nuts sprinkled over the tops at the last minute.

VARIATION

Turn this Spanish dessert into a Sicilian-style one by using the blood-red oranges that grow in great profusion on the island.

Creamy Fruit Parfait

Serves 4–6

INGREDIENTS

8 oz/225 g fresh, juicy cherries
2 large peaches
2 large apricots

3 cups Greek Strained Yogurt
(see page 182), or plain,
thick yogurt
½ cup walnut halves

2 tbsp flower-scented honey, or
to taste
fresh red currants or berries, to
decorate (optional)

1 To prepare the fruit, use a cherry or olive pitter to remove the cherry pits. Cut each cherry in half. Cut the peaches and apricots in half lengthwise and remove the pits, then finely chop the flesh.

2 Place the prepared cherries, peaches, and apricots in a bowl and gently stir the fruit together.

3 Spoon one-third of the yogurt into an attractive glass serving bowl. Top with half the fruit mixture.

4 Repeat with another layer of yogurt and fruit mixture, then top with the remaining yogurt.

5 Place the walnuts in a small food processor and process gently until chopped but not finely ground. Sprinkle the walnuts over the top layer of the yogurt.

6 Drizzle the honey over the nuts and yogurt. Cover the bowl with plastic wrap and chill for at least 1 hour. Decorate with a small bunch of red currants, if using, just before serving.

VARIATION

Vary the fruit to whatever is best in the market. Berries, figs, seedless grapes, and melons are also delicious in this simple family-style dessert. In winter, replace the fresh fruit salad with a dried fruit compote; cover dried fruit, such as apples, apricots, pitted dates, and figs, in orange juice until they plump, then proceed with the recipe.

Peaches with Amaretto-Mascarpone

Serves 4–6

INGREDIENTS

8–12 ripe peaches
1 large lime
2 cups fruity dry white wine
1 tbsp black peppercorns,
   lightly crushed

3 inch/7.5 cm cinnamon
   stick, halved
finely pared rind of
   1 unwaxed lemon
½ cup superfine sugar
fresh mint sprigs, to decorate

AMARETTO-MASCARPONE
   CREAM
2 tbsp amaretto liqueur, or
   to taste
1 cup mascarpone cheese

1 Fill a large bowl with iced water. Bring a large pan of water to a boil. Add the peaches and cook for 1 minute. Using a slotted spoon, immediately transfer the peaches to the iced water to stop the cooking process.

2 Squeeze the juice from the lime into a bowl of water. Peel the peaches, then quarter each, and remove the pit. Drop the fruit into the lime water as it is prepared. Cover and refrigerate for 24 hours.

3 Meanwhile, make the amaretto-mascarpone cream. Stir the amaretto into the mascarpone, cover, and refrigerate.

4 Place the wine, peppercorns, cinnamon, lemon rind, and sugar in a pan over medium-high heat, and stir until the sugar completely dissolves.

5 Boil the syrup for 2 minutes. Reduce to a simmer. Remove the peaches, add them to the

syrup, and poach for 2 minutes, or until tender— (they should not end up falling apart).

6 Using a slotted spoon, transfer the peaches to a bowl. Bring the syrup to a boil and continue boiling until thickened and reduced to about ½ cup. Pour the syrup into a heatproof bowl and cool. When cool, pour over the peaches. Cover and chill until required. To serve, decorate with mint.

Creamy Rice Dessert with Lemon & Pistachio Nuts

Serves 4

INGREDIENTS

1 tsp cornstarch	about 2 tbsp sugar, or	freshly squeezed lemon juice,
scant 3½ cups milk	1 tbsp honey, to taste	to taste
¾ cup short-grain rice	finely grated rind of	½ cup shelled pistachio nuts
	1 large lemon	

1 Put the cornstarch in a small bowl and stir in 2 tablespoons milk, stirring until no lumps remain. Rinse a pan with cold water and do not dry it out.

2 Put the remaining milk and the cornstarch mixture in the pan over medium-high heat. Heat, stirring occasionally, until the mixture simmers and forms small bubbles all around the edge. Do not let it boil.

3 Stir in the rice, lower the heat, and continue stirring for 20 minutes, until all but 2 tablespoons of the liquid has evaporated and the rice is tender.

4 Remove from the heat and pour into a heatproof bowl. Stir in sugar to taste. Stir the lemon rind into the dessert. If a slightly tarter flavor is required, stir in freshly squeezed lemon juice. Let cool completely.

5 Tightly cover the top of the cool rice with a sheet of plastic wrap and chill in the refrigerator for at least one hour—the colder it is, the better it tastes with fresh fruit.

6 Meanwhile, using a sharp knife, finely chop the pistachio nuts. To serve, spoon the dessert into individual bowls and sprinkle with the chopped nuts.

COOK'S TIP

It is important to rinse the pan in step 1 to prevent the milk from scorching on the sides or bottom of the pan.

Spanish Tart

Serves 4–6

INGREDIENTS

butter, for greasing	4 tbsp water	1 vanilla bean
¾ cup plus 2 tbsp superfine sugar	juice of ½ lemon	2 large eggs
	2 cups milk	2 large egg yolks

1 Lightly grease the sides of a 5 cup soufflé dish. To make the caramel, put a scant ⅓ cup sugar with the water in a pan over medium-high heat and cook, stirring, until the sugar dissolves. Boil until the syrup takes on a deep golden-brown color.

2 Immediately remove from the heat and add a few drops of lemon juice. Pour into the soufflé dish and swirl around. Set aside.

3 Pour the milk into a pan. Slit the vanilla bean lengthwise and add it to the milk. Bring to a boil, remove the pan from the heat, and stir in the remaining sugar, stirring until it dissolves. Set the pan aside.

4 Beat the eggs and egg yolks together in a bowl. Pour the milk mixture over them, whisking. Remove the vanilla bean. Strain the egg mixture into a bowl, then transfer to the soufflé dish.

5 Place the dish in a roasting pan filled with enough boiling water to come two-thirds up the side.

6 Bake in a preheated oven at 325°F/160°C for 1¼–1½ hours, until a knife inserted in the center comes out clean. Cool completely. Cover with plastic wrap and refrigerate for at least 24 hours.

7 Run a round-bladed knife around the edge of the dish. Place an upturned serving plate with a rim over the top of the soufflé dish, then invert the plate and dish, giving a sharp shake halfway over. Lift off the soufflé dish and serve.

COOK'S TIP

The lemon juice is added to the caramel in step 2 to stop the cooking process, to prevent it from burning.

Orange Crème à Catalanas

Serves 8

INGREDIENTS

4 cups milk	9 large egg yolks	3 tbsp cornstarch
finely grated rind of 6 large oranges	1 cup superfine sugar, plus extra for the topping	

1 Put the milk and orange rind in a pan over medium-high heat. Bring to a boil, then remove from the heat, cover, and let cool for 2 hours.

2 Return the milk to the heat and simmer for 10 minutes. Put the egg yolks and sugar in a heatproof bowl over a pan of boiling water. Whisk until creamy and the sugar is dissolved.

3 Add 5 tablespoons of the flavored milk to the cornstarch, stirring until smooth. Stir into the milk. Strain the milk into the eggs, whisking until blended.

4 Rinse out the pan and put a layer of water in the bottom. Put the bowl on top of the pan, making sure that the bottom does not touch the water. Simmer over medium heat, whisking, for about 20 minutes, until the custard is thick enough to coat the back of a wooden spoon. Do not boil.

5 Pour into eight ⅔ cup ramekins and let cool. Cover each with a piece of plastic wrap and put in the refrigerator to chill for at least 6 hours.

6 When ready to serve, sprinkle the top of each ramekin with a layer of sugar.

Use a kitchen blowtorch to melt and caramelize the sugar. Let stand for a few minutes until the caramel hardens, then serve at once. Do not return to the refrigerator or the topping will become soft.

COOK'S TIP

A kitchen blowtorch is the best way to melt the sugar quickly and guarantee a crisp topping. Blowtorches are sold at good kitchen-supply stores. Alternatively, you can melt the sugar under a preheated hot broiler.

Italian Drowned Ice Cream

Serves 4–6

INGREDIENTS

about 2 cups freshly made espresso coffee	VANILLA ICE CREAM	⅔ cup superfine sugar, or Vanilla-Flavored sugar (see page 254)
chocolate-covered coffee beans, to decorate	1 vanilla bean	2¼ cups milk
	6 large egg yolks	1 cup heavy cream

1 To make the ice cream, slit the vanilla bean lengthwise and scrape out the tiny brown seeds. Set aside.

2 Put the egg yolks and sugar in a heatproof bowl that will sit over a pan with plenty of room underneath. Beat the eggs and sugar together until thick and creamy.

3 Put the milk, cream, and vanilla bean in the pan over low heat and bring to a simmer. Pour the milk over the egg mixture, whisking. Place 1 inch/2.5 cm of water in the bottom of a pan. Place the bowl on top, ensuring the bottom does not touch the water. Turn the heat to medium-high.

4 Cook the mixture, stirring constantly, until it is thick enough to coat the back of a spoon. Remove from the heat, transfer to a bowl, and let cool.

5 Churn the mixture in an ice-cream maker, following the manufacturer's instructions. Alternatively, place it in a freezerproof container and freeze for 1 hour. Turn out into a bowl and whisk to break up the ice crystals, then return to the freezer. Repeat 4 times at 30-minute intervals.

6 Transfer the ice cream to a freezerproof bowl, smooth the top, and cover with plastic wrap or foil. Freeze for up to 3 months.

7 Soften in the refrigerator for 20 minutes before serving. Place scoops of ice cream in individual bowls. Pour coffee over them and sprinkle with coffee beans.

Mint-Chocolate Gelato

Serves 4–6

INGREDIENTS

6 large eggs
¾ cup superfine sugar
1¼ cups milk

⅔ cup heavy cream
large handful fresh mint leaves,
    rinsed and dried

2 drops green food coloring
    (optional)
2¼ oz/60 g dark chocolate,
    finely chopped

1 Put the eggs and sugar in a large mixing bowl. Using an electric mixer, beat the eggs and sugar together until thick and creamy.

2 Put the milk and cream in a pan and bring to a simmer, where small bubbles appear all around the edge, stirring. Pour onto the eggs and sugar, whisking constantly. Rinse the pan. Turn the heat to medium-high.

3 Transfer the mixture to the pan and cook gently, stirring constantly, until it is thick enough to coat the back of a spoon and leave a mark when you pull your finger across it.

4 Tear the mint leaves and stir them into the custard. Remove the custard from the heat. Cool, then cover, and infuse for at least 2 hours, chilling for the last 30 minutes.

5 Strain the mixture through a small plastic strainer, to remove the pieces of mint. Stir in the food coloring, if using. Churn in an ice-cream maker for 20 minutes, adding the chocolate pieces when the mixture becomes thick and almost frozen. If you don't have an ice-cream maker, freeze and whisk as in step 5 of Vanilla Ice Cream (see page 228).

6 Transfer to a freezerproof bowl, smooth the top, and cover with plastic wrap or kitchen foil. Freeze for up to 3 months. Soften in the refrigerator for 20 minutes before serving.

Lavender Ice Cream

Serves 6–8

INGREDIENTS

flowers from 10–12 large sprigs fresh lavender, plus extra to decorate	6 large egg yolks ¾ cup superfine sugar, or Lavender Sugar (see Cook's Tip)	2 cups milk 1 cup heavy cream 1 tsp vanilla extract

1 Strip the small flowers from the stems, without any brown or green bits. Place them in a small strainer and rinse, then pat dry with paper towels. Set aside.

2 Put the egg yolks and sugar in a heatproof bowl that will sit over a pan with plenty of room underneath. Using an electric mixer, beat the eggs and sugar together, until they are thick.

3 Put the milk, cream, and vanilla in the pan over low heat and bring to a simmer, stirring. Pour the hot milk over the egg mixture, whisking constantly.

Rinse the pan and place 1 inch/2.5 cm water in the bottom. Place the bowl on top, making sure that the bottom does not touch the water. Turn the heat to medium-high.

4 Cook the mixture, stirring, until it is thick enough to coat the back of a spoon.

5 Remove the custard from the heat and stir in the flowers. Cool, then cover, and set aside to infuse for 2 hours, chilling for the last 30 minutes. Strain the mixture through a plastic strainer to remove the flowers.

6 Churn in an ice-cream maker, following the manufacturer's instructions. Alternatively, freeze and whisk as in step 5 of Vanilla Ice Cream (see page 228).

7 Transfer to a freezerproof bowl, smooth the top, and cover with plastic wrap or kitchen foil. Freeze for up to 3 months. Soften in the refrigerator for 20 minutes before serving. Decorate with fresh lavender flowers.

COOK'S TIP

To make Lavender Sugar, put 1lb 2 oz/500 g sugar and 4½ oz/125 g lavender flowers in a food processor. Process until blended, then leave in a sealed container for 10 days. Sift out the flower pieces. Store the sugar in a sealed jar.

Orange & Bitters Sorbet

Serves 4–6

INGREDIENTS

3–4 large oranges
1 cup plus 2 tbsp superfine sugar

2½ cups water
3 tbsp red Italian bitters, such as Campari

2 large egg whites
fresh mint leaves and Candied Citrus Peel (see page 178), to decorate (optional)

1 Working over a bowl to catch any juice, pare the rind from 3 of the oranges, without removing the bitter white pith. If some of the pith does come off with the rind, use the knife to scrape it off.

2 In a pan, dissolve the sugar in the water over low heat, stirring. Increase the heat and boil for 2 minutes without stirring. Using a wet pastry brush, brush down the sides of the pan, if necessary.

3 Remove the pan from the heat and pour into a heatproof, nonmetallic bowl.

Add the orange rind and let it infuse while the mixture cools to room temperature.

4 Roll the pared oranges back and forth on the counter, pressing down firmly. Cut them in half and squeeze ½ cup juice. If you need more juice, squeeze another orange.

5 When the syrup is cool, stir in the orange juice and bitters. Strain into a container, cover, and chill for at least 30 minutes.

6 Put the mixture in an ice-cream maker and churn for 15 minutes. Alternatively, follow the instructions in step

5 of Vanilla Ice Cream (see page 228). Whisk the egg whites in a clean bowl until stiff.

7 Add the egg whites to the ice-cream mixture and continue churning for 5 minutes, or according to the manufacturer's instructions. Transfer to a shallow, freezerproof container, cover, and freeze for up to 2 months.

8 About 15 minutes before serving, soften in the refrigerator. Scoop into bowls and serve, decorated with mint leaves and the Candied Citrus Peel (see page 178), if desired.

Lemon Granita

Serves 4–6

INGREDIENTS

4 large unwaxed lemons
½ cup superfine sugar

scant 3 cups water
scooped-out lemons (optional)

mint sprigs, to decorate
(optional)

1 Pare 6 strips of rind from one lemon, then finely grate the zest from the remaining lemons, being very careful not to remove any bitter white pith.

2 Roll the lemons back and forth on the counter, pressing down firmly. Cut each in half and squeeze ½ cup juice. Add the grated zest to the juice. Set the mixture aside.

3 Put the pared strips of lemon rind with the sugar and water in a pan and stir over low heat to dissolve the sugar. Increase the heat and boil for 4 minutes, without stirring. Use a wet pastry brush to brush down any spatters on the sides of the pan. Remove from the heat, pour into a nonmetallic bowl, and cool.

4 Remove the strips of rind from the syrup. Stir in the grated zest and juice. Transfer to a shallow metal container, cover, and freeze for up to 3 months.

5 Chill serving bowls 30 minutes before serving. To serve, invert the container onto a cutting board. Rinse a cloth in very hot water, wring it out, then rub on the bottom of the container for 15 seconds. Give the container a shake and the mixture should fall out. If not, repeat.

6 Use a knife to break up the granita and transfer to a food processor. Quickly process until it becomes granular. Serve at once in the chilled bowls (or in scooped-out lemons). Decorate with mint sprigs, if desired.

VARIATION

Lemon-scented fresh herbs add a unique and unexpected flavor. Add 4 small sprigs lemon balm or 2 sprigs lemon thyme to the syrup in step 3. Remove the herbs and discard, with the pared rind in step 4.

Espresso Granita

Serves 4–6

INGREDIENTS

1 cup superfine sugar
2½ cups water
½ tsp vanilla extract

2½ cups very strong espresso
coffee, chilled

fresh mint, to garnish

1 Put the sugar in a pan with the water and stir over a low heat to dissolve the sugar. Increase the heat and boil for 4 minutes, without stirring. Use a wet pastry brush to brush down any spatters on the sides of the pan.

2 Remove the pan from the heat and pour the syrup into a heatproof nonmetallic bowl. Set the bowl in the kitchen sink filled with iced water to speed up the cooling process. Stir in the vanilla and coffee and let the syrup cool completely.

3 Transfer to a shallow metal container, cover, and freeze for up to 3 months.

4 Thirty minutes before serving the granita, place serving bowls in the refrigerator to chill.

5 To serve, invert the container onto a cutting board. Rinse a cloth in very hot water, wring it out, then rub on the bottom of the container for 15 seconds. Give the container a sharp shake and the mixture should fall out. If not, repeat.

6 Use a knife to break up the granita and transfer to a food processor. Quickly process until it becomes grainy and crunchy. Serve at once in the chilled bowls, decorated with mint.

COOK'S TIP

A very dark, full-flavored espresso is the only choice for this Italian specialty, otherwise the flavor will be marred by the freezing.

Italian Ricotta-Lemon Cheesecake

Serves 6–8

INGREDIENTS

1¾ oz/50 g golden raisins
3 tbsp marsala or grappa
butter, for greasing
semolina, for dusting
1½ cups ricotta cheese, drained
3 large egg yolks, beaten
½ cup superfine sugar
2 tbsp semolina

3 tbsp lemon juice
2 tbsp Candied Citrus Peel,
homemade (see page 178) or
store-bought, finely chopped
finely grated zest of 2 large
lemons

TO DECORATE
confectioners' sugar
mint sprigs
fresh red currants or other
berries (optional)

1 Soak the golden raisins in the marsala or grappa in a small bowl for about 30 minutes, or until the spirit has been absorbed and the fruit is swollen.

2 Meanwhile, cut out a circle of baking parchment to fit the bottom of an 8 inch/20 cm round cake pan with a removable bottom that is about 2 inches/5 cm deep. Grease the sides and bottom of the pan and line the bottom. Lightly dust with semolina and shake out the excess.

3 Using a wooden spoon, press the ricotta cheese through a plastic strainer into a bowl. Beat in the egg yolks, sugar, semolina, and lemon juice, until blended.

4 Fold in the golden raisins, candied peel, and lemon zest. Pour into the prepared pan and smooth the surface.

5 Bake the cheesecake in the center of a preheated oven at 350°F/180°C for 30–40 minutes until firm when you press the top, and slightly coming away from the sides of the pan.

6 Turn off the oven and open the door. Let the cheesecake cool in the turned-off oven for 2–3 hours. To serve, remove from the pan and transfer to a plate. Sift over a layer of confectioners' sugar from at least 12 inches/30 cm above the cheesecake to dust the top and sides lightly. Decorate with mint, and red currants if desired.

Tarte au Citron

Serves 6–8

INGREDIENTS

grated zest of 2–3 large lemons
⅔ cup lemon juice
½ cup superfine sugar
½ cup heavy cream or
    crème fraîche
3 large eggs

3 large egg yolks
confectioners' sugar, for dusting

CRUST
1¼ cups all-purpose flour

½ tsp salt
8 tbsp cold unsalted butter, diced
1 egg yolk beaten with 2 tbsp
    ice-cold water

1 To make the crust, sift the flour and salt into a bowl. Using your fingertips, rub the butter into the flour, until the mixture resembles fine crumbs. Add the egg yolk and water and stir together to make a dough.

2 Gather the dough into a ball, wrap in plastic wrap, and refrigerate for at least 1 hour. Roll out on a lightly floured counter and use to line a 9–10 inch/23–25 cm fluted tart pan with a removable bottom. Prick the bottom all over with a fork

and then line with a sheet of baking parchment and baking beans.

3 Bake in a preheated oven at 400°F/200°C for 15 minutes until the crust looks set. Remove from the oven, then remove the paper and beans. Reduce the oven temperature to 375°F/190°C.

4 Beat the lemon zest and juice and sugar together until blended. Slowly beat in the cream or crème fraîche, and finally beat in the eggs and yolks, one by one.

5 Set the crust on a cookie sheet and pour in the filling. Transfer to the preheated oven and bake the dessert for 20 minutes until the filling is set.

6 Cool completely on a wire rack. Dust with confectioners' sugar. Serve with Candied Citrus Peel (see page 178).

Chocolate Pine Nut Tartlets

Makes 8 tartlets

INGREDIENTS

2¼ oz/60 g dark chocolate with
at least 70% cocoa solids
4 tbsp unsalted butter
¾ cup plus 2 tbsp supérfine
sugar
5 tbsp light brown sugar
6 tbsp milk
3½ tbsp corn syrup

finely grated rind of 2 large
oranges and 2 tbsp freshly
squeezed juice
1 tsp vanilla extract
3 large eggs, lightly beaten
3½ oz/100 g pine nuts

CRUST
1¼ cups all-purpose flour
pinch of salt
7 tbsp butter
1 cup confectioners' sugar
1 large egg and 2 large egg yolks

1 To make the crust, sift the flour and a pinch of salt into a bowl. Make a well in the center and add the butter, confectioners' sugar, whole egg, and egg yolks. Using your fingertips, mix the ingredients in the well into a paste.

2 Gradually incorporate the surrounding flour to make a soft dough. Quickly and lightly knead the dough. Shape into a ball, cover in plastic wrap, and let chill for at least 1 hour.

3 Roll the pastry into eight 6 inch/15 cm circles. Use them to line eight 4 inch/10 cm tartlet pans with removable bottoms. Line each with baking parchment to fit, and top with baking beans. Chill for 10 minutes.

4 Bake in a preheated oven at 400°F/200°C for 5 minutes. Remove the paper and beans and then bake for another 8 minutes. Cool on a wire rack. Reduce the oven temperature to 350°F/180°C.

5 Meanwhile, break the chocolate into a pan over medium heat. Add the butter and stir until blended.

6 Stir in the remaining ingredients. Spoon the filling into the tartlet cases on a cookie sheet. Bake for 25–30 minutes, or until the tops puff up and crack and feel set. Cover with baking parchment for the final 5 minutes if the crust is browning too much. Transfer to a wire rack and let cool for at least 15 minutes before removing from the cookie sheet. Serve warm or at room temperature (not chilled).

Baklava

Makes 25 pieces

INGREDIENTS

2 cups walnut halves

1¾ cups shelled pistachio nuts

¾ cup blanched almonds

4 tbsp pine nuts, finely chopped

finely grated rind of 2 large
   oranges

6 tbsp sesame seeds

1 tbsp sugar

½ tsp ground cinnamon

½ tsp ground allspice

about 1¼ cups butter, melted

23 sheets phyllo pastry, each
   10 inches/25 cm square,
   defrosted if frozen

SYRUP

3 cups superfine sugar

2 cups water

5 tbsp honey

3 cloves

2 large strips lemon rind

1 To make the filling, put the walnuts, pistachio nuts, almonds, and pine nuts in a food processor and process gently, until finely chopped but not ground. Transfer the ground nuts to a bowl and stir in the orange rind, sesame seeds, sugar, cinnamon, and allspice.

2 Butter a 10 inch/25 cm square ovenproof dish that is 2 inches/5 cm deep. Cut the stacked phyllo sheets to size, using a ruler.

Keep the sheets covered with a damp dish towel.

3 Place a sheet of phyllo on the bottom of the dish and brush with melted butter. Top with 7 more sheets, brushing with butter between each layer.

4 Sprinkle with a generous 1 cup of the filling. Top with 3 more sheets of phyllo, brushing each one with butter. Continue layering until all the phyllo and filling

are used, ending with a top layer of 3 sheets of phyllo. Brush with butter.

5 Using a sharp knife and a ruler, cut into twenty-five 2 inch/5 cm squares. Brush again with butter. Bake in a preheated oven at 325°F/ 160°C for 1 hour.

6 Meanwhile, put all the syrup ingredients in a pan, stirring to dissolve the sugar. Bring to a boil, then simmer for 15 minutes, without stirring, until a thin syrup forms. Cool.

7 Remove the baklava from the oven and pour the syrup over the top. Let set in the dish, then remove the squares to serve.

Cannoli

Makes about 20 rolls

INGREDIENTS

3 tbsp lemon juice
3 tbsp water
1 large egg
1¾ cups all-purpose flour
1 tbsp superfine sugar
1 tsp ground allspice
pinch of salt

2 tbsp butter, softened
sunflower oil, for deep-frying
1 small egg white, lightly beaten
confectioners' sugar, to dust

FILLING
3¼ cups ricotta cheese, drained
4 tbsp confectioners' sugar

1 tsp vanilla extract
finely grated rind of 1 large
  orange
4 tbsp very finely chopped
  candied fruit
1¾ oz/50 g dark chocolate, grated
pinch of ground cinnamon
2 tbsp marsala or orange juice

1 Combine the lemon juice, water, and egg. Put the flour, sugar, spice, and salt in a food processor and quickly process. Add the butter, then, with the motor running, pour the egg mixture through the feed tube. Process until the mixture just forms a dough.

2 Turn the dough out onto a lightly floured counter and knead lightly. Wrap and chill for at least 1 hour.

3 Meanwhile, make the filling. Beat the ricotta cheese until smooth. Sift in the confectioners' sugar, then beat in the remaining ingredients. Cover and chill until required.

4 Roll out the dough on a floured counter until ¹⁄₁₆ inch/2 mm thick. Using a ruler, cut out 3½ x 3 inch/ 9 x 7.5 cm pieces, re-rolling and cutting the trimmings; you should be able to make about 20 pieces.

5 Heat 2 inches/5 cm oil in a pan to 375°F/190°C. Roll a piece of dough around a greased cannoli mold, barely overlapping the edges. Seal the edges with egg white, pressing firmly. Repeat with all the molds you have. Cook 2 or 3 molds until golden, crisp, and bubbly.

6 Remove with a slotted spoon and drain on paper towels. When cool, carefully slide off the molds. Repeat with the remaining dough.

7 Store unfilled in an airtight container for up to 2 days. Pipe in the filling no more than 30 minutes before serving. Sift over the confectioners' sugar and serve.

Lavender Hearts

Makes about 48 cookies

INGREDIENTS

1⅔ cups all-purpose flour, plus
extra for dusting
7 tbsp chilled butter, diced
6 tbsp Lavender Sugar (see
page 232), or ordinary
superfine sugar

1 large egg
1 tbsp dried lavender flowers,
very finely chopped

TO DECORATE
about 4 tbsp confectioners' sugar
about 1 tsp water
about 2 tbsp fresh lavender
flowers

1 Line 2 cookie sheets with baking parchment. Put the flour in a bowl, add the butter, and lightly rub in with your fingertips until the mixture resembles fine crumbs. Stir in the sugar.

2 Lightly beat the egg, then add to the flour and butter mixture with the dried lavender flowers. Stir the mixture to form a stiff paste.

3 Turn out the dough onto a lightly floured counter and roll out until about ¼ inch/5 mm thick.

4 Using a 2 inch/5 cm heart-shape cookie cutter, press out 48 cookies, occasionally dipping the cutter into extra flour, and re-rolling the trimmings as necessary. Transfer the pastry hearts to the cookie sheets.

5 Prick the surface of each heart with a fork. Bake in a preheated oven at 350°F/ 180°C for approximately 10 minutes, or until the cookies are lightly browned. Transfer to a wire rack placed over a sheet of baking parchment to cool.

6 Sift the confectioners' sugar into a bowl. Add 1 teaspoon cold water and stir, until a thin, smooth frosting forms, adding a little extra water if necessary.

7 Drizzle the frosting from the tip of the spoon over the cooled cookies in a random pattern. Immediately sprinkle with the fresh lavender flowers while the frosting is still soft so that they stick. Leave for at least 15 minutes until the frosting has set. Store for up to 4 days in an airtight container.

Almond Cookies

Makes about 32 cookies

INGREDIENTS

generous 1 cup unblanched
  almonds
1 cup butter, softened

6 tbsp confectioners' sugar, plus
  extra for dusting
scant 2 cups all-purpose flour

2 tsp vanilla extract
½ tsp almond extract

1 Line 2 cookie sheets with baking parchment. Using a cook's knife, finely chop the almonds, or process them in a small food processor, taking care not to overprocess them into a paste. Set aside.

2 Put the butter in a bowl and beat with an electric mixer until smooth. Sift in the confectioners' sugar and continue beating, until creamed and smooth.

3 Sift in the flour from above the bowl and beat it in until blended. Add the vanilla and almond extracts and then beat again to form a soft dough. Stir in the chopped almonds.

4 Using a teaspoon, shape the dough into 32 round balls about the size of walnuts. Place on the prepared cookie sheets, spacing them apart. Bake in a preheated oven at 350°F/180°C for 20–25 minutes until set and just starting to turn brown.

5 Remove from the oven. Let stand on the cookie sheets for 2 minutes to firm up. Sift a thick layer of confectioners' sugar over them. Transfer to a wire rack and let cool completely.

6 Lightly dust with more confectioners' sugar, just before serving. Store the cookies in an airtight container for up to one week.

VARIATION

Although not a true Mediterranean ingredient, pecans can be used instead of the almonds. Alternatively, add 2 teaspoons finely grated orange zest to the dough in step 3.

Vanilla Cake with Candied Fruit

Makes 12–15 slices

INGREDIENTS

8 oz/225 g quality candied fruit, such as cherries, and orange, lemon, and lime peels, or Candied Citrus Peel (see page 178)

¾ cup ground almonds

finely grated rind of ½ lemon

generous ½ cup all-purpose flour

generous ½ cup self-rising flour

¾ cup butter, softened, plus extra for greasing

¾ cup plus 2 tbsp vanilla-flavored sugar (see Cook's Tip)

½ tsp vanilla extract

3 large eggs, lightly beaten

pinch of salt

candied fruit, to decorate

1 Grease an 8½ x 4½ x 2 inch/ 22 x 12 x 5 cm bread pan, and line the bottom with a piece of baking parchment.

2 Chop the fruit into small pieces, reserving a few of the larger slices for the top. Combine with the ground almonds, lemon rind, and 2 tablespoons of the measured flour. Set aside.

3 Beat the butter and sugar together until creamy.

Beat in the vanilla extract and eggs, a little at a time.

4 Sift both flours and the salt into the creamed mixture, then fold in. Fold in the fruit and ground almonds.

5 Spoon into the pan and smooth the surface. Arrange the reserved fruit slices on the top. Loosely cover the pan with foil, making sure that it does not touch the cake. Bake in a

preheated oven at 350°F/ 180°C for about 1½ hours, until risen and a skewer inserted into the center comes out clean.

6 Cool in the pan on a wire rack for 5 minutes. Turn out and remove the lining. Cool completely. Wrap in foil and store for up to 4 days in an airtight container. Serve decorated with candied fruit.

COOK'S TIP

Make your own vanilla-flavored sugar by storing a sliced vanilla bean in a closed jar of superfine sugar.

Index